Simply
the
Best

ALSO BY SUSAN ELIZABETH PHILLIPS

Simply the Best

A Chicago Stars Novel

SUSAN ELIZABETH PHILLIPS

AVON

An Imprint of HarperCollinsPublishers

SIMPLY THE BEST. Copyright © 2024 by Susan E. Phillips, LLC. All rights reserved. Printed in the United States of America. No part of this book may be used or reproduced in any manner whatsoever without written permission except in the case of brief quotations embodied in critical articles and reviews. For information, address HarperCollins Publishers, 195 Broadway, New York, NY 10007.

HarperCollins books may be purchased for educational, business, or sales promotional use. For information, please email the Special Markets Department at SPsales@harpercollins.com.

FIRST EDITION

Food truck art © Shutterstock / Nerthuz

Library of Congress Cataloging-in-Publication Data has been applied for.

ISBN 978-0-06-324856-4

23 24 25 26 27 LBC 5 4 3 2 1

To Vicky Joseph, dear friend and guiding light, whose vision and hard work have enriched the lives of countless families.

PROLOGUE

Rory held out her bundle. "Hey, lady, do you want a kid? You can have him for free."

"Child, where did you get that baby?"

"I found him in a . . . in some bushes. He hardly ever cries. He's a real good baby, and you don't have to pay nothing for him. You can just take him."

But instead of taking her baby brother, the lady called the police.

1

Rory was drunk, and she'd earned the right to be drunk, and anybody who wanted to judge her for it could go to hell. Not that anyone at this party should be judging. "Juliet," she said, extending her hand to the man who'd made his way out onto the hotel balcony to her side. "As in Capulet."

"Darth," he replied. "As in Vader."

His voice was deliciously husky, his smile silky, and she was surprised to hear herself laugh. "Tell me, Mr. Vader, are you really evil?"

His mouth ticked up at the corner, a mouth with thin, finely carved lips. "It depends on who you ask."

"I'm asking you." The three fruity, high-octane cocktails she'd already gulped down in an attempt to erase her resentment over having to attend a party where she didn't fit in made it easy to be flirtatious with this arrogant, cocksure, very sexy jock who had football money written all over him, from his slicked-back hair to his athletic body to his luxury watch.

"I bend the rules here and there." He touched the red velvet flower in her hair with the tip of his finger. "Tell me you aren't really thirteen, Ms. Capulet." His finger moved to her cheek.

She let it rest there for a moment before she took a long sip of her fourth cocktail. "What do you think?"

"I think you left thirteen behind a while ago."

She'd left thirteen behind a good twenty-one years ago, so how could she take offense? She tossed her dishwater-blond curls like a pro at this hypermasculine hunk of man. "Correct. And what do you do for a living, Mr. Vader? When you aren't destroying Jedis, that is."

"I make money."

"Really?" His gaze was brash and dangerous, exactly what she needed right now, and the alcohol numbing her brain made caressing the front of his dress shirt seem perfectly appropriate. "Any tips on how I could do that?"

He gave her a cocky, bone-melting grin. "I have a few ideas."

*
*

When Rory woke up, she was alone, nauseated, and naked except for the red velvet flower hanging crookedly by her ear, a black garter belt, and a pair of fishnet stockings. She blinked at the drizzle of streetlight seeping through the window of a hotel room she dimly recalled being located in the same hallway as the party suite. After a couple of years of sexual judiciousness, she'd gone rogue.

She thought she remembered a condom, but maybe not, and what if he had some horrible disease that thumbed its nose at condoms? The room spun, right along with her stomach. She'd had a one-night stand—something she could check off her bucket list, except it had never been on her bucket list—but she'd been despondent and stupid, no longer herself, and this obscenely rich jock, bloated with arrogance from too much adulation, had seemed like the perfect escape. Not only had she agreed—she'd encouraged him.

The party teemed with beautiful women years younger than her, each one decked in a skimpy outfit and stilettos with hair all silky and swishy trying to snag the attention of the bevy of professional football players in attendance. Rory, thirty-four years old with runaway curls and a vintage cocktail dress that now lay in a black tulle puddle on the hotel room floor, had been the outlier, and yet Vader had singled her out.

She vaguely remembered he'd had a quarterback's build, tall and broad shouldered. His asshole arrogance and slicked-back hair should have sent her running. Instead, they had somehow signaled *do me* to her impaired brain. Now here she was, alone in a strange hotel room at three o'clock in the morning, her stomach churning with self-disgust from having sex with a stranger who possessed every quality she most disliked—and was almost certainly married.

Groaning, she staggered to the bathroom, held her hair back from her face, and threw up. She rinsed her mouth and splashed her face with water, all the while trying not to look at the wreck in the mirror but looking all the same, taking in the mascara smudges under her eyes, leftover smear of bright red lipstick, and eruption of unleashed curls around her head. At least it was still dark. She could sneak out of the hotel and hope she didn't run into anyone.

Her hands were clumsy, her head throbbing, and it took forever to get her clothes back on. She snatched up the red satin evening bag that was all she had left of her mother—*Are you proud of me, Mom?*—and headed for the door, but just as she reached it, she spotted something lying on the desk. Something that shouldn't have been there.

Five one-hundred-dollar bills.

He thought she was a sex worker.

*.

The party was winding down. The caterers had left along with the bartender, but three couples and a few strays remained in the suite. Brett Rivers's most important client, Clint Garrett, sat alone on the couch, his head in his hands.

Brett had arranged tonight's party ostensibly to celebrate Clint's birthday, but in reality to restore their relationship, which had hit an unexpected speed bump thanks to a slight error on Brett's part. Brett wasn't used to making mistakes. Mistakes were for losers. But then so were regrets. Winners fixed what they'd gotten wrong and came out stronger.

Brett calculated how to approach another conversation. Clint was normally a dream client—smart and talented, with a sterling character and a passing arm that put him in the same league as Robillard, Tucker, Brady, and Manning. Signing him as a client had placed Brett in position to move up to senior vice president, second in command, at Champion Sports Management. Things had been going perfectly until Brett had tried to warn Clint that his current girlfriend was only after his money.

Brett was always right about people. It was built into his DNA. But this time he'd gotten it wrong. Not only had he seriously misjudged Ashley Hart's character, but he'd underestimated the depth of Clint's feelings. He'd tried to retreat, but his accusatory words had been said, and Clint hadn't forgiven him, not even after Ashley dumped him. Brett had talked trash about the woman he loved.

Brett hated being wrong. It went against everything he knew to be true about himself. Everything he'd built his career on. Now he had to fix the damage.

The balcony doors opened and Darius Beale, a veteran Chicago Stars offensive lineman, appeared, his arm wrapped around a beautiful brunette with mile-long legs. "Wassup, man?" Darius cocked a thumb at Brett. "Laila, this is my personal barracuda, Brett Rivers. Best agent in the NFL."

Brett smiled at Laila, fairly sure she wasn't the same woman the lineman had arrived with. "It's easy to do good work when you have the great Darius Beale for a client."

Darius grinned. "See what I told you? The River, man. He runs swift and deep, fast and furious. No mercy. The guy's ruthless. Where you been hiding yourself, dude?"

"I had some business to take care of." No need for his client to know Brett's business involved an oddball woman with a round face, baby-doll cheeks, and crazy honey-blond curls. The city's exclusive escort services offered more variety these days.

The lady didn't fit the escort mold, with the exception of that bright, crimson mouth and lacy black garter belt. She was no twenty-year-old working her way through college, a big point in her favor. He'd probably stiffed her by leaving only five hundred, but that was all the cash he had on him.

He'd never understood paying for sex, but it had been a tough week, a long time since he'd been able to fit a woman into his schedule, and something about her had caught his admittedly jaded attention.

Darius's lady friend Laila turned out to be an econ major at the

University of Chicago. As Brett chatted with them both, he kept an eye on Clint. Despite all the beautiful women in attendance, the party hadn't cheered him up. If anything, he seemed more depressed, and Brett needed to fix that.

He excused himself from Darius and headed for the couch where Clint slouched, his head still in his hands. Brett broke the ice. "Things'll look brighter in the morning."

Clint thrust out his empty glass without lifting his head. "Get me another drink."

Brett didn't like Clint's belligerence. Didn't like it at all. But he swallowed his dignity. "Sure."

Garrett was already drunk, but Brett was his agent, not his mother, something he wished like hell he'd remembered before he'd told Clint his ladylove almost certainly cared more about Clint's money than about the quarterback himself. But the lady had dumped him, pointing out the error of Brett's accusation, and Clint was holding a grudge. Losing credibility with a client made Brett break out in a cold sweat. So far, Brett's boss hadn't caught wind of the problem, and Brett intended to make damn sure he never did.

He grabbed a sparkling water for himself and splashed Glenlivet into Clint's tumbler along with a few ice cubes and a generous amount of water. As he dropped a final ice cube into Clint's drink, he thought about "Juliet" and hoped she'd left the hotel by now instead of hanging around looking for another customer.

He'd booked extra rooms for party guests who got too shit-faced to drive home, but he'd never expected to use one himself. He was thirty-five, too self-disciplined for casual hookups, and his encounter with Juliet had been out of character. But she'd had good times stamped all over her, and he was under a hell of a lot of pressure. You didn't get to the top in this business by second-guessing, and no way he'd beat himself up about it.

Brett knew his strengths. Maybe it was arrogance, but who ever said that was a bad thing? He was smart, driven, and, as Darius had mentioned, ruthless when he knew he was right. He had razor-sharp instincts, and he worked smarter and harder than anyone else. Nothing was going to get in his way. Before the summer was over, he'd be the new senior vice president and heir apparent at Champion Sports Management. All he had to do was repair his relationship with one of the agency's biggest clients.

Brett carried the watered-down drink back to the couch. Clint accepted it with a snarl. "Happy now?"

"I'm not happy at all. I know how much you loved her." Something he sure as hell wished he'd realized earlier.

"I still do." Clint gazed into his drink. "She's beautiful and smart. She knows sports, she's funny, and she cared 'bout me as a person, not just a football player." His eyes darkened with anger. "She didn't give a shit about my money!"

That was true. By dumping Clint, Ashley had proven Brett had misjudged her. He should have known better than to butt into a client's love life. Ashley was hot, one of the most beautiful women Brett had ever seen, but there'd been something avaricious about her, an air of entitlement that worried him. Still, if he'd kept his mouth shut, he wouldn't be in this position. "I was wrong." The words were poison in his mouth.

"Damn right you were. Now she's goin' out with Karloh Cousins, who doesn't make half what I do." Garrett's bloodshot eyes turned mean, a word Brett would never have associated with his easygoing client. "Did you fix 'em up?"

Brett never lost his cool, no matter the provocation, but he could barely rein in his temper. "I wouldn't do that." Cousins was a power forward for the Chicago Bulls, a great guy, but as Clint pointed out, not nearly in the same league financially. Brett sat on the couch and risked resting his hand on Clint's solid shoulder. "All I want is what's best for you. You know that."

"You don't know what's best for me. You just think you do." Garrett shrugged off his hand. "She loved me, but she couldn't take the pressure when the press started following her around and people kept taking photos. It freaked her out." Clint's expression grew bitter. "You should have taken care of the press. You should have kept them off her back."

Making his clients' lives easier was what they paid him for, but Brett had limited powers when it came to controlling the media. Still, if he'd known this was a problem, he would have done something.

Clint rubbed his beard, which was looking more street-corner homeless than manicured scruff. "You didn't know her at all. You just thought you did. I was goin' take her to Vegas. Ask her to marry me. I had the ring and everything. That's how sure I was. Cost me a quarter million." Garrett rolled the tumbler over his forehead, his words beginning to slur. "One day Ashley and I were okay. The next day we weren't."

"I hate to see you hurting."

Clint took a long, slow sip from his glass. "If you were so wrong about her, what else are you wrong about?" Without warning, he drew back his thirty-four-million-dollar arm and hurled the tumbler across the room, where it exploded against the wall, drawing a gasp from the other guests. "You and me. Once the trust is broken, what's left?"

Brett's customary iron stomach lurched. This was bad. Worse than he'd calculated.

Garrett came unsteadily to his feet and headed for the bar, glancing at Darius on the way. "Did you see her leave?"

Darius peeled his attention away from the broken glass. "See who?"

"My sister."

An icy finger tapped the base of Brett's spine. "Sister?"

Garrett filled a fresh glass with scotch, sloshing some over the sides. Bristling with hostility, he looked at Brett. "I saw you talking to her earlier. Where'd she go?"

Fate couldn't be this much of a bitch. Not to him. He was The River. Swift and deep, fast and furious. He didn't screw up. Never. "I talked to a couple of women. I'm not sure which one . . ." But he knew, and the icy finger turned into a hard fist.

"Curly blond hair. Weird black dress." Clint took another slug of scotch. "She was actin' strange. Not much of a drinker. Hates parties like this. Doesn' like me much. She only came 'cause it's my birthday and I made her."

Cold dread shot right through him. Careful not to look as if he were rushing, he came off the couch and made his way to the door. Never show weakness. Always in control. "I'll check it out. See if she's still in the hotel." See if she was still in the room where he'd left five hundred dollars.

He cut around the hallway corner. If Garrett found out about this, he'd fire Brett for sure. As for Brett's boss . . . If he knew Brett had slept with the sister of one of his agency's biggest clients, Brett could kiss his career good-bye.

He started to sweat. He was always careful. Always planning.

Looking ahead. Positioning himself. This couldn't be happening. Not to him. Not to The River.

He picked up his stride until he was practically running. He hadn't been gone long. She'd still be asleep. This would all work out. He'd shove the money in his pocket and leave without waking her.

But what if she woke up? What then?

He'd figure it out. He always figured it out. He'd do whatever he needed to. Whatever it took. Failure wasn't an option. He'd never lost a client, and he didn't intend to start now.

He fumbled with the key card and finally got the door open.

The bed was empty, but the money was still there. Each bill ripped in half.

*

Rory rushed down the stairs of the Ravenswood three-flat apartment building where she'd been living for the past six months. In her hand, she clutched the latest violation notice from the City of Chicago. She rounded the landing, hurried past the door to Ashley's second-floor apartment and down another flight to the first floor where her landlord lived. At the back of the three-flat, she pushed open the screen door.

The early June day was already hot, not a good harbinger for the summer. Her sneakers slapped the porch's wood floor. She jumped off the top step, avoiding the ugly green pottery frog at the bottom, and ran past Mr. Reynolds's vegetable garden toward the old wooden garage she'd been forced to rent for an extra one hundred dollars a month.

One hundred dollars times five equaled five hundred dollars, the exact amount that bastard had left in the hotel room three nights ago.

Just when she'd thought her life couldn't become more dismal, she'd met a sexy stranger at a party and, in a drunken, misery-fueled lapse of judgment, decided it would be a terrific idea to jump into bed with him. She'd had one too many encounters with bastard men lately, and she had only her own shitty lack of judgment to blame.

She turned the lock and pushed hard on the garage's warped side door. It squeaked open to reveal the Royal Palace of Sweets, an ancient pink-and-purple food truck. At least that bastard Jon hadn't driven off with her truck.

In the dim light seeping through the cobweb-festooned garage window, she gazed at the envelope she was holding. It came from the City of Chicago. Her so-called business partner had scrawled a message across the front. *Leaving town. Too fucking many rules.*

Inside the envelope was a citation from the city for violating one of Chicago's draconian food truck laws. Their first fine had cost them a thousand dollars. This second fine was going to cost *her* two thousand dollars.

Before she'd moved to Chicago from Manhattan—before she'd invested her savings in this food truck Jon had found on eBay— she should have taken into account her old housemate's habit of jumping into new projects only to abandon them when he lost interest.

She opened the pink-and-purple passenger door of the Royal Palace of Sweets, stepped inside, and settled into the worn, butt-sized indentation in the driver's seat. Where was she going to get two thousand dollars? She'd already been working twelve-hour days, six days a week. With Jon gone, she'd have to work seven days.

On the other side of the windshield, the garage's overhead bulb lit up, and Ashley Hart swept into the gloomy interior like a queen into a peasant's cottage. Exquisitely beautiful, charismatic, and self-centered twenty-six-year-old Ashley Hart, with her silky red hair, glorious breasts, endless legs, and husky laugh. It was no wonder every man she met fell at her feet, including Rory's half brother.

Rory wanted to hide. Ashley didn't know how badly Rory had betrayed their friendship, and Rory didn't want to face her. She and Ashley couldn't have been more different, and Rory doubted they'd have become friends if Ashley'd had any other girlfriends, and if Rory hadn't been so lonely for female companionship after she'd moved here. Ashley was shallow and narcissistic, but she'd grown up in Chicago, and she'd been generous with her time, showing Rory the city and helping her get her bearings.

"There you are," Ashley said in her throaty bedroom voice. She stopped at the truck's open door but didn't climb in. Royalty only entered carriages, not rubbish food trucks. She regarded Rory's high-rise canary-yellow shorts and vintage Scooby-Doo T-shirt with her customary bewilderment. Rory liked the way she dressed, even if her evil stepmother and Ashley hated it. Rory's thrift-store finds—some vintage, some merely cheap—kept her in interesting outfits without her having to spend a fortune.

Ashley tossed her long, shampoo-commercial hair. "Why are you sitting out here, sweetie?" Everything Ashley said sounded seductive, even when she asked Rory to feed her cat.

"Jon quit," Rory said. "I was afraid he'd driven off with the truck."

Ashley's perfect lips made a small moue. "Jon's quitting is a blessing. You can do so much better than selling cheap candy from a food truck. Jon was a loser."

A fact Ashley had understood from the beginning and that Rory should have admitted to herself long before she'd spent the last of her rainy-day funds restocking the shelves with a fresh supply of candy bars, bubble gum, and fizzies. She'd have to find more Little League games to park near, locate more street festivals and swimming pools. She'd work longer hours. She might be able to convince Mr. Reynolds to give her an extension on her rent, but then what?

Ashley, still standing on the cracked cement floor, braced her elegant hand against one side of the door and tilted her head so her hair flowed perfectly over her shoulder. "I went out with Karloh Cousins again last night."

The ease with which Ashley had moved on from Rory's half brother, Clint, to the basketball player should justify what Rory had done, but Clint was desolate, and Rory was growing concerned. He hadn't answered any of her phone calls in the three days since his birthday party when Rory had jumped into bed with a stranger.

"Karloh loved those chocolate truffles you gave me," she said with her effortless, seductive charm. "Could you pretty please make some more?"

How could anybody resist Ashley when she looked at them with such dazzling, wide-eyed eagerness, as if they were the most fascinating person on the planet? "And maybe you could put the Bulls logo on top?"

Rory didn't want to give away another batch of her ancho chili chocolate truffles, let alone add the Chicago Bulls logo on top, but betraying the only female friend she'd made since she'd arrived in Chicago six months ago required some kind of penance. "I'll make them next week."

"You're the absolute best!" Ashley's smooth forehead knitted in a charming little crease. "I hate to ask, but I'll love you forever if I can give them to him tomorrow."

"Sure." Living with guilt was a bitch.

Ashley regarded her mischievously. "Your apartment door was unlocked, and I knew you wouldn't mind, so I borrowed that sick retro evening bag of yours to go with my black tank dress. Karloh loves everything bodycon. Clint did, too." For a fraction of a second, Ashley seemed to soften. Maybe she'd genuinely fallen for him. But love wasn't what motivated her friend. Or maybe Rory had made a big mistake by interfering.

Mistakes were Rory's thing. Trusting Jon, lying to Ashley, and betraying herself by jumping into bed with a rich football player who'd left money on the desk. She'd eventually get over that last mistake since she'd never have to see him again, but the others weren't so easily dismissed. Who was she to play God with people's lives when her own kept falling apart?

Ashley quickly pulled herself back together. "Gotta go. Thanks for the evening bag, sweetie." With a quick wave, a dazzling smile, and a toss of her glorious hair, Ashley left the garage.

Once again, Ashley had manipulated her. She knew Rory wouldn't voluntarily lend out her mother's evening bag, so she'd gone into Rory's apartment and taken it. Every time Rory opened that red satin clutch, she imagined the lingering notes of her mother's perfume. But Ashley went after what she wanted whether it was the evening bag, free artisanal chocolate truffles, or a rich athlete.

Rory gazed blindly through the dirty windshield. She'd only been five when she'd lost her mother, and she was no longer certain which of her memories was real and which she'd conjured over time. It was ironic. She'd been shocked and sad when her father had died two years ago from a sudden heart attack, but her father had been an emotionally distant figure all her life, and her deepest grief would always be for her mother.

She couldn't keep sitting here feeling sorry for herself because her life was going nowhere. She had to find Clint. Talk to him. Make sure he was all right, because he hadn't looked all right the last time she'd seen him. She needed to get to work.

As she turned to climb out of the truck, she saw what she'd been too distracted to notice when she'd climbed in.

The shelves she'd so freshly replenished with candy were stripped clean. Jon had taken everything but the truck and run.

2

Clint's house was ridiculously ornate, a château-style white limestone mansion with chimneys, balconies, sloping slate roofs, and a turret. Nothing was too good for Gregg and Kristin Garrett's little boy. The house couldn't be more different from the redbrick Colonial on Minneapolis's Lake Harriet where Rory and Clint had grown up.

Rory pulled the Royal Palace of Sweets around to the back, out of sight of the other palatial residences in the wealthy neighborhood of Burr Ridge. Chugging along the right lane of Interstate 55 in an ancient pink-and-purple food truck that burped exhaust had been humiliating, but because of the choices she'd made, this oil-burning junker was her sole mode of transportation.

She curled her hands over the top of the steering wheel and rested her forehead there. She was thirty-four years old, no longer a kid, and the food truck business she'd only entered because she'd wrongly viewed it as a stepping-stone to fulfilling her real passion had gone bottom up. Ever since her sophomore year in college when she'd cut psych class to attend a chocolate-making work-shop, she'd dreamed of a career as a chocolatier.

Over the years, she'd worked food service jobs with restaurants and catering companies to support herself as she served unpaid apprenticeships with every fine chocolatier who'd have her. She'd learned how to properly temper the highly technical ingredient by taking into account climate, temperature, and humidity. She'd studied molding and finishing, and discovered she could identify a cocoa bean's terroir simply by smell. As the years passed, she'd come to understand how beautifully made fine chocolate awak-ened all the senses: sight and smell, taste and mouthfeel, even the sense of hearing with the distinctive snap of a well-made bar. Unlike human beings, impeccably fashioned chocolate never disappointed.

She forced herself to climb out of the truck. The long serving window was shuttered, the pink-and-purple awning stowed in the empty interior. She slammed the door twice before the latch caught. As hard as she'd worked, she wasn't any closer to making her dreams come true and supporting herself as a chocolatier than when she'd first started. She was paralyzed—stuck in place—with no plan for the future and no idea how to move forward.

She rounded the house and made her way up the sidewalk. Topiaries presided over each side of the mansion's massive front doors. She caught her reflection in one of the sidelights: dishwater-blond curls snagged on top of her head, sleeveless red-and-white-checked blouse with a Peter Pan collar, blue pedal pushers from the 1950s, Walmart flip-flops, and red Bakelite heart earrings that hadn't cheered her up as she'd hoped.

She rang the electronic doorbell and heard the distant chime of "Hail to the Victors," the University of Michigan's fight song. *Seriously?* Boston University, the college that would have been her alma mater if she'd stayed past sophomore year, had a fight song, but not a football program—the primary reason she'd chosen it, along with its geographical distance from her Minnesota home.

No one answered. The doorbell was wireless, so she should be showing up on his phone. She waved. Tried to smile. Nothing happened. Shouldn't he have a butler or something?

She subjected herself to another two rounds of "Hail to the Victors," but the door went unanswered. She thought of all the times she'd wanted Clint to ignore her and how payback was a bitch.

She dug into her leather patchwork boho bag, one of her best tag sale finds, and withdrew the key he'd given her, despite her protests that she'd never use it. But as usual, he'd been right. He was the Golden Boy, with a list of achievements that made her hodgepodge life even more pathetic by comparison. Rory Meadows Garrett, college dropout, failed business owner, general screw-up. Clint Garrett, all-American multimillionaire NFL quarterback adored by the world.

She entered the marble foyer and took in the Grecian pedestals, sparkling chandeliers, and gilded console. "Clint! Clint, it's Rory!"

The empty house echoed. She made a quick search: sumptuous living room, spacious great room, elegant dining room—all of it expensive and overdecorated, although who was she to criticize anyone else's decor? Returning to the foyer, she called out again, but the house felt empty.

Her gaze drifted to the arched ceiling. A fresco of frolicking cherubs dancing around the chandeliers mocked her. Those cherubs might be a reflection of her half brother's sensitive side, or they could be ironic. With Clint, she never knew, and she flipped them the bird.

The kitchen lay at the end of the long marble hallway. Two more crystal chandeliers hung above the central island. Of course he had chandeliers in his kitchen. What megamillionaire professional quarterback with fleet feet and a golden arm didn't? She took in the stone floor, ice-white lacquered cabinets, and cold, black-granite countertops, any one of which would make a great mortuary slab. Or a perfect place to hand-temper chocolate. If only she were tempering chocolate right now.

She set down her bag. The kitchen had a designated coffee bar with a high-end espresso and coffee maker. No basic Mr. Coffee for Clint Garrett.

"Hail to the Victors" blasted into the kitchen. Her brother? Maybe he'd gotten drunk and lost his key. Ignoring the cherubs cavorting overhead, she hurried down the slippery black marble hallway floor. This was her chance to make things right. She flung open the door.

Darth Vader stood on the other side.

* *

Rory slammed the door in Vader's face and marched back down the marble hallway to the kitchen.

How much time had really elapsed before Vader had dragged her away from the party four nights ago? Twenty minutes? Thirty?

Or, more accurately, she'd dragged him.

Where can we go? She shuddered to remember saying those very words.

He was a jock in designer clothes—almost certainly a *married* jock—and that breathy, drunken voice shouldn't have belonged to her. But he'd been slick and practiced and oh-so-seductive, and she'd been dizzy and drunk and oh-so-needy.

"I have a room," he'd whispered.

"Show me."

Alcohol and self-pity were a lethal combination.

*
*

As Brett stared at the front door that had been slammed in his face, his brain fired, weighing his next move. This mess wouldn't go away on its own, and running from trouble wasn't his mode. He needed to assess his opponent, unearth her weakness, and use it to his advantage. Depending on how she reacted, he might need to put her on the defensive, or he might have to charm her. Worst case, he could profess love at first sight, although that stuck in his craw. He was aggressive and occasionally ruthless, but he was never unethical.

This would be a challenge.

*
*

Another round of "Hail to the Victors" echoed through the house. Rory slapped her hands over her ears and threw herself onto a white leather counter stool, the image of those five one-hundred-dollar bills forever seared in her brain—the payment for services rendered.

The back door clicked open. Her head shot up.

Vader stepped into the kitchen, commanding the space just by breathing its oxygen. She jumped from the stool. "Get out!"

He stayed where he was, taking her in with a pair of steel-gray assassin's eyes. At the party, the balcony light had been dim, the bedroom dark, and seeing him now was like seeing someone you only dimly recognized but were certain you never wanted to see again. White oxford dress shirt without a crease, dark pants with a perfect crease, burgundy loafers with the trademark Gucci horse-bit toggles. Everything about him represented skewed values and a devious mind.

"Juliet," he said with a nod. "Where's Clint?"

"You tell me," she retorted.

He was tall and lean, probably around her age, with a power broker's slicked-back dark hair the exact shade of her Irish cream chocolates. His jaw was too square, cheekbones too sharp, eyes too assessing to belong to a pretty boy. This dude was all about dominance and control.

She glared at him. "Does your wife know about your dirty little habit of sleeping with random, shit-faced women?"

"Wife?" The slight dip at the end of his nose gave him a vaguely predatory look.

"It's easy to forget about the little woman waiting for you at home, isn't it? The one who's watching the clock while the kids sleep upstairs and you're out doing your man-whore thing." A horrifying new thought hit her. "I'll bet she's pregnant! *I'd* better not be because, I swear to God, if I am, I will personally murder you and convince your wife to help me hide the body."

His lip curled. "Ease up, will you? When a man has four kids, he needs a break."

"Four!" Was he sneering at her?

"Five. I forgot about Roland. We gave him away because he made too much noise. And, frankly, Ambrose is on shaky ground. Asthma."

She let out an unintentional sigh of relief. "You don't have kids."

"No."

"Wife?"

"No."

"Fiancée?" Once again, she gathered steam. "Don't lie to me! I know there's someone you were unfaithful to."

He hesitated for a moment before he spoke. "My principles."

"*Your* principles? What about mine?"

"I have no idea what yours are," he said evenly. "We're strangers, remember?"

"Exactly!" She took a moment to recalibrate. "How did you get in?"

"I have a key."

How many people did Clint give keys to?

"Who are you?" she said. "Other than a face I prayed never to see again?"

If anything, those cold-steel eyes grew even colder and steelier. "I'm Clint's agent. Brett Rivers. And you're Rory Garrett, his sister, a piece of information I wish you'd passed on to me before our . . . encounter."

Was he really blaming her? "It's Rory *Meadows*. And why should I have mentioned it? So you could suck up to me?"

"As opposed to going down—" The corner of his mouth ticked. "Apologies. My tongue sometimes gets away from me."

She stared at him incredulously.

He didn't seem embarrassed by his horrifically inappropriate remark. "Is your brother around?"

"My half brother, and he's not here, so get out."

"Where is he?"

"I don't know."

He pulled out his phone, checked the screen, and re-pocketed it before he glanced toward the coffee station. "Any coffee in there?"

"Why? Do you need to sober up? Again."

"With all due respect, Ms. Garrett . . ."

"Again. It's Meadows. I use my mother's maiden name."

"Ms. Meadows. I wasn't the only person who drank too much four nights ago." He had her there, and he wasn't done. "I used protection, so if you're pregnant, I'm not the one who got you that way."

She flashed back to what she could remember of a naked Brett Rivers. He had a patch of dark hair on his very athletic chest, and a narrow, hard-muscled butt she'd almost certainly dug her fingers into. She didn't remember much else, including the condom. On this, however, she trusted him. He was too calculating to take chances. "Of course. You're one of those men who go around with pockets stuffed full of condoms in case you run into some . . . some . . . *floozy*." The word popped into her head from a vintage 1920s flapper poster hanging over the bookcase in her shabby apartment.

"Floozy?" He lifted one dark eyebrow. "Your attitude toward your own sex is outdated and offensive." With an air of disappointment, as if she'd failed his personal test of political correctness, he strode toward the coffee station.

She couldn't believe he'd managed to put her on the defensive. She shoved aside an unwelcome memory of a long, deep kiss from that glib, deceitful mouth. "Hey, I'm not the one going around with fistfuls of condoms in my pants, and I'm sure there's a Starbucks nearby if you're jonesing for caffeine."

"Probably, and the condoms were already in the hotel room." He pulled the lid off a canister of beans and dumped some in the grinder. As it whirred away, he surveyed her as if he had to come to terms with what he saw—an odd, curly-haired woman who bore little resemblance to her high-powered brother except for the color of their eyes and definitely no resemblance to the women he almost certainly had in his contacts list, probably listed by bust size.

He filled the carafe at the sink, dumped it in the machine, and started the brew. As he waited, he checked his phone again.

The silence was getting to her, and the tightness she'd been carrying in her stomach pinched harder. "When did you see him last?" she asked.

"At the party. Four nights ago. What about you?"

"The same. And he's not here, so you can leave now."

He leaned against the edge of the coffee bar, phone in his hand. "Where does he go when he's hurting? You're his sister. You must have some idea."

"Half sister," she repeated. She and Clint had never been close, and, no matter how pure her intention, she should have let his affair with Ashley play out on its own terms. Sooner or later, he would have come to his senses. But almost certainly not until after a quick Vegas marriage with no prenup.

She shoved the tips of her fingers in the pockets of her capris. "I don't know where he goes."

He regarded her more closely. "Why's that? You're his only sibling, as I understand."

"He's six years younger. We're not close."

"I do remember you calling him an asshole the night we met."

"I never." Except in her drunken state, she could have.

He gestured toward her with his phone. "At the time, I thought you just weren't a sports fan, but it seems there's more to it. Interesting that Clint was concerned about you the night of the party when you disappeared."

"I disappeared with *you*!" She couldn't hold back any longer. "And you left *money* for me!"

He lifted his free hand. It was big and square with blunt-tipped fingers the perfect size to find the laces on a football. "An error in judgment I deeply regret."

"Who does that? Who leaves money? What kind of man are you other than a former football player who couldn't cut it on the field and decided to masquerade as a sports agent?"

"Now that's harsh." It was his turn to go on the offensive. "To refresh your memory, we were having a conversation about making money."

"So?"

"You asked me if I had any ideas how you could make money."

"And you assumed that meant I was selling myself?"

"It was the way you said it." He abandoned the coffee he'd been about to pour. "You were coy."

"Coy? I've never been coy in my life."

"You were coy. And some of those guys at the party have been known to show up with beautiful, paid escorts."

She planted her hands on the hips of her blue pedal pushers. "If you think I look like a beautiful paid escort, you need your eyes checked." She stopped herself before she pointed out her flaws: too-curly hair, eyes too big, face too round, mouth too small, legs too short.

"In the light of day, I can see my mistake. You're beautiful, but it's not a surface beauty. You're far too interesting for that. That's why you intrigued me."

She curled her lip at him. "You're such a bullshitter."

Instead of denying it, he smiled. "I'm an agent. We have to be adaptable."

His slick, practiced charm might work on egotistical athletes, but not on her. "Do you have any idea how insulting it was to leave money?"

"The way you tore up those bills might have clued me in."

"And I could have used the cash!"

He stared at her over the rim of his coffee mug.

She retrenched. "I think we're done here."

He took a slow sip of coffee. It smelled good, but no way was she pouring any for herself. With a snake like him, she was keeping her distance.

He tilted his head. "That pink-and-purple food truck parked out back . . . The Royal Palace of Sweets? I assume it's yours. Unusual to see something like that in Clint's driveway."

"My car's in the shop." Her old Nissan had needed a brake job when she'd sold it to help pay for supplies, so that might be true. "I'm actually a chocolatier." A chocolatier without a business. Someday she'd figure it out. Except she'd been telling herself that for years.

"You don't seem to have much to sell," he said.

"You looked inside the truck?"

"It wasn't locked." Instead of pursuing the topic, he picked up his mug and made his way through a door near the butler's pantry.

She shot after him. "Where are you going?"

"To see if he's left any clues."

"You can't search his house without permission."

"Come with me to make sure I don't steal anything."

She didn't really believe he'd steal anything, but she stomped after him—or at least as close to stomping as her Walmart flip-flops would allow—and stopped cold.

She'd been in Clint's house only once before, but she hadn't made it as far as his office. A three-tiered crystal chandelier hung from a ceiling free of cherubs. The crown molding, along with the elaborate marble fireplace, displayed a riot of scrollwork and acanthus leaves. A Persian rug covered the stone floor, and a pair of built-in bookcases with more scrollwork held an array of books her brother had probably read. The room's most dramatic feature was the large, square bay jutting from the back of the house, with sweeping Palladian windows looking out on the home's formal garden. The room was weird but oddly arresting, if you were into gross over-ornamentation.

His desk, a massive Louis-something with scalloped edges, cabriole legs, and brass marquetry, sat in the center of the square window bay facing the garden. It was a ridiculous desk for a football player, and Rivers was opening the drawers.

Seemingly out of nowhere, the top slid open and a very modern computer rose from the interior like the ghost of Vince Lombardi. Rivers booted it up. "Let's see what we've got."

"Try 'IMTHEGREATEST' for a password. One word, all uppercase."

He didn't look up from his task. "You seem more than a little hostile toward your brother."

"Normal sibling rivalry." Not so normal. Growing up in the shadow of a younger brother who excelled at everything, while Rory only excelled at getting in trouble, had left scars she should have gotten over by now. Still, she'd cared enough about him to get rid of Ashley, hadn't she?

And look how that had turned out.

She tugged one of her Bakelite heart earrings. "Maybe he needs some alone time." But Clint was a social creature, and only a major crisis would make him go off by himself.

Rivers was all business. "I know him better than that."

Had she really had sex with this arrogant asshole who was as foreign to her current life as an NFL locker room? "It's only June," she said. "Training camp doesn't start until next month, so what's the rush?"

Apparently "IMTHEGREATEST" wasn't working, nor any of the other passwords Rivers had been trying, because he abandoned the computer. "I need to find him, that's all."

"I need to find him, too." She offered up the same stubborn look he'd just given her.

He set off, leaving her to trail in the back draft of his luxury aftershave. She wanted to be able to tell Clint that she'd tried her best to keep his rampaging agent from searching his house without permission. "Stop!"

Rivers ignored her, which was fortunate, because she was as anxious as he to see if Clint had left any clues to his whereabouts.

They traveled from one room to the next, with Rivers occasionally stopping to fire off a text. They checked out the gym and sauna. The house had formal areas, casual areas, a vast media room, a gym, and five bedrooms. No one should be this rich.

Clint had offered her money more than once, and each offer was a tangible reminder of the gap between them. Gritting her teeth, she'd thanked him for his generosity and assured him she was doing just fine on her own. If he recognized the lie, he didn't call her on it. She'd wait tables for the rest of her life before she'd take money from her little brother.

"Have you talked to your mother?" Rivers said as they approached the master bedroom.

"My mother died when I was five."

"Apologies. And I know you lost your father two years ago. Have you talked to Clint's mother?"

"Kristin and I avoid each other as much as possible."

"Your brother, your stepmother, me. That's quite an enemy list you have, but you still need to call Kristin. If I do, it'll only worry her."

True. Kristin was a champion worrier when it came to her baby boy. "Clint didn't go home to Minneapolis."

"You're sure of that?"

"He's upset about his breakup with Ashley Hart, and the last person he'd visit when he's upset is his mother. Have you met Kristin?"

"Sure. She's great."

Not the word Rory would use to describe her judgmental step-mother. "Clint knows if he went home now, Kristin would insist on taking him out for ice cream and buying him a new video game."

Rivers didn't have suffocating memories of Kristin coddling Clint, and he smiled. "Sounds about right." He opened the door to Clint's bedroom.

All the bedrooms were well-appointed, but this was like step-ping into Marie Antoinette's personal boudoir. The sky-blue tray ceiling displayed a fresco of fluffy clouds, leafy trees, and rosy-cheeked shepherdesses. An elaborate fireplace took up much of one wall, and a pair of tall, narrow doors opened onto one of the small Juliet balconies she'd spotted from the back.

"I don't know how he sleeps in here." But even as she said it, she thought it might be comforting to fall asleep with those rosy-cheeked shepherdesses keeping watch over her.

As she retreated toward the balcony doors, Rivers glanced at the ceiling. "I'm sure he does a lot more than sleep here." He approached the bedside table only to hesitate before he opened the drawer. "Maybe it would be better if you checked this out."

"Not in a million years." Who knew how many sex toys were inside? She shuddered, opened one of the double doors, and stepped onto the small, iron-railed Juliet balcony. From here, she could see the rear gardens and the pool glistening in the afternoon sunshine.

Something else caught her attention. Something so out of place it took her a moment to register what it was.

A body lay on the stone patio beneath the balcony, its torso twisted, long legs sprawled, silky red hair trapped in a pool of blood.

3

Ashley wore a breezy summer dress, silver bangles, and the same strappy sandals she'd worn yesterday when they'd last talked in the garage. Even in death she was beautiful . . . as long as you didn't look at her head.

Rory couldn't stop trembling. The June sun beat down on her. Ashley's body lay on the patio in front of her. "She must have . . . fallen off the balcony."

Rivers was cool and efficient, as if he stumbled on dead bodies all the time, although that might have been part of his supervillain act because he nearly dropped his phone while he was pocketing it after calling the police. Now he gazed up at the balcony. "Those doors were closed until you opened them."

A fact Rory had already taken in but couldn't process. She frantically looked around at the pool and garden. "Maybe she didn't fall. Maybe she came out here, tripped on one of the stones, and hit her head."

"Do you believe that?"

No, she didn't. The patio pavers were smooth, and even to Rory's untrained eye, something about the spread of Ashley's arms, the sweep of her hair, suggested she'd fallen from a height. "There has to be a logical explanation."

"I'm sure there is," he said grimly. "But we might not like it."

"What do you mean by that?" She knew what he meant. If Ashley had gone out onto the balcony and accidentally fallen, the doors would have been open when Rory and Rivers had entered the bedroom.

Rivers had looked in the window of the five-car garage and told her Clint's Range Rover was missing. Rory hadn't known Clint owned a Range Rover or any of the other three cars Rivers had informed her were still inside. Where was Clint?

"Go in the house and wait for the police," he said. "I'll stay here."

She wouldn't hide inside while he stood guard, but she couldn't look at Ashley's body. Turning away, she remembered the quote on a silly T-shirt some of her friends had given her before she moved. *Chocolate is to women what duct tape is to men. It fixes everything.*

But not even chocolate could fix this.

⋆

Rivers went off with the younger of the detectives, while the older, Detective Strothers, a man who reminded her of a very unfunny Eddie Murphy with his receding hairline, black-rimmed glasses, and neatly trimmed moustache, interrogated her in the kitchen. "You and Mr. Rivers were in Mr. Garrett's bedroom because you were both concerned about him?"

She'd already gone through this. "He hadn't answered my calls, and I needed to talk to him."

"Tell me again why that was so urgent."

She wasn't a deceitful person, but she wouldn't confess the part she'd played in breaking her brother's heart. "His mother and I have a difficult relationship. I wanted to talk to him about it."

He brushed his moustache with his thumb. "How long did your brother and Ms. Hart date?"

"A few months. My brother dates a lot of women, and Ashley was one of them." She wouldn't tell him that Clint had fallen in love with her.

"But you said they'd broken up, so why do you think she came here?"

A question Rory had been asking herself. The only answer she could come up with was too awful to contemplate. What if Ashley had discovered Rory had lied to her, and she'd come here hoping to reconcile with Clint? "I have no idea."

She expected the detective to press her, but he moved on. "The doors that lead to the balcony. You said they were closed. Were they locked?"

"Only latched, so it's possible the wind blew them shut." There hadn't been a trace of a breeze all morning.

"Why did you open them?"

Because she'd needed to do something that didn't involve looking at Rivers and remembering the particulars of their lost night. "I wanted to see the view."

He pushed his glasses higher on his nose. "You met Ms. Hart the day you moved into your apartment. That was six months ago, correct? Why did you move to Chicago?"

He'd already asked her this. "An old housemate of mine wanted me to partner with him operating a food truck selling candy."

Since Chicago was Clint's city, Rory had hesitated to make the move, but Jon had wrongly insisted Chicago was the best place to start their business. She'd also been ready for a change, and somewhere in her brain, selling candy from a food truck seemed like the next step toward becoming a full-time chocolatier.

He stroked his trim moustache. "The van that's parked in back. You drove it here from your apartment in Ravenswood. That has to be about thirty miles."

"It's currently my only means of transportation."

"And yet your brother is a wealthy man."

It wasn't a good idea to lose your temper with the police, and she forced herself to speak calmly. "Clint is wealthy. I'm not."

"I see." Detective Strothers stroked the lapel of his suit coat. "Did either of you look in the bathroom off Mr. Garrett's bedroom?"

"No. We hadn't looked there yet."

"You seem to have looked everywhere else." He moved on before she could respond. "Did she talk about any of the other men she dated?"

"She'd just started seeing Karloh Cousins, the basketball player. She also told me about someone she broke up with when she met my brother. She called him Real Estate Man and said he didn't take their breakup well, but I never met him."

The detective wrote in his notebook. "She never mentioned his name or told you where he worked?"

"No."

He closed the notebook. "Would you mind showing me your truck?"

His request took her by surprise. "All right," she said hesitantly.

The truck was hot, and she was already perspiring from nerves when they stepped inside. Strothers took in the empty shelves.

There were no Skittles for the grade school kids, Kit Kats for teens, or M&M's for moms and dads. The Milky Ways had disappeared, the Starbursts, the boxes of Reese's cups and packets of Gummi Bears. Jon had taken it all.

"Did Ms. Hart usually carry her cell phone?" the detective said.

"Always."

"Interesting." He had to be hot in his suit, but unlike her, he wasn't sweating. "We found Ms. Hart's purse in Mr. Garrett's bathroom, but not her cell phone."

That explained why he'd asked if she or Brett had gone in the bathroom. He gestured toward Rory's leather patchwork boho bag. "Could you empty your purse for me?"

Her attempt at staying calm evaporated. "You think I have her phone?"

"Routine," he said smoothly. "So I can complete my report."

If she refused, she'd only make herself look as if she had something to hide. A trickle of perspiration slid between her breasts as she dumped the contents on the driver's seat: wallet, keys, gum, tampons, loose change, a snack bag of almonds, and her cell phone.

He gestured toward the phone. "Unlock it, please."

Her fingers wouldn't work, and it took her two attempts to open it. The screen showed a photo she'd always liked of a tarnished antique spoon drizzled with chocolate. She handed it to him.

When he was satisfied the phone was hers, he returned it and gestured them both outside.

A metallic red Mercedes sedan that looked as though it cost a million dollars was parked next to the truck. It could only belong to Brett Rivers. In the yard, uniformed officers combed through the shrubbery.

"One more thing." For the first time since he'd begun

interviewing her, the detective regarded her pleasantly. If she'd had more experience with being interviewed by the police, she would have seen it for what it was. A sign he intended to strike. "How long were you alone in the house before Mr. Rivers showed up?"

Rory's stomach lurched. She would never again watch another Eddie Murphy movie. "I— I don't know exactly. Maybe ten minutes?"

"I see." He nodded, but nothing about that nod looked friendly. "Thank you, Ms. Garrett. I'll be in touch."

*
*

She was a suspect! She had no alibi for the ten or so minutes she'd been alone in the house before Rivers had arrived and while Ashley lay dead on the flagstones outside.

The EMTs began loading the stretcher with Ashley's body into an ambulance. Rory swallowed hard against the ugly reality of knowing Ashley would never again borrow one of Rory's vintage pieces, tell a dirty joke, or remind Rory that she was destined for more than selling Sour Patch Kids from the window of a food truck.

She dredged up everything she could remember from watching crime shows, and one disturbing fact emerged. Pathologists only provided the approximate time of death, so unless Ashley had died hours before Rory arrived, Rory was a potential suspect.

She had to leave. She jumped back in the truck and eventually made her way through the throng of emergency vehicles to the front. Detective Strothers stood on the porch speaking with a slim woman in jeans, a dark T-shirt, and sneakers. Judging by the grocery sacks at her feet, she must be Clint's housekeeper and one more person who had a key.

A ripped guy carrying a coiled hose stood near a swimming pool maintenance service van parked behind a landscaping truck. This was a busy household. The only person missing was its owner.

*
*

The Royal Palace of Sweets had disappeared. Brett got into his Benz, plugged in his phone to charge it, and left the house. He didn't like questions without answers, and there were so many questions. Where was Clint? Why had Ashley come here? And why did his instincts insist Rory Meadows Garrett knew more than she was telling?

*
*

Rory parked the Royal Palace of Sweets in the garage. As she came out to lower the cranky garage door, she saw Rivers leaning against the side of the red Benz she'd noticed earlier. With his slicked-back hair and tailored clothes, he couldn't have looked more out of place. "I passed you on 55." He pocketed his phone. "Your truck is burning oil."

Something she knew too well. "What are you doing here?"

"What kind of car did Ashley drive?"

He'd been wondering the same thing she had. "That kind." She pointed toward the sporty blue Toyota Supra sitting in one of the three narrow parking slots behind the apartment house. "More specifically, that's Ashley's car."

"Then how did she get to Clint's house?"

"Another question I can't answer, Detective." The garage door squealed as she yanked it shut. "*I'm* a suspect!"

"You're just figuring that out?"

"Leave me alone." She stalked past him and around the side of the garage to the apartment building. The back door opened, and her landlord emerged. Mr. Reynolds was tall and thin, with the exception of a slight belly protruding above the belt that held up his shorts. He had severely combed white hair and, like Detective Strothers, a moustache, but his was gray and shaggy.

She made her way along the cracked sidewalk, past Mr. Reynolds's vegetable garden, and toward the house, uncomfortably aware that Rivers wasn't far behind. Mr. Reynolds gave her his customary, crusty nod. His first name was Oscar, but she couldn't imagine calling him that. "Trash pickup is tomorrow," he grumbled. "If you see that Toby fellow, you remind him."

"I will." "That Toby fellow" was her third-floor neighbor, a twenty-three-year-old IT guy who had earned her landlord's wrath by setting off the smoke alarm making French fries because Ashley said she was in the mood. Like every other male, Toby was smitten with her.

The reality that Ashley was dead hit Rory all over again. Ashley had been shallow, self-absorbed, and manipulative, but she hadn't been evil, and she didn't deserve to die.

Rory couldn't summon the will to tell Mr. Reynolds what had happened, not with Brett Rivers snapping at her heels. She'd tell him later.

The old man gave Rivers the twice-over, but Rory wasn't making introductions. As she opened the screen door to go inside, Rivers caught the edge over her head so she couldn't slam it on him and followed her. The king of the universe could apparently go wherever he wanted.

Mr. Reynolds's greystone three-flat apartment house was a

mainstay of Chicago neighborhood architecture. With recessed front porches and bowed windows extending to the roof, these two-story, three-story, and four-story flats still peppered the city. Most had been built in the early twentieth century by the children of European immigrants to serve as multifamily residences. Now many of them had either been torn down or converted into pricey, single-family homes, but elderly Chicagoans like Mr. Reynolds were holding on.

He occupied the ground level and Ashley the second floor, while Rory and Toby rented the two smaller, and much shabbier, apartments that had once been a single unit on the top floor. As Rory reached the second-floor landing, she couldn't look at Ashley's door. She wondered if the police had called her sister. They hadn't been close, but Rory knew Ashley's sister was her only immediate relative.

Rory's apartment was exactly as she'd left it, but nothing felt the same. Rivers came in behind her. She imagined him judging her based on what he was seeing—once-white walls, uneven wood floors, and a yellowing ceiling. But the place was clean, and the building had a great location.

He closed the door, and she rounded on him. "What do you want?"

He observed her mismatched furniture and the rope espadrilles she'd left by the couch. "Tell me about Ashley. You two were good friends?"

"I'm not telling you anything."

He seemed comfortable standing uninvited right where he was. "I know we've both had a tough day, but a couple of questions are eating at me, and unlike the police, you can tell me anything."

The stubborn set of his square jaw suggested he wasn't going anywhere, and she had questions, too. It was easier answering him than fighting about it. "We weren't good friends, but she was good to me when I moved here." She sucked in some air. "I can't believe I'm a suspect."

"You don't have a motive." He paused. "Do you?"

"Of course I don't!" Except the police might not see it the same way. Loyal sister furious with ex-girlfriend for dumping her beloved brother pushes ex-girlfriend off the balcony in retaliation.

His gaze fell on the framed poster of the Twenties flapper she'd hung over her bookcases, the word "Floozy" in navy script over a peach background. "Clint's a more plausible suspect than you."

"Don't say that!" Even though it was exactly what the police had to be thinking. Either Clint or herself.

"Why should you care? He's an asshole, remember?" Rivers wandered toward one of the room's two side windows.

"He's only an asshole in my eyes," she said. "He could never murder anyone."

Rivers gazed out at the view of the neighboring four-flat's brick wall. "Clint's big. He's strong. He has a temper. You've seen him get into it on the field."

"You're supposed to be on his side," she retorted.

"I am, so let's hope wherever he is, he has a good alibi."

Rory's mouth was dry, her throat scratchy. She needed water, and she headed for the kitchen.

Between the buckled linoleum floor, the warped white metal cabinets, and the single window that looked out over the backyard and the alley, her kitchen was a relic of the past. Naturally, he followed her—his right as ruler of the world. "You do know how to live the life of luxury," he said. "Out of curiosity, and I realize it's a sore point, but does your megarich brother know you live so . . . rustically?"

"I haven't gotten around to inviting him." She opened the refrigerator and took out a pitcher of water with floating slices of orange and cucumber. Clint had also never been to Ashley's more luxurious apartment downstairs, because Ashley had always insisted on meeting him elsewhere. *Image is everything,* she'd told Rory with her impish smile. *No need for him to see me in a Ravenswood three-flat.*

"What's this?"

She turned to see Rivers standing by her drop-leaf kitchen table. He'd spotted the rack holding two dozen of the truffles Ashley had asked her to make yesterday in a rush job for her new boyfriend. Rory swallowed hard. "Those are my ancho chili truffles." Technically, they were bonbons because Rory had enrobed them in a chocolate shell, but in the US the terms "bonbon" and "truffle" tended to be used interchangeably.

As she took a glass tumbler from the cupboard, she saw the novelty wineglass she'd picked up at a stoop sale. It had a crown and the word "Queen" etched in the glass. Ashley had always insisted on using it when she ate dinner here. Rory's eyes stung. Ashley had loved Rory's curried eggplant with turmeric and coconut milk.

"Is that the Bulls logo on top?" he asked.

"It is." Because she'd made adjustments to the flavoring, she wanted another opinion, even his. "Help yourself."

Instead of popping the whole thing in his mouth as most people did, he bit it in half and tasted. She couldn't imagine him appreciating the complexity of the flavors—the marriage of sweet and tart, the hint of lime and almost imperceptible breath of cinnamon.

He studied the uneaten half. "This might be the best piece of chocolate I've ever tasted."

He was still an arrogant ass, but he did know good chocolate. She filled her water glass. "Ironic, isn't it, for someone who, until recently, earned her so-called living wearing a plastic tiara and selling Tootsie Rolls."

"Until recently?"

"I'm not in the mood to share the sad story of my undoing with a man who drives a Benz and considers the rest of humanity grit under the soles of his Gucci loafers."

He smiled. "Unfair, but I do enjoy my luxuries."

She took a long drink of water. He was still studying the uneaten half of the truffle, almost as if he were looking for the key to its flavors. Years of experimentation had gone into perfecting that glossy shell—not as bitter as bad dark chocolate, nor as sweet as inferior milk chocolate. Her small tempering machine sat on the counter. She'd stuffed the cupboards and drawers with her bowls and molds, spatulas and piping bags, all the tools she'd acquired over the years.

He finished the piece. "You're damn good at this."

"But not good enough to make a living at it." She hated how self-pitying she'd sounded.

"Plan better. Work harder."

She wanted to punch him. "You have no idea how hard I've worked, but as it turns out, no matter how good you are, you can't make a living wage selling artisanal chocolates at farmers' markets." When Rory had lived in Manhattan, she'd rented booths at markets all over the five boroughs, but between fees, gas, and refusing to compromise by using cheaper ingredients, she'd still had to support herself by working for catering companies and waiting tables.

He leaned against the doorjamb, filling the space with his wide shoulders and slicked-back hair. "So you came to Chicago to make your fortune."

Minneapolis to Boston to New York and now Chicago. An unwelcome bitterness dusted her reply. "I somehow convinced myself that selling Snickers from a food truck would bring me closer to my goal."

"Which is?"

She could see the chocolate shop in her mind. Something small and cozy with a sparkling front window displaying everything from her silky opera creams to her black raspberry truffles. Instead of a starkly intimidating European-style fine chocolate emporium, her shop would have friendly Wedgwood-blue walls, colorful rugs, and painted cupboards with glass doors. She'd offer tastings at the worn white marble counter, everything from cognac-infused bonbons to exquisitely simple vanilla nougats. In the winter, she'd serve steaming cups of single-source Peruvian hot chocolate at round bistro tables with curly ice-cream parlor chairs. In the rear of the shop, she'd have her own well-stocked kitchen where she made everything. But she couldn't tell Rivers any of that. Instead, Ashley's words popped into her head. "My goal? Finding a rich husband, of course."

To his credit, he didn't miss her sarcasm. "Like your friend Ashley?"

"You figured that out about her?" she said.

"It's true, then."

"Yes."

"Then why did she dump him for Karloh Cousins? Karloh does all right for himself, but he's not nearly in the same pay bracket as Clint."

Rory had the stupid urge to confess what she'd done. Instead, she gestured toward the truffles. "I don't know. Help yourself to another."

He made his selection and once again bit it in half. There was something sensual in the way he savored the chocolate that seemed out of character for a workaholic who'd checked his phone at least three times since he'd walked in the door.

"Clint didn't shove Ashley off the balcony," she said. "And it's past time for you to take your cash-stuffed wallet and leave." She'd earned her grudge against him, and she was holding it tight.

"You're not going to let that unfortunate money incident go, are you?"

She rubbed her earlobe, feeling the tiny bumps from old piercings she'd let close up. "I've had a lot of crappy things happen to me lately, but that night is right near the top."

"If it's not number one, that means I can redeem myself." He polished off the chocolate.

"Save your oily charm for someone susceptible." She tugged on the end kitchen drawer. It was old and warped from decades of paint, and if she pulled too hard, it would fall out. She opened it just enough to retrieve Ashley's key from underneath a pad of sticky notes. "I'm searching Ashley's apartment."

That brought him to full attention. "Bad idea."

She bumped the drawer closed with her hip. "It isn't a crime scene, and when she's not around, I feed her cat."

"There's been a murder. Going in there could be seen as tampering with evidence."

"What are you? A lawyer?"

He followed her from the kitchen. "As a matter of fact, I am, like most NFL agents."

"You were never one of those nice-guy lawyers serving the downtrodden, were you?" she retorted. "You interned at some big firm that charges a thousand dollars an hour and loves hiring ex-jocks. A place where everybody works a hundred hours a week and spends their free time drunk on top-shelf liquor."

His brow furrowed, lips narrowed. She'd finally managed to annoy him. "How do you know I'm an ex-jock?" he said.

Now she was the one with the patronizing tone. "Your shoulders. Your body. Your entitled attitude."

"You're a very judgmental person. Did anyone ever tell you that?"

"Sue me. Oh, wait. You could."

The furrows eased. "I don't practice law now."

"Not enough money in it?"

Instead of taking the bait, he came after her. "I love money and I love my job. I work hard, I work smart, and that's why I'm the best at what I do."

There had to be a soft spot beneath all that egotism. Every human being—even a master of the universe—had weaknesses, skeletons hidden in the back of his custom-built closet. She headed for the door. "I need to get into Ashley's apartment before the police seal it off. Maybe she talked to Clint. Maybe she wrote something down."

He blocked her. "You can't go in, and you definitely can't tamper with any possible evidence. No one wants to find Clint more than I do, but—"

She shoved past him. "Obviously not true, or you'd be with me on this."

As she entered the hallway, the door across the landing opened, and Toby Griffin emerged, scrawny as a scarecrow with a shrub of sandy brown hair exploding around his head. In jeans that didn't fit and a black T-shirt that read, "Battery Full," he was the techie of a thousand memes. "Hey, Rory. Have you seen Ashley?"

It felt like a body slam. Once again, she saw Ashley splayed on the flagstones.

"I told her I'd put in a dimmer switch for her," Toby went on.

This was another example of Ashley's less attractive qualities. She had no interest in Toby, but she knew he was crazy about her, and she paid him just enough attention to give him hope and get him to do things for her.

Toby regarded Brett Rivers with curiosity. "I'm Toby Griffin."

"This is Brett," Rory said, before the conversation could go further. "I'm showing him out."

"If you see Ashley, let her know I'm looking for her." He disappeared back into his apartment.

As the door shut, Brett lifted that dark eyebrow again. "You're not going to tell him?"

"Later." When she could say the words without falling apart.

She slipped past Brett down the stairs. She hesitated at Ashley's door, then turned the key and pushed it open.

The tail of Ashley's cat, Luther, disappeared under the couch. Like so many other men, he wanted only Ashley's company. Rivers followed her inside. "I'm acting against my better judgment."

"Slap a couple hundred dollars on her dresser. You'll feel more like yourself."

"That hurt."

He didn't seem hurt. He seemed alert. Like an eagle who'd spotted an especially juicy creature worthy of his attack. She turned away from him.

Ashley's ultrafeminine white-on-white color scheme couldn't be more different from her own decor. The couch, chairs, and carpet-brushing drapes at the big bay window were all white, broken up by an array of sherbet-colored throw pillows and an abstract painting in the same pastel hues. The painting was an original oil Rory happened to know her brother had paid for, along with the delicate crystal chandelier dangling from a ceiling hook in the corner. If a woman admired a multimillionaire football player's crystal chandeliers enough times, apparently he'd buy her one of her own. Then she'd get a love-smitten nerd to install a dimmer switch for it.

Clint had tried to buy things for Rory, but unlike Ashley, Rory had refused until he'd stopped offering.

"Clint is so generous," Ashley had gushed. *"He's the man I've been waiting for. I just know it."*

The reality that Ashley was no longer alive hit her anew. Rory made herself look around, but nothing seemed out of place. An abandoned wineglass rested on the coffee table by a bottle of nail polish. A *People* magazine lay open on the white carpet next to the tip of Luther's tail.

Luther. What was Rory supposed to do about Ashley's cat?

"It looks like she got dressed in a hurry." Rivers spoke up from the largest of the two bedrooms. Rory went over to look for herself.

Discarded outfits covered the sloppily made bed, shoes littered the floor, and jewelry lay in a tangle on her dresser. Rory remembered Ashley's last outfit: the summer dress that showcased her endless legs, the ankle-wrap sandals, and the silver earring obscenely sparkling in a pool of blood.

The bathroom was equally messy, with makeup spread across the counter, a towel crumpled on the floor, and a fat curling iron turned off but still plugged into an outlet.

"Ashley wasn't the neatest person, but she wasn't normally this messy."

"It looks like she was in a hurry."

A hurry to get Clint back.

Rory found a stack of mail on the kitchen counter. The idea of going through it left her squeamish. Besides, that wasn't what she was looking for. Maybe Clint had called her from a different phone, and Ashley had written down his number.

But the only note she found in Ashley's handwriting read: *Love fades. Money doesn't.*

* * *

Unlike him, Rory Garrett had no poker face. When Brett asked a question she didn't like, she developed a fascination with his right ear. He'd also noticed her nibbling on her bottom lip whenever she was troubled. Yes, she had a grudge against him, but more than that grudge was bothering her. For someone who professed to dislike her half brother, she seemed awfully concerned.

He checked his phone. One missed text could cost him a client, but nothing needed his immediate attention. He looked around. Even Rory's shabby apartment was better than Ashley Hart's place with its white upholstery and way too many throw pillows. He hated throw pillows. Since they always ended up on the floor, he didn't understand why women liked them so much.

Rory was standing at the kitchen counter, which opened into

the too-white living area. "Let's get out of here," he said as she emerged from the kitchen.

"But the cat . . ."

"Is a cat," he said.

"I knew it! You hate cats, don't you?"

"I don't hate cats." Her hostility was about more than cats. Her distant relationship with Clint, combined with her feisty nature, stubborn pride, and regret over their hookup, made him hopeful she wouldn't run to Clint with the story of what had happened in that hotel bedroom, but hope was far from certainty. "If you can manage to forget about that night, I can, too."

"You're afraid I'll tell Clint."

"It has occurred to me."

"Agents should never get intimately involved with a member of a client's family." She sounded uncomfortably smug. "That would be an unforgivable breach of your professional code of conduct."

Yes, it would be. "I didn't know you were related."

"And now you're totally freaking out."

"I never freak out." He projected a calmness he was far from feeling. "Granted, I'd rather no one found out about this."

"I'll think about it."

She was bluffing. She had to be. Or was she? She marched from the apartment into the hallway, and he followed her out.

"Why are you still here?" She glared at him from her perch three steps above, one of her red heart earrings tangling in the curls escaping from the top of her head.

"I'd rather not leave without another chocolate." As well as some answers to his questions and more assurance about what she would or wouldn't tell Clint.

"Everyone wants my chocolates, but nobody wants to pay for them!"

"I'll pay you."

"Yes, you're good at that."

"What can I say? I like my sensory pleasures." He hadn't meant to sound quite so sleazy, but he couldn't take it back, so he dug in. "I'm talking about food and wine. Not what you're thinking."

She hurried up the stairs, flip-flops spanking her heels. "If you know what I'm thinking, then you meant it exactly the way it sounded."

He didn't completely follow her logic, but he still understood her point.

He slipped inside her apartment before she could slam the door on him.

Brett headed for the chocolates while Rory ducked into the apartment's only bedroom. The kitchen had one window painted shut and an old green refrigerator wedged next to a four-burner gas stove. It reminded him of his college apartment, not a place where Clint Garrett's thirty-four-year-old half sister should be living.

As he considered having another of the chocolates on the table, he heard a muffled scream. He raced toward its source and found Rory standing at the foot of a neatly made double bed, her hand pressed to her mouth. A red evening bag lay in the center of the bedspread, its satin fabric slashed to ribbons.

"What's going on?"

Rory's blue eyes met his, and her voice shook. "It was my mother's. The only thing of hers I had left. Ashley borrowed it yesterday. The last time I saw her alive."

"Why did Ashley cut up that bag?"

"I—I didn't want to lend it to her. She knew that. But she took it anyway." She rubbed her cheek. "I was out all morning. She must have come in when I was gone and left it here."

Something ugly had happened between these two recently, something that made the word "motive" flash in his lawyer's brain like a cherry light on an old police cruiser. He didn't know what Rory had been up to before he'd arrived at Clint's house. What he did know was that she'd been anxious to get rid of him. Was that only because she hated his guts or for a more pressing reason?

She dashed from the bedroom and headed to the kitchen, a place he was beginning to suspect was her sanctuary. He took another look at the ruined purse before he followed her, stopping inside the door.

"Are you *ever* going to leave?" she exclaimed.

"You and I need to have a heart-to-heart."

"Good luck finding one."

"That's cold." He commandeered a chair at the kitchen table closest to the chocolates. "Conversations like these always go better with food. Consider that a hint."

"If you stay any longer, I'm charging you rent!"

"Fair." With the drop leaves down, only one of his legs fit comfortably underneath the table. He extended the other, careful not to trip her as she moved around. Maybe she wasn't all that anxious to be alone, because she pulled two bottles of beer from the refrigerator and set them on the table. "I can't afford a charcuterie board, so you'll have to make do with chocolate and peanuts."

For a moment, he thought she'd said "penis." He couldn't believe his mind had fallen into the gutter so quickly. "Penis is fine," he said, only to hear his mistake a second later.

Shit. This was Rory Garrett standing in front of him, Clint's sister, and also not the kind of woman who'd impress his clients. The younger guys surrounded themselves with gorgeous, long-stemmed bottle blondes. Even the older guys had their share of current and former wives who looked strikingly similar and nothing at all like Rory with her mop-top, honey-colored hair; ragamuffin's cheeks; and pugnacious attitude.

He chose the women he publicly dated as shrewdly as he chose his clothes. Nothing personal about it. It was good business for his clients to see him with beautiful women, but he was a pragmatist, not a sleaze, and he didn't take any of those showpieces to bed unless they had a genuine connection and a no-strings understanding. He'd gotten good at keeping his pants on . . . right up until the incident with Rory. Too much alcohol and unease over Clint's state of mind had dimmed his normally acute judgment, and he'd ended up falling into bed with a woman who seemed to have frivolity stamped all over her.

He couldn't have been more wrong about that. Rory Garrett's only frivolous parts were those blue eyes the color of a Bombay Sapphire gin bottle and a body like a World War II pinup on the nose of a B-29. Less lean and leggy—more shapely—with curvy hips, a neat waist, and commendable breasts.

She rummaged in the cabinet without noticing that he couldn't seem to differentiate between "penis" and "peanuts." How long had she really been at Clint's house before he'd arrived? If she'd pushed Ashley off the balcony, his client was in the clear, but that didn't ease his mind.

"What am I supposed to do with a cat?" She opened a bag of shelled peanuts and poured them into a small pottery bowl. "This is going to traumatize Luther."

"Does she have any relatives?"

"Luther's a he, not a she. And cats don't exactly have responsible relatives."

"Not the *cat*. Ashley. Talking to you is like talking to a client with too many concussions." *Damn*. He kept forgetting she was Clint's sister. He needed to stop insulting her, and he quickly regrouped. "Fortunately, you're charming enough to be forgiven."

She greeted his unctuousness with a sneer. "Have you always been an arrogant dickhead or is it more recent?"

He could be a dickhead when he needed to be, so this wasn't exactly an unfair criticism. Now he had a weird urge to dig in and argue with her that she was, indeed, charming. She was also a pain in the ass, but interesting to be around in a twisted sort of way.

She put the peanut bowl on the table next to the chocolates. "Ashley has a sister who lives somewhere around Midway. They don't get along. Or *didn't* get along. Don't eat that!"

He dropped the truffle he'd been about to consume. "I thought you were offering chocolate."

"Ancho chili truffles don't pair with that oatmeal stout." As she gestured toward the beer she'd put in front of him, she sounded as offended as if he were once again offering her hooker money.

"Excuse my stupidity," he said dryly.

She extracted a Christmas cookie tin from the cupboard, stepped over his extended leg, and took the chair across from him at the table. She opened the lid, revealing a jewel box of her chocolate creations. Domes of bright red and purple, yellow and green, some of them dappled with metallic flecks. Glossy squares of dark and milk chocolate made those bright colors stand out even more. His hand crept toward a brilliant green dome dusted with tiny purple stars. He reconsidered just in time. "Any objections?"

She pointed out a chocolate square glimmering with salt crystals. "Stouts need a really good milk chocolate, preferably with caramel and sea salt. If you're drinking a hoppy IPA, dark chocolate is best. With pilsner, semisweet chocolate. Easy to remember."

He intended to forget as soon as possible. But after the first taste, he knew she was right. The chocolate she'd recommended intensified the beer's creamy malt, and the salt crystals brightened the finish. But he had something more important on his mind than chocolate and beer pairings. "Tell me about the evening bag."

She grabbed the pottery peanut bowl and got up from the table. "Let's go into the living room. You look weird sitting in my kitchen. Actually, you look weird sitting in my apartment."

"Why is that?" He picked up the beer and considered bringing along the tin of chocolates, but Rory's work was designed to be savored, not gulped down like a handful of M&M's.

"Because you belong in one of those rich bachelor pads where everything is painted gray with some black thrown in for added masculinity." She set the peanuts on a spindle-leg coffee table that looked as if she'd dragged it up from a curb. "Abstract paintings that your decorator picked hang on the walls. Maybe there are some antelope horns in your bookcase instead of books."

He settled on her lumpy couch. "Antelope horns?"

"Okay, maybe not that, but a hardback of *Infinite Jest*, which you haven't read, but you like to display alongside a copy of, let's say, *Das Kapital* for irony. You keep the Marvel comics you really read hidden in your bedroom."

"You do love your stereotypes."

She chose an oversized armchair draped with an Indian cotton tablecloth. "*And* you have a collection of silver cocktail shakers. Am I wrong?"

She wasn't entirely wrong. He did have *Infinite Jest* in his book-case, but he'd also read it. And the way she'd nailed the gray-and-black color scheme in his condo made him wish he hadn't given his decorator free rein. He didn't like how Rory had pigeonholed him, and he momentarily forgot his intention to worm himself into her favor. "You're not exactly the person to cast aspersions on other people's homes. This place is—excuse the term—a rathole."

So much for his intention not to insult her, but instead of call-ing him out, she shrugged. "I sold every decent thing I owned to scratch together the money to buy the food truck."

"What happened?"

"I don't want to talk about it."

He'd allowed her to deflect his questions long enough. "Ashley was sending you a message when she cut up that evening bag, right?"

"I don't want to talk about that, either."

He draped his arm across the back of the couch and ambushed her. "Are you the one who pushed Ashley off the balcony?"

She jumped from the armchair, knocking over her beer. "Now look what you've done!" She dashed into the kitchen.

He followed her. "Are you?"

"Get out of my way." She grabbed a couple of paper towels and rushed back to the living room, digging a sharp elbow into his ribs as she passed by him.

"Ouch!"

Only a little beer had spilled on the floor, but she made a big show of cleaning it up. He rubbed the ache in his rib cage. "Here's the thing, Rory. You're probably not the one who pushed Ashley off that balcony, but—"

"'Probably'?" She rounded on him, an avenging angel with birthday-candle curls and lollipop eyes. "You think I killed her?"

"Something was wrong between the two of you, and there's a good chance the police will figure that out, so you might as well tell me first."

She dropped back into the chair, landing so hard she pulled off the tablecloth covering it to reveal unsavory brown upholstery beneath. "You're a lawyer. I'm hiring you."

"I'm not currently practicing, as I told you. And if I were, you couldn't afford me."

"You're freeloading off my beer and practically living here. It's called barter."

Following her train of thought was like trying to play chess with a Pomeranian. "I'm afraid to ask why you're so anxious to hire a lawyer."

"Because you keep asking me questions, and I'm not answering any of them unless I have attorney-client privilege."

He rubbed the back of his neck. "God, you *did* kill her."

"Don't be an idiot."

"So you didn't kill her?" He sank into the lumpy couch.

"Of course, I didn't kill her! Do we have a deal or not?"

He gave her his badass stare. "I need a retainer."

"Grab a dozen of those chili chocolates."

"How about you just tell me the truth?"

"I don't want to."

"Really? I'm shocked. Since you've already been so forthcoming."

"I hate sarcastic people."

He conjured all the sarcasm he could muster. "I'm wounded."

She leaped up at the sound of a knock. He shot to his feet and grabbed her arm. "Don't answer that."

"I have to answer."

"It might be the police, and you're not ready to talk to them again."

"My attorney is right here." She pulled free and threw open the door.

It wasn't the police.

A woman stood on the other side, frizzy gray hair, maybe sixty, wearing too many clothes for such a hot day. She stared at Rory, not saying anything at first, and then: "I'm Claudia."

"Of course, Claudia. We've met before. Come in."

Claudia gave him a wary eye. "If it's a bad time, I can come back later."

"It's a perfect time. You can ignore him. He only cares about making money." She stepped aside. "The clothes you left here last week are clean, and I'll put some fresh towels in the bathroom."

"I left my clothes here?" Claudia was still regarding him suspiciously.

"You did. And I'll get them for you while you take a bath."

Thunderstruck, he watched Rory lead the strange woman toward the bathroom. On the way, she took a couple of towels and a small stack of clothes from the closet. She emerged a few minutes later, still talking to the woman, as water ran in the background. "Leave whatever you want me to wash on the floor. You can get it next week." She shut the door behind her.

He aimed his finger toward the bathroom. "What in the almighty hell is *that* about?"

"I don't want to talk about it."

"There is a *hell* of a lot you don't want to talk about!"

She shrugged and headed for the kitchen. He grabbed his beer and followed her. "Do you know that woman?"

"She comes here every week or so, but she has memory issues, so she keeps forgetting who I am." Rory filled a pot with water.

He'd witnessed a lot of recklessness in his career—drinking, fighting, gambling—but this was a whole new category. "Is that woman homeless?"

"We say 'unhoused.'"

She delivered way more sarcasm than he'd used earlier, and he set the flat of his hand against the doorjamb. "Are you in the habit of letting random street people use your apartment?"

She put the pot on the stove and turned on the burner. "They're not entirely random."

"'They'? You mean she's not the only one?"

"A friend of a friend works in social services. If I'm home, I try to help a few of the women she sends to me." She began pulling ingredients from the refrigerator: butter, a package wrapped in butcher paper, a wedge of cheese. She retrieved a cutting board and chef's knife. "They can take a bath or shower. I wash some clothes. Give them a meal. No big deal."

He lost it. "You know how you help the unhoused? You do what I do. You support programs that deal with food, jobs, and mental health. You don't go around—"

"Says the rich boy."

He advanced on her. "It doesn't have anything to do with rich. It has to do with common sense. Some of these street people could be dangerous. You don't invite them into your home. For God's sake, Rory. Volunteer at a shelter or a soup kitchen."

She slammed her knife on the cutting board. "I'm the one who broke up Clint and Ashley!"

If the abrupt change of topic was a strategy to shut him up, it worked. She grabbed a head of garlic from a wire basket and turned away from him. "I thought I was doing the right thing, but . . ." Her voice developed the woolly edge of a woman determined not to cry. "But now Ashley's dead and Clint has disappeared."

He sat at the kitchen table, temporarily abandoning the discussion they needed to have about the woman in the bathroom. Since Rory didn't like questions, he took another route. "Tell me more about Ashley."

She smashed the head of garlic on the cutting board in a way that made him nervous. "Ashley was smart, ambitious, and single-minded. She knew exactly what she wanted from life."

"Which was?"

"To marry rich. And once she met Clint, she found her dream man."

Rory confirmed what he'd intuitively known.

Her chef's knife drummed against the wood as she began chopping. "Ashley was a pragmatist. She wanted love, but more than that she wanted luxury." She poured olive oil into a skillet. "Over drinks one night, she told me straight-out she was willing to marry anyone to get it. She even joked about it. She said her only other criterion was that he had to be under seventy unless he had a heart condition. I was almost jealous. She was so clear about what she wanted and how to get it." The oil sizzled as she tossed the garlic in the skillet. "After she met Clint, she tried to convince me she'd only been kidding about money and that Clint was the love of her life, but I knew better. I tried to talk to him about her, but he'd already bought a ring, and he cut me off before I could say anything." She poked at the garlic with a wooden spoon and turned down the heat under the burner. "He was getting ready to take her to Vegas to elope. Without a prenup! I knew if I said anything negative about her, he'd only dig in deeper. I couldn't let that happen."

"And so, you . . ."

"I broke them up," she said flatly. The kitchen began to fill with the scent of garlic. "I swore Ashley to secrecy and told her Clint was a compulsive gambler. That he'd lost all his money and that the Stars were going to cut him because . . ." She kept her gaze focused on the skillet, not looking at him. "Because they found out he was betting on his own games."

Brett nearly knocked over his beer. "Betting on Stars games? Do you have any idea how serious that is?"

"It was the first thing that popped into my head."

"It should have popped right back out again." He temporarily forgot that she'd given him exactly the information he needed to save his relationship with his most valuable client. "Clint plays a ten-dollar Nassau on the golf course. And nobody wants to sit at a poker table with him because he insists on a fifty-cent limit. Setting that aside, even a rumor that he was betting on his own games could have damaged his career."

"I swore her to secrecy. I told her if she cared about him, she'd never tell anyone." She pulled a package of pasta from the cupboard, only to drop it on the floor. "I even made myself cry, which wasn't hard because I knew what I was doing was wrong." She picked up the pasta she'd dropped. "But Clint really loved her, and I broke his heart."

Brett considered what this meant to him. Once Clint found out about this, he'd know Brett had been right about Ashley from the beginning and had only been trying to protect him. Brett would be off the hook. But Rory's sadness tempered his excitement. "Not to put too fine a point on it," he said, "but Ashley broke his heart."

Rory took the pasta ribbons from the package. "Ashley wasn't a bad person, just mercenary. And she was good to me even before she knew I was Clint's sister."

"You must have introduced them."

"An ugly coincidence. Ashley and I went to see an exhibit of Nick Cave's work at the MCA. Afterward, we were passing the Peninsula as Clint came out from some kind of event and saw me. I'd never let Clint come to my apartment, and I tried to avoid introducing them, but Ashley did it for herself, and that was all it took. One look at her, and Clint was smitten. Now she's dead, Clint's gone, and I'm responsible."

Someone with her overdeveloped conscience wouldn't last a minute as a sports agent. He finally had an answer to the missing piece of the puzzle—why Ashley had dumped Clint for a less wealthy basketball player. He risked a direct question. "How do you figure you're responsible for what happened to Ashley?"

"You saw that evening bag. Ashley knew what it meant to me. Somehow she found out I lied and took her revenge on me by destroying it."

"How do you think she found out?"

"I don't know." She snatched up a dish towel and dried her hands. "Something happened after I saw her yesterday, because everything was okay then." She tossed prosciutto in the skillet with the garlic and dumped the pasta into the pot of boiling water. "I was gone most of this morning. She must have come in here then, thrown the purse on my bed, and raced out to do whatever she needed to get Clint back." She bit her lip. "I think she'd genuinely fallen for him."

"But not hard enough to stay with him when she thought he was going broke." He finished his beer. "Someone else had to have been in his house."

"The person who pushed her off the balcony." She fumbled with a wedge of Parmesan cheese. "If I hadn't lied to her in the first place, she wouldn't have broken up with him, wouldn't have gone out there, and she'd still be alive."

His leg was trapped under the table and beginning to go to sleep. He pushed the chair back and stood up, calculating all the angles. "Right now, the police have two suspects in their crosshairs. You and Clint."

"Her ex did it," she said bitterly. "Real Estate Man. I know it. The guy was stalking her." As the pasta finished cooking and she prepped the peas, Rory told him about Ashley's old boyfriend and how he'd harassed her after she met Clint and broke up with him. "I just wish I knew his name." A cloud of steam rose from the sink as she drained the pasta into a colander.

"That's for the police to figure out. Your problem is that Ashley had a grudge against you, and you have no alibi for the time you were in the house before I got there."

"I know," she said dismally.

"But the fact that Clint has disappeared makes him the prime suspect."

"I've got to find him."

He leaned against her old green refrigerator. "For someone who professes to hate her brother, you seem awfully concerned about him."

"Half brother." She began grating the block of cheese into a bowl. "I never said I hate him. I just don't want anything to do with him."

"Clint's a congenial guy unless he's on the field. What happened to make you resent him so much?"

"Your bathroom smells like flowers," an uncertain voice said.

He turned to see Claudia standing barefoot in the doorway, her lank gray hair hanging wet around her shoulders.

"It's the lavender bath salts," Rory told her. "Sit down, both of you. The pasta is almost ready—tagliatelle with peas, prosciutto, and Parmesan."

And that was how he found himself having dinner with a homeless woman who wore her clothes inside out and a broke chocolatier with a guilty conscience.

* *

Rory couldn't put off talking to her stepmother a moment longer, and as soon as she was alone, she reluctantly picked up her phone. The one good thing Brett had done before he left was insist on taking the red evening bag with him so Rory didn't have to look at it.

Kristin answered on the third ring. "My caller ID says this is someone named Rory Garrett, but I don't recall the name."

Instead of sounding frantic, Kristin greeted Rory with her habitually annoyed voice, which meant the police hadn't yet contacted her, something they were certain to do very soon. "I've been busy." Rory set the abandoned beer bottles next to the sink where the dirty dishes awaited. Shockingly, Brett had volunteered to wash them, but she only wanted to get rid of him.

"You're always busy," Kristin said, "and yet your brother, who's even busier, never seems to have trouble finding time to call me."

Because you fawn on him, and you can barely tolerate me. Rory dropped the beer bottles in the recycling bin. "We both know he's the better person."

"Self-pity doesn't become you."

Neither did Rory's wardrobe, hairstyle, chosen career, or choice of friends—only a few of the many things Kristin had criticized over the years.

Kristin had been pregnant with Clint when Rory's father had married her less than a year after Rory's mother's death. Rory had been five at the time. Clint had been a beautiful baby; a sunny, bright little boy; and a gifted teen athlete. Both Kristin and Rory's father had been smitten with him, and Rory had become a footnote in their lives, the child who lived in their house and required attention only when she got into trouble with her talent for disruption. Kristin didn't understand the deep roots of Rory's unhappiness, and instead of a hug, she offered punishment.

Rory remembered spring of her sophomore year in high school when Jason Williams, the senior she'd had a crush on for months, had finally asked her out. But as she'd been getting ready to leave, Kristin had grounded her. "You can't ground me!" Rory had cried. "I have a date with Jason tonight!"

"You should have thought about that before you hit your brother. For God's sake, Rory, you're fifteen. He's nine."

"He's a brat! And he hit me first."

"Do you hear yourself? You sound like *you're* nine."

Rory had erupted, punishing Kristin for the misery her teenage self couldn't articulate. "And you sound like you're being a bitch!"

Any hope she'd harbored that Kristin would relent vanished, right along with her date with Jason.

Her father, as always, refused to intervene. "Do what Kristin says."

Looking back, Rory felt as if she'd lived her childhood permanently grounded. She'd even had her bedroom door removed for a week because she'd slammed it one too many times.

Eventually, she'd outgrown her bratty behavior, but that hadn't eased her relationship with Kristin. Her stepmother could no longer ground her, but she could still let her displeasure with Rory be felt.

"To what do I owe the honor of this rare phone call?"

Rory gritted her teeth. "Have you talked to Clint?"

"It's been over a week." The familiar note of displeasure colored her stepmother's voice, but for once it wasn't directed at her.

Rory turned on the kitchen faucet, then turned it off. She'd deal with the dishes tomorrow. "I've been trying to reach him."

Kristin was many things, but she wasn't stupid. "What's wrong? I knew something was wrong when he didn't call on Monday."

"I'm sure Clint mentioned Ashley Hart."

"I think he's falling in love. I can't wait to meet her. She sounds perfect for him."

"She wasn't." Rory had to tell her. "Ashley's dead."

Kristin gasped. "What happened? How's Clint? This is going to devastate him."

Not to mention what it did to Ashley. But, as was typical, Kristin's first thoughts were always of the Chosen One.

Rory told her the rest, omitting only her role in the breakup. "The fact that he's disappeared makes him a suspect," she said. "The police are already looking for him."

"That's outrageous! Clint would never hurt anyone."

A few NFL defensive players might disagree, but Rory understood. "The police don't know that."

"I'm flying out right away. I'll text you as soon as I have my arrival information. Pick me up at the airport."

The image of Kristin in the pink-and-purple food truck was too bizarre to contemplate. "My car's in the shop. You'll have to call an Uber or take a limo."

"Honestly, Rory, could you just once in your life—" She emitted her best long-suffering sigh. "Never mind. As much as I hate it, I should probably drive anyway so I have my car. You can meet me at Clint's house. I'll stay there."

Since Clint's house was officially a murder scene, Rory wasn't certain Kristin would be able to get inside, but her stepmother could sort that out. And like everyone else in Clint's universe, Kristin surely had a key.

Learning that Clint had missed his regular phone call with Mommy made Rory even more anxious to find him. She wished she knew more about his friends and where he hung out. She needed that information, and there was only one person she could think of who could give it to her.

★
★

The story of Ashley Hart's murder hit the news early the next morning, and every reporter in the city wanted to talk to Clint Garrett. Not being able to reach him, they pummeled his agent. Most of the reporters were polite, a few weren't, but the toughest call came from Stars headquarters wanting to know why Clint's agent couldn't locate their quarterback.

Heath Champion, the head of Champion Sports Management, sat behind his office desk studying Brett. Known in business as "The Python," Heath was a good-looking guy with dark hair just beginning to gray at the temples, alert green eyes, and a tough demeanor that only relaxed when he was with his family. "You really don't know where he is?"

"I'll find him." Brett leaned back in the chair across from him, trying to look more relaxed than he felt. He'd worked too hard to get where he was to let anyone—especially his boss—see him sweat. Brett had put himself through law school, passed the bar on his first attempt, and come up through the ranks at Champion by working harder than anyone else. He lived in airplanes, kept his phone on him twenty-four hours a day, and never forgot a birthday, anniversary, or career milestone. He scouted players, signed them, and groomed them for the NFL. He hugged grandmothers and kissed babies and took phone calls at three in the morning from drunken clients who owned too many firearms. All that hard work had made him rich, but more important, he had the success he'd craved since he was a kid, and he wasn't going to blow it now. "Everything's under control," he told his boss.

"Knowing you, I'm sure it is." Heath toyed with one of a pair of purple origami frogs perched on the desk in front of him. Brett had a nearly identical set on his own desk, a gift from the Champion kids. "There's a rumor floating around that Tyler Capello is less than happy with Tommy Landom."

Capello, who played for the Eagles, was one of the top running backs in the League, and Brett sat straighter. "Maybe Tyler's finally figured out Tommy's a sleaze."

"Maybe." Heath picked up a pen and balanced it between his index fingers. "It was bad enough losing Tyler, but I'll never get past losing him to Landom."

"Nate got stupid," Brett said. Nate Douglass had been a rising young agent at Champion when his relationship with Tyler had blown up in his face, and Nate's career at Champion had come to an abrupt end.

The Python set down the pen. "Anyone running a company like this has to know when to cut their losses. Nate had to go."

Brett shifted uncomfortably in his seat. "Let me know if you hear anything more about Tyler. We might have another chance at him."

Heath nodded. "Your first priority is finding Garrett before the police get to him. Do whatever you have to."

Brett rose and headed for the door. "I'll find him."

"I know you will." Heath gave him a Python's smile. "You're The River."

A photo gallery ran along the hallway outside Heath's office. Brett had seen the photos a thousand times, but this time he took a moment to look at them again. Heath's photo hung next to portraits of Portia Powers and Brodie Gray, a married couple who'd left Chicago for LA a few years ago to set up and run Champion's West Coast office. There were photos of every Champion client as well as all the agents, including an unsmiling portrait of Brett. One photo wasn't in the hallway. Instead it had been moved to the break room where only the employees could see it hanging, turned to the wall. If anyone cared to turn it around, and all of them had, they'd see a photo of Nate Douglass's face as an ever-present reminder of what happened when an agent embarrassed the company.

*
*

Detective Strothers was even less friendly toward Rory than the first time they'd met. "How many people have your brother's house key?"

Apparently, half the world. "I have no idea."

It was the day after Ashley's murder, and Rory stood with the detective in the backyard next to Mr. Reynolds's vegetable garden. She'd broken the news about Ashley to both her landlord and Toby last night. Mr. Reynolds had been stoic, more concerned with getting Ashley's things out of her apartment so he could find a new tenant, but Toby had taken it hard. "She was starting to like me," he said, his eyes welling with tears.

Rory would never tell him the truth—that it was his adoration Ashley had liked, not him.

The police had temporarily cordoned off Ashley's apartment, and now Rory had scratch marks on her arms and Toby had a traumatized cat hiding in his kitchen cupboard. She was grateful Toby had agreed to take him. "It's the least I can do for her," he'd said.

Detective Strothers had his notebook in hand. "You don't seem to know much about your brother's habits." The afternoon was warm, and he must've been suffocating in his suit coat, but she was the one sweating. "You don't know who he might have given house keys to, and you don't know where he is."

She touched the scratch mark Luther had left on her wrist. "I told you, Detective. Clint is my half brother, and we're not close. What about Ashley's ex-boyfriend? The one I told you about who was harassing her."

"We're looking into that." He thumbed his moustache. "You said you went to Mr. Garrett's house to talk to him about your relationship with your stepmother. If you're not close to your brother, why do that?"

Why, indeed? She grasped for straws. "I thought he might have some ideas about how I could get along better with her."

Strothers couldn't know that Rory cared more about staying away from Kristin than getting along with her.

*
*

Brett took a shower to wash off the stench of failure from the day's events and slipped into a pair of gym shorts. The longer Clint was missing, the guiltier Clint looked. Brett had to get to him before the police did.

As for the matter of Clint's grudge . . . Once Clint learned how Rory had lied to Ashley, Brett would no longer be his client's scapegoat. Admittedly, Rory's motives had been pure, but that was her problem to deal with, not his.

Just after eleven, his phone rang. It was the concierge announcing Brett had a visitor.

5

Rory Garrett wore jeans, a Hawaiian shirt, and bright red sandals. She'd snared her curly hair through the back of a Yankees ball cap she'd better not wear anywhere near Wrigley Field. "Some people underdress for a party," she said, as he let her in. "I'm underdressed for your *building*."

"I only hope my neighbors didn't see you." In truth, she looked . . . cute, a word he'd never utter aloud. Those bright blue eyes eating up her face, curls at her cheekbones, pinup body not entirely concealed by her quirky outfit. If she were more of a show-piece and not the sister of his most important client, he might have been into her. Although, technically, he had been into her. He only wished he remembered it better.

As he drew his T-shirt over his head, he noticed his chest had caught her attention. Since he spent an hour at the gym most days—an hour he could better spend a thousand other ways—he took his time pulling the T-shirt down because . . . why not?

Did she redirect her gaze a little too quickly? "Your condo looks exactly like I knew it would," she said. "You're living in a cliché."

"As opposed to living inside an episode of *This Old Rathole*."

"That's good."

Her smile made him push it. *"Fixer Downer?"*

"Dated, but okay."

He closed the door. *"Loathe It or Dump It?"*

"You're surprisingly familiar with old home renovation shows," she said. "And you'll be laughing out of the other side of your smug mouth when I get back on my feet and buy a decent place with my first million."

A flicker of pain that he didn't like seeing tugged at the corners of her eyes. He directed her into his living room and pretended not to notice. "I had an old girlfriend who was an HGTV addict. We broke up because I wouldn't let her redo my place with shiplap."

"Wise decision on your part."

"She said it showed a lack of commitment."

"Did it?"

"Damn right."

She smiled again and took in the view of the Chicago Municipal Opera house on the opposite bank of the Chicago River. "I heard Olivia Shore is the newest board member at Muni Opera."

It wasn't the non sequitur an outsider might have perceived it to be. In addition to being one of opera's most accomplished mezzo-sopranos, Olivia Shore was also the wife of Thad Owens, Clint's former backup with the Chicago Stars and one of Clint's closest friends. Rory returned her attention to Brett. "Have you talked to Thad?"

He nodded. "He and the kids are on tour with Olivia, and he hasn't heard from Clint."

She took in his bookshelves, undoubtedly disappointed to discover they contained actual books instead of animal bones. "I want to talk to Karloh Cousins. Can you make that happen?"

He saw his opportunity. "Maybe."

"Meaning what?"

"I have a few conditions."

Rory's blue eyes narrowed suspiciously. "I'm not sleeping with you again."

"You weren't invited." Although, if things were different—if she didn't have such a prickly personality, if he hadn't sobered up, and most important, if she weren't Clint's sister—he'd be more than a little tempted to enjoy a rematch. Her twisted sense of humor and lack of personal vanity were interesting. And her refusal to take him seriously had become a challenge. "Clint's not in a good place right now," he said, "and at this point he's more likely to talk to you."

"I don't believe it! He's mad at you, Captain Super Agent. What did you do? I can't wait to hear."

She was sharp. He'd give her that. He looked down his nose at her, an expression designed to intimidate, although she was so pleased with herself, he doubted it would work. "I didn't say he was mad at me."

"Dude, you might be able to BS your clients, but I see right through your oily, deceitful ways."

"I'm not oily or deceitful," he retorted. "And anything that transpires between an agent and a client is confidential." Not exactly true, but her attitude pissed him off.

"That's too bad, because this partnership can't go any further without mutual trust." She picked up a copy of *Sports Illustrated* with Clint on the cover. The magazine sat on an ugly concrete table he kept knocking his shins on.

He weighed the pros and cons of telling her the truth and,

since he knew her secret, concluded he had nothing to lose. "I suspected Ashley's motives right from the beginning. She was used to men falling at her feet, and she didn't like not being able to charm me."

"She trashed you to Clint."

Rory didn't miss much.

"I'm sure she did, but that wasn't the issue. Unfortunately, I tried to warn him about her."

"Judging from my experience, he didn't take it well."

"He was furious. One of the first rules of a good agent is to never disparage a client's girlfriend, wife, or mother. Even when she broke up with him, he wouldn't let me off the hook. He even accused me of trying to buy her off."

"You wouldn't do that." She hesitated. "Would you?"

"I'm never unethical."

"*Ha!*" She slapped the magazine facedown. "You said I was *charming*. That was unethical!"

"I was being manipulative, not unethical."

She laughed, which made him like her even more. Handling Rory Garrett was tricky. Once Clint discovered his sister was at fault for his breakup, Brett was in the clear. But what if she decided not to tell him the truth? As much as he hated the idea, he'd have to do it for her. He had too much at stake.

He dropped into a hard-edged leather chair that looked good but was uncomfortable as hell. "There's a predictable pattern when things go wrong in a client's life. It's always easier to blame the agent than take personal responsibility."

"Clint hates being wrong, and now he's pouting because you were right." She settled into a more comfortable upholstered chair across from him. "He's a spoiled brat. I could have told you that. Baby Brother isn't used to people arguing with him."

Clint might be pigheaded, but he was neither spoiled nor a brat. He was the consummate professional and normally rational, which was why Brett had thought he could be honest with him about what he saw unfolding with Ashley. "Interesting, isn't it, that both of us have gotten into trouble trying to do our best by him?"

"Except he's still talking to me," Rory said pointedly. "Or at least he would be if he'd answer his phone." Brett had never witnessed bright blue eyes look so calculating. He waited to see what was transpiring in that brain of hers, and sure enough . . . "Even if you find Clint, you're worried he won't talk to you. Or worse. Fire you on the spot."

She was right.

"Maybe."

She kicked off her sandals, drew up her heels, and sat cross-legged in the chair. "It seems as if I'm your best hope for reconnecting with him."

"A perfect example of how unfair life can be." He leaned forward, arms balanced on his thighs. "I need to smooth things over with him before he digs in deeper." And before The Python discovered Brett had made a misstep.

"So yesterday when you drove to Clint's house to see him, you went there to grovel?"

"Exactly."

She'd gotten very good at smirking. "You really screwed up when you told him the truth."

He cocked his head. "Unlike you, who took the high road by claiming he was betting on his own games?"

She winced. "Once we find him, your troubles aren't over. You need someone to help heal the breach. To remind him you were looking out for his best interests. Basically to convince him to grow up and stop shutting you out."

She'd nailed it.

"I'm not the only one with a problem."

She regarded him warily.

He stretched his legs, which didn't do anything to improve the comfort of the chair. "If you want to purge your guilt-ravaged conscience, you need to find him, too, so you can confess. But you can't do that without me and my contacts, right?"

"Unnecessarily blunt, but true."

Neither of them stated the bigger problem. The longer Clint was missing, the more suspicious the police would be.

"Let's make a deal," he said. "I'll let you in on my contacts, and you'll help me get back in his good graces."

She uncrossed her legs and rose. "I'm not sure I can do that."

"I'm sure you can if you try." He wasn't sure, but he needed all the help he could muster to make sure he didn't lose his client and—along with him—the senior vice presidency he deserved.

She turned away from a boring painting of a rusty oilcan his decorator had insisted would give the place an edgy contemporary vibe. "If we're going to work together, we need a few rules. Mainly, you pay all our expenses."

"Agreed." He got up from the chair. "And you promise never again to wear that shirt in my presence."

"What's wrong with it?"

"It burns my eyeballs."

"Fine. Now get me to Karloh Cousins."

*
*

The next morning, as Rory walked the six blocks from the Sedgwick L station to Cousins's home in Chicago's Old Town, her mind ping-ponged from Ashley to Clint to her job crisis to her bank account to the parking fine she didn't have the money to pay. As her brain skipped from one problem to another, she wanted the world to stop spinning long enough to get her bearings.

She reached Cousins's mansion just as Brett pulled up in his luxury-mobile. She watched him get out, all lean grace and cool authority, a man with no self-doubt. Her resentment festered even as she noticed the way the sunlight played in his dark hair, as slick as he was. She wanted to dress him in a torn T-shirt and baggy jeans. Sort of the way he'd been dressed last night except the T-shirt hadn't been torn and the baggy jeans had been a pair of well-fitted gym shorts.

He scowled at her. "What? Why are you looking at me like that?"

"Trying to find your Satanic markings. Idle question: Do you ever let your hair run free?"

"Really? You're criticizing *my* hair?" He passed her on the walkway and hit the doorbell.

She shoved a few rampant curls behind her ears. The door opened, and the giant on the other side extended his hand. "It's The River. How you doin', man?"

Rory's gaze shot from the basketball player to Brett. *The River?* He even had a hotshot nickname. The only nickname she'd ever had was Poodle Head.

"Karloh, thanks for seeing us." Brett gestured toward her. "This is Rory Garrett, Clint's sister. Don't mind the way she looks. She's color-blind."

Not only had Brett disapproved of yesterday's Hawaiian shirt, he now had an aversion to the green-and-crimson octopus-print, puffy-sleeve blouse she was wearing with perfectly ordinary 1970s bell-bottoms and her favorite espadrilles. He apparently thought women should dress as conservatively as he did, another black mark against him.

"Come on in." Ashley's last boyfriend was tall—very tall. He was also clean-shaven and muscular, with huge hands and an enviable set of locs. Rory felt like an elf in comparison.

He led them through the atrium into a glass-walled living room. As he gestured toward a pair of oversized white leather couches, Rory thought about asking for a booster seat.

"The police were already here." Cousins dropped his head into his hands. "I can't believe Ashley's dead."

Rory sat on the edge of the couch so her feet would touch the floor. "I know she really liked being with you." *And with your money.*

His head came up, his locs brushing his shoulders. "She was fun for a while."

"When did you last talk to her?" Brett asked.

"Two days ago, the morning of the day she died, like I told the cops. The team was flying back from playing the Rockets, and I called her from the plane."

"You had a good game," Brett said.

"The shots were falling."

Rory didn't want to talk basketball, although she did plan to look for a photo of Cousins in his uniform. "Could you tell us what you and Ashley talked about?"

He shifted his big frame. "Mainly, what we were going to do that night, but then she mentioned some presents Clint gave her one too many times, and I got pissed, like she was saying he bought her more shit than I did. She knew I was torqued, and she tried to bullshit me about how Clint was such a loser compared to me, that he was gambling on games and the League was ready to ban him. I said whoever told her that was a liar—that Clint was Mr. Clean, the last guy in the NFL to get involved with gambling."

Rory's stomach got queasy. This was exactly what she'd feared. Karloh had unknowingly exposed her lie.

Brett gave her a quick glance. "How did Ashley take that?"

"She acted like she wanted to get off the phone, and I knew right then she'd been playing me. I always suspected she wasn't over Garrett. I told her we were done, and she didn't even seem to care. Now she's dead. Man, if I'd known what was going to happen, I wouldn't have been so cold."

Rory mentally reconstructed the time frame. Karloh had talked to Ashley that morning, probably while Rory had been mindlessly wandering around Lincoln Square trying to figure out where she could get a decent-paying job. Rory hadn't gone back into her apartment before she'd left for Burr Ridge, so Ashley had plenty of time to send Rory a message by destroying the evening bag and then heading to Clint's house. But how had she gotten there without her car, and had Clint known she was coming?

* *

Brett had work to do, calls to return, and he didn't want to go with Rory to see Kristin Garrett. They stood in Karloh's driveway arguing about it. "There's no reason for me to go," he said. "You already know Clint hasn't called her."

"You're Clint's agent. You have a responsibility to keep Kristin updated."

"On what? I have no information you don't have."

"You'll think of something to ask her that I won't. You have a different perspective."

He regarded her suspiciously. "You don't want a different perspective. You want a ride because you're afraid that oil-burning junker of yours won't make it."

"You caught me." Better he think that than know how much she hated being alone with her stepmother. If Brett was with her, she and Kristin wouldn't be able to go after each other's throats. Rory was surprised the police had given Kristin permission to stay in the house, but Kristin had her ways.

"How about I rent you a car?" he said.

"How about you just drive me there? We're a team, remember?"

She won, but her teammate spent most of the trip with a Bluetooth headset in his ear, talking to clients and ordering a three-hundred-dollar flower arrangement for someone named Sophie with a card that said, "Thanks for a great evening."

"'Evening'? Not night?" she said when he was done. "You're losing your touch. And only three hundred dollars? Shame on you."

He tilted down the mouthpiece. "Don't you think it's time we put the past behind us?"

"A lifetime wouldn't be long enough to put that behind us."

"I wonder what the penalty is for dumping a dead body on the expressway."

She smiled, then realized the only time she smiled these days was with him, a depressing thought that wiped away any trace of humor. "Both hands on the wheel."

"Tell me more about the debacle that led to your hooking up

with the irresponsible Jon and getting stuck with an empty pink food truck." Traffic was getting heavier, and he turned off the car's cruise control.

"First, it's a pink-and-*purple* food truck, and Jon and I never hooked up. We were friends. *Were*." Telling someone as successful as Brett Rivers about her bad judgment didn't strike her as a fun way to enjoy the rest of the drive, but since nothing about this drive was fun, she plunged in.

"Jon found the food truck on eBay and convinced me to partner with him. Food trucks have low overhead, and their owners can make decent money. I needed a fresh start, and peddling candy seemed nominally connected with what I really wanted to do."

He nodded. "Make a living selling chocolate."

"Selling *artisanal* chocolates. Specialty chocolates that I create."

"I'll testify to how good you are."

It was true. She was good. As she experimented with techniques and flavor profiles, she lost track of time. Instead of simply taking up space on the planet, she was offering the universe something beautiful. But Brett only valued things that earned lots of money, and he wouldn't understand. "I massacred my savings and set off," she said.

"But things didn't go as planned."

"Jon neglected to research Chicago's very restrictive food truck laws, and I neglected to take into account Jon's general unreliability. The truck kept breaking down, and he wouldn't follow city regulations. He'd park over the legal four-hour limit or too close to brick-and-mortar stores that sold food. First offense—a thousand-dollar fine. Second offense, two thousand dollars. He cleaned out the truck the night before Ashley died and skipped town, generously leaving me with the fine and without any product to sell."

"You should have seen that coming."

"Exactly the kind of insight that explains why you earn the big bucks and I don't."

He didn't know who he was more pissed off with, her for being naive or Jon for being a class A dirtbag. "You'll be smarter in the future."

"I doubt it." She gazed out the window, studying the billboards flying by. "If you haven't noticed, all the brains in the family went to one person, and I'm not him."

Damn if he didn't feel sorry for her. "Everybody makes mistakes."

Her head whipped around. "Stop right there! The River doesn't go soft on someone who's made as many mistakes as I have."

He gave a deep sigh. "Even for a bastard like me, it's hard to kick a person when she's this far down."

"I appreciate your self-restraint."

He glanced over at her. "You know Clint would bail you out in a second."

"Not in a million years. I handle this myself."

Her response didn't surprise him. She had the same stubborn pride as her brother. He swung onto the Tri-State exit ramp and merged onto the Stevenson Expressway. "What's your plan?"

"Find Clint, clear my conscience, and get a job as fast as I can. Something temporary and, hopefully, well paying."

"And yet, you passed on that five hundred dollars." As long as he was being a jerk, he might as well go all the way. "Do I remember a small birthmark inside your left thigh?"

He braced himself for her to throw a punch. He kind of wanted her to because it would be the perfect ending to a shitty couple of days, but she disappointed him. "I believe you're confusing me with one of the hundreds of other strumpets like myself who've stumbled into your bed."

"First you were a floozy, and now you're a strumpet? You do have a low opinion of yourself."

"A *drunken* strumpet."

"I hardly think a too-short hour of mutual pleasure makes you a floozy or a strumpet."

"I have standards."

So did he. Or at least he'd always thought he had. As he slowed for road construction, he remembered that pasta dish she'd made for Claudia, the homeless woman. Best thing he'd tasted in weeks. "Why don't you set up a catering business or work as a personal chef instead of making chocolates? There'd be more money in it."

"Because I'm a chocolatier, not a caterer or a personal chef. But if you ever need either one, I'll do you a favor and take the job. Although you should know up front that I only use the best ingredients, and I'm very expensive."

Not new information. She was already costing him his peace of mind.

6

Kristin answered Clint's front door before the second round of "Hail to the Victors" came to an end. Just looking at her put Rory's teeth on edge. Kristin should have had dyed black hair and fangs instead of a blond bob with professional highlights. And villainous black would fit her personality better than that long-sleeved emerald-green blouse and those immaculate white capris Rory would have gotten cooking stains on in no time.

Kristin looked like every toned, blond socialite who popped up in photos of charity events. In fact, she was a member of the League of Women Voters and volunteered at an animal shelter, but she could have been a socialite. Or a Real Housewife of Minneapolis if only she'd had a lip job, boob job, hair extensions and wore a lot more makeup. Rory wished her uptight stepmother were a free-flying Real Housewife. She'd be more likeable.

Clint's mother had arrived the night before, and apparently sleeping in a house where someone had been murdered hadn't bothered her because she was her normal cool self. "Brett, it's lovely to see you."

"You, too, Kristin." Brett gave her a polite hug.

There was a perfunctory hug for Rory, over so quickly that Rory barely felt it. Considering the way Kristin eyed Rory's red-and-green octopus shirt, she probably believed it was contagious.

"Rory, you should have told me Brett was coming with you." She stepped aside to let them enter. "I would have made us lunch."

"Lunch for Brett but not for me?"

"My cooking never meets your standards."

True. Kristin was a terrible cook. Rory's childhood was filled with bad casseroles, burned hamburgers, overcooked vegetables, and more dessert desecrations than one woman should have been able to produce. Rory had taken over desserts when she was ten. "Brett decided to come at the last minute."

"I'm so glad." As Kristin led him down the hallway toward the kitchen, Rory hung back, which afforded her another opportunity to give the supercilious cherubs on the ceiling the finger, a distraction from thinking about Ashley standing in this very hallway the morning she died.

"Would you like iced tea?" Kristin asked, as she slipped behind the kitchen island. "I just made some."

"Sure," Brett said.

"No thanks," Rory said at the exact same time.

Rory set down her summer straw bag, embroidered with multi-colored raffia flowers and the word "Nassau." Kristin moved it off the counter as if it were contaminated and poured a glass for Brett from a fat pitcher. "Rory doesn't like my iced tea because it's unsweetened. I offer her sugar, but that doesn't seem to make a difference."

Rory held her tongue, even though everyone knew sugar didn't dissolve properly unless the water was hot.

Kristin added ice to a glass of what already looked like barely tinted water. "I don't have a sweet tooth like Rory."

Something she never failed to mention.

She added a sprig of wilted mint. "I wanted Rory to get a teaching certificate."

"I didn't want to be a teacher." Rory heard a vacuum cleaner running somewhere.

Kristin regarded her critically. "You're good with children, and it would have been a more stable career than working in food services."

Food services, as if Rory made her living serving mashed potatoes from behind a cafeteria steam table, admittedly a more admirable job than passing Skittles through the window of a food truck.

"Why don't we sit on the patio?" Kristin handed the iced tea to Brett.

The depth of her stepmother's insensitivity never ceased to amaze. "You do know that's where we found Ashley's body."

"We can't stop using it just because something unfortunate happened there."

"'Unfortunate' is an understatement, don't you think?" This was exactly why Rory had wanted Brett with her today, so she didn't sink to the level she'd just sunk to.

Kristin gave an exasperated sigh. "All right, Rory. Where do you want to sit?"

The kiss-up sports agent jumped in. "The patio's fine. We'll sit on the other side."

"Go ahead." Rory turned toward the sound of the vacuum. "I want to talk to the housekeeper."

"The police already talked to her," Kristin said.

Ignoring that, Rory left Jerry Maguire and Evil Stepmother to each other and followed the sound of the vacuum through the downstairs to a large media room with wooden paneling and a cherub-free coffered ceiling. A combination of loungers and couches sat in front of the big screen, and a linear fireplace with black, tempered glass "ashes" occupied the wall beneath.

The housekeeper was the same woman Rory had seen talking to the police two days ago. She looked to be around Rory's age. Slim, with long brown hair caught in a messy bun on top of her head, tight jeans, and a black T-shirt. She turned off the vacuum and regarded Rory warily. "Can I help you?"

"I'm Rory. Clint's sister."

The woman didn't wear much makeup—a bit of lip gloss—but then she didn't need more. "I'm Gabby."

The carpet was so soft and plush Rory could have happily taken a nap on it, something she'd rather do than play detective. "I know you've already talked to the police, but do you mind if I ask you a few questions?"

She eyed Rory's octopus blouse. "I don't know what else I can tell you."

Rory sat on the arm of the closest lounger, trying to put the housekeeper at ease by making her posture and questions seem casual. "Have you worked here long?"

"Two years. I come four times a week."

"Good job?"

Gabby nodded. "Clint's the best boss I ever worked for."

Also the most generous, Rory guessed. "Do you know who has keys to the house?"

"A few of his friends stay here when he's gone. Maybe some maintenance people. I told the police all that."

"Did you ever meet Ashley?"

The corners of Gabby's mouth tightened. "They were eating breakfast a couple of mornings when I got here. I don't think she even noticed me."

Gabby hadn't liked Ashley. Was it because Ashley had ignored her or because she didn't like any woman who caught Clint's attention? "When I came in the house the day Ashley died, there was no security system. Doesn't he have one?"

"Yes, but he hardly ever bothered with it. I kept telling him he needed to be more careful. He'd agree, but then he'd forget again. He thinks he's invincible."

Gabby sounded like every woman who cared about a man. "Do you have any idea where he could be? Did he mention a trip? Are any of his suitcases missing?"

"He didn't say anything to me about leaving. I don't know about his suitcases, and he could have gone anywhere." She busied herself straightening the vacuum cord even though it didn't need smoothing.

Rory was no Detective Strothers, but she had the feeling Gabby was hiding something. "You know the police are looking for him."

"I don't know where he is," she said stubbornly.

"But you have an idea, don't you?"

"He didn't hurt her!" she exclaimed. "He's not like that."

"You and I know that, but the police need convincing." She rose from the chair arm and met Gabby's eyes. "If you care about him, tell me where he is so I can get to him first."

Gabby switched on the vacuum. "I have to go back to work."

Rory wouldn't get more out of her. She walked over to a curved glass console and wrote her phone number on the Chicago Stars notepad that sat there. As she gave it to Gabby, she spoke over the sound of the vacuum. "If you decide you can trust me, call."

Gabby stuffed the paper in the rear pocket of her jeans without looking at it and turned the vacuum toward the movie screen. Rory had just reached the door when the vacuum went quiet. "He has a cabin," Gabby said.

"A cabin?"

Gabby rubbed her arm. "Sometimes I'd find credit card receipts or a couple of business cards from a town called Ludlow, Michigan. It might be near there. I don't know."

"You don't have an address?"

Gabby shook her head.

"Call me if you find it."

Gabby gave a brief nod and got back to work.

*
*

"Cabin? Clint doesn't have a cabin." Kristin gave Rory the same patronizing look Rory had seen a thousand times growing up.

"You're not really going to wear that."

"Another romance novel? Your brain is going to rot."

"You already know everything, of course. So why should you stay in college?"

More recently: *"And how do you expect to open your own chocolate shop when you can barely pay your rent?"*

She'd found Kristin and Brett chatting at a white metal patio table. Brett had kicked back in the chair, Marchand watch glimmering on his wrist, strong hands bare of rings. He couldn't possibly be as self-assured as he looked.

It was already hot, and Rory wished she hadn't refused the iced tea, sugar or not. Kristin uncrossed her legs, and as Rory took the chair across from her, she was shocked to see her stepmother wore a delicate gold anklet with a tiny infinity sign dangling from the chain. The incongruity of Kristin, a conservative, fifty-one-year-old suburbanite, wearing an anklet was so wrong Rory momentarily lost track of their conversation.

"The idea is ludicrous," Kristin said to Brett. "If he bought a cabin, he would have mentioned it."

Apparently, Baby Boy doesn't tell Mommy everything. Rory dragged her gaze away from the anklet. A landscape worker was trimming shrubs by the fence. "Maybe Clint uses it as some sort of hideaway."

Kristin cupped her glass, jigging the melting ice. "If he needed a hideaway he'd come home."

Rory resisted pointing out all the reasons Clint wouldn't do that, beginning with Kristin's smothering. "Gabby doesn't have an address," she said. "But the cabin might be near Ludlow, Michigan."

"There's no cabin," Kristin said. "I know my son better than his housekeeper."

"Maybe not as well as you think." Rory had once again broken her vow to remain pleasant, and Brett, ever the slickster, cut in.

"What else did you learn?"

The landscaper set down the hedge trimmers and glanced toward the patio. He was big and buff. "That the housekeeper might be in love with Clint."

"I could have told you that," Kristin said. "I've had years of practice watching girls fall for Clint."

"Always irresistible, my brother." Rory heard her petulance and wished she'd kept her mouth shut. Brett regarded her with pity. She was thirty-four-years-old, long past the age when she had to react to everything Kristin said, and she didn't like letting him witness this immature side of her.

"I don't understand any of this," Kristin said.

Brett rose from the table. "I'll look into it. I promise."

Rory corrected him. "*We'll* look into it."

⋆
⋆

Rory buckled the seat belt of the luxury-mobile. "What time are we leaving for Michigan?"

Brett pushed the ignition switch. "Who says we're going to Michigan?"

"Oh, sure. We'll let the police find him first."

Brett slipped the car into reverse and checked the dashboard touch screen as he backed into the turnaround. "Amazing all this trouble you're subjecting yourself to for a brother you seem to have spent years avoiding."

She retrieved her rhinestone cat's-eye sunglasses from her bag. "If I help clear his name, I'll also be able clear my conscience."

He shifted and headed down the drive. At the end, he stopped for a slender runner in pink shorts and a racer-back top to pass. Rory watched her. "I could look like that if I'd been born with her body. And had the motivation to run every day, which I don't."

He pulled onto the street. "There's nothing wrong with your body."

"As you clearly know, having seen way too much of it." She pushed her sunglasses up on the bridge of her nose.

The devil frisked in those cold gray eyes. "My memory's foggy. You might have to show me again."

She gaped at him. "Did you just come on to me?"

"Why would I do that?"

"You tell me."

"You're imagining things." He gave her a smarmy smile. "Not to be hurtful, but you're no Sophie."

Rory remembered the three-hundred-dollar flower order he'd placed. "You mean your lingerie model girlfriend who moonlights making artisanal cocktails and believes she has a deeply spiritual side?"

"You know Sophie so well."

Rory laughed.

He smiled. "Sophie is my aunt, a retired phys ed teacher who plays mahjong, swims every day, and gave up *Jeopardy* after Alex Trebek died." He braked for a stop sign. "Tell me more about your sibling rivalry."

"There is no rivalry. I declared defeat long ago."

"You're six years older. I don't see how there could be much of a competition."

"And yet you've met Clint. Imagine growing up with a baby brother who starts outshining you in grade school. Clint was good at everything right from the beginning—academics, athletics, making friends. Of course Kristin and my dad doted on him. Can you imagine having a sibling who never does anything wrong?"

"No. I have four younger brothers, and they did plenty wrong."

"You were an oldest child. That explains your pathological ambition. No sisters?"

"No sisters. Our mother says that's why we were feral children."

"I can't imagine you as a feral child."

"Very feral."

"You're lying. Nobody changes that much."

"Alcohol. Drugs. Attempted murder. I did it all."

"Liar. You're the one who had to set the example, right?"

He seemed surprised that she'd figured out the obvious.

"You were perfect, just like Clint. When your brothers got in trouble, your parents held you up as an example, which is why they're now miserable failures and they all hate you."

The corner of his mouth curled. "A firefighter, accountant, marine, and a teacher at the elementary school in Fresno three blocks from the house where we grew up. There goes your theory."

She wasn't giving up. "You'd probably started slicking back your hair in second grade."

"I was too busy running my pet-sitting business to care about personal grooming."

"A pet-sitting business? You were—what? Seven?"

"I liked money then just as much as I like it now. I also sold the grapefruit that fell on our side of the fence from the neighbor's tree, but that was seasonal work."

"You're scary." She touched the dashboard. "I do like this car, though. What other businesses did you have when you were a kid?"

"I sold snacks at school with a fifty-percent markup. Amazing what kids will pay for a bottle of Mountain Dew. I started my first franchise in sixth grade."

"You franchised?"

"An errand-running business, then a tutoring business and a lawn-mowing service. I would have done more, but I was playing sports. The big money came in high school when I started flipping sneakers. I kept at it right through college, which is why I graduated without any debt."

"You parents should have put you in therapy. Who has that kind of ambition so early?"

"I'm not apologizing for being ambitious." As they sailed onto the Stevenson Expressway, Brett punched the accelerator a little harder than he needed to. "Make a goal and go after it. That's how I got you in bed half an hour after I met you."

She couldn't let that pass. Slipping her sunglasses down on her nose, she peered at him over the top. "I'm the one who got you in bed, not the other way around. And do you know why? Because I'm a woman who goes after what she wants." *Generally, in the wrong direction.* "And right then, drunken me stupidly wanted you."

He flew by a pair of semis clogging the right two lanes. "You finally admit you wanted me."

"I was suicidal." She shoved the sunglasses back in place.

"You were not suicidal. Depressed, maybe, but . . ."

"I was depressed and drunk. I would have done any guy who came out on that balcony." Most definitely not true. There had been something about his brashness and complete lack of self-doubt she'd needed that night.

He sighed. "Naive guy that I am, I left money for your dubious services."

"'Dubious'? Now you're saying I wasn't good in bed?" He'd baited her, and she'd jumped right into his trap. "Not that I care about your opinion."

They shot beneath an overpass. "Now that you admit you were the aggressor," he said, "let's talk about how you took advantage of me at a vulnerable time."

"You haven't been vulnerable since you were in diapers."

"I've been vulnerable. Very vulnerable. You think it's easy always being at the top of your game?"

He said it as if it were a joke, but his fingers tightened around the steering wheel. Maybe he wasn't as arrogant as he pretended to be. She decided to poke around. "Tell me more about being an overachieving firstborn so I can mock you."

"I'm not telling you anything except that we need to find Clint before things get worse. Phoebe Calebow takes a dim view of criminal investigations involving her players."

Even Rory knew that Phoebe Calebow, the legendary owner of the Chicago Stars, was not a woman to be trifled with.

They rode in silence until they reached the Kennedy Expressway. "If your parents made you feel inferior," he finally said, "they were the ones who screwed up, not Clint."

"Mainly my father. He left me in Kristin's evil clutches."

"Did she beat you? Lock you in a closet? It's strange. Kristin doesn't seem evil."

"Cruella de Vil." Kristin wasn't really evil. Instead, she was rigid, overly critical, and so enamored with her own child that she'd had nothing left for the child who'd been foisted on her. As for Rory's father . . . He'd been a shadow in her life, animated only by Clint's accomplishments.

Brett kept glancing over at her, as if waiting for her to say more. She reached for her purse. "Don't you have phone calls to make?"

"As a matter of fact, I do."

While he talked to someone in Dallas, Rory pulled her own phone from her purse, along with Detective Strothers's card. She reached him right away. "You need to investigate Clint's housekeeper. I think she might have been in love with him. And the guy who works for Clint's landscaping service. He's really big."

But Strothers only cared about one thing. Whether she'd talked to her brother and what Ashley's phone case looked like.

"I haven't talked to Clint," she told him. "Ashley's case is white leather with some kind of designer logo. Triangle. Prada, I think. Have you found it?"

"Thanks for your help, Ms. Garrett."

He hung up before she could remind him that Clint was innocent.

They were back on the Tri-State, and Brett was still busy fielding calls. She made a business out of scrolling through her messages. There was nothing new, but she wanted to look like someone with important matters to take care of instead of a person whose life had stalled in place.

⁎

The coffee shop smelled like espresso, spice, and air-conditioning. "A small matcha tea, please. Iced." Kristin had just drunk iced tea with Rory and Brett, and she wasn't thirsty, but she couldn't stay in that house a moment longer. She wished she'd gone to a hotel coffee shop instead of this place with its hard surfaces, uncomfortable metal chairs, and gray cement floor. She wanted faded Persian rugs, deep-seated wing chairs, and Alicia Keys singing instead of a throbbing electronic soundtrack. She also wanted her youth back without its mistakes. She gazed at the anklet she'd started wearing in a foolish attempt to reimagine herself. It looked ridiculous, and she was taking it off as soon as she got home.

She carried her tea to a table that sat beneath an abstract black-and-white painting of an upside-down woman's head. If Gregg were still alive, he'd be complaining about the art, the electronic music, and the prices. His fatal heart attack two years ago had changed so much in her life, and she still hadn't found her footing.

Her phone pinged. She looked at the screen and saw that

someone had AirDropped a photo taken seconds ago, a photo of herself sitting at this very table. Creepy. She declined it and looked around.

A few teenagers ignored their textbooks to play on their phones. An older man huddled over his laptop. A pair of young mothers with babies in strollers visited near the far windows, and an elderly woman perused the newspaper, reading glasses perched on the end of her nose.

It was easy to spot him, a smarmy-looking kid ogling her from behind his hipster sunglasses. Cocked back in his chair with his legs extended, his smirk suggested she should be flattered that a young stud like himself was hitting on a withering hag like her.

She gave him her iciest glare, changed chairs so her back was to him, and took a sip of her tea. It could benefit from sugar, but she'd tried to set an example of healthy eating while Clint was growing up, and it had become a habit. Rory, being Rory, had begun smuggling candy into her bedroom when she was seven.

Today had been upsetting. Rory had been her normal hostile self, and every time Kristin thought about Ashley Hart, a weight settled in her chest. Rory had called Kristin insensitive, but Rory hadn't spent the night alone in a house where a woman had been murdered. Kristin prayed Clint would be waiting at the house when she got back so she didn't have to do it again.

She understood why the police wanted to talk to Clint, but regarding him as a suspect was unfathomable. How could anyone believe her son, one of the most honorable men alive, was responsible?

She cradled the tea in her hands, feeling brittle and off-balance. She'd always believed she knew everything about her son, but she didn't know why he'd broken up with a woman he loved or why he hadn't mentioned buying a cabin, and she especially didn't know why he wasn't answering her calls. She felt as if she was gradually losing parts of herself.

She'd just turned twenty-two when she'd discovered she was pregnant from an unwise affair with a man fourteen years older than herself—a man still mourning his dead wife. Gregg hadn't wanted to marry her. She'd always known that, although he'd never said it aloud. But he was a good man, and he believed in doing the right thing. Over the years, he'd grown to love her, but it was the love of familiarity, not the passionate love he'd felt for Debra Meadows, Rory's mother.

Accomplished, beautiful Debra, who'd remained forever young in his memory. Perfect Debra, who'd never had to deal with a hostile stepchild, had never suffered through menopause, and had never been forced to nag her husband about taking his heart medication. But Kristin had done something Debra couldn't. Kristin had given Gregg the bright, athletic son he'd always craved.

Her phone pinged. It was Clint! Finally! She grabbed it.

But it wasn't Clint. It was another AirDropped photo of her, this one also taken only seconds ago.

She shot up from her chair, the metal legs shrieking on the hard cement floor, and stalked across the coffeehouse to the smirking Gen Z–er hiding behind his hipster sunglasses and pretending not to look at her.

Kristin screeched to a halt next to the Gen Z–er's table. "Really? You think this is a good way to approach a woman? By sneaking photos? Do you have any idea how disrespectful that is? Little boys like you give your entire generation a bad name." On and on she went, all the steam that had built up in her internal teakettle finally finding an outlet. "If you want to talk to someone, be man enough to approach that person and say hello. And take off those ridiculous sunglasses. We're inside a coffee shop, not outside in a—"

"Excuse me. I— I think— I don't—"

She broke off her rant mid-sentence as the man she'd spotted earlier working at his laptop came up next to her.

The Gen Z–er's baffled expression finally penetrated the shrieking teakettle of her frustration. She noticed the kid's earbuds, his gray T-shirt, the way his sunglasses wrapped around his temples . . .

His white cane.

She gasped. "Oh, my God, I'm so sorry!" Her skin burned as the reality of what she'd done hit home. "I'm so . . . I didn't know . . . I thought you were— Oh, shit. Please forgive me. I assumed . . ."

"It's my fault," the older man said.

As the kid continued to look baffled, Kristin exclaimed, "Wait! I'll— I'll be right back." She grabbed her purse, flew to the counter, and stood in line behind a soccer mom who couldn't make up her mind between a caramel mocha frappé or cookies and cream. From the corner of her eye, Kristin saw the older man talking to the younger one.

She finally made her purchase and dashed back to set it on the table. "Here's a—a gift card. I know you can't put a price tag on what I did, but—"

"How much?" the kid said.

"A hundred dollars. Maybe I should have—"

"Cool." With a cocky grin, the kid found the card, leaned back on one hip, and tucked it in his jeans pocket. "Have a nice day, lady. Even if you are crazy."

She couldn't take any more. Clutching her purse, she dashed out the door, leaving her drink behind. She tried to be a decent person—open-minded and caring. She loved animals and made meals for sick friends. She—

"It was me," a deep voice said from behind her.

She spun around, blinking against the sunlight.

He was tall—vaguely familiar—with olive skin and graying dark hair beginning to thin at his high forehead. He had a grip on his laptop, the charging cord still hanging from it like Linus's blanket. "I—I'm the one who AirDropped the photos to your phone."

"You? Why would you do such a thing?"

"Because my daughter told me to."

She stared at him. "Your daughter told you to photograph strange women?"

"Not exactly. I'm—" He held on to his laptop but detached the charging cord and handed it to her for some reason. "Please . . . Would you let me apologize? Despite what you think, I'm harmless. Except maybe to myself." Without waiting for an answer, he turned to go back inside.

She stared down at a charging cord she had no idea why she was holding. She was away from home, staying in a haunted house, her son was missing, and she'd just falsely accused a visually impaired person of stalking her. She was losing her mind.

He was back before she'd sorted through the muck of her feelings, and she saw he'd gone inside to retrieve the tea she'd abandoned on the table. "I'm Daniel Hanbridge."

Daniel. That was why he seemed familiar. He resembled a slightly heavier Daniel Day Lewis. Not as handsome, but not unattractive. He had the same long, lean face and neatly spaced eyes. He was probably somewhere in his fifties, and although he didn't have a paunch, he wore his clothes a little too big like a lot of men his age.

He gestured toward an empty umbrella table with her cup. "Would you sit down with me?"

She took her cup from him but didn't move.

"I'm quite embarrassed," he said.

"*You're* embarrassed? I'm mortified. How could you do something so asinine?"

"It's a new experience," he said seriously. "Although I do have a tendency to be obtuse."

"I'll say."

He gave a slow nod and took the cable from her.

Maybe because his morose expression reminded her of Eeyore—the book illustration, not the Disney version—she decided to hear what he had to say. Or maybe she wasn't ready to return to that haunted house. For whichever reason, she pasted on a scowl and moved to the table he'd indicated.

"I didn't mean to be an ass," he said, after he claimed the chair across from her and placed his laptop next to him. "The truth is, my daughter's sick of me. She says I'm turning into an old fart."

"So you decided to reclaim your youthful vigor by taking photos of me without permission?"

"I only recently learned about AirDropping," he said. "You were nearby, I saw your AirDrop was activated, and I was trying to be amusing by sending that photo." If anything, he looked even more morose. "I'm not good at being amusing."

Neither was she.

He extended his legs, the movement a bit awkward, as if, after all these years, he still wasn't comfortable in his lanky body. "You appeared to be around my age. You're quite attractive, as I'm sure you're aware, and I decided to act, if for no other reason than so I could tell my daughter I'd done something impulsive."

"Insult a woman you don't know?"

"It played out differently in my head," he said. "That sometimes happens. I planned to send you a photo of myself next."

"And what was I supposed to do with it?"

"I thought maybe you'd look around, see me, and come over to say hello. In which case I intended to buy you a pastry."

"A pastry?"

"It was all I could think of."

He was so clueless, so unlike Gregg, whose self-assurance had made her own insecurities more acute, and Kristin found herself warming to him. "How old are you, Daniel?"

"Fifty."

And she'd just turned fifty-one. Even if only by a few months, she liked being older. "I'm assuming you're unmarried?"

"Divorced. I discovered my wife—ex-wife—had opened numerous credit cards without my knowledge and run up sizeable debt. When I attempted to put limits on her spending, she accused me of being controlling. She was also having an affair."

"Those sound like good reasons for a divorce."

"I wasn't without fault. I'm not completely on the spectrum, but I do push the boundary, and my seeming indifference was difficult for her."

Now Kristin really was intrigued. "How so?"

"I'm not good at reading people's feelings. As an example, I can't tell if you're still angry with me."

She wasn't. "Mildly irritated."

He smiled. "Then will you let me take you to dinner?"

"Whoa, cowboy. You're missing a little nuance here."

He nodded. "I do that. I suppose we should know more about each other before I invite you to dinner. You're not wearing a wedding ring, but you could be seeing someone. Are you?"

"No. I'm a widow."

"How long have you been a widow? Did you love your husband? You seem quite intelligent, although I don't know that for a fact."

She smiled. "Everything is upfront with you, isn't it? No innuendo. No hidden agenda."

"I understand that my bluntness can be perceived as rude, but I don't intend it that way."

"No offense taken. I've been a widow for two years. I loved my husband, but I didn't always like him." She'd never said those words aloud, yet it seemed natural to confess her dark secret to this strange man. "He was older. Better educated. He loved me, but he didn't respect me. He didn't see me as his equal."

"Because someone isn't your intellectual equal doesn't mean they aren't superior to you in other ways. For example, I'm sure you're not my intellectual equal either, but it's quite easy to see you are far superior when it comes to dealing with people."

She burst out laughing. "How do you know I'm not your intellectual equal?"

"Hardly anyone is." He didn't look happy about that.

The sun was in her eyes, and she shielded them with her hand. "What do you do for a living, Daniel?"

"I own a small engineering consulting company." He repositioned the umbrella so she was once again in the shade. The simple courtesy touched her. He might not be good at reading feelings, but he'd noticed this.

"Electrical engineering," he said, "is an ideal career for people who are good at abstract thinking. We're logical and highly focused, but we're not always comfortable with ambiguity, and we don't tend to handle change well."

"I see." She didn't see, but she could tell he didn't expect her to. Right then, she decided to go out to dinner with him. "Daniel—" She broke off as she spotted a sticker with the Chicago Stars logo on the bottom right corner of his laptop. She hesitated. "You're a football fan."

"My daughter put the sticker there. She's turned me into quite a Stars fan."

"Why the Stars? Why not the Bears?"

"We live in the western suburbs. How could we be Bears fans?" He smiled. "Watching the Stars play is something my daughter and I always do together."

The old tension returned. She'd been burned too many times since Gregg had died by perfectly nice men who turned out to be more interested in getting close to Clint than to her. But Daniel didn't know she was Clint's mother . . .

"You haven't told me your name," he said.

"Kristin. Meadows." Of all the names she could have chosen, why had Debra's maiden name slipped out?

"And what do you do, Kristin Meadows? Tell me about yourself."

"Let's save that conversation for dinner."

He grinned. "You're going out to dinner with me? That's surprising. And gratifying. How about tonight?" His face fell. "Too soon?"

"Too soon." She smiled. "Let's say tomorrow."

"Tomorrow it is. Give me your address, and I'll pick you up."

"I'll meet you at the restaurant."

"It's wise to be cautious. I should have thought of that myself."

How fascinating that this obviously brilliant man made her feel as though she were the most insightful woman in the world. She exchanged information with him and rose from the table. "Thanks for the interesting company, Daniel Hanbridge. Tell your daughter the old man still has game."

He grinned and, in the process of rising, knocked over what remained of her iced tea.

She laughed and headed for her car.

She'd laughed twice, in the space of minutes. How long had it been since anything had amused her? She wanted to phone one of her friends and share what had happened, but they'd be more alarmed than intrigued. None of them would understand why Kristin had agreed to have dinner with such an odd man. The only person who might get it was Rory, and that relationship had been ruined long ago.

More than anything, she wished she could have a do-over. Except she was very much afraid she'd make the same mistakes.

*
*

Late that afternoon, Rory and Brett headed for Ludlow, Michigan. Brett spent the early part of the trip talking on the phone while Rory pondered her brother's whereabouts. Did he know Ashley was dead, and if so, why had he run?

Rory had finally endured enough of Brett's talking while driving and ordered him to pull over. Not surprisingly, he protested. "I like to drive."

She glared at him. "No, what you like is talking on the phone and sucking up to your clients."

He flipped up the end of the earpiece. "I'm not turning this car over to a woman who drives an oil-burning junker that shouldn't be allowed on the road."

"I got bored with my Maserati. Now let me drive or I'll tell Clint how his hotshot agent seduced his poor drunken big sister."

"Am I the only one who notices you keep changing your story about who took advantage of who?"

"Of *whom*. If you'd spent more time in the classroom and less time in the gym, you'd know that."

He'd spent far more time in the classroom than she, but instead of calling her on it, he pulled over and let her take the wheel.

For the next few hours, she was almost happy speeding toward northern Michigan in a high-performance car that drove like a miracle while she did her best to ignore the man next to her. If only Ashley were still alive, Clint hadn't disappeared, she could support herself, and she hadn't gotten tangled up with a slick sports agent, her life would be perfect.

Brett had pushed the passenger seat all the way back to accommodate his long legs. He'd rolled the cuffs on his blue-and-white striped dress shirt, revealing a great set of forearms with just the right amount of hair and a watch that probably cost nearly as much as his car. He was a sexy man in the way rich, powerful men were sexy. He was also funny, smart, and charismatic. But he belonged in Clint's world, not hers. Like so many men in professional sports, Brett Rivers's identity was built on money, power, and ambition.

They sailed through the small town of Ludlow. It was almost dark, and they hadn't seen another car for a few miles. The GPS kept cutting out, and Rory decided to pull over and take a screenshot of the directions before they lost it completely.

"We're not going to lose service," Brett declared, as if saying it would make it a fact. "We'd better not."

"I understand. Without cell service, you're only half a man."

"It's not funny, Rory. I have to be reachable twenty-four seven."

"Or the world as you know it will come to an end. Let's hope for the best."

But hope wasn't enough, and a few minutes later, as they turned onto still another county road, they lost the signal permanently. Brett looked so upset, she nearly took pity on him, but she wasn't that good a person. "Do you need a paper bag to breathe into?"

He shot her a visual death ray. "We'd better not be here for long."

She held her peace until they reached their destination.

Dick's Salvage Yard.

Rory turned into a gravel lot presided over by a cinder-block building where a single caged light bulb above the front door cast shadows over the graffiti spray-painted on the walls. As Brett muttered an obscenity, she double-checked the directions on the screenshot she'd taken, but there was no mistake. Dick's Salvage Yard was the end of the line.

She brought the car to a stop, eyeing the stacks of hubcaps growing like giant mushrooms through the weeds by a chain-link fence. Behind the fence stretched a graveyard of car husks. She gazed from the sign to the weed-infested lot. "Do you think Dick knows there's a difference between a salvage yard and a junkyard, which this actually is?"

"Dick's clearly a believer in aspirational thinking."

"Another person with a failed dream."

Brett tore out his earpiece and tossed it aside.

She touched the switch that opened the driver's-side window. A dog howled in the not-so-far distance, and the musky night air held the metallic smell of an oncoming thunderstorm. "Now might be a good time to tell me the real story about how you got this address."

He slid down his own window. "Clint's business manager's assistant is an old friend."

"An old girlfriend, you mean."

"How do you know that?" He checked his phone again, as if he expected a signal to have miraculously appeared.

"I know because we're sitting in front of Dick's junkyard instead of Clint's cabin. This is your ex-girlfriend's way of getting revenge for the heartless way you dumped her."

He set his phone aside. "She dumped me, and no revenge was involved. She also warned me that the print was blurred on the document she located with the cabin's address."

"Why did she dump you?"

"Why do you care?"

"I don't." The dog that wasn't so far away howled again. "This place is creeping me out."

"His cabin should be somewhere around here."

"There has to be a better way to find it. Maybe you should—" She let out a soft shriek as someone rapped on the roof of the car right above her head. She spun around to see a bearded man in full camo with a rifle slung over his shoulder standing right outside her open window.

"What the hell?" she cried.

Brett opened the passenger door and got out for no ascertainable reason. "Howdy."

Howdy? Who said "howdy" anymore?

Maybe he wanted to divert Camo Man's attention from her? Surely not. But if he had, it was working, because Camo Man stepped away from the window toward the hood of the car.

The engine was still running. All she had to do was hit reverse and peel out. Which she couldn't do because the ruler of the universe wasn't in the car.

"We seem to be lost," Brett said.

"Looks that way."

Every part of her bristled at Camo Man's undiluted hostility. He couldn't have made it clearer that he wasn't some friendly local anxious to help a couple of strangers.

Brett regarded him across the hood of the car. "We're supposed to be visiting a friend who has a cabin out here, but my girlfriend . . ." A nod toward the front seat. "She wrote down the wrong address, and my buddy's not answering his phone."

Sure. Blame it on the girlfriend.

"Who're you looking for?" Camo Man's free hand came to rest on the butt of his sidearm. He had a rifle and a sidearm? Definitely overkill.

Bad choice of words.

"That's where it gets tricky." Brett put his hand on the hood. "Our friend's a big deal in Chicago and a privacy nut. Likes to keep a low profile so he won't get hassled when he comes up here. He wouldn't appreciate me tossing his name around."

"Hard to find him without a name."

"He lives somewhere nearby, maybe along this road. Only shows up for a few days here and there and doesn't rent out his place."

Brett couldn't know any of this for sure, but he'd made good guesses. "Anybody fit that description?" he went on.

"Hard to say."

Brett turned back to the passenger door. "Thanks for your help."

Which was nonexistent.

"Hold it right there." Two men stepped out from the side of the building. In the reflection coming from the headlights, they looked like younger clones of Camo Man. They were both bearded white guys wearing ill-fitting jeans, camo shirts, and some kind of military vest displaying an olive-green patch showing an American eagle with a gun in its beak and the words "In God We Trust" imprinted on a bar beneath.

The fake soldier boys were armed, and she was growing more pissed off by the second. She'd read about these guys—small-minded men with so little self-esteem that they were threatened by anyone who didn't fit their narrow concept of who was an American. Men so bored by their real lives that they needed to manufacture excitement. More women should do their patriotic duty by screwing these losers to keep them off the street. Or, in this case, out of the junkyard.

Her temper flared. Leaving the engine running, she opened the door and got out. "Guys, what the hell?"

"Rory . . ." The warning note in Brett's voice told her he wasn't happy with her intrusion. Maybe he was being protective, but more likely, he didn't want to tell Clint he'd witnessed his sister getting shot. Bad for his career.

She didn't care. She'd had enough of the obstacles standing in the way of her moving forward with her life. "Do you guys go around pointing your guns at everyone you don't recognize?"

Camo Man stuck out his jaw. "We do if we think they might be from the gov'mint."

"Sweet Jesus." She made a wild gesture toward Brett. "He wears Gucci loafers and drives an S-Class Benz. Does he look like he's from the government?"

The three exchanged glances. Finally, the youngest and possibly brightest of the group—although that was relative—saw the flaw. "What about you?"

"I make chocolate. Or at least I try to."

"Prove it."

She turned to Brett. "How do I open the trunk?"

"You don't have to prove anything." Brett's snarl sounded as mean as the proverbial junkyard dog.

"Apparently I do," she said, "because these guys are morons."

"Rory . . ." He turned her name into a long warning note.

"Well, they are!"

"Ignore her," Brett said. "She's been smoking a lot of weed lately."

"I wish." Thunder sounded in the distance. "Judging by those fierce-looking patches on your vests and your general attitude, I suspect you men see yourselves as guardians of the Constitution—a document you clearly haven't read. And pointing your phallic symbols at me and my candy-ass *boy*friend makes you look ridiculous."

Brett rounded on her. "I am *not* a candy-ass—"

She wasn't done. "When you idiots take over the federal government from the deep state, exactly what do you intend to do with it?"

"I'll open the trunk," Brett said quickly.

Ignoring him, Camo Man strode toward her. "You've got a big mouth, Curly. When the shit hits the fan, we're the only ones who can save your sorry ass."

"You're the shit that's gonna—"

"The trunk's open!" Brett exclaimed, blocking off the rest of what she'd been about to say. "Here you go, guys. Some of the best chocolate you'll ever taste."

The trunk contained a dozen small, brown cardboard sample boxes—leftovers from her farmers' market days—each containing six pieces of the most recent chocolates she'd made. She'd packed them with the vague notion that they might come in useful if someone needed a little encouragement to talk to them.

All three men approached the trunk, rifles ready in case her truffles decided to open fire. Brett picked up one of the boxes. Like the others, it held six confections: passion fruit, praline, bourbon maple pecan, and vanilla buttercream, along with a luscious sea salt caramel and a creamy coin of perfectly melded dark and milk chocolate.

As the taller moron opened the sample box, Rory was struck

with an unwelcome rush of patriotic fever that made her think about all the good people in the military, in government, in churches and volunteer work—people who cared about each other, about their country, and about their country's place in the world. Decent, caring people who had too much good work to do to spend their time trading outrageous conspiracy theories and training for insurrection. Then she thought about the oath that naturalized citizens had to take to protect the Constitution from all enemies, foreign and domestic. Yet here she was, appeasing idiots with her precious bonbons. She stormed forward. "Forget it! I'm not sharing my chocolates with traitors to our country!"

She was too late. The bonbons were disappearing into their stomachs. "She's got a mouth on her," Camo Man said to Brett as he licked his lips.

"Tell me about it."

"It seems a guy like you could do better."

"I've often thought so," Brett said with a nod.

Suddenly, these two were buddies? She should have known. It was her chocolates. This wasn't the first time she'd seen strangers come together over her handiwork, although never quite such an unlikely pairing.

Camo Man spoke around her caramel. "If you're looking for Clint Garrett, he has a place a couple of miles down the road. A big trout mailbox."

So much for Clint's supposed anonymity.

"Thanks." Brett began to move around the hood of the car, ready to take over the driving. She jumped inside before he could get there and settled behind the wheel. No way was she abandoning the driver's seat in front of these Neanderthals.

To his credit, Brett made a smooth reverse back toward the passenger's side.

"You let a woman drive your car?" Young Moron said.

"Why not?"

All three men regarded him with smirks that conveyed their pity for his lack of manhood. He smiled and curled his hand over the top of the passenger door. "Just so you know, I agree with every word Curly said, although I'd have been more tactful about it. You guys need to find another hobby."

Instead of jumping in the car so she could peel away in a hailstorm of loose gravel, he took his time settling in and closing the door.

"Hurry up," she hissed, not liking the way they'd shifted their rifles.

He nodded to the men through the windshield. At the same time, he spoke to her in a low, warning whisper. "Don't you dare peel out of here."

Exactly what she'd been prepared to do.

She made herself back slowly away. At the same time, she prepared for her tires to be shot out.

Sure enough—

A bullet exploded in the gravel in front of the car. *Damn it!* Another shot hit the dirt, and then another. Close, but purposely falling short of the tires. She stuck her head out the open window. *"Assholes!"*

"*Now* you can peel out," Brett said.

8

Once they were out of firing range, Brett took her to task. "You really thought it was a good idea to call them assholes?"

"I'm a patriot."

"If you'd gotten shot—"

"Clint would have blamed you." She grinned. "I love our relationship. As long as you're Clint's agent, which—let's be honest—you might not be much longer if he doesn't change his attitude toward you . . . I have all the power."

"It sucks to be me."

She laughed.

He reached for his cell only to abandon it when he couldn't get a signal. She drove slowly, her headlights on high beam, raindrops beginning to splatter the windshield. Occasionally, a driveway cut through the dense tree growth on each side of the dark road, but none of those driveways had a mailbox that looked like a trout.

The windshield began to cloud up. He reached over to adjust the defrost and brushed her arm, an inconsequential touch that made her aware of how close they were sitting. He glanced at her. "Despite what I told them, I didn't agree with everything you said. I am *not* a candy-ass."

She moved her arm on the wheel, creating more distance between them. "Probably not. But I didn't want you to get shot."

"Something you quickly forgot about when you started calling them names."

"That's another difference between Clint and me. The Golden Boy seldom loses his temper. I, on the other hand, am a human time bomb." The headlights picked out the glowing eyes of a coyote or fox darting into the underbrush. "We've gone well over a mile. What do you think a trout mailbox looks like?"

"A fish?"

"That kind of sharp insight explains how you managed to pass the bar." Smirking at him made her feel better about herself. He was the kind of man who could overwhelm a woman, and she'd been overwhelmed enough.

"We must have missed it," he said. "Look for a place where you can turn around without destroying my car. Wait! Right there."

She saw it at the same time he did. A post holding a mailbox shaped like a gape-mouthed trout. The car lurched as she made an abrupt turn into the two-track dirt driveway. Brett's shoulder hit the window. "Don't you dare bottom out this car."

"Roger that. You'd think with what Clint makes, he'd buy a load of gravel."

"This is a good way to discourage visitors." The headlights swept the wet underbrush and came to rest on a log cabin not much bigger than the garden shed at Clint's fake château. "I can't wait to send Kristin a photo of the place," Rory said. "She'll come unglued."

"You'll let me know, won't you, when you graduate from third grade."

She deserved that. Through the rain, she studied the rustic cabin. Two steps led to the front door, and no light shone through the single window facing the drive. "Maybe he's asleep," she said. "Or out for a night hike."

"Or planning insurrection with the fake soldier boys."

"More likely wearing a wire for the feds. He's such a Boy Scout."

Rain hammered the roof of the car even as Brett reached for the door handle. "I'll check it out. No need for both of us to get wet."

She turned off the engine and watched him, in the glow of the headlights, dash up the front steps. He was a big man, not big in the way of football players but leaner and more long-limbed. The square overhang offered little protection from the rain. He banged on the door a few times before he tried the knob. When that didn't work, he leaned across the wooden side rail to peer in the window.

It felt wrong sitting in the dry car while he was getting soaked. She made her own dash to join him on the now-crowded landing.

"I can't see a damned thing," he said, as he straightened from the window. His tailored dress shirt had gotten wet so that it clung to his broad shoulders, while rain glistened in that slick, whiskey-brown hair.

The car's automatic headlights dimmed and went out. "Maybe he went into town," she suggested.

"Or maybe he never came here in the first place."

"Stop being so negative." The wind had picked up, and the overhang offered little protection. She tried the knob herself, but it was firmly locked.

He turned on his phone flashlight and swept it across the

porch. The beam landed at the base of the front stair rail. "Look at this."

A metal key box was chained to the bottom. "It has a combination lock," she said. "Try his college jersey number and his pro jersey."

"Eighteen fifteen? It won't be that simple."

"Clint doesn't have much imagination when it comes to home security."

He gestured toward the key box, raindrops sliding over his admirable cheekbones. "Be my guest."

The box was angled so the only way to work the combination involved crouching in a muddy puddle by the lock. She took his phone and redirected the beam to the lockbox. "I couldn't possibly deprive you of the opportunity to show off your manhood, not to mention earning those millions you collect in commissions."

"I have a helluva lot better way to show off my manhood." The low, husky note in his voice, the rainwater spiking his dark eyelashes, and the wet shirt clinging to a really, really decent set of shoulders distracted her. He grinned.

She waited too long to curl her lip at him. "So juvenile."

"Not sorry."

The rain was falling harder, and one of them needed to get completely wet. She tucked his phone between her knees to free her hands. "Rock, paper, scissors. Two out of three. Loser works the lockbox."

"You're on."

Paper over rock.

Scissors cut paper.

Rock breaks scissors . . . He lost, and he was all injured dignity. "You cheated."

"There's no crying in rock, paper, scissors."

He snorted, gazed up at the leaky overhang, and stepped into the downpour. She pointed the light beam toward the lock as he knelt before it. By the time he returned to the landing, he was drenched. "You were wrong about the combination. Fifteen eighteen."

"Clint got creative."

Brett's wet shirt now outlined not just his shoulders but also the well-developed tendons of his back. He moved inside ahead of her, whether as a deliberate discourtesy or to protect her from squatters, she could only guess.

The simple, one-room interior lacked squatters, as well as a crystal chandelier and gaggle of simpering cherubs. Gray chinking sealed the log cabin walls and angled beams supported the pitched roof. The open kitchen held a small refrigerator, an old four-burner range, and a single pair of cabinets. Instead of a fireplace, a wood-burning, cast-iron stove sat between a nondescript, rust-colored couch and a table with two straight-backed chairs. Rory pushed aside a heavy curtain that hung across the only interior doorway. On the other side was a tiny bathroom with a sink, toilet, and shower stall that looked too small for Clint's large frame. She grabbed some hand towels.

When she emerged, she found Brett gazing up at the sleeping loft, reachable by a flat-rung, wooden ladder. She passed over one of the towels. He wiped his face and ran it over the top of his head. Unlike hers, his hair stayed in place.

"Clint thrives on being around people," she said. "It's hard to imagine him coming here." She went to the ladder, looped her towel over one of the rungs, and climbed far enough to see a bed taking up most of the plank floor. Even if there'd been more room, Clint would only have been able to stand upright in the center.

A bolt of lightning lit up the window at the far end of the loft. She saw jeans and a couple of jackets dangling from wooden pegs, along with open shelving holding a stack of T-shirts, some underwear, and a few pairs of high-end sneakers. Everything about this cabin disconcerted her.

She climbed down the ladder to see Brett standing in front of the refrigerator, wet shirt molded to his skin, towel draping his neck. "Someone's been here recently. There's an open milk container with next week's date. Also, an empty bottle of very expensive scotch in the trash."

"Clint only drinks beer."

"Are you sure you know your brother? He was drinking eighteen-year-old Glenlivet the night you and I . . ."

"Met?"

"Did we ever."

A shaft of lightning lit up those laser-cut cheekbones. The storm was nearly overhead, but also brewing inside her. She wasn't good at holding grudges against anyone except her family, and her animosity toward him had faded. Brett lived in a world filled with high-class escorts, and—face it—she was flattered he thought she was sexy enough to be an employee.

She told herself to focus on finding Clint, not on this powerhouse of a man who made her feel both fearless and woefully inadequate. She gestured toward the fishing poles leaning in the corner. "Maybe he went out night fishing and decided to hole up until the storm passes."

He moved toward the kitchen. "The tackle box is still there. It looks like we've hit a dead end."

Discouraged, she studied the cabin for another clue, but the space was too small to hide much. She thought she knew Clint. Why did her normally social brother need this kind of isolation?

The lights flickered twice and went out, plunging the cabin into darkness. "That's it," he said. "We're done here."

She reached for her phone and turned on the flashlight. "This can't be the first time he's lost power. He must have a lantern or some candles."

"We don't need them," he said firmly. "We're getting out of here."

"I'm staying." She swept the flashlight beam around the cabin. "He's clearly been here recently, and he could be on his way back right now. Besides, it's raining like crazy."

"We're already wet, and I need to check my calls."

"Is your phone all you care about? Never mind. Rhetorical question." She directed the flashlight into one of the kitchen drawers looking for a candle but saw only a collection of rubber bands, nail clippers, spare change, and a broken pair of sunglasses.

"Staying connected is my job," he said. "One missed call, and I could lose a client."

"If that's all it takes to lose a client, you must not be very good at what you do."

He bristled. "You have no idea what my job entails."

"Making lots of money," she retorted.

"Has it occurred to you," he said, "that, at this very minute, Clint might be trying to get in touch with me?"

He was right. She closed the drawer. "Go on. I'll stay here in case he comes back. You can get me in the morning."

"I can't go off and leave you alone," he said indignantly. "Those clowns at the junkyard know where we are."

"I seriously doubt they'll be taking a late-night hike in this weather. They're probably holed up in a bar somewhere plotting the next insurrection. Besides, I can take care of myself." She opened the top cupboard and spotted a fat candle on the high shelf. She stretched to reach it but wasn't tall enough.

"Yeah, I saw how well you did that at the junkyard. Remind me again what you called them. Morons? Traitors?"

"And assholes."

He snorted and retrieved the candle for her. His height, the breadth of his chest, his general maleness, gave her goose bumps. This cabin wasn't all she found disconcerting. She needed to put distance between herself and Brett Rivers.

She took the candle from him and returned to the junk drawer for matches, but as she began to light the candle, a blue-white blaze of lightning followed by a deafening whipcrack of thunder shook the walls. The splintering sound of a tree falling sent them both dashing to the front window.

Another zigzag of lightning showed a tree had fallen across the drive exactly where Brett's car was parked.

"Son of a bitch!" He made a dash for the door, coming to an abrupt halt only because she grabbed his shirttail.

"You're not going out in all this lightning."

"The hell I'm not." Another boom rattled the cabin. "My car is out there."

She blocked the door. "It'll still be there when the worst of this storm passes." She reared up on her tiptoes, which still didn't put them at eye level. "Or would you rather get fried? I hear lightning does great things for the brain."

He gazed down at her. Their eyes locked and an invisible fireball zapped between them. He quickly backed away. "All right.

But the minute this storm passes . . . Damn, if that tree hit my car . . ."

"You'll buy a new one. Probably two." It seemed safest to hide behind her snark.

He returned to the window. "It's too dark to see if the car got a direct hit."

"The storm will pass. I'm drying off, but you're still wet." *And tempting.* "Why don't you find something of Clint's to change into while I see if I can scrounge up a meal?" They hadn't stopped for dinner on the way, and he had to be as hungry as she, although maybe not in exactly the same way.

"Food isn't going to make me forget about that car," he grumbled, heading up the ladder.

She breathed a sigh of relief at having him out of sight. As she investigated the kitchen, she found a lone can of beer, an unopened box of rice, a package of freezer-burned hot dogs, and a can of spray cheese that made her shudder. Even worse than the fake cheese, her brother had been eating from an open box of Choco Whorls cereal that was a desecration of everything she believed chocolate should be. She dumped it in the trash.

Gazing at the pitiful ingredients left, she tried to pretend she was on *Chopped.* Except *Chopped* would at least have given her a kumquat and some squid ink.

Resigned, she made the rice, set it on one of the stove's four burners, and ran warm water over the hot dog package before she pried it open.

Brett reappeared in a pair of gym shorts and a Chicago Stars T-shirt. He looked way more delicious than the meal she was preparing. He stole the candle from her. "There has to be a flashlight somewhere."

As he searched the cabin, his silhouette cast hazy shadows on the walls, ironic for a man who knew exactly who he was, what he wanted, and how to get it. A man who wasn't a drifter like her.

He emerged from the bathroom and showed her a flashlight, placing the candle on the kitchen countertop. "I found this under the sink."

"All the better for Clint to study his good looks in the mirror."

"You're hopeless."

She adjusted the flame under the rice and tossed the half-frozen hot dogs into the cabin's only skillet. As the flashlight beam bounced across the far wall, she repositioned the candle so she could better see what she was doing. Unfortunately, the glow gave her just enough light to watch his very fine butt once again disappear up the ladder to the loft.

Her memory of what had occurred in that hotel room was so foggy it no longer seemed real. She couldn't imagine him in the throes of passion. He was too controlled. She was almost sure she remembered that he was a lousy lover, one of those guys who focused only on closing the deal.

He came back down the ladder. "I thought I might have missed some kind of clue up there, but no luck."

She refocused. "Your gourmet dinner is almost ready. Prepare to be dazzled." She plated the rice and held the can of spray cheese over the hot dogs, but she couldn't make herself press the nozzle. He'd have to eat them straight.

"Fair warning," she said, as she set the plates near the candle she placed in the middle of the table. "This is the worst meal I've ever made."

He studied her for a disconcerting moment then focused on the hot dogs. "I don't suppose there's any mustard."

"Not even a packet of drive-through ketchup."

He reluctantly scooped up a forkful of rice. As she poked at her food, he took another forkful. Seconds later, he gazed at her in surprise. "This rice is great. What did you do?"

"Half beer and half water. I could have cooked the hot dogs in beer, but that would have been overkill."

"You're good."

His words were slow and sexy. Flustered, she looked down at her plate. "I'd kill for a glass of Sangiovese."

"I'd kill for a cell signal."

His obsession with his phone brought her back to reality. "Tell me more about growing up with four younger brothers and without a sister who could have taught you so much about human relationships not involving money."

"If we'd had a sister, we'd have known that chest bumps and noogies weren't the best way to get a girl's attention." He smiled. "Girls—and I'm sure you already know this—also don't think burping in someone's face is nearly as hilarious as my brothers did."

She poked at a hot dog. "It's hard to imagine you as a child. I'll bet you came out of the birth canal with hundred-dollar bills wrapped around the umbilical cord."

"A disturbing image."

"Your poor mother."

"She tried her best, but she was too busy keeping us from killing each other to worry about the finer points of gracious living."

"What about your dad?"

"He was her sixth kid. A happy, unreliable alcoholic. He left fake snakes in our beds, pretended to cut off his finger with his hunting knife. Once, when we got home from school, we found all the porch furniture missing and a Sold sign on the house. That made Robbie cry." He smiled. "The best was the night we were camping in the backyard, and he jumped out at us with a Leather-face mask and a chain saw."

"That's horrifying!"

"We were perverse little bastards, and we loved it. Everybody but Robbie. He had to sleep with a night-light on for years. But he's a master gunnery sergeant in the Marines now, so the trauma didn't last forever." Brett set down his fork and gazed at her across the candlelit table. "Unlike your beef with Kristin."

"I'll say this for Kristin. She wasn't into chain saws. She was a little more subtle."

"How so?"

The cabin lights flickered back on, but the rain continued to pound the roof. "Eat your rice," she said.

*⋆

After dinner, Brett cleaned up the kitchen. She wasn't sure if he did it because he was enlightened or to keep himself from obsessing over his cell phone trauma.

The rain finally stopped, and they could go outside to assess the damage. Avoiding the puddle at the bottom of the porch steps, Rory inhaled the earthy scent of clean, scrubbed night air along with a whiff of sandalwood as Brett strode past her. The glow from the porch light showed a fallen tree barricading the driveway behind the Benz.

"It missed your car," she pointed out, as he uttered a series of locker-room swears. "You should be relieved."

"Relieved? We're stuck here!"

Stuck with you, she thought.

He attacked the tree, but it quickly became evident that, without a chain saw and truck, his car wasn't going anywhere. "Things will look better in the morning." She tried to sound cheerful. He practically bared his teeth at her.

Eventually, they cleared enough branches to open the car's trunk. Her backpack and the Trader Joe's shopping bag where she'd packed what she needed leaned against his leather Montblanc weekender, a visual reminder of the gap between them. After he'd handed over her bag and claimed his weekender, he reached for the remaining boxes of chocolates she'd brought along for bribes. "You can leave those in the car," she said.

"Like hell." He tucked them under his arm and struggled unsuccessfully to open the driver's door.

"We can't do anything about this tonight," she pointed out.

"You think I don't know that?" It was more a snarl than a statement. He stepped back from the car and ran his hand through his no-longer-perfect hair. "Sorry. I'm being a jerk." He looked as regretful as a buff, megarich professional sports agent could look.

She cocked her head at him. "Are you really sorry or sister-of-my-biggest-client sorry?"

He gave her a rueful smile. "Both."

She grinned. She liked this sexy weasel way more than she wanted to.

9

Less than an hour later when she came out of the bathroom, he stopped pacing long enough to take in the vintage mint-green kimono she used as a robe. The way he looked at her made her even more conscious of him as a lust-inspiring man instead of a symbol of raw ambition. She pulled herself together. "Are you going to complain about this, too?"

He took her in from toe to head, his gaze lingering at the draped neckline. "No complaints necessary."

Maybe the aftereffect of the storm made her feel as if an errant electrical charge buzzed between them. She searched for something to say that would break the tension. "You're too big for the couch. You can have the bed." *Unless you want to share it with me.*

He looked up at the loft. "Thanks."

"Aren't you going to argue with me?"

"First rule of being a successful negotiator. When someone offers you a good deal, take it."

"I'll remember that."

He peeled his eyes away from her to check his ever-present

phone. With no bars in sight, he started to pace but only got as far as the table. He gazed at the small sample boxes. "Go ahead," she said.

"Are you sure?" He didn't wait for reassurance but opened a box and studied its contents. "Which of these pairs best with disaster?"

"The bourbon maple pecan at the end. Unless you have a flask with the real thing tucked away somewhere."

"I didn't plan that well."

She sat on the couch. He bit the truffle in half as usual and savored it before he ate the rest. Slow and deliberate. If only he'd been this way in bed instead of a dud. A total dud. She was sure of it. Unless she was making that up to cool herself down.

"You don't want any?" he said, as she waved off the proffered sample box.

She wanted some, all right, and if he'd been one of the men she was normally drawn to, she would have made a move. Unfortunately, he wasn't a loser.

She didn't like those memories, and she shook them off. "I try to eat chocolate only when I'm testing a batch or creating a new flavor."

"A chocolatier who doesn't eat chocolate?"

"I love it. Obviously. But I have to eat mindfully or I'll screw up my palate." He seemed genuinely interested, and talking to him about what she did was smarter than ogling him. "I love experimenting with flavor combinations. It's trendy for chocolatiers to use herbs—rosemary and thyme, lavender, a few others—but it started to feel gimmicky, and I gave it up. Also, no Parmesan cheese, garlic, or, God forbid, Pop Rocks."

He stopped by the door. "Garlic?"

"Not kidding." She sat on the couch, choosing the end farthest from the door where he was standing. "Some chocolatiers pride themselves on weird combinations—the stranger, the better—but that feels like posturing to me, more about experimenting for the sake of experimenting than about producing something truly delicious. I believe in honoring the product. I won't even use bacon."

"You might have gone too far there."

She smiled. "Maybe."

Silence fell between them. Instead of looking at his phone, Brett was looking at her. The deep V neckline of the kimono continued to draw his attention, and she told herself to tighten the sash, but she didn't. "Tell me why Clint's business manager's assistant broke up with you."

He started pacing again. "This is what you want to talk about? Why a former girlfriend broke up with me?"

"I'm only making conversation." She drew up her knees and wrapped the kimono around them. "Let me take a wild stab. She got tired of waiting for a ring."

"Not exactly." He stopped pacing to take in the way the fabric draped her legs. "She wasn't ready to get married."

Rory extended her foot a few inches. "But she wanted to move in with you."

"A little less subtle." He drew his attention away from her legs. "She wanted to be with a man who loved her."

"Which you didn't."

He resumed his pacing, unable to settle down without a cell signal. Or maybe the lack of cell reception wasn't the sole reason for his restlessness. Maybe he, too, felt the same discomfiting awareness. "She was smart, and she didn't want to slap shiplap on my walls, so it wasn't her." He reached the cast-iron stove. "The bottom line is, I'm not open to romantic love."

"You're bitter toward women. I get it."

"Now why would you say that?" He stopped walking. "I'm not bitter. I like women, sometimes more than I like men. And I definitely like sex." He hesitated, his eyes returning to the outline of her legs under her robe. "Do we have to talk about this?"

She clasped her hands more firmly around her knees. "You know my secrets. It's only fair I know yours."

"Mine will only give you more reason to hate me."

"Shockingly, I don't hate you anymore. I don't *trust* you, that's true. We both know you'd throw my body to the sharks if you could make a profit from it, but—"

"I would *not* throw you to the sharks." Despite what he said, he looked like a pissed-off barracuda.

"Whatever. Go on. Spill your terrible secret."

He shoved his hands in the pockets of his gym shorts, inadvertently pulling the fabric tight across his flat abdomen . . . and below. "I grew up in a big family with no privacy. Now I only want one person at the center of my life."

"Yourself."

He extracted his hands from the pockets, spoiling her view. "I'm not apologizing so forget whatever it is you're thinking."

She was thinking that she wished he'd put his hands back in his pockets.

"It doesn't mean I'm self-centered, at least not completely. I'm just not a guy who's into romantic love. Whatever that thing is that makes people fall in love, I don't have it."

"I've heard that about sociopaths." She held up her hand before he could respond. "Never mind. Another low blow. You've never been in love?"

"I love my family. My brothers. My nieces and nephews are the cutest kids ever. And I'm not a cynic. Or a sociopath. Romantic love makes the world go round. I get that. But, no, I've never been in love, not even when I was a teenager. It's outside my realm of experience."

"How weird. You're like a three-piece-suit version of the lonesome cowboy roaming the Wild West on his faithful steed with only the stars to be his guide."

"I'd never wear a three-piece suit, and I get lost without a GPS."

"Still . . ."

He approached the couch. "I put my career first. Always. I'm upfront about that. My job is how I keep score of the way my life is going."

She shifted uncomfortably at the idea of using the jobs she'd worked as a way to assess her own life.

He finally looked as though he wanted to settle on the couch, so she pulled her legs closer to her body, giving him room. "I like having my own space," he said. "Working as long as I want, going where I want, when I want. What's wrong with that?"

"You tell me."

"Nothing." He sat next to her, only keeping a few inches between her toes and his hip. "My boss, Heath Champion. Real name, Harley Davidson Campione—"

"There's a story behind that."

"A good one. Anyway, Heath has a great marriage and great kids, but he's had to make a lot of business sacrifices I'm not willing to make."

"So no marriage. No kids."

"You sound as judgmental as my mother. Being single isn't a crime. Unmarried women talk about how happy their lives are. Why isn't it okay for men?"

"I didn't say it wasn't okay. I've never had any interest in marriage either, and I can't imagine having kids. But I also can't imagine never having been in love."

"It's saved me a lot of angst, and I'll bet you can't say the same."

"True." She'd had more than her fair share of angst. The worst was the result of her involvement with the brilliant French chocolatier she'd apprenticed herself to. André had made her do the impossible: fall even more deeply in love with the art form. From him, she'd learned the science of making chocolate, not just the skills of tempering, molding, and decorating. Along the way, she'd also fallen in love with him. She hadn't understood that—like Ashley's—André's ego demanded complete devotion. Once he'd secured that, he moved on.

But Brett Rivers wasn't André, and Brett's disinterest in romantic love would have made him a perfect candidate for a no-strings affair except for two things: his relationship with her brother and the fact that breathing his rarefied, overachieving air made her even more conscious of the sense that she was drifting aimlessly through her life. On the other hand, it was dark, they were in the middle of Nowhere, Michigan, and he had that dangerous thing going on—killer cheekbones, knife-blade nose, and gray gangster's eyes.

Only the rattle of wind in the trees intruded on the strained silence between them. His hand found her bare foot. He cupped her toes, grazed his thumb along the arch. A jolt of pure lust sped through her body. She straightened her other leg and laid it across his lap. Her calf brushed against all the proof she needed that he felt the same heat storm she did.

He pushed her leg aside and rocketed from the couch. "I'm going to bed. I'll pull up the ladder after me."

*
⋆

Brett didn't have to see that small nose tilt disparagingly in his direction to know he'd insulted her. "Don't bother with the ladder," she said icily. "I'm not interested."

The hell she wasn't. The tension that had been crackling between them all evening had reached its breaking point. His body thrummed, and he'd broken a sweat under his T-shirt. He had to either get away from her or do something stupid, and he didn't do stupid.

She dropped her feet over the side of the couch, clearly done with him. Her robe parted, revealing bare, shapely legs to just above her knee, which wasn't nearly high enough.

"You're not as hot as you think you are." She waved her fingers dismissively toward the ladder. "Off you go. Scurry on up to your hidey-hole."

"Damn it, Rory! I'm trying to be the good guy here."

"Aw, thanks," she scoffed. "Because I need you to protect me."

"That's not what I meant."

But he'd insulted her, and she was on a roll. "For your information, you're not the big prize you seem to think. Do you know what you really are?"

He had a feeling she was going to tell him.

"You're an arrogant, egotistical workaholic! You're cocky and pretentious and shallow and—and a total douche who had to get a woman *drunk* to get her in bed!"

"I did not have to get you drunk! You were already—" He shoved his hand through his hair. "You know as well as I do this is a bad idea! You're the sister of my—"

"Your biggest client. Blah. Blah. Oh, yes, I know." She practically spat the words at him as she stalked toward the bathroom. "Discussion over. We are *not* happening." Shoving the curtain back from the door, she disappeared inside.

He was The River. Laser-focused. Shrewd. Disciplined. But his single-mindedness had developed a fault line, and she was it. He went after her.

The bathroom was basic. Log walls, a shower stall, and a mirror above the sink. The bare window over the toilet looked out into the dark woods behind the cabin.

She stood scowling at him, her curvy hips propped against the sink, arms crossed over her round breasts, sneer out of place on that sweet, floozy face.

"I'm sorry for whatever I did that has you so pissed off, even if I don't know what I did." For a straightforward guy, he was lying. Big time. He knew exactly what he'd done. He'd had foreplay with her foot, and when she'd responded, he'd done the last thing he wanted to do and rejected her. He rubbed his arm. "Okay. I do know what I did. I panicked, okay?"

That didn't go over well, as evidenced by the curl of her lip. "The River, panic? I don't think so."

"I'm human, for God's sake. Not just a—what did you say?— egotistical, arrogant bully."

"I didn't call you a bully. I called you a douche."

"Point made." *Never apologize. Never explain. Unless it's to a client . . . or a coach . . . or a general manager.* He also remembered groveling to a couple of team owners and a few ad executives, but only to cover a client's ass, not his own, like he had to do now. "I was trying to do the right thing."

All the steam she'd been building up erupted. "How? By protecting the little lady from something she clearly wanted. Note the use of the past tense. Past tense means—"

"I know what past tense means!" He'd dealt with impossible people before, and he turned on The River charm. "Do you think we could start over?"

"From exactly what point?"

"You pick."

"How about when I said, 'Fuck you'?"

"I don't think you actually said—"

"I was thinking it!"

"I'm sure you were. Okay. You win. I'm out of here. But first . . ." One long stride closed the distance between them. He took her by the shoulders, gazed down into those beautiful blue eyes, and kissed that Cupid's bow mouth hard and deep, the way he'd been wanting to all day.

His heart battered his chest at the taste of her, and his body caught fire. He pressed against her, going half-crazy . . . heat sizzling through his blood . . . until the whole consent thing hit him like a bucket of ice water—the permission he should specifically have asked for but hadn't. Because he was an ass!

Appalled, he shot back from her as if she'd turned radioactive. "Sorry." Another apology. "I might have gotten my signals wrong. If I did—"

"It's hard to be you, isn't it?" She looped her arms around his neck and went in for her own kiss, taking command like the most accomplished floozy in the universe. Their bodies pressing together. His hand—his wayward hand—fumbled with the tie on the robe she wore like a 1930s movie star.

What felt like a short, fluffy nylon gown lay beneath. A gown no woman her age had worn in decades. His hand touched the hem and drifted beneath to a pair of panties he couldn't imagine any girlfriend of his would ever have worn. Not a thong. Not even a bikini. Real panties that went all the way to her waist and had this idiotic ruffle around the leg holes. He'd never touched anything sexier. He toyed with the lace, slipped his fingers—

A gentle pressure against his chest made him freeze. She pushed him away and gave him a shaky smile. "See you in the morning." Her hand brushed his very rigid crotch—accidentally, on purpose, he didn't know. "You can have the couch. I'm taking the bed."

Dumbfounded, he watched her slip out of the bathroom. *What the hell just happened?*

✦

Rory's wobbly, lust-ravaged legs barely carried her up the ladder's six rungs. Her kimono gaped open and her short nightie stuck to damp skin. The loft was hot, but she was hotter. Still, she'd somehow held on just enough to remember that, for her, sex with someone she cared about had to be more than joining body parts. She couldn't risk any more involvement with him, not while she was slogging through the muck of her own existence, not while she might be in danger of looking for a solid rope to cling to. He was bigger than life, a man who took over a room simply by walking into it. She already had a brother who made her feel incompetent. She didn't need a lover who made her feel the same way. So she'd done the nearly impossible. She'd pushed him away.

Peeling off her robe, she edged around the bed to the window at the end, but the warm, humid air did little to cool her off. That would take a January blizzard.

She lifted her damp curls off her neck, remembering the heady rush of that kiss. What woman wouldn't be turned on by that hot mess of a man, and how many of them would have the fortitude to walk away? In addition to lusting after him, she cared about the jerk. Yes, he was a badass, but he was also straightforward in his own way, intelligent, perceptive, and more decent than he'd ever admit.

He'd looked so stricken when he'd retreated from that kiss, as if he feared she didn't want it as much as he did. But she wanted it all right. She wanted it very much. Instead, here she was, getting ready to lie down in a bed with only a sheet and a pillow for company.

It would be a long time before she fell asleep.

*
*

Brett's neck was stiff and his back ached. It was barely six, and he'd spent a miserable night on the couch. As he climbed the ladder to the loft to retrieve his suitcase, the dim morning light coming through the open window fell on Rory asleep in the comfortable, oversized bed that took up most of the space. The robe she'd worn last night lay on the floor, and the temptation to crawl in next to her was so overwhelming, he had to force himself to look away. He retrieved his weekender and almost made it back to the ladder without looking at her again. Almost, but not quite.

She lay on her side, the curl that had drifted across her cheek gently lifting and falling with the slow rhythm of her breath. She'd kicked the sheet to the bottom of the bed, and her lips were puffy. Either she'd been nibbling on them while she slept or they were a result of last night's kiss.

The nightgown part of that outfit no one under the age of eighty should own had hitched up to her waist while she slept, revealing those old-fashioned white bloomers that left everything to the imagination. Maybe it was the aftereffect of his sleepless night, but they were sexier than the scantiest thong.

Watching her sleep made him hard all over again. He forced himself down the ladder and headed for the bathroom. As much as he craved a cup of coffee, he craved getting out of this place more.

After he showered and dressed, he emerged from the bathroom to see Rory peering down at him from the edge of the loft.

"What're you doin'?" She rubbed her eyes and yawned.

"Go back to sleep." He growled at her, as if she were the world's biggest annoyance, which she was. "I'm walking down the road to the closest neighbors. I'll see if I can hire someone with a pickup to pull the tree away so I can get the car out."

She swung herself onto the ladder. "Give me a minute. I'm coming with you."

At first, he was too caught up in a perfect view of that round butt in the ruffled panties descending the ladder to respond, but he finally found his voice. "Stay here and have some coffee ready for when I get back."

"You expect the little woman to make coffee while you go off adventuring? Not gonna happen. Give me three minutes." She padded for the bathroom.

"Like any woman can get ready in three minutes," he called after her.

"You're on, butthead. Make it two and a half minutes."

"You wear granny panties!"

"You're a pervert," she shot back.

He smiled despite himself.

10

As it turned out, he barely had time to fill the coffeepot with water before she emerged in yesterday's clothes, no makeup, her tangled hair snared through the back of her Yankees ball cap, a smug smile on her face. "Next time, remember who you're talking to."

"I saw your underwear," he retorted, since their conversation had regressed to a grade school playground.

"That had to make your day." She grabbed some of her sampler boxes and put them in her backpack. "We might need bribes."

She was out the door ahead of him as if last night had never happened.

✦

Rory detoured around a muddy pothole in the gravel road. Brett hadn't said a word about last night. It was as if he'd forgotten all about it. She gazed over at him from under the visor of her ball cap. "Even out here in the wilderness, your hair is ridiculous."

He frowned at her. "What's this thing you've got about my hair?"

She pushed thoughts of last night out of her head. It hadn't happened. It was only a dream. A wet dream. "I get thrown off when you look like one of those cheesy men's hairstyle photos."

"Living with all that jealousy must be painful."

"Not really. I'm used to it." She wished she could wear her hair like he did, slicked back from her face in that consummate power look, but she didn't have either the personality or the career for it.

They passed a shredded trash bag tossed on the roadside. He batted away a buzzing mosquito. "Last night got a little out of control."

He'd finally brought it up. "Not really. I was toying with you."

"*Toying* with me?"

She had to be smart about this, which meant no serious conversation. "You really need to learn to keep your hands to yourself."

"Hey, I wasn't the only one with wandering hands."

The mosquito headed for her, and she took a swipe at it. "I was having a fantasy about an old boyfriend."

"Is that so?" The gravel crunched under his loafers, which were not nearly as practical for walking along a muddy country road as her sneakers. He dug his phone out and checked the screen. His disgruntled expression indicated he was no closer to cell phone nirvana than he'd been at the cabin. He shoved the phone back into his pocket. "The thing is—"

"Here's what your addled brain keeps missing, Rivers. I'm not a hookup person. I'm a relationship person, a dating-and-getting-to-know-you person. Despite what happened last night—despite what happened in that tawdry incident at the hotel—I need something more than a couple of gropes and a fast poke."

"A fast *poke*? Lady, the way we were headed—"

"I need emotional intimacy way more than immediate gratification. I would have aced that marshmallow test."

"Yeah?" He practically sneered at her. "Well, I'd have been smart enough to bargain for the whole bag!"

He was probably right.

A mustard-yellow ranch house came into view. Strands of Christmas lights still dangled over the porch, and an old mint-green kitchen sink filled with wilting geraniums served as lawn art. A late-model pickup sat in the drive.

"Bingo." Brett strode toward the front porch and rang the bell while she waited by the truck. No one answered, but the distant sound of voices carried from the back of the property. "You stay here," Brett said.

Ignoring that, she followed him around the side of the house. As they reached the backyard, she was dismayed to see Camo Man emerge from behind a galvanized metal shed. He wore last night's uniform along with his phallic sidearm. "I didn't expect to see you two again."

"We didn't expect to be here," Brett replied. "The storm knocked a tree down at the cabin, and my car's trapped in the driveway."

Camo Man nodded as if he didn't expect anything better from them. "And now, you need help."

"Do you know anyone I could pay to haul the tree out of the way?" Brett said smoothly. "The sooner the better."

"Now how would a *moron* like me know how to help smart people like you?"

Rory stepped forward. "I might have misspoken," she said hastily. "But in my defense, I can't support men who spend their time—"

"You know anybody I could hire?" Brett cut in.

"I brought chocolates," Rory said.

Camo Man moved his hand to the butt of his sidearm, and she got rattled. "I'm only offering them if you promise not to shoot at us again. Or at least me. My boyfriend is on his own."

"What the hell, Rory?" Brett exclaimed.

Camo Man shook his head. "Pal, you got yourself more trouble than a fallen tree."

"You're not wrong," Brett said.

Since Rory's attempt to lighten the mood hadn't worked well, she decided it was prudent to ignore the insult. Camo Man jerked his head toward a narrow path through the woods in the general direction of the voices they'd been hearing. Once again, Brett gave her a look that warned her to stay where she was, but she couldn't in good conscience let him go off alone, so she hurried ahead of him.

"Rory . . ."

"Be careful you don't ruin those loafers," she called over her shoulder.

They hadn't gone far before the trees opened into a muddy grove with a couple of soggy tents, some pop-up campers, an old trailer, and a few pickup trucks. The smell of leaf mold, coffee, and gasoline hit her nostrils. She spotted the two younger morons sitting on a log near a crude wall made of raw planks where a spray-painted human outline had been riddled with bullet holes. A couple of others lounged in white plastic lawn chairs clutching insulated coffee mugs. Behind them, someone had hung a banner that said "Jesus Is King," a proclamation she was certain her old Sunday school teachers would have regarded as woefully out of place.

All the men were looking at her. Brett seemed right at home. "You guys have quite an operation here."

"It's not much, but it's home," Camo Man said, showing a surprising sense of humor, although nobody laughed.

Rory couldn't help herself. "Now that we've seen this place, you don't have to kill us, do you?"

"You never heard of the right to assemble?" Camo Man said. "It's guaranteed in the Constitution. And Shelby Smith over there is the county sheriff."

Sheriff Smith nodded at them.

Rory decided now was a good time to bring out the chocolate, but as she slipped off her backpack, she suddenly found a rifle pointed right at her chest.

"I'm not armed!" She spun toward Sheriff Smith. "Are you seeing this? Arrest him!"

"For all Bobby knows, you're going to pull a gun," the sheriff said.

"I'm a chocolatier! Why would I have a gun?"

The sheriff shrugged. "Lot of crazies around."

Brett stepped between her and the rifle. "You guys are starting to piss me off."

"Put it away, Bobby," Camo Man said. "The only dangerous thing about her is her big mouth."

Rory clutched her backpack. "Forget it! I'm not giving my chocolate to any of you."

"What's this thing she's got about chocolate?" the sheriff asked.

"In her defense, it might be the best chocolate in the country," Brett said. "Ask your pals. You've never tasted anything like it."

"And you're not going to," Rory declared.

"Well then," Camo Man said. "Sorry we can't help you with your tree problem."

Brett grabbed her backpack and proceeded to distribute all the sampler boxes. Within minutes, she was forced to watch these turncoats polish off her hard work, complain because she hadn't brought more, and lecture her about government tyranny, all this punctuated by Sheriff Smith pulling out his pistol and firing a bullet through the head of the spray-painted figure on the wooden wall.

*   *

Even though half a dozen pickups circled the campsite, no one volunteered to help move the tree. Camo Man, however, loaned them his chain saw. "Leave it on the cabin porch when you're done. I'll pick it up this afternoon." He chuckled. "And good luck figuring out how to use it."

"Well, at least they didn't kill us," Rory said, as she and Brett trekked along the road with the chain saw.

"My life didn't seem to be in danger. Yours, however . . ."

"I still say if the women around here would start dating some of these losers . . ."

"I remember your theory."

She glanced at his mud-caked loafers. "Your shoes are ruined."

"I don't care."

"What's it like being so rich that you can ruin a pair of thousand-dollar shoes and not care?"

"They didn't cost a thousand dollars, and here's what you should understand. I don't give a crap about shoes or clothes or my hair, despite what you believe. But the players I represent are young, a lot of them grew up poor, and they're making up for lost time. If I show up in twenty-dollar sneakers, I lose all credibility."

"Clint's not like that."

"He didn't grow up poor."

She saw his point.

"I've got a signal!" he exclaimed, sounding like someone stranded on a desert island who'd spotted a rescue helicopter. He began thumbing frantically at his phone with one hand, chain saw dangling from the other.

She pulled out her own phone, but her bargain-rate carrier wasn't up to servicing the wilds of Northern Michigan.

His phone began chiming with incoming texts, and his thumb sprinted across his screen. She took the chain saw from him.

"Damn it! I'm losing it!" He held his phone over his head and hurried to the other side of the road.

"You could climb a tree," she suggested.

He was too busy navigating a cell phone signal obstacle course to respond.

With the chain saw in tow, she left him behind and continued her trek. As she turned into the cabin driveway, a pair of wild turkeys scuttled in front of her. She'd barely gone ten more feet before she came to a sudden stop. Parked just ahead was a dirty blue Range Rover.

She broke into a run.

11

Clint sat on the front step of the cabin, bare feet shoved into dirty, checkerboard Vans, a coffee mug in his hand. He was shaggy, his beard unkempt, wearing khaki shorts and a dirty white T-shirt.

"Clint!"

His head came up. "Rory?"

All the old resentment rushed back. Why hadn't her dad cared as much about her as he did about Clint? Why couldn't Kristin have been a real mother to her? And why was Rory no further along in her life than she'd been ten years ago?

He set his coffee mug on the stoop but didn't come to his feet as she approached. She pushed all her resentment back inside where it needed to stay.

His hair, a shade darker than Rory's dishwater blond, looked as though it hadn't seen either a comb or scissors in weeks. His square face and hard jawline, softened only by his beard, couldn't have been more different from her round face, but they'd inherited the same blue eyes from their father.

"What are you doing here?" He didn't sound as if he much cared, which was different from his normal, overly enthusiastic way of greeting her.

She took in his red-rimmed eyes and understood. "You've heard about Ashley."

"Yeah." He propped his elbows on his knees and dropped his face in his hands. "Yeah, I heard."

"I'm sorry." The chain saw couldn't weigh more than ten pounds, but it felt much heavier. She set it down and sat on the porch next to him.

She wasn't used to seeing him like this or to the heavy silence that fell between them. On the few occasions they'd been together recently, Clint filled their silences with a funny story about one of his friends or a place he'd visited. He did the heavy lifting in their conversations. Now, he didn't seem to care.

She had to tell him the truth, but not when he was so overwhelmed. "Your agent and I drove up together."

He dropped his hands but kept his head down. "Just like him to rope in my family."

He had no idea exactly how much she'd been roped in. She extended her mud-caked sneakers. "He mentioned that you haven't been happy with him lately."

His head finally came up. "He trashed Ashley."

"I'm sure that was tough to hear, but he seems to have your best interests at heart."

"You don't know him. He only has his commission at heart."

Clint had never been cynical, but then she'd never known him to be this upset.

Brett came around from behind Clint's muddy car and tilted his head in its direction. "You've been camping," he said, as he stopped in front of them.

Rory had also noticed the outdoor gear in the back of Clint's car when she'd run past it.

"I've been in the U.P." He took another sip of coffee.

Rory remembered Kristin complaining about a fishing trip Clint had taken last year to Michigan's Upper Peninsula. Kristin considered the area too sparsely populated for her baby boy. *"What if he has some kind of emergency?"* she'd complained to Rory. *"Why can't he visit Miami like every other pro player?"*

"But think of all the STDs he'll avoid by going fishing in Michigan instead," she'd retorted.

Kristin had bitten her head off for that.

"I've been trying to reach you," Brett said evenly.

Clint shoved his hand through his too-long hair. Unlike hers, his hair had natural waves instead of renegade curls. "I locked my cell in the glove box. Didn't check it until I got to Newberry last night. I figured whatever was happening in the world, I didn't need to know about it." He looked up at them. "Obviously, I was wrong."

So he hadn't heard about Ashley until last night.

"I'm sorry about Ashley." Brett sounded as inadequate as she felt.

"Yeah, I bet," Clint said bitterly. "They're calling her death suspicious. What does that mean? And what was she doing at my house?"

"You need to get in touch with the police," Brett said.

"They think I had something to do with it, don't they?" Anger clipped his words.

"They need to ask you some questions," Brett said quietly.

"And here I told myself the world would keep turning if I unplugged."

All Rory could think to do right now was what came naturally. She tapped her sneakers on the ground to dislodge the muddy clumps stuck to the bottom. "Is there any food in your car? I'll make breakfast."

"In the cooler," Clint said. "But I'm not hungry."

"I'll make something anyway."

She retrieved an unopened package of smoked salmon, some spinach tortillas, and a few rings of dried pineapple. As the chain saw screamed in the driveway, she made four sandwich wraps. Whenever her curiosity became too much for her, she paused to watch them from the front window. Brett operated the chain saw with an efficiency that would have shocked Camo Man. Clint hauled away the brush, moving mechanically, neither of them speaking.

She set the breakfast tortillas on the table and brewed a pot of coffee, but the coffee beans were old and the results bitter. The cabin door opened and the men came in.

". . . call Bert Perkins," Brett was saying. "Don't talk to the police without your attorney."

"I'm sick of people telling me what to do."

Where was the amiable brother she'd always known?

"You hired me to look out for you," Brett said flatly. "That's what I'm doing."

"Are you?" Clint snatched up the car keys he'd tossed on the counter. "I'm going back to the city."

He was out the door without eating breakfast or offering to take her with him.

*
 *

Even though the breakfast tortillas were tasty, they didn't settle well in her stomach, and the cabin coffee had been undrinkable.

They stopped in Ludlow for a decent cup. Mainly, however, they stopped for Wi-Fi.

As Rory sat at a table outside the combination bakery-coffee shop, Brett paced the sidewalk a few yards away, his cell pressed to his ear and the lenses of his sunglasses flaring in the sunlight whenever he changed direction. She heard lots of *yes*es and *couldn't be better*s, combined with flying-fingered texts as he appeased demanding clients. In one conversation, he seemed to be talking to his boss, and she heard him say he was "on it." She'd hate such a high-voltage job, but she had to respect the way he did it. She wanted to work like that—with single-minded dedication and a sense of accomplishment at the end of the day.

He finally set his phone aside and lowered himself into the white plastic chair across from her. He took a sip of coffee and ran his thumb around the rim of the paper cup. "You didn't tell him what you did."

She knew he meant her lie to Ashley. "I didn't have a chance."

"The hell you didn't. We were clearing that driveway for a good forty-five minutes. All you had to do was stick your head out the door and tell him you needed to talk."

He'd put her on the defensive. "He only learned Ashley was dead the night before. It didn't seem like the best time to dump even more on him."

"The best time for him or for you?"

"That's unfair."

"You can't put this off, Rory."

He was right. She dabbed at a spot of spilled coffee on the table with the bakery's napkin and nodded. "I'll talk to him as soon as we get back."

"Good." He regarded her through the trendy, clear-plastic frames of his sunglasses. "Before then . . . How would you like a job?"

"Do I have to kill anyone? Never mind. Bad timing on my part."

"I have to make a slight detour before we drive back to Chicago, and it turns out that I need a temporary assistant for the day." He idly tapped his phone.

"What are you paying?"

He sipped his coffee. "What do you want?"

She had a two-thousand-dollar fine hanging over her head, an oil-burning food truck with empty shelves, and apartment rent due soon. "A thousand dollars," she said, just for the hell of it.

"I'll give you two fifty."

"Thousand?"

"Hundred."

"The story of my life." She'd been so intent on having income, she'd failed to consider what she might have to do to earn it. "What's the job?"

"You drive. I'll tell you about it in the car."

They headed out of Ludlow with her again at the wheel. She watched him set the car's GPS for the Detroit airport. "We're flying? St. Barts? Maui? Paris?"

"Philly."

She sighed. "Of course. By the way, I'm not bringing you coffee. I mean, I *might* bring you coffee, but only if it's not part of my job."

"Noted."

Between phone calls, he told her about Tyler Capello. "He's a third-year player with the Eagles, and one of the best running backs in the League. My former coworker, Nate Douglass, signed him right out of Florida State. During Tyler's second season, things went south between him and Nate. Tyler ended up firing Nate and signing with a weasel named Tommy Landom—Landom Sports Management. My boss, in turn, fired Nate."

"That seems harsh. Surely things like this happen."

"Not this way. Nate couldn't handle Tyler's mother."

"What was the problem?"

"Callie Capello hit on him, something she's prone to do with men. She's one of a kind."

Rory put the pieces together. "I'm guessing Nate didn't say no."

"Callie is apparently very persuasive. Still Nate should have known better, and their affair went downhill fast a few months later when Nate tried to end it. He quickly became Tyler's ex-agent."

"Tell me how you figure into all of this."

"One of the calls I had this morning was with Heath, my boss. Tyler's suddenly decided he wants to talk to me. Only me."

"And you're dropping everything—including the fact that Clint could be headed to jail—so you can fly to Philadelphia and meet with Tyler?"

"Nothing critical is going to happen with Clint before tomorrow, and Tyler wants to see me right away. I'm hoping he's figured out that Landom is a big talker and a lousy agent." He checked his phone. "Landom's a bottom-feeder with shady recruitment tactics and a tendency to make side deals that only benefit him. There's even a story flying around that he's funneling money from a couple of endorsement deals into his own pocket."

"Interesting, but where do I fit into all this?"

"If Tyler's getting rid of Tommy, I want to sign him, but I need to be certain his mother isn't part of the deal. I'm probably being overly cautious, but if she's around today, your job is to make sure I'm not alone with her."

"Aw, how sweet. You're afraid she'll come on to you. Totally understandable if she's desperate."

"You never let up, do you?"

She smiled at him. "Never."

Several hours later, as she emerged from Detroit's Wayne County Airport security checkpoint minus an eight-ounce bottle of her favorite lotion, she was still pondering the difference between Brett and Tommy Landom. Brett was brash and competitive, but from everything she'd witnessed, he was also honorable. Unlike her. If she'd kept her mouth shut, Clint would most likely be married by now. He'd have ended up miserable and with a sizeable dent in his fortune, but Ashley would still be alive.

Brett pocketed his driver's license and dodged a man juggling golf clubs. "We have time before the plane boards, and we need to do some shopping."

"I could use a nice set of luggage."

"True." He gazed pointedly at her Trader Joe's bag. "But I'm thinking more about that mess you have on."

"Mess?" She wore baggy linen overalls rolled at the cuffs, an unremarkable tie-dyed tank top, and, instead of her muddy sneakers, campy canvas flats with Frida Kahlo on the toes. "I love this outfit."

"Two of you could live inside those overalls."

"That's what makes them cute." She hitched her backpack higher on one shoulder. "You have zero sense of style."

He snorted. "Don't think for a minute you can show up at the Capellos' house like that. I have a reputation."

She was on weak ground professionally speaking, and she tried a diversion. "I'm kind of going to be your bodyguard."

"However you want to look at it."

*

Brett smiled to himself as Rory stalked out of the airport's chain clothing store ahead of him. The light blue-and-white striped cotton shirtwaist dress he'd chosen for her while she'd huffed and puffed about artistic expression and individual freedom didn't look like anything she would choose, but it did look like something his assistant might wear on a warm summer day. He'd also made her trade in her crazy canvas shoes for the only dress-leather sandals the store carried.

As she took off toward the gate, overstuffed Trader Joe's grocery bag in one hand, backpack on her shoulders, he felt a stab of regret. Making her wear something as conventional as a shirtwaist dress was like dimming the lights on one of Clint's chandeliers. No other woman he knew could have pulled off those ugly linen overalls she'd been wearing, but on her they had been distracting—as distracting as those granny panties she'd slept in—because of the way that strap kept slipping off her shoulder. When it slid down her bare arm, those overalls looked as if they were ready to tumble to her ankles at any moment.

He flashed back to his first sight of her on the hotel balcony when she'd been all honey-blond curls, black net gown, and hot red lipstick. *Admit it.* He was enjoying the hell out of Rory Garrett. He liked her smart-ass sense of humor and her sharp insights, her guilty conscience and out-of-this-world chocolates. He even admired the way she'd stood up to those fake soldier boys, although he'd nearly had a heart attack at the time. He also liked how she drove a car. Unlike him, she wasn't prone to sudden bursts of speed or his habit of riding some asshole's bumper when he got impatient. She was steady.

But there'd been nothing steady about the loose strap on those baggy overalls. One little slip . . . He reminded himself what had happened last night. She was Clint's sister. Forbidden fruit. A poisoned apple. Off-limits. Do Not Disturb. No Entry.

Definitely *No Entry.*

He sidestepped a family of five loaded down with a stroller, car seats, backpacks, and rolling suitcases adorned with panda bears and pink unicorns. He regarded them with pity.

When they reached the gate, Rory flounced into a seat. "You've broken my spirit," she said petulantly. "I hope you're satisfied."

He grinned. "Nothing could break your spirit. You're indomitable."

She tugged at the skirt. "I feel like an eighty-year-old on her first outing after hip surgery."

"You look professional. Or at least semiprofessional."

"What's the 'semi' part?"

He regarded her hair.

"Don't you dare criticize my hair!" she exclaimed. "Only I'm allowed to do that."

"I love your hair."

"Then why are you frowning at it?"

"It's a little too . . . bedroomy for business."

"'Bedroomy'?"

"You know what I mean. Like you just woke up." *In a man's arms.*

"Fine. I'll tie it up."

Tie me up, he thought, as she, her backpack, and her Trader Joe's bag marched off for the ladies' room.

He pulled out his laptop, refocusing on his most important client. Clint should be arriving in Chicago anytime now. He didn't have a good feeling about what might happen next.

*   *

Tyler Capello opened the massive wooden door of the imitation Tuscan villa he'd built in the Philadelphia suburbs with his riches. He had dark, curly hair; great cheekbones; and burnished skin. He also possessed the ideal body for a running back—a little under six feet tall and compact. He wore a gray hoodie and clay-colored shorts that revealed a set of powerfully sculpted legs designed for speed and strength.

"Tyler, it's great to see you again. This is Rory, my assistant."

When she didn't immediately respond, Brett's elbow dug into her ribs. She reluctantly pulled her gaze away from those legs. "Tyler, I'm happy to meet you. I'm a fan."

"Yeah?" He eyed her from head to toe with bratty skepticism. "How would you describe my running style?"

"You've got the bursts and the speed. You're agile. You have great balance. And when you hit the hole, it's game over."

Out of the corner of her eye, she saw Brett's left eyebrow twitch. He didn't realize how well she knew the game, but she'd been required to watch Clint's games growing up. Later, she'd watched only so she could share follow-up commentary with her father, one of their few interactions after she'd left home. As for Tyler Capello's particular skill set . . . She'd regurgitated what every egotistical running back wanted to hear whether it was true or not.

"I like her," Tyler said to Brett, as he led them through the multistory entry into a vast living room.

"She's very efficient."

Not a word she'd ever use to describe herself except when it came to making chocolate.

As they entered the massive great room, a woman who could only be Callie Capello swept through an archway bordered with Tuscan columns. She was big, bold, and beautiful—like one of Renoir's women, except painted in primary colors instead of pastels.

Tyler must have been born when she was very young, because she barely looked forty. She had a tumble of long dark hair, hazel eyes, and full lips. She reminded Rory of a plum so ripe that biting into it would send juice dripping down your chin.

Callie's towering fuchsia stilettos clicked on the parquet floor as she approached. "Brett." She uttered his name like a coo. "We met in Chicago when the Eagles played the Bears."

"Mrs. Capello. It's good to see you again." Brett addressed her with the formality of an English butler. "This is my assistant, Rory—"

"Rory Meadows," she quickly inserted. "Lovely to meet you, Mrs. Capello."

Ignoring Rory, Mrs. Capello had eyes only for Brett. "Please. I'm Callie." She made a broad gesture toward the sofa. "Have a seat."

Contrasted against the cool modernism of Karloh Cousins's home, the Capello home looked as if a polluted Venetian canal ran below its heavily draped windows. Barrel arches; walls painted faux-gold; oversized, claw-foot furniture. Rory guessed Callie had done the decorating herself. Interesting that Tyler still lived with *madre*.

Brett chose an overstuffed armchair upholstered in garnet bro-
cade. Rory took the couch.

"Ma, get Brett a beer. Rory, what are you drinking?"

Vodka on the rocks. "Just water."

"C'mon, you can do better than that. Ma, forget the beer. Open
the Dom."

"Ma" exited the way she'd entered, her curves lusciously outlined in a tight purple print mini dress. Instead of wearing stilettos, Rory would have accessorized the dress with her campy cork
sandals, the ones with the kicky yellow bows across the toes.

Brett and Tyler began talking about the Eagles' season. Brett
didn't fawn over Tyler. He was complimentary but factual. Callie
returned carrying a tray holding four champagne flutes and a
bottle of Dom Pérignon. Tyler made a show out of popping the
cork.

Rory had consumed more than a few leftover glasses of Dom
when she'd waited tables at a couple of high-end restaurants. Personally, she'd rather have a decent IPA. "How impressive."

"Only the best." Callie smiled.

After the bottle was uncorked and poured, Tyler made a toast.
"To the future."

Brett raised his glass, but merely nodded. Nobody could accuse
him of being a suck-up, although Rory dimly remembered having
accused him of exactly that.

The way Tyler put his champagne aside after barely taking a sip
made Rory suspect he'd also rather have an IPA. "So I'm guessing
you're wondering why I wanted to see you," the running back said.

Without a shred of self-consciousness, Callie settled on the
overstuffed arm of Brett's chair, leaning across the ornately carved

back until she was within inches of his shoulders. He acted as though he didn't notice, although nothing escaped The River's predatory gaze. "I'm guessing it's because you've figured out you deserve better representation."

"Right to the point. See, Ma. The River's a straight shooter."

"Indeed." The word dripped from her plum-juice lips. Callie Capello oozed sex. No wonder Brett was being cautious.

The doorbell rang. Callie rose reluctantly from her armchair perch and disappeared, only to return a few moments later escorting a pumped-up guy with a swarthy complexion, oily curls, and heavy features. A lot of women might find him good-looking in a Neanderthal kind of way, but Rory didn't.

"Tyler, my man!" As he pointed his finger toward the running back, his shirt cuff rode up, revealing a hairy wrist encircled by a chunky gold link bracelet.

"What are you doing here, Tommy?" Tyler didn't seem happy.

"In the neighborhood, kid."

He could only be Tommy Landom, Tyler's shady agent. Rory sat straighter. This should be interesting.

Like Brett's, Tommy's clothes were expensive: a mint-green-and-white striped dress shirt with a crest on the pocket, black pants that broke perfectly over the vamp of his—yep—luxury loafers. Did shoe designers offer a discount to sports agents?

Landom pressed a kiss to Callie's cheek and slipped an arm around her shoulders. "What are you doing here, Rivers? Poaching my territory." He presented it as a joke, which it clearly wasn't.

Callie shrugged off his arm. "Brett, let me show you the garden while Tyler and Tommy talk. We put in a new pool house."

Brett didn't reveal any unease about leaving Tyler and Landom alone, but he did stop in front of Rory. A few seconds ticked by. He stepped on her foot.

"Ouch!"

"Sorry." He bored straight through her. "Clumsy of me."

She'd become so fascinated by what was about to unfold between the sleaze and the running back that she'd forgotten her duty. "I'd like to see, too." She jumped up. "This is such an amazing house."

She followed them into another gilded room featuring four arched doorways opening onto a loggia. In Rory's opinion, the whole place could use some of Brett's detested shiplap.

Callie opened one of the doors and turned to Rory. "I need to talk to Brett alone, if you don't mind."

Rory's brain searched wildly for an excuse to come with them. "But I'm so crazy about this house, I have to see what you've done in the garden. I won't bother you. I promise." She tucked her hand through Callie's elbow, drawing her outside away from Brett. "What perfume are you wearing? It smells incredible."

Callie was momentarily distracted. "Really? You like it? You don't think it's too heavy?"

"On someone else, maybe, but not on you. You're a woman who needs a bold scent. Gardenia?"

They'd stepped into a U-shaped courtyard with a rectangular swimming pool across the open end. Callie turned her attention to Rory while Brett moved farther away and made a great play of studying the loggia's exterior columns. "It might be gardenia. I'm not sure."

"It's perfect for you." Rory improvised. "I'm detecting middle notes of sandalwood and maybe ylang-ylang." She had only the barest idea what ylang-ylang was, let alone how it smelled. With her arm still linked through Callie's, she made a grand gesture toward the house. "Where did you get your inspiration? You designed it. I can tell."

Now she had Callie's full attention. "I had an amazing architect. Tyler's worked so hard, and I wanted something special for him. Something no one else has. A place he could grow into when he gets married and—God willing—has children. I did all the interior design."

"Of course you did." Brett had made it to the other side of the pool deck. "You don't have to answer, of course, but how did someone as special as Tyler end up with . . ." She tilted her head toward the back of the house. "You know. Him."

"Tommy?"

"Please forget I said anything. Brett would fire me if he knew I made a negative comment about a competitor. Brett's all about integrity." She tugged on the skirt of her shirtwaist. "You and your son seem to have a close relationship."

"We'd do anything for each other. I feel so guilty. A while ago, I wasn't in a good place, and Tyler ended up having to fire his agent because of it. Afterward, he signed Tommy in a rush. It's not working out. I blame myself."

Rory played the wise elder. "Everyone makes mistakes. It's how we recover from them that matters." *And how are you going to recover from your mistakes, Rory Garrett?*

Callie touched the plunging neckline of her mini dress. "Tyler needs different representation, but we're smarter now. We're going to take our time. Talk to all the best agents. I don't want to make another mistake."

"You're making a great start meeting with Brett," Rory said, joining Team Rivers.

"Mmm . . ." Callie brushed a curl away from Rory's cheekbone, a soft, intimate gesture. "You have beautiful hair."

Rory was too taken aback to reply.

Callie gazed into Rory's eyes and trailed a finger along her jaw-line. "I'd like to see you again when we come to Chicago next week." With that, she pressed a quick kiss to Rory's lips and glided back into the house.

12

"I t's all your fault for making me wear this stupid dress!" Rory was still railing at him as they cleared security at the Philadelphia airport. She was heading to Chicago while he flew back to Detroit to claim his car. "She thinks I'm gay. I wish I were. The most interesting women are gay, and if I were gay, I wouldn't have to deal with the memory of a man who paid me for sex."

He looked up from his phone. "Question. If you and Callie decide to have a twosome, can I pay to watch?"

His stupid grin almost disarmed her. Almost but not quite. "The worst is that you've decided to host some kind of big party for them this weekend when they come to Chicago, and you promised her I'd be there!"

"In my defense, I didn't know about the kiss when I said you'd be at the party. Was it good?"

"I was too shocked to evaluate. That woman is hot." Remembering how she'd taken Callie's arm and praised her perfume, Rory could understand how Callie might have concluded Rory was hitting on her. She was jealous of Callie's boldness. Lately, everyone had more confidence than she did.

"I'll make sure you're not alone with her at the party," he said, as he pocketed his phone.

"Not a problem because I won't be there."

"You have to be. You're catering."

"I'm what?"

"I've just decided," he said. "You'll be catering a small party at my place. Thirty or so of the city's most prominent athletes and their significant others. I need to impress Tyler. He needs to see the kind of connections I can set him up with if he signs with me."

"That's five days from now! And I'm a chocolatier not a professional caterer. I can't plan a party that fast." Even as she said it, she reminded herself she wasn't in any position to turn down a job, even one she wasn't entirely qualified for.

"You'll figure it out," he said. "It's in your employment contract."

"I don't remember signing a contact."

"Verbal agreements are binding. Trust me. I'm a lawyer."

"You're a snake."

"A snake who pays well." He studied the departures board.

"You could rent out a restaurant." *Don't rent out a restaurant,* she thought. *I need a job, even one I'm not qualified to pull off.*

"That isn't personal enough." They started walking again. "The party has to feel special. I texted my assistant, and the invitations are going out right now."

"Throwing a party like this is going to be *very* expensive," she said. "Especially with only five days to prepare."

He lifted an eyebrow. "Now who's the snake?"

"Fair warning. After the party, I'm resigning as your assistant to pursue other opportunities."

"I admire your ambition. Hold on." Moving to the side, he set down his weekender and pulled out a notepad. He wrote something on it and showed it to her. "Is this enough to compensate you for the short notice? Above expenses, of course."

She looked at the number he'd jotted down. *$2,000.00.* The exact amount she needed to pay off her fine. She hesitated for only a moment before she took the pen and notepad from him, made her counteroffer, and held it out.

He gazed at it, stupefied. "You're crazy! Five hundred dollars?"

"I don't need your pity money." She shoved the notebook into his chest. "Five hundred. Not a penny more."

If his hair weren't slicked back, it would be standing straight up from outrage. "What's *wrong* with you?"

"Stupidity. Pride. Maybe even integrity. Call it what you will. Five hundred after expenses is more than generous for a party like this, despite the short notice. Plus, that number's symbolic, isn't it?"

He looked as serious as she'd ever seen him. "I don't understand you."

"Two of us." She walked away from him to her gate.

*
*

The Allovar & Ivy had crisp white tablecloths and wood-paneled walls. The fireplace held a pyramid of leafy Boston ferns instead of logs, and each table displayed a white orchid. Best of all, the thick carpet muted the tinkle of cutlery and the conversations of the restaurant's well-heeled guests.

The quiet was a balm to Kristin's shredded nerves. After she'd returned from the coffeehouse yesterday, so many reporters had begun ringing the doorbell that Kristin had to stuff her fingers in her ears to mute the notes of "Hail to the Victors." That musical battle cry used to give her goose bumps when her son had been commanding the field at Michigan Stadium, the sun glinting off the maize and blue of his helmet, but now she wanted to scream every time she heard it. And this evening when she'd left for her date, a reporter had followed her car. She'd only managed to lose him because he ran a red light and a patrol car pulled him over.

A woman had been murdered, she hadn't heard from Clint, and she was in no shape to be anyone's dinner companion tonight. But she couldn't stay in that house a minute longer, so she hadn't cancelled the date.

In the low light, it took her a moment to spot Daniel Hanbridge sitting at a corner table, his back to the wall, big hands clasped in front of him. Kristin wondered if anyone ever called him Dan or Danny. She couldn't imagine it.

He sprang to his feet as he spotted her, bumping the table so water sloshed over the edge of his glass onto the tablecloth. "You came. I wasn't sure you'd show up. I'm glad you're here."

She fixed a smile she didn't feel on her face. She was sick with worry about Clint, and unlike Daniel Hanbridge, she was more frantic than nervous.

The outside temperature had hit the high eighties today, and even though Allovar & Ivy was a fine-dining restaurant, Daniel was the only man wearing a suit coat. He had to be hot. She'd dressed less formally in a boat-neck wrap dress.

"You look beautiful as always," he said.

"'As always'? This is only the second time we've met."

"True." He nodded awkwardly and pulled out a chair for her. Once they were both settled, he didn't seem to know what to say, which meant she'd have to carry the burden of the conversation. Even thinking about it made her tired. She'd have a glass of wine, plead a headache, and beg off dinner.

He picked up the menu, only to set it back down again. "You're regretting this, aren't you?"

"You said you weren't good at reading people's feelings."

"I'm not. But it's only logical. You're a beautiful, sophisticated woman who could go out with anyone, and here you are with me."

"You don't hold a very high opinion of yourself." She remembered their previous conversation. "Except intellectually."

"That's true. I'm very confident when it comes to business."

A young woman in a white shirt and black pants appeared tableside, cutting off their conversation. Her name was Courtney, and she was happy to be their server for the evening.

Kristin ordered sauvignon blanc and Daniel zinfandel. "This is my first date in twenty-eight years," he said, when they were alone again. "I suspected I wouldn't be good at it."

"I remember my first date after Gregg died. It was a disaster." She'd gone out with a Minnetonka accountant who only wanted to talk about Clint and expected her to arrange a meeting.

He shifted uneasily in his chair. "In case you're wondering, I won't try to kiss you. It's my understanding women sometimes can't enjoy an evening out because they're concerned about what will happen at the end."

"I'm not concerned."

"That's good." He smiled. "Before I left, my daughter texted me and told me that—whatever I did—I shouldn't act like myself."

Kristin heard herself laugh. "Your daughter sounds interesting."

"She's my pride and joy. Do you have children?"

Kristin carefully smoothed the napkin in her lap. "A stepdaughter.

My husband was a young widower when we married. Rory lives in the city." What some might consider a lie by omission, she regarded as self-protection.

"And what about you?" he said. "I assume you live in the western suburbs."

"No, I live in the Minneapolis area."

His face fell. "Why were you at the coffee shop?"

She hesitated. "I'm visiting here."

Courtney appeared with their wine. Daniel ordered two appetizers, even though Kristin protested that she'd never be able to eat that much. "You won't know until you try," he said, as the server left.

"Your jacket looks hot," Kristin said. "Feel free to take it off."

He gave her a sheepish grin. "I can't. I sweated through my shirt."

She laughed again. Everything was out front with this man, so different from all the years of pretending with Gregg. Pretending they had a wonderful marriage. Pretending he loved her with all his heart. Pretending they had more in common than their son.

He lifted his glass. "To Kristin Meadows, a brave lady who agreed to have dinner with a bumbling fifty-year-old."

His use of the last name she'd appropriated from Gregg's dead wife made her fumble with the stem of her wineglass. She recovered and lifted her own glass. "To the bumbling fifty-year-old, who also happens to be a very interesting man. Thank you for inviting me."

Gradually, their conversation grew more comfortable. Over walleye for him and a strawberry spinach salad for her, they discovered a mutual love of travel, hiking, and true crime podcasts. They had a similar take on politics, and they both enjoyed photography. She liked watching movies. He didn't. He liked reading science-centered nonfiction. She loved memoirs. It was surprisingly lively conversation, spoiled only by her failure to tell him she was Clint Garrett's mother.

As he walked her to her car afterward, his former nervousness returned. "I— This was— I don't know how much longer you'll be in town, but— Do you want to go out with me again?"

She tilted up her head and gave him a soft kiss on the lips. "Yes, I do."

★
★

Since Kristin had left the house for her date with Daniel, the number of cars and news vans in the street had multiplied. All her good feelings from the evening disappeared. As the reporters spotted her car, they made a run for the end of the driveway, shouting out questions. She nearly hit one of them when she turned in, and by the time she reached the garage, she was shaking.

She rushed inside the house but didn't turn on the lights. The big kitchen windows had no shades, and she couldn't shake the feeling reporters were lurking in the bushes outside, watching her.

Her phone pinged. She pulled it from her purse. It was Clint.

I'm back in the city staying at some friends' house. Don't worry.

"Don't worry"? How could she not worry? She punched in his number. As the call went to voice mail, the invisible cracks in their relationship grew wider.

She tried calling Rory again, but she didn't answer, either. She stumbled through the dark house to the home theater where she'd made a bed for herself on one of the couches. In addition to a big screen and comfortable furniture, the room had no windows.

She washed her face in the adjoining bathroom and changed

into the pajamas she'd left there. She called Clint again. No answer. But just after midnight, Rory finally picked up.

"Where have you been?" Kristin clutched the phone. "I've been trying to reach you."

"I was in the air. Flying back to Chicago from Philadelphia. A long story."

Kristin didn't care about Rory's story. "Clint texted me. He said he was back in the city and staying with friends, but he's still not answering my calls." Admitting this made her ache. Since the day he was born, Clint had been the center of her life. She'd been a good mother, always there for him, and she was proud of the relationship they'd forged as adults. She'd secretly pitied her friends who didn't share the same closeness with their grown children. Yet now she had to go to Rory for information. "Who are the friends he's staying with?"

"I don't know. But I saw him early this morning at his cabin in Michigan." Rory emphasized the word "cabin," letting Kristin know how wrong she'd been when she'd insisted Clint wouldn't have bought something like that without telling her.

Kristin twisted a lock of hair around her finger so tightly it pulled at the roots. "You talked to him? And you didn't tell me?"

"It's been a weird day, and I just got home. Clint was fishing in the U.P. and he'd only learned about Ashley late last night. He said he was driving back to Chicago, and he'd talk to the police. That might be where he is now."

"At midnight? This is a nightmare. I want to kill those piranhas from the press. They've surrounded the house, won't leave me alone. They keep ringing the doorbell. How do I turn that thing off? It's making me crazy!"

"Clint probably has to disable it from his phone," Rory said. "Maybe you could trip the circuit breaker or something."

"Like I'd know how to do that. Just once, could you tell me something helpful?"

She heard Rory's sharp intake of breath and wished for the thousandth time she would stop using Rory as a target for her own insecurities.

"I'm hanging up now," Rory said.

Kristin didn't blame her.

* *

". . . and we have identified a person of interest in Ashley Hart's death. We'll keep you informed when we know more."

Rory wondered if Kristin was watching the hastily called morning press conference. Last night's frantic phone call testified that it wouldn't take much to push her over the edge.

"I have no further statement to make at this time." The police chief picked up his notes and turned from the microphone as the press began shouting out questions.

"Is Clint Garrett the person of interest?"

"Have you talked to him?"

"Where was Garrett when the murder took place?"

Clint was being tried without a jury, and Rory couldn't watch any longer. She called Detective Strothers. "This is ludicrous! Clint couldn't kill anyone. Did you investigate his housekeeper? I think she might be in love with him."

"His housekeeper was at her niece's quinceañera," Strothers said. "She has at least fifty witnesses."

Rory dug her fingers into her curls. "What about Ashley's ex-boyfriend?"

"We're investigating all possible suspects, Ms. Garrett. As I told you."

The police believed they had the man who'd killed Ashley, and they weren't interested in looking any further.

The call ended, and she pocketed the phone in her fuzzy bathrobe. She understood why Clint hadn't gone back to his house, with the press everywhere, but he should call Kristin instead of leaving it up to Rory. The police would surely have told him not to leave the area, so where was he? The brother who had once been everywhere was now nowhere.

She went into her bedroom and kicked the detestable blue-and-white striped shirtwaist dress she'd discarded last night to the back of her closet. When she was dressed, she wandered into the kitchen. It was exactly as she'd left it two days ago, but it felt empty without a tin of her chocolates stashed in the cupboard. The last of her work had gone to feed a band of hairy Michigan insurgents.

She put water on to boil for oatmeal and tried texting Clint again.

> Kristin is seriously freaking out. Stop being an ass and tell me where you are.

She gazed out the kitchen window into the alley. Ashley's car was still there.

The kitchen table held the notes she'd made on the plane for Brett's party. She didn't like that she was missing him—this arrogant jerk of a man she'd met under the worst of circumstances eight days ago. She settled down to finalize her party plan so she could stop thinking about him.

Brett had given her the number of his real assistant, and Kyle Simmons turned out to be a nice guy who Venmoed her an advance for the food.

Her phone pinged. It was Clint.

> C: If I tell u swear to keep it to yourself.
>
> R: I swear.
>
> C: Not Mom and not Brett.
>
> R: Brett isn't your enemy. You should talk to him.
>
> C: Forget it.
>
> R: Never mind. I swear.
>
> C: At Olivia and Thad's house. Leave me alone.

*
*

Brett spent the day after returning from Michigan fielding calls and trying to track Clint down, all while dodging his boss. He slept fitfully that night and woke the next morning to rain pounding on his bedroom windows. He wished he could have gotten at least a partial commitment from Tyler Capello, but Clint was still his biggest problem. The best way to repair their relationship was to make certain Clint knew Brett was firmly in his corner. To do that, however, he had to find him—again. All he knew was what Kristin had told him when she'd called, that Clint had returned to the city but wasn't at his house.

He ducked into the shower, but instead of sorting through his options, he thought about how great it would be to start a rainy day with Rory, the two of them mulling over life as they ate one of her inventive breakfasts after a round of hot morning sex. He shook off the image. He relaxed too much when she was around, had a little too much fun, and this wasn't the time for it.

His hand stalled as he reached for a towel. He suddenly knew where Clint had almost certainly holed up.

*
*

Brett climbed the flight of eight steps to the front door of the imposing, limestone Gold Coast mansion belonging to former Stars player Thad Owens and his wife, the great mezzo-soprano Olivia Shore. They were close friends of Clint's, and neither Olivia nor Thad was in Chicago now, so their house must be empty—a bonus to a man who clearly wanted to be alone.

Even as he rang the bell, Brett figured Clint wouldn't answer, so he sent a text.

Answer the fucking door.

Tough love might work better than tact, but if Brett had miscalculated and Clint was somewhere else, the text should at least elicit a phone call.

As it turned out, Brett had calculated correctly.

Clint looked even worse than he had two mornings ago at the cabin. His shaggy hair lay flat against one side of his head while it stuck out on the other, and the shadows under his eyes reminded Brett of divots in stadium fields with real grass.

Clint had apparently tried to clean up before he talked to the police, but he'd missed a few patches on his neck when he'd gotten rid of his beard, and he looked as if he were molting. If anyone saw him now, he'd have to turn over his title as Chicago's most eligible bachelor.

"So much for promises," Clint growled. "I should never have told Rory where I was."

If Rory had known where Clint was, why hadn't she let Brett know? "Rory didn't tell me anything. You've seen her? Talked to her?"

"Hell, no."

Disappointment curdled his stomach. Rory still hadn't told Clint the truth. Brett had expected better of her, and he didn't like being wrong about anyone, especially a woman he'd grown to like so much. Not only did it make him question his judgment, it also meant Brett was still Clint's whipping boy.

Clint braced his hand on the doorjamb. "What do you want?"

"I want you to remember whose side I'm on." Brett pushed past him into the foyer, angry at Rory and at himself.

The interior of the Owens-Shore residence couldn't have been more different from the stuffy Romanesque exterior. Light green walls, colorful artwork, and a laundry basket overflowing with kids' toys. The comfortable surroundings steadied him. "Remember Bert Perkins? Your attorney? He called to tell me he never heard from you."

"I don't want to talk about it."

Not wanting to talk seemed to be a quality the Garrett siblings shared. Brett moved closer. "Showing up at the police station without legal representation was stupid."

"Leave me alone." Clint turned his back on Brett and retreated down the hallway.

Brett strode after him, passing a sunny room with a glossy black grand piano sitting before a pair of long windows and another more masculine room that must be Thad's office. Clint jerked open a door off to the side of the hallway and disappeared down a set of carpeted stairs. Brett followed him into a brightly lit, luxuriously finished basement with a pool table, a fireplace, and a pair of ceiling-mounted televisions. A stuffed unicorn sat on top of a rectangular wooden platform at one end of the room. Judging by the sequined blue child's microphone and mike stand next to it, this must be a kid's performance stage. Nothing like starting them early in Mom's career.

Clint racked the balls on the pool table, broke them, and began picking them off, all without looking up. "Two fucking hours they interrogated me, asking me the same questions until I told them I wasn't saying any more without my attorney. A little late, right?" He aimed for the side pocket and missed. "I have buddies on the force. Stadium security, guys who work special events. I've known 'em for years. I thought . . ."

"You thought the police would give you a break." Rory referred to her brother as the Golden Boy. Clint didn't know how to handle anything other than life going his way. Rory was the one who'd had to develop street smarts.

Clint turned on Brett. "How does it feel now that Ashley's dead to remember the way you trashed her? Does it make you feel good? Righteous?"

Brett had been Clint's scapegoat long enough. "So you haven't talked to Rory?"

"What am I supposed to say to her?"

It's what she should be saying to you. Clint still believed Ashley had left him because the pressure of his celebrity was too much for her. Twice now Rory had passed up her chance to come clean—

two days ago at the cabin and all day yesterday. It was time Clint knew the truth.

But as Brett framed the words, he found himself remembering how Rory drove a car and laughed and was so brutally honest about herself. He remembered the way that silky green robe had clung to her curves, how those ridiculous overalls looked as though they'd slip off her. He remembered her granny panties, hoodlum curls, and wild-blue-yonder eyes.

Enough. He shoved sentiment into the lockbox of his brain. Rory was a logjam, and he was The River. Business always came first.

"That's something I need to tell you."

13

Rosehill Cemetery provided a shady oasis from the heat that had gathered since this morning's rainstorm. Rory side-stepped the Canada geese's mess on the sidewalk and gazed at the grassy expanse dotted with simple gravestones, elaborate monuments, winding pathways, and ponds. At three hundred fifty acres, this was the largest cemetery in the city, and since she'd moved into her apartment, she sometimes took advantage of its nearby green space.

Now she was here to postpone, if only for a bit longer, her walk to the L station. She'd received the text from Clint yesterday morning telling her where he was, and she should have gone to see him right away. Instead, with all the work she had to do for the party, she'd decided she could put it off for a day.

Her straw purse held a package of the chocolate bars she'd made as a potential peace offering, even though she knew peace wasn't the most likely outcome. She still hadn't heard from Brett, and she hated that he hadn't at least texted her, but she couldn't contact him until she'd talked to Clint.

A pair of deer emerged from the trees. It was strange having wildlife in proximity to car horns and sirens. The spacious grounds held the remains of Chicago bigwigs from Montgomery Ward to Oscar Mayer, along with hundreds of Civil War soldiers and fourteen of that war's generals. Since this was Chicago, Rosehill was also the final resting place of the notorious murderers Leopold and Loeb, as well as the victims of the St. Valentine's Day massacre. The cemetery was a microcosm of Chicago history.

Her cell rang. "I'm at your place," Brett said, as she answered. "Where are you? I need to talk to you."

His abruptness suggested it might not be a pleasant conversation. She hoped he wasn't going to fire her. She'd already hired two people to work the party: a friend of Jon's with catering experience to help serve and her neighbor Toby, who'd bartended in college. "I'm at Rosehill."

"The cemetery? That's just great." She didn't miss his sarcastic drawl. "What street are you close to?"

"Peterson. I came in the Western Avenue entrance."

"Stay there."

Brett found her in an alarmingly short period of time on a bench near a willow bank. He'd rolled up the sleeves of his button-down shirt in deference to the warm weather and traded in his clear-rimmed sunglasses for a pair of aviators. Even in a cemetery, he looked like a power player.

As he stopped at the bench, he took in her halter-neck rockabilly sundress with its swirly blue floral skirt. She'd bought it for ten dollars in a Pilsen thrift shop, and normally she loved wearing it, but today it wasn't doing its customary job of lifting her spirits.

"I figured out where Clint was," he said, as he loomed over her. "No thanks to you."

"He swore me to secrecy."

"So he said."

She nervously smoothed her skirt. "You've talked to him?"

"I was just there."

"How did it go?"

"How do you think it went?" He stood before her, legs spread, arms crossed over his chest, and she could feel accusation rolling off him in waves.

"I'm on my way to see him now," she said.

A muscle ticked in his jaw. "You seem to have taken a detour."

She came to her feet. "I only found out where he was yesterday."

He dropped his arms, and the fingers of one hand curled into his palm. "I only figured it out this morning, yet I've already seen him. But you don't seem to have found the time."

His reproach stung. She should have gone to her brother with the truth right away, but she'd kept finding excuses to put it off. Now, here she was in the cemetery, still stalling. "I told you. I'm going now."

"Are you? You didn't talk to him when he showed up at the cabin. Yesterday, you knew where he was, but you didn't get around to visiting him. Now here it is, almost noon, and you've been walking around this cemetery for God knows how long. Yet I'm supposed to be the bad guy—the one who unfairly slandered the ex-girlfriend he still sees as a perfect human being." He shook his head, his lip curling. "You know the worst of it? If I'd told him the truth about what you did, all the heat would be off me. I started to. The words were all ready to come out, but instead, I stood there and let him throw more crap at me. I didn't say anything in my defense."

She gripped the strap of her straw purse, not meeting his eyes. "I'll set the record straight."

"I'm sure you will eventually, but that's not really the point, is it?" His shoulders set with his trademark grim determination. "I give a hundred percent to my job."

"As you've mentioned a few hundred times."

He ignored the dig. "If anyone other than you had been involved, I'd have told Clint straight-out what I knew. I meant to, but I didn't."

"I forgive you for not being ruthless." She was in the wrong, and she should be apologetic. Instead, she'd come across as flippant. "I get the message. I'll take care of it."

Now he looked more troubled than angry. "You can't always avoid doing tough things, Rory."

She wasn't an angry person, but a jolt of panic made her erupt. "Are you, a master workaholic, seriously lecturing me on how to live my life?"

"Take it however you want." With a curt nod, he walked away, leaving her fuming in the gravestones.

What an ass! What an arrogant, presumptuous ass! This man who saw no point in close relationships with anyone other than his clients, this man who lived only to work—this same man believed he had the right to criticize her!

Her eyes burned from the sting of his accusation. With the toe of one sandal, she brushed away a leaf that had fallen across the toe of the other. The sun slipped behind a cloud, and her anger faded as she saw the truth. He was right. When it came to doing tough things, she dodged. She didn't want to deal with the consequences of telling Clint the truth, so she'd used work as an excuse to put it off.

It was humiliating that Brett had seen what she'd hidden from herself, especially in light of all the grief she'd thrown at him about his character defects. Until this very moment, she hadn't realized how much she valued his respect. And now she'd lost it.

A streak of gray-brown fur raced across the path. An urban coyote, the trickster in mythology. She watched it disappear into the shrubbery. The trickster—that's what she was. She'd been tricking herself into believing she was moving forward toward her dream of owning a chocolate shop, but all she'd done was fall further behind. The only tangible step she'd taken toward making chocolate her real profession was selling small batches within the safe confines of farmers' markets, and she'd abandoned even that. She drifted from one job to the next and—in her ultimate example of self-sabotage—spent the money she'd saved not to go toward her shop, but on a food truck.

Sitting here surrounded by gravestones, she saw the truth. She didn't have the guts to put herself on the line. Big dreams without follow-through was her mode, and the reason was blindingly clear. As long as she didn't really try, she didn't have to risk failing.

For as long as she could remember, she'd let herself be shaped by the notion that she'd never be as good as her brother, so why should she try? But she wasn't a kid any longer, and it was long past time she stopped using Clint's success as an excuse for her own lack of courage. If she wanted to keep living with herself, she had to commit to her future. She had no money and no job, and she didn't know how she'd do it, but she needed to figure it out. Even if she failed, she had to try something.

She rose from the bench and made her way toward the cemetery gate. The first step toward moving forward with her life was taking responsibility for what she'd done.

*
  *

As she waited for Clint to answer the door of the Owens-Shore home, the old memories came rushing back. When Clint had started to read at four, her father had reminded her that she couldn't read until she was seven. She'd loved playing soccer until one summer afternoon her pip-squeak little brother had kicked the ball around the yard with so much skill that she couldn't get close to him. After that, she'd told everyone soccer was boring. She'd dropped out of college with middling grades at the same time Clint was thriving academically. It had always been easier to drift than to set a goal and go after it, but no longer.

She rang again. Clint was almost assuredly inside, and by ignoring the bell he was giving her the perfect excuse to turn around and leave. But she was done with taking the easy way out. As the breeze from the lake whipped her skirt around her legs, she texted him.

Answer the door. I'm pregnant.

What was one small lie in the face of the much bigger one she'd told?

Less than thirty seconds later, Clint flung open the door. "What the hell, Rory?"

She ducked inside. "I lied. It isn't the first time. I'm not pregnant."

He gritted his teeth. "Then why did you say you were?"

She closed the door with her butt and pressed against it with her spine. "It was the only way I could think of to get you to see me."

"I don't *want* to see you. I don't want to see anyone."

"I understand. This won't take long." Despite the foyer's high ceilings and open doorways, the walls were closing in on her from the weight of what she had to do. "It's hot in here. Can we go outside?"

"I'm not exactly free to roam the neighborhood." Sarcasm didn't suit him nearly as well as it suited her.

"I know that, but . . ." She plucked at the halter neck of her sundress. "I think I'm having a hot flash." More likely an anxiety attack, but either way, she needed fresh air.

Maybe he decided the fastest way to get rid of her was to give in, because he tilted his head toward the rear of the house. "C'mon. Say what you have to say and leave."

Clint wanted nothing to do with her right now, and Rory wanted nothing to do with Kristin. What a sad family they were.

She followed him down the hallway, through the kitchen, and onto a shady urban patio with vine-covered walls of whitewashed brick and lush foliage spilling from an array of copper-toned planters. In addition to an adult seating area, one end of the patio held a cedar playhouse with a bright blue door, a pair of windows framed by white shutters, and a shingle roof. "Lucky kid," Rory said.

"Kids. They have two."

The window boxes held red plastic geraniums, and a garden gnome sat outside the front door. Giving herself a moment to get her thoughts in order, Rory ducked her head to peek inside. She saw a tiny sink and stove, a table and chairs, and a wall-mounted clock with moveable hands. She straightened back up. "My old pink plastic playhouse was low rent compared to this."

"I liked that playhouse."

"What do you mean? You never played in it."

"Hell I didn't. I told my friends pink was the ninja color of invisibility, and I turned it into a fort." He pushed aside a pair of marine-blue throw pillows and slumped on the couch. "I used to climb on the roof with my Nerf Lock 'n Load and try to pick off the neighbors. I also used the roof to jump over the back fence. I got in big trouble for that."

"You never got in trouble."

"You have a lousy memory. Every time Mom caught me, she'd add another day to my grounding."

Rory couldn't recall Kristin ever grounding Clint. She tugged nervously at her purse strap. "I made you some chocolate bars last night. Hazelnut and milk chocolate from organic Peruvian fair-trade beans." She dug in her bag, pulled out the package she'd wrapped in kraft paper, and set it next to him on the couch.

He didn't even glance at it. "I'm sure you have good intentions, but I don't need you or Mom trying to make me feel better. I have to deal with what happened to Ashley by myself."

"I understand that, but—" She returned to stand by the play-house. "I need to tell you something." She dug her fingernails into her palms. "It's going to upset you."

He gave a harsh, humorless laugh. "Nothing could upset me more than knowing some fucking psychopath murdered Ashley."

She couldn't fall apart now. She had to do this. "It might be my fault."

He straightened. "What are you saying?"

"The truth is . . ." She clenched her fists. "I'm not saying Ashley didn't care for you because I know she did. But she cared even more about your money."

He shot to his feet. "You've been talking to Rivers." He pointed toward the door. "Go. Now. I'm going to fire his ass!"

"No!" The words tumbled out. "Brett was right. Not long before you met her, Ashley and I were having dinner at my apartment, drinking too much wine. She told me how tired she was of working. She said she wanted real luxury—designer clothes, jewelry, travel. She wanted to live in a mansion and have people take care of it."

"That doesn't mean—"

"She came right out and said it. She told me she was an old-fashioned gold digger, and she wouldn't apologize for it." Rory bit her lip. "I actually admired that about her. She said she was willing to marry anyone to get what she wanted." Her nose had started to run, and she swiped at it with the back of her hand. "She genuinely cared for you, Clint. Maybe she even loved you. But she loved money more. I tried to tell you, but you wouldn't listen. I wouldn't have done anything more, but then you said you'd bought her a ring and were taking her to Vegas . . ." Rory's voice broke. "I— I couldn't let that happen."

His words were flat, devoid of emotion. "What did you do?"

She pressed a hand to her stomach. "I swore her to secrecy and told her you had a gambling addiction and you'd lost all your money. I said you were in debt and the Stars were going to cut you." This was the worst part. "And I said no other team would take you because you'd been betting on Stars games."

"You *what*?"

"I'm sorry!" she cried. "It was spur-of-the-moment, but she believed me. Don't you see? She broke up with you the next day!"

He stared at her as if she were a worm he wanted to crush under his foot. Her kind, genial little brother . . . He ground out the words. "Why did she go to my house?"

She clutched her hands in front of her stomach. "Because she talked to Karloh the morning she was killed. He—he set her straight about you. Told her whoever had given her that information had lied." Her throat constricted. "She drove to your house to get you back."

"And I wasn't there."

"But somebody else was." Rory didn't try to plead her case or point out that her motives had been pure even if her methods weren't. "I don't expect you to forgive me."

His lips barely moved. "I never want to see you again."

She nodded and turned toward the back door, but she had one more thing to say. "Two people tried to warn you about Ashley. Brett was upfront about it and I wasn't."

"Keep Mom off my ass." His lips barely moved. "You owe me that."

"I don't know if I can."

"You figured out how to break up Ashley and me," he said bitterly. "I'm sure you can manage this. Now get out of here."

Her sunglasses didn't hide hot tears as she rode the L back to Ravenswood, but this was the Midwest, and her fellow riders were polite enough to look the other way.

*
*

Kristin curled in the recliner and stared at the dark movie screen. Clint's home theater was the only space in the house where she felt safe. A room without windows. A place where the predators lurking outside couldn't get to her.

She had to stop being so fearful. The rear of the house was fenced. No one could get to the backyard, and she needed to stop hiding in here.

During her dinner with Daniel Hanbridge two nights ago, she'd been able to temporarily forget about the trouble hanging over her son and simply be herself—not Clint's mother, Rory's stepmother, or Gregg Garrett's widow. She'd felt like carefree, twenty-two-year-old Kristin Shaw again with her fresh bachelor's degree in kinesiology and plans to become a physical therapist.

That hadn't happened. When she'd told Gregg she was pregnant, he hadn't proposed. He'd simply stated that he'd marry her. So magnanimous of him, she thought bitterly.

She'd never let Rory know how little she missed the underlying tension in her marriage, the sense that she was somehow supposed to be everlastingly grateful to Gregg. What would her life have been like if she'd done what she should have and said, "Thanks a lot, but I'm not marrying a man who doesn't love me, and I'm not moving into your dead wife's house. My baby and I will do just fine without you"?

But she'd loved him, and with the naive optimism of a twenty-two-year-old, she'd been certain she could make him love her back. In a way, she'd succeeded. He'd grown to love the familiarity of her. The comfortable life she'd made for him, and the way she'd shouldered the responsibility for his daughter. He definitely loved the son she'd given him. But never had she seen the same respect in his eyes that Daniel Hanbridge, a man she barely knew, had shown her two nights ago.

Maybe if Daniel had come into her life at a different time—a time when her son hadn't been accused of murder—she could continue to see him, but not now.

"Do you have children?"

"A stepdaughter."

She didn't regret not saying more.

She couldn't keep hiding in here like a scared rabbit, and she made herself get up and head for the kitchen. She'd already cleaned up the remnants of the frozen Lean Cuisine she'd had for dinner, and she couldn't think of anything more to do. Clint's office with its comfortable furniture and wall of bookcases was her favorite room in the house. She needed to stop letting the wall of windows there intimidate her.

She turned on a floor lamp and tried to settle on the couch with a book. She had friends. She volunteered. She did everything a woman was supposed to do to fill a life that had grown empty.

She dreamed of the way it had been. The little-boy smell of a sweaty head; the litter of cleats, backpacks, and jackets she'd trip over. She wanted to plan birthday parties, and drive car pools, and sign permission slips for school field trips. She'd committed the cardinal sin of making her child her life, and that child had rebelled. He wouldn't call her, wouldn't tell her where he was. He was a man now, and he'd lost patience with her intrusions into his life.

*
*

Dispirited and defeated from yesterday's encounter with Clint, Rory couldn't concentrate on the party preparations. Instead, she kept thinking about all the times she'd wished she weren't Clint Garrett's sister. *Be careful what you wish for.*

She stared up at the sign. Gilford Graphic Design sat above a hair salon on a shady street in the Roscoe Village neighborhood. If the police weren't willing to question Ashley's stalker ex-boyfriend, Rory would do it. Ashley's former boss might have some answers.

It wasn't only guilt that had driven her here. The injustice of Clint's public reputation being shredded was horrible to witness, and even with the party only two days away and a hundred jobs left to do, she had to come here. She was no longer taking the easy way out. She could do difficult things, and she needed a name.

She trudged up the stairs and opened the door. Two state-of-the-art computers sat on top of sleek black workstations in the small, well-organized studio. The walls displayed framed photos of the studio's work, mainly logos and ad designs. The man sitting at the closest workstation didn't look up. "The job's filled."

"I'm not here about a job."

"Then?"

"I'm here about Ashley. I was her friend."

"Good luck with that." He had a trendy pompadour haircut, high and sculptured on top, a fade at the sides. He wore skintight olive motorcycle jeans and a sleeveless black T-shirt that revealed a rainbow-colored tattoo of a DNA strand.

Rory took a hesitant step into the office. "It doesn't sound as if you liked her much."

"Loved her work. Loved the money she brought in. But girlfriend was a bitch." He set down his pen. "You sure you're not a reporter?"

"Definitely not. Her neighbor. I'm—I'm having a hard time handling what happened, and I thought maybe if I knew more about her life it would help. I'm Rory Meadows."

"Duncan Gilford." He cocked his head. "Wait. Are you the Rory who lives in the apartment over hers? A—quote—'dreary place furnished with Goodwill rejects'?"

"That's me."

He patted the rolling stool at the next workstation with the flat of his hand. "Have a seat."

As she made her way to the stool, she took in more details of the studio: the company's GGD logo above the center desk, a pothos plant trailing from black metal shelving, a Mason jar filled with loose change. She had no clue how to get the information she needed, and she searched for a starting point. "You don't seem too broken up about Ashley."

"No one expects someone they know to be murdered, and I was temporarily devastated. But, honestly, if it had to be someone that I know, at least it was Ashley."

Rory lifted an eyebrow. "Explain to me why you aren't the lead suspect."

"Airtight alibi. I was at a breakfast meeting that morning with a potential client and two of her admins." As he tilted back in his ergonomic chair, his tight T-shirt outlined a set of ripped pecs. "If you want to know what I think, I think the football player killed her. He wouldn't be her only ex-boyfriend to have a motive."

She focused on his mention of an ex-boyfriend and not his opinion of Clint's guilt. "I keep thinking about the real estate guy she broke up with. I know he took their breakup hard."

"He was a client—a major player in residential real estate. She made a big mistake dumping him for Garrett, but Ashley was always on the lookout for a fatter bank account."

Rory tried to appear pensive. "I can't remember her ex's name, the real estate agent."

He straightened in his chair and turned back to his computer. "I gave it to the police."

So they had his name, but since they were sure Clint was guilty, how closely had they questioned him? "Would you give it to me?"

"Why do you want it?"

"I want to talk to him."

"Playing girl detective?"

"Maybe the police missed something." The stool rolled a few

inches beneath her. "Ashley was friendly to me when I moved here from New York. My only friend. I owe her."

She had his attention again. "I'm not sure you owe her anything. She liked you, but she still called you Loser Girl behind your back. And I'm not telling you this to be a bitch, honey, merely to help you overcome your grief."

She refused to feel hurt. "What else did she say about me?"

"Do you really want to know?"

"Yes. I need solace."

"She said you were frumpy, but if what you're wearing today is an example, she was wrong. That blouse is everything."

Her baby-blue cotton blouse had a portrait neckline and a tiny hole at the hem that she'd hidden by tucking it out of sight beneath the waistband of her Audrey Hepburn–ish navy pedal pushers. He gestured toward her mint-green resin hoop earrings. "Ashley only wore twenty-four karat. She knew fashion, but she didn't have any individual style, if you know what I mean. The only thing distinctive about her clothes was that everything looked expensive, the same as hundreds of other women."

"Except she was more beautiful."

"And didn't she know it."

Rory squirmed on the stool. "I'm not really comfortable trashing her."

"She had no trouble trashing you."

"I'm a bigger person."

"She did say you were too nice for your own good and that the world was going to chew you up and spit you out in pieces. Yet she's the one who got spit out." He shook his head. "I'm going to miss her work, though. When she put in a full day, she was damn good, and she definitely knew how to attract clients."

Rory tried again. "Her ex-boyfriend . . . ? The real estate agent?"

"Leave the detective work to the police, honey. I'm not getting involved."

"You wouldn't be involved. You're only giving me a name. And I brought chocolate." She reached into her purse and took out a package of six deliciously creamy raspberry truffles that she'd created between planning hors d'oeuvres and making phone calls to rent tables and dishes. "Try this."

He bit into the truffle and, as the flavors hit his palate, rolled his eyes. "Where have you been hiding all my life? God . . ." He held out his hand for the box. She moved it just out of his reach.

"The name?"

"Seriously?"

"I'll give you the rest of these and drop off another dozen next week. All you have to do is turn over the name of Ashley's ex."

He reached for a notepad, scrawled something on it, and gave it to her. "Just leave me out of this, Nancy Drew. And hand over the chocolates."

"Done." She passed them over and glanced down at his draftsman's penmanship.

GRANT PADDERSON

*
*

A few minutes later, as she stepped out into the late afternoon, she spotted a familiar figure coming toward her. It was too late to pretend she hadn't seen him, and her stomach performed an uncomfortable flip-flop.

Brett stopped in front of her and looked up at the sign for

Gilford Graphic Design. "You've been talking to Ashley's boss? Really, Rory? There's a murderer wandering around, and you've decided it's up to you to investigate?"

"What about you? Did you just happen to be wandering by?"

He shoved his hands in his pockets. "That's different."

She reared up on the toes of her yellow cork sandals. "Because?"

"Because it is."

"Because you're a tough, overachieving American success story, and I'm not?" There she went again, poking at his character and putting herself down. When was she going to give that up?

He shifted uneasily on his feet. "I'm sorry about what I said. I was having a bad morning and took it out on you."

She made herself meet his gaze. "You didn't say anything that wasn't true."

"I have too many faults of my own to throw stones." His eyes lingered on her hair in a way that made her want to grab a comb from her bag. "And I left out the great things about you."

She regarded him quizzically. "Name one."

"How about your sense of honor?"

She blinked. "No one's ever said that about me."

"You feed homeless people and are worried about the brother you profess to hate."

"I never said I hated him. I only—"

"You're smart and funny, and you're also a good kisser."

His attempt to ease the tension between them fell flat, but she appreciated his effort. "I'll save you time," she said. "Gilford didn't like Ashley much, but he was at a meeting all morning and has an airtight alibi." She wasn't sharing the name of Ashley's ex until she had a chance to figure out her approach. "I have to get in your condo so I can check your kitchen and begin transferring some things into your freezer."

"I'll leave a key for you with the concierge at the desk."

He'd said she was honorable, and it was time to prove it. "I talked to Clint yesterday. You're off the hook."

His phone hummed in his pocket. He pulled it out and glanced at the screen. "I need to take this."

Of course, he did. His clients always came first. He was a man who knew exactly what he wanted.

*
*

Two muscled men were wrestling Ashley's white couch down from the second floor when Rory returned. After they'd passed, she climbed the steps and stopped at the open door to the apartment. Inside, a woman was tossing throw pillows into a packing box. She had bleached platinum hair and the stub of a ponytail that couldn't contain all her jaw-length straight hair. Rory knocked on the doorframe. "You must be Stacy. I'm Rory."

"Come on in." Ashley's sister had a tough face—wide cheekbones, small mouth, and tired eyes. Rory knew from Ashley's disparaging comments that Stacy had married young, now worked at Family Dollar, and already had three kids. Judging from the shape of her bulging belly, she had another baby on the way.

"I couldn't find your number, or I would have called," Rory said. "I'm sorry about Ashley. Is there anything I can help with?"

"I've got it under control." She gestured toward the boxes. "Ashley would hate me having all her stuff."

Rory wasn't sure what to say. "Relationships can be tough."

"If you knew Ashley, you probably know we didn't get along. Ashley wasn't exactly subtle about it. Still . . ." She sank back on her heels. "I never thought anything like this could ever happen to her."

"It's awful."

Stacy abandoned packing and flopped into the remaining chair to rest her feet on the coffee table. "I'm only seven months, and I already feel like shit, but at least I've stopped throwing up." She looked around. "I wish to hell she'd left money instead of all this white furniture, but Ashley spent whatever she made."

"She has some beautiful things."

Stacy made a vague gesture toward the place where the couch had been. "I'll throw some sheets over her furniture. Even if the kids get it dirty, it's better than what we've got. And I'm selling her clothes. I'm sure as shit not gonna wear all that designer stuff."

"Not many women could."

"I can't have a funeral until they release her body. And I'm not sure anyone would come."

One of the men had returned, a swarthy guy with sleeve tats. He headed for the chair where Stacy was sitting and extended his hand to help her up. "Move it, babe. I need that chair."

"What you need, Jake, is a goddamn vasectomy."

He grunted, hoisted her up, and wrestled the armchair out the door. She tilted her head after him. "There wasn't a guy Ashley couldn't charm, even Jake. It was like, if a man walked in a room, she couldn't relax until she had him wrapped around her finger. He's taking it harder than I am. He wants to keep her car, probably so he can smell her perfume, but I want to sell it so we can start saving some money." Stacy picked up the last of the throw pillows and tossed them in the open box. "Hand me those, will you?"

Rory retrieved the pair of ceramic candleholders Ashley had arranged in a grouping along with a seagrass basket and a stack of coffee-table books she'd probably never looked at. "Are you sure you don't need any help? I can go change."

"Ashley stashed the moving boxes under her bed. If you'd just pull a couple more out for me, that'd be great."

Rory began moving toward the bedroom only to freeze. "Ashley lived in this apartment for at least three years. Why did she still have packing boxes?"

"Those are new ones. She wanted to move out. She didn't tell you that?"

Rory hadn't seen any boxes when she'd searched the apartment the day Ashley had died, but then she hadn't thought to look under the bed. "Ashley never mentioned moving."

Stacy shrugged. "She was acting weird about it."

"What do you mean?"

"I don't know. The last time I talked to her, she said she planned to move in a few weeks, but she wouldn't tell me why."

Was she moving because her ex, Grant Padderson, was stalking her? Or did she plan on moving in with Karloh?

Rory retrieved the boxes for Stacy and left. As soon as she got to her apartment, she called Detective Strothers and told him about the boxes.

"We have them in our inventory," he said.

"But she never said anything to me about moving. Don't you think that's strange? I think she was afraid her ex would find her, and she didn't want anyone to know where she was going."

"Thanks for the information, Ms. Garrett. I apologize for cutting you off, but I have an appointment."

Once again, she'd been dismissed.

*
*

A few hours later, a knock interrupted her as she jammed another batch of party appetizers into her already overstuffed freezer. She dried her hands and went to the door. Brett stood on the other side wearing khaki and the face of doom.

"What's wrong?"

He stormed in. "They've arrested Clint and charged him with Ashley's murder."

14

She gave Brett a locally brewed double IPA with some nuts and a raspberry truffle. She was too upset to care that the beer and truffle didn't pair well. Brett slumped on her couch, half a truffle in one hand, beer in the other. "They found his hair samples on her."

"She was in his bedroom!" Rory exclaimed. "That doesn't prove anything."

"She was also clutching his ring."

"What ring?"

"His National Championship ring from his senior year at Michigan."

"He hasn't worn that ring in years."

"He was photographed wearing it two nights before Ashley died, at a reunion with some of his old Michigan teammates." Brett finished the truffle and set his beer on her coffee table. "The police haven't released the news yet, and when it goes public— I don't know, Rory. Maybe he did—"

"Don't say it. Do *not* say it."

He braced his arms on his thighs and gazed out at nothing. "He has one of the best-known faces in the NFL. How could no one have seen him that morning when he left the house?"

"He probably left early." She slumped into the cushion next to him. "If I hadn't lied to her . . ."

"This wasn't your fault." He slipped his arm around her. "You look tired."

"I haven't been getting much sleep."

"It's the party, isn't it? The way I sprang it on you last minute."

"Sleep is overrated." More than putting together the buffet had robbed her of sleep. Last night as she'd worked, all the obstacles preventing her from opening her own shop had seemed so insurmountable that she'd begun making excuses for why she couldn't follow through. But this time she'd stopped herself. She had a food truck, didn't she? Once she came up with enough money to pay her fine and refurbish the truck, she could get it back on the road, but this time she'd sell her own chocolates from the window instead of gum, lollipops, and Pez dispensers. It might not be the chocolate shop of her dreams, but it would still be a chocolate shop, only on wheels.

She'd dragged herself back into the kitchen and pulled out the last of her tiny, white-cardboard, four-piece sample boxes. With the supplies she still had left, she set to work. When she was done, she'd have beautiful chocolates to fill the containers, each one bearing a label that displayed her cell number and the words "Custom Orders Accepted." Those boxes would be waiting for Brett's wealthy guests to take with them as they left the party. Maybe no one would call, and she'd have wasted her diminishing supplies. Maybe nothing would happen at all, but she was going to try . . . even if she failed.

Overcome with exhaustion and the comfort of being near him, she leaned against his shoulder. He smelled of soap and spice with a hint of beer. It felt right being here. As if they fit.

He pulled her closer, and her sense of comfort vanished. His fingertips brushed her chin. She gazed up at him, taking in those storm-cloud gray eyes, and she did what she shouldn't. She brushed her lips against his.

It was the merest touch. A friendly little butterfly of a kiss. *Hey there, pal . . . It's me. Your good buddy Rory sayin' hello. Nothin' personal. Just a little peck.*

*   *

The moment Brett felt Rory's lips on his, common sense flew out the window. That light touch against his mouth made him forget that he was The River, cool and rational. Made him forget that discipline was his superpower. Instead, his body took over from his brain, and every part of him needed this calamity of a woman.

Their mouths locked. He delved right into her.

She reached under his shirt, and he tunneled his fingers into those rampaging curls. Her hands dug into his back, giving him permission to dig into her.

He found her breast through her *Purple Rain* T-shirt but lost his bearings as she moved on top of him. Their bodies tangled on the uncomfortable couch. With one foot on the floor, the other who-knew-where, he cupped her butt, pulling her down hard against him. She bracketed his head in her palms, taking over the kiss, a beautiful velociraptor ready to eat him alive.

God, she was sweet. So sweet.

He reached under her T-shirt. Grappled with the clasp on her bra. He'd always been good at unhooking bras, but this bra seemed to be out of the 1940s, with a clasp designed to withstand German artillery. As it finally gave, she reared up and whipped the T-shirt over her head, her bra still on, satin straps falling down her arms. He reached for the damn thing to pull it off, but his leg hit the coffee table, knocking over the beer bottle.

He was half on, half off the couch. They were firecracker hot, wild, and ridiculous. She fell on him, and they were both on the floor, wedged between the coffee table and couch, beer soaking the sleeve of his T-shirt.

"Bed." His voice sounded as though it were coming from the bottom of the ocean.

"Bed," she whispered back. But instead of rolling off him, she held him tight, and they were kissing again, mouths and tongues, teeth bumping, and the sides of her breasts were in his hands, and the world was a roller coaster of plunge and climb until he banged his head against the leg of the fucking coffee table.

Enough.

He extricated himself and pulled her up. He lifted her off her feet, his arms under her butt. She wrapped her legs around his waist. They kissed again as he duckwalked her to the bedroom. "We're really doing this?" she whispered.

He threw away a lifetime of good judgment. "We really are."

She smiled against his mouth.

A pounding. Not coming from his heart.

Someone was knocking! *Really?*

Maybe she didn't hear.

But she did, and she broke the kiss. "Ignore that," she whispered.

"Damn right," he whispered back.

But the knocking wouldn't stop. Instead, it grew louder.

She rested her cheek against his jaw with a groan.

He gave in to the inevitable and set her down.

The door began to rattle.

Rory grabbed her *Purple Rain* T-shirt. "Go away!"

An angry woman's voice shouted, "You have my clothes!"

With a Rottweiler's growl, Rory pulled the T-shirt over her head and stomped to the door, taking the Lord's name in vain with every step.

He tried futilely to adjust his shorts, cursing the intruder, cursing Rory for answering, cursing his hard-on.

"Claudia?"

He risked a look over his shoulder.

The straps of Rory's still-unfastened bra looped down her arms from beneath her T-shirt sleeves, her hair was a shambles, and the unhoused woman he'd shared dinner with six nights ago had once again appeared at exactly the wrong time.

It only got crazier.

"If anybody needs a shower, it's me!" he hissed after Rory handed over Claudia's clean clothes and showed her to the bathroom. "A cold one!"

"This is a sign from God that we went too far."

"It's a sign from Satan!" Now he was the one stomping into the kitchen to grab paper towels and clean up the mess he'd made when he'd knocked over his beer.

"How did Kristin take the news about Clint?"

He paused, paper towel in hand, and looked up at her. "I haven't talked to her."

"You didn't call her?"

"I didn't think about it."

"You're The River!" she exclaimed. "You think of everything!"

"I was stressed."

"You don't do stress!"

How wrong she was, he thought, as he took in those sturdy legs emerging from her lemon-yellow shorts.

He pulled himself together and checked his phone. "You're the one who should call her."

"And tell her over the phone that her precious darling has been arrested? Even I'm not that heartless." She dead-eyed him. "You need to drive there right now and tell her in person. Before the news breaks."

He dead-eyed her right back. "You tell her."

She stared at him.

He stared back.

She held out her hand.

Rock . . . Paper . . . Scissors . . .

Scissors cut paper.

Which was how he ended up feeding Claudia a ham sandwich and listening to her opinions about climate change while Rory headed west in the Royal Palace of Sweets to talk to her stepmother.

*   *
   *

Rory forgot her sunglasses and squinted against the last of the setting sun. They'd almost hooked up. She'd been on the brink of a no-hands orgasm when Claudia had pounded on the door. What was wrong with her? She only formed relationships with losers, not barracudas. But sex with Brett Rivers felt inevitable.

She needed to stop obsessing over him and figure out how she was going to get to Kristin so she could break the news. She couldn't simply walk up to the front door and ring the bell, not with all those reporters camped out, and not driving the Royal Palace of Sweets. They'd figure out who she was and make her life hell. She could phone Kristin and ask to meet her somewhere, but Kristin would be followed. Besides, she would immediately demand to know what was wrong.

Only as Rory drew closer to the house did she remember Clint had mentioned one of DuPage County's many small forest preserves butted up to the rear of his property. Maybe she could get in that way. She didn't have much daylight left, but after a few wrong turns, she found the preserve on a dead-end street that ran somewhere behind his house. She parked the truck two blocks away and set off.

The trail into the preserve reminded her of the path she and Brett had slogged through only three days ago to get to the militia camp. This trail, however, was covered in wood chips instead of mud. Bracket fungi grew in half saucers from the trunk of a fallen tree, and a scurry of squirrels, attracted by the many oaks, scampered through the undergrowth.

It didn't take long to reach the stockade fence that marked the rear boundary of Clint's estate. Unfortunately, it was at least eight feet tall. She walked the length of it, looking for a way over, but found nothing she could climb on—no handy abandoned ladder or perfectly positioned tree stump. The only access she could see was a sugar maple growing close to the fence, with a limb that hung across it. The limb didn't look all that sturdy, but her only other option was delivering the news to Kristin over the phone, and she already had enough on her conscience.

The hell with it. She was no longer looking for the easy way out, and she was going over that fence. But she needed something to stand on to help her get into the tree. She cased the area and found a gnarled log. By the time she'd dragged it to the base of the maple, her T-shirt was damp with sweat, and she'd broken two fingernails, which wasn't exactly a big loss since she didn't take that great care of her nails anyway. The log wobbled as she climbed on top, but she had just enough leverage to grab the bottom limb. She pulled herself up, wishing she'd changed into jeans before she'd left instead of wearing her yellow shorts.

The limb that hung over the fence was still at least five feet above her head. Climbing trees had been fun when she was a kid, but this wasn't fun. She looked down once and didn't make that mistake again.

By the time she'd maneuvered to the branch she needed, her knee was bleeding and her thighs chafed. The sun had set. It was full twilight. She gritted her teeth and eased herself out on the branch. It began to sway—not much, just enough to make her cling tighter.

She crept forward. She was over the fence now. A few more inches—

An ominous crack sounded like a gunshot. The branch gave, and she hit the ground so hard the wind was knocked out of her. She was going to die. She lay helplessly in the grass. No breath.

A nocturnal raptor swooped above her searching for prey, and the first gurgle of air trickled into her lungs. With a wheeze, she grabbed another breath and then another. When she could finally sit up, she realized she'd barely missed impaling herself on the fence.

She staggered to her feet. She was scraped and bruised, her back hurt, and her right foot didn't feel all that great, but she'd done it.

She hadn't given up. She hobbled toward the house, going around the swimming pool and through the garden. One dim light shone from Clint's office, but the rest of the house was dark. She edged through the rosebushes to the office windows, avoiding looking at the place on the patio where Ashley had fallen.

Kristin sat on the couch under a single lamp, her legs tucked under her, a book in her hands. Rory tapped gently on the window. Even through the glass, Rory could hear Kristin's scream. Kristin jumped to her feet; the book fell to the carpet. Clutching her chest, her gaze shot toward the windows.

Rory waved.

Kristin stormed toward her, murder in her eyes. Rory flashed the peace sign, gestured toward the back door, and tried to extricate herself from the rosebushes without more damage to her legs.

Eventually, Kristin flung open the back door. *"What are you doing?"* she screamed. "What's *wrong* with you?"

So much. Rory limped toward her. "I climbed over the back fence. It didn't go exactly the way I hoped."

"You couldn't ring the bell like everyone else?"

"I didn't want reporters stalking me, too. Can I come in?"

Kristin threw up her hands and flipped on a kitchen light.

Rory had never seen her stepmother look so undone—no makeup, unwashed hair caught up with a cheap plastic banana clip. Her top was wrinkled, her tan capris stained on the front.

By the time Rory was inside and had closed the door behind her, Kristin was already regarding her dirty shorts and battered legs with disapproval. "You look like you've been mauled." She pointed toward the bathroom off the kitchen. "Clean yourself up. I'll get some ointment."

Rory had just washed off the last of the dirt and blood when Kristin appeared with a tube of ointment. "I couldn't find any Princess Jasmine Band-Aids. Don't throw a fit."

Rory had forgotten all about the Princess Jasmine Band-Aids. "I don't think I'll need a Band-Aid."

"God is merciful."

Kristin's familiar sharpness was vaguely reassuring. "Was I that much of a drama queen?"

To her surprise, Kristin took the question seriously. "You were pretty stoic. Do you remember when you cut your forehead on that nail in the garage and had to go to the emergency room?"

"Vaguely."

"I've never seen so much blood in my life. But all you cared about was negotiating for ice cream afterward."

"Dad was pretty easy to manipulate when it came to ice cream."

"You got your sweet tooth from him. Of course, I'm the one who took you. Clint had T-ball, and Gregg went with him."

The mention of Clint's name was an unnecessary reminder that Rory had a mission. She recapped the ointment. "Instead of ice cream, how about wine? Maybe Clint still has some of that Napa Valley Promontory I heard him talking about. Let's treat ourselves."

"I'm happy with Yellow Tail."

"I'm not."

Clint's wine cellar was, in fact, a beautiful, glass-walled room with wooden racks displaying the bottles on their sides, exposing the labels. Rory found the Napa Valley Promontory and imagined how it would pair with her seventy-percent dark chocolate bars, the ones she made from the best Madagascar beans.

She carried the bottle reverently to the kitchen. Kristin had turned off all the lights except the ones under the cabinets. She'd set out two goblets designed for white wine instead of red, but Rory refrained from sounding like a pretentious ass by pointing that out.

As Kristin handed her the corkscrew, the doorbell rang "Hail to the Victors." Kristin rubbed her forehead. "I thought they'd finished hounding me for the day." Her fingers crept to the neckline of her wrinkled top. "Last night, I caught someone—a reporter maybe—looking in the house through a front window."

Rory frowned. "No wonder I startled you. Sorry."

Kristin's hair had come loose from its clip and hung lank over her cheek, but she didn't seem to notice. "The doorbell won't stop ringing, even though I never answer it. As I'm sure you saw, cars and news vans are everywhere. Clint's housekeeper, Gabby—one of the tabloids offered her a thousand dollars for a story."

Rory remembered the pretty housekeeper well, the one who had a key to the house, was probably in love with Clint, disliked Ashley, and had an alibi. The bell rang again. Kristin's hand trembled as she reached for the glass Rory had poured for her. "They don't usually bother me this late."

The news must have broken.

Kristin searched her face. "Why are you here? This isn't a friendly visit. Of course not. We don't do friendly visits."

"Let's find a more comfortable place to drink." Rory cocked her head toward the ceiling. "Preferably where the cherubs won't be judging us."

"I'll never understand why Clint won't let me redecorate this place for him."

Rory had a fairly good idea.

Instead of returning to Clint's office, Kristin led her to the home theater. "It's more comfortable in here." She chose one of two couches centered in front of the dark screen. Rory set the wine bottle on a circular table and settled next to it.

"I assume you watched that press conference yesterday morning." Kristin gazed at the empty movie screen. "It was nothing short of a public lynching."

Rory gripped the stem of her glass. A wine as fine as this deserved the best treatment. It should be studied for its color, carefully swirled to observe its legs, and sniffed for key fragrances. Instead, she took a deep slug. It slid down her throat, one of the best wines she'd ever drunk, but she should have chosen Yellow Tail because she couldn't appreciate a drop of it.

In the distance, the doorbell intruded. Kristin squeezed her eyes shut. "It's too much."

Rory had never heard her sound so defeated. She set her glass on the end table and tried to find the right words only to realize there weren't any. "I'm afraid I have some bad news."

Kristin's eyes flew open. "I knew it. Why else would you be here?"

Rory hesitated before she said what she had to. "Clint's been arrested."

Kristin moaned and covered her face with her hands.

Rory wanted to offer a hug, some kind of comfort, but Kristin wouldn't welcome it. She tried to sound reassuring. "Clint's attorney will have him out on bail by morning."

Kristin's head came up, her expression fierce. "Clint did not murder Ashley!"

"We know that. It's only a matter of time before the police find the right person." She took another gulp of wine, praying that was true.

Kristin jumped up from the couch. "I have to get to him."

"You can't do that. Brett's all over this. By now he's probably hired an army of attorneys and the best private detectives in the city."

Kristin sagged back into the cushions. "You can't be sure of that."

"I know Brett Rivers. He's got this, and there's nothing you can do for Clint right now except give him the room he needs. He has enough to deal with without having to deal with you, too."

Kristin's eyes filled with tears. "That's mean, even for you."

Rory hadn't meant to be mean, but as usual, she'd said the wrong thing in the wrong way. "I only meant that Clint loves you and seeing how distraught you are would only make this harder for him. He needs to take care of himself now. You don't want him worrying about you, too."

Kristin grabbed her glass and emptied its contents as if she were drinking Two Buck Chuck instead of a wine that cost over eight hundred dollars a bottle. "I hate this house! I never understood why he bought it."

Rory refilled Kristin's glass. "Some kind of rebellion, I guess."

"What does Clint have to rebel from?"

"Beats me." But that wasn't quite true. Now that it was too late, she'd begun to see her brother differently—a man who'd bought a bare-bones cabin so he could escape being himself. Unlike her, he always had to be on guard. While she could talk freely to anyone, he had to watch what he said because he knew he'd be quoted. Every morning she got out of bed without her joints aching. She didn't have to worry about early dementia from too many concussions. And she wasn't being publicly tried for the murder of a lover. Her world shifted as she absorbed what had escaped her for too long.

Being Clint Garrett was as much a curse as a blessing.

Kristin pulled a rumpled tissue from her pocket and wiped her eyes. "I went out with someone a couple of days ago."

Rory blinked at the sudden change of subject. "Dad's been gone for two years. Fine with me."

"I wasn't asking permission. And it was only one date." Her eyes filled with tears again, and Rory knew she was thinking about Clint.

"Did you sleep with him?" Rory asked, as a distraction.

"God, no. I hardly know him."

"But you wish you had."

Kristin shoved the hair out of her face and polished off another glass of wine. "I can't imagine getting naked in front of someone again."

"I'm sure you look better naked than I do."

"Hardly." She curled her hands into fists. "What if they've locked him up in a cell with all kinds of degenerates?"

Rory refilled Kristin's glass. "If they have, the degenerates will be falling all over themselves trying to be his best friend."

"I can't understand how any of this happened. One day everything's wonderful, and the next day, life has fallen apart."

"He'll get through this. You both will."

Kristin shredded the tissue she'd pulled from her pocket. "Daniel doesn't know I'm Clint's mother."

"Daniel? The new boyfriend?"

"He's fifty years old, and I'm not going to see him again." She drank more of the wine Rory had poured. "I introduced myself as Kristin Meadows."

"That's weird."

"The men I've dated are more interested in Clint than in me. That's why I didn't tell him."

Rory understood. Years ago, she'd stopped using her last name unless she had to. The doorbell kept ringing, and Kristin finally flew off the couch. "I can't stay in this house a moment longer! I have to get out."

Rory's own nerves were jangled. "Maybe you could find a hotel." Even as she said it, she knew that would be difficult. Reporters would follow Kristin wherever she went, and if she managed to elude them, someone on the hotel staff would leak her whereabouts.

Kristin regarded Rory with her familiar pinched expression of disappointment, the creases around her lips compressing like the bellows of a mini accordion. Rory should have been used to it after so many years, but guilt and wine made her fold. "Or I guess you could spend the night at my apartment," she muttered.

Her stepmother grabbed the nearly empty wine bottle and headed none-too-steadily toward the door.

"Where are you going?" Rory asked.

"To pack a suitcase."

⋆
⋆

An hour later, they approached the back fence. It was pitch-dark now, Kristin was more than a little drunk, and she kept banging the suitcase she was carrying against Rory's legs—a suitcase, Rory noted, big enough to hold more than an overnight's worth of clothes. Rory was dragging the six-foot ladder she'd found in the garage while Kristin had custody of the flashlight. "Point it ahead of me!" Rory complained.

Kristin shifted the beam. "You're walking too slow."

"Do you want to carry this instead?"

"You don't have to get your knickers in a knot."

"Who the hell under ninety says 'knickers in a knot'?"

"I'm an old soul. Watch out!"

Rory had snagged the end of the ladder on some undergrowth. She stumbled but managed to hold on to it. "I could be home eating bonbons now. Literally."

"Stop complaining," Kristin retorted. "That's all you've done since we left the house."

"If it hadn't taken you an hour to pack, we could have done this before it turned pitch-black. And we didn't have to do this at all. We could have taken your car."

"No! I need to disappear."

"What you need is to take a shower. How long has it been?"

"You worry about yourself."

They'd been bickering like this even before they'd left the house, because it was easier to bicker over small things than to think about Clint in jail.

When they finally reached the fence, Rory leaned the ladder against it and gingerly climbed to the top. It was even darker in the woods than in the more open yard. "Hand me your suitcase."

After a great deal of pushing and lifting on both their parts, Rory managed to balance the suitcase on the top rail.

"Be careful with that. All my toiletries are inside. We should have brought a rope. How are you going to—"

Rory dropped the suitcase over the fence. It hit the ground with a satisfying thud.

"I can't believe you did that!" Kristin cried.

"How else did you think we were going to get this monstrosity over the fence?"

"You could at least have leaned farther down so it didn't have to fall so far."

"If I'd done that, the suitcase would have taken me along with it."

"A blessing," Kristin muttered.

"I heard that." Rory eyed the ground beneath her and awkwardly straddled the fence. Clinging to the top rail, she eased her other leg over, held her breath, and dropped.

She somehow managed to stay on her feet.

Kristin's head appeared above the fence. "What am I supposed to do?"

"What I did."

"I'll break a leg."

"I'll catch you."

"You can't catch me."

"I know. But pretend that I can." Rory moved the suitcase out of the target zone.

"Oh, God . . ." Compared with Rory's awkward scramble, Kristin looked almost graceful as she positioned herself. Rory moved aside, giving her plenty of room.

"What are you doing over there?" her stepmother screeched. "You're supposed to catch me."

"Oh, yeah . . ."

Rory couldn't catch her, but at least she could break her fall. Kristin groaned as she picked herself up off the ground. "I'm too old for this."

Rory retrieved the flashlight and pointed it toward the trail that led from the woods. "Stay out of sight of the houses while I get the truck."

"Truck?"

Kristin would understand soon enough.

A little over five minutes later, Rory pulled to the trailhead, got up from behind the wheel, and opened the passenger door.

Kristin looked inside, horrified. "Where's your car? What is this?"

"Welcome to the Royal Palace of Sweets."

15

Rory couldn't go to bed until she'd finished filling the four-piece sample boxes for the party, so she offered Kristin her bedroom and resigned herself to catching whatever sleep she could steal on the lumpy couch where she and Brett had gone so much further than they should have. As she flipped on the kitchen light, she resolved to focus on her work and never put herself in that impossible situation again.

By one in the morning, the boxes for Brett's guests were finally done. Each held four bonbons enrobed in glossy, gold-dusted shells: a French praline, raspberry cream, coconut rum, and her beloved ancho chili. She stuck the labels Toby had printed for her onto each box.

LUXURY CHOCOLATES
Custom Orders Accepted

She could only list her cell number for now, hoping it would create the impression of exclusivity and personalized service. As soon as the party was over, she'd come up with a name for her business and start building a rudimentary website. A small online business wouldn't give her the capital she needed to go much further with her plan, but it would be a positive step in the right direction. In the meantime, she'd have to find a roommate to save on rent, even though it meant she'd end up sleeping on the couch. She'd take as many jobs with catering companies as she could get and work eighteen hours a day if she had to for as long as it took. First she'd pay off the fine. Then she'd start saving for everything she needed done to the truck. She already had food sanitation certification from the city, but she'd have to rent space in a commercial kitchen before she could sell chocolates from the truck. In addition to repairs, the Royal Palace of Sweets would need a makeover since the garish pink and purple colors and tacky name didn't exactly scream fine chocolate. If she thought too hard about everything she needed to accomplish and how much could go wrong, she'd be paralyzed, so instead of thinking about it, she'd simply plow ahead.

She slept for a couple of hours and got up at six the next morning to marinate shrimp for the party and make a wild mushroom lasagna for the vegetarians. Brett called at eight with the news that Clint was out on bail. At nine, she knocked on the bedroom door. "Upsy-daisy!" She imitated the cheery voice Kristin had tortured her with when Rory had been a teen, even though she felt anything but cheerful.

"Go away," Kristin groaned from inside.

"I have some good news," Rory called through the door. "Clint's out on bail."

The door swung open. Kristin had a crease in her cheek, and her hair made a lopsided lump on the side of her head. For a change, she looked every one of her fifty-one years. "Did you talk to him? I have to talk to him!"

"I talked to Brett. Clint will be holed up with his attorney all morning. I'm sure he'll call you."

"Where is he? Is he going back to his house?"

"I doubt it. Hurry and get dressed. You have a breakfast date."

"Breakfast date?" Kristin shoved her hair out of her eyes. "What are you talking about?"

"Daniel Hanbridge called. Naturally, when I saw his name on your phone I answered."

"You picked up my phone! Rory, what have you done?"

"He wanted to know if you were free for breakfast this morning, and I told him you'd be delighted."

"You had no right! I'm calling him right now and canceling." Kristin stalked past her into the living room where she'd unwisely left her phone.

"Bad idea. All you'll do is sit around and worry. I suggested he take you to the Busy Chicken. It's a neighborhood place. Wear sunglasses if you're worried someone will recognize you."

"I can't believe you did this."

"It's for your own good." It was also for Rory's good. She needed Kristin out of the way so she could meet Ashley's stalker, Grant Padderson, this morning. She'd easily located him with a quick Google search. The meeting would put her further behind with party prep, but this new version of herself couldn't postpone something so important. "Daniel's picking you up in half an hour, and you look like hell, so you'd better hurry."

Kristin gritted her teeth. "You have crossed so many boundaries."

With a familiar hiss of displeasure, Kristin marched into the bathroom and slammed the door. Since she didn't take her phone with her, Rory knew the breakfast date was still on.

*

Kristin was still getting dressed in the bedroom when Daniel Hanbridge arrived, so Rory answered the door and introduced herself. "We spoke on the phone," she said, wiping her hands on the dish towel she'd brought with her. "Kristin'll be out in a few minutes."

He was an interesting-looking man—tall and lanky, with a high forehead and knobby wrists, kind of a more attractive Abraham Lincoln. He nodded and gazed around her apartment, pausing when he spotted her floozy poster.

"It's meant to be ironic," Rory explained. "Mostly."

He regarded her with interest. "How so?"

"We don't know each other well enough for me to explain."

A slow smile tugged at the corners of his mouth.

Kristin emerged from the bedroom, looking almost like herself in turquoise slacks and an asymmetrical white top, her hair in its customary blond bob. As Daniel took her in, he flushed. "I apologize for calling at the last minute. I hope that didn't offend you."

"Very little offends me these days," Kristin said.

Not quite true. Rory offended her.

"You look lovely," he said earnestly.

He was so serious, the kind of rock-solid man who only knew how to speak the truth. Unlike Brett Rivers, he wouldn't have a clue how to bullshit an insecure client or schmooze a prickly general manager. Yet something about the two men felt similar. Maybe a sense that, at their core, they were both decent.

As the older couple moved toward the door, Rory couldn't help herself. "Before you leave, Mr. Hanbridge . . . What are your intentions toward my stepmother?"

"Rory!" Kristin gasped. "Ignore her, Daniel. She likes to make trouble."

But he didn't ignore her. Instead, he faced her squarely. "I'm enchanted by her."

Rory smiled. "Good enough."

*
*

The party was the next evening. Rory still had chicken to marinate, meat to prep, and more specialty food to buy, but it would have to wait. Clint had been arrested. If the police wouldn't do their job, Rory would do it for them. And she was going to handle this alone, without a big-name sports agent charging in.

She could blame her attraction to Brett on his great body or the slight asymmetry of his face that made him even better looking. She could blame it on those gray assassin's eyes or his thick, Irish-cream-chocolate hair, but her attraction to him was more than physical. She was drawn to his competence, his confidence, his take-charge nature. Now, she needed to look past all that and rein in her growing feelings for him. Their lives were too different, their personalities too dissimilar. Theirs was a relationship with no future. She needed to keep all her focus on her work.

"I have an appointment to see Mr. Padderson."

The receptionist sat behind a gray granite desk in the posh fourth-floor office of Padderson Realty. Rory had made the appointment yesterday, right before Brett had shown up to tell her about Clint's arrest.

"I'll let him know. You're welcome to have a seat."

Instead of sitting, Rory took in the perfectly lit photos on the lobby wall showcasing mansions with spectacular interiors, none of which looked like places where a person could hang up a floozy poster.

Thanks to raiding Kristin's suitcase while her stepmother was on her breakfast date with hunky Abe Lincoln, Rory fit in with her surroundings. She'd borrowed a silky mid-calf wrap skirt in a Pollock-influenced spatter print and paired it with one of Kristin's boring black tops, along with her even more boring silver hoops and nude, mid-heeled sandals that were a size too small. Rory had even semi-tamed her hair with a diffuser, flat iron, and one of Kristin's prissy headbands. She hoped she looked like the wife of a man making a fortune at the Chicago Board of Trade, but she felt ridiculous. Why would anyone dress like this when they had the entire world of fashion to choose from?

She didn't second-guess her decision not to share the name of Ashley's ex with Brett. If he were here, he'd take over—that was his nature—and she didn't need him barging in. She had to do this alone.

"Mrs. Meadows? I'm Grant Padderson."

He was diminutive, maybe in his early forties, with a shaved head and manicured scruff. His all-black outfit included a silky, long-sleeved shirt open at the throat, perfectly tailored pants, and shiny black loafers with no socks. If only Ashley had stayed with him instead of setting her sights on Clint.

"Mr. Padderson." She inhaled the reek of expensive cologne as he shook her hand.

"Please. Call me Grant. I have a feeling we're going to be good friends."

And I have a feeling we aren't.

"Is Mr. Meadows—"

"Unfortunately, my husband had a work emergency, but I'm the decision maker."

"Of course."

He led her to his office where two cubic towers supported a black granite desktop. Gray marble floors, original canvases, and sleek, European-style furniture proclaimed that poor people needn't waste their time here.

As he directed her toward one of the comma-shaped chairs in front of his desk, she noticed the tasteful display of wooden wall plaques recognizing Padderson as a big charity donor. If Rory were a big charity donor, she wouldn't give her money to any organization that spent its funds on donor plaques. Which reminded her that it had been over a week since she'd taken sandwiches to the street people who camped in the underpass. She hated thinking about anyone going hungry, and she'd been feeding them whenever she could ever since she'd come to Chicago.

"Would you like coffee? I can also offer you a mimosa . . . unless you prefer your champers straight?"

"Champers"? Really? The word went along with his cologne and manicured fingernails. "Nothing, thank you."

"Tell me about yourself." He clasped his hands on top of his desk and regarded her as if she were the most fascinating woman on the planet, something she clearly wasn't. His high-end clients might view his interest as genuine, but a low-ender like herself had a stronger bullshit meter.

She crossed her ankles off to the side like a royal. "As I mentioned to your receptionist when I made the appointment, Ashley Hart gave me your name"—her throat tightened with genuine emotion, unlike everything else that was unfolding—"before . . . A few weeks ago."

"Ashley . . ." He swept his hand over his face, pinky ring catching the light. "What an ugly thing to happen."

His distress seemed real, but distress about what? Being caught? "This has been very hard," she said.

"Hard for everyone who knew her. Now tell me exactly what you're looking for."

And just like that, he dismissed Ashley's death. She needed to reintroduce the subject, but in the meantime, he was waiting for an answer. She should have thought ahead. "Well . . ." She pleated a fold in the Pollock-printed skirt. "My husband and I are looking for a place on the North Shore." She paused. "Preferably Winnetka, but we'd also consider Glencoe or, in a pinch, Kenilworth." Warming to the subject, she went on. "Nothing over seven million. Open floor plan, a minimum of six bedrooms, four-car garage with heated floors." She channeled HGTV. "A chef's kitchen with granite countertops and stainless-steel appliances. A pool and fenced-in yard for our dogs. My husband would prefer beach access. And, of course, plenty of room for entertaining."

"You have exquisite taste."

What a suck-up. But was he also dangerous? She needed to bring the conversation back to Ashley, but before she could do that, the office door opened and the receptionist appeared. "Mr. Meadows is here."

In walked—who else?—Brett Hot-as-Sin Rivers.

Grant Padderson immediately shot to his feet, even as he shrank in stature—not because of his smaller frame but because the real power player had arrived, slicked-back hair, designer suit and all.

And the real power player was not happy.

"Hello, *darling.*" Those killer eyes shot flames at her as he crossed the room. "I finally made it."

"Yippee," she said weakly.

Padderson came around the side of his desk. Brett extended his hand to shake. "Luther Meadows."

He named himself after Ashley's cat?

"Apologies for being late. I forgot when we were meeting, and I had to call your receptionist. *DeeDee* wasn't picking up her phone." His gaze swept over Rory's nauseatingly perfect outfit and, if anything, grew even more disapproving. Did this man make it his life's mission to dislike everything she wore?

The real estate agent greeted him enthusiastically. "Your lovely wife and I have been getting acquainted."

"I was just getting ready to tell Grant about the shiplap," Rory said, chipper as all hell. "My husband adores it, but I find it dated. You can't have everything you want, pumpkin."

Brett gave her the stink eye before he said smoothly, "Then no shoe closet for you, DeeDee." He tried to make himself comfortable in the comma chair. "You know how women can be about shoes. It's as if their adorable *wee brains* have ended up in their feet."

Rory missed those very early days when Brett had at least tried to be conciliatory to his most important client's sister.

"Now, now, sweetheart." She patted his knee. "Remember that only one of us graduated from Harvard." She gave Grant a conspiratorial smirk as he resettled behind his desk. "My husband was forced to attend a *state* school, of all things, but look what he's made of himself."

Brett shot her a *Did you really say that?* look.

Grant was a whiz at practicing diplomacy with bickering couples. "High achievers like the two of you deserve an elite property. I have two in mind that have just come on the market. The first is new construction, a six-bedroom contemporary with gated entry . . ."

She barely listened as he ticked off a floating staircase, retractable glass walls, and a pergola with a motorized roof. How could she bring the conversation back to Ashley?

Brett beat her to it, taking over as usual. "An interesting property. Did my wife mention we heard about you from Ashley Hart?"

So much for subtlety.

"She did." Grant pushed back from his desk, as if he wanted to create more distance from them. "Tragic what happened."

Brett rearranged himself in the too-small chair. "Did DeeDee also mention that Ashley was my last serious relationship before I met her?"

What the hell?

He crossed an ankle over his knee—good-ol'-boy time. "I know it sounds callous—nobody deserves what happened to her—but the day she dumped me was the luckiest day of my life."

She'd already told Grant *she* was Ashley's friend, and Brett was screwing everything up. She jumped in. "The irony is that Ashley and I still became close. What happened to her has been more difficult for me to deal with than my husband."

"Because you weren't the one who got dumped at the end of a seven-hundred-dollar meal at a Michelin three-star restaurant." He gazed at Padderson. "What do you say, Grant? Should we form a Dumped by Ashley Hart Club? I heard you went through the same thing not too long ago."

Grant toyed with a pen on his desk. "Everything happens for a reason."

Anyone who used that expression knew nothing about the atrocities of human existence. "So brave . . . " she said.

"It was dreadful at first," Padderson said. "I didn't behave well. I don't like to think about it. Then I met someone at a conference in LA who changed my life." Padderson's smile seemed genuine. "All's well that ends well." He recomposed his face. "Except for poor Ashley, of course. I never had a chance to apologize for bothering her. Now, let me tell you about a second property. It's an ideal house for entertaining. It has—"

"The person you met . . ." Rory leaned forward. "Are you still together? I love happy endings."

"We are." He adjusted his computer so they could see the screen. "This is a magnificent Tudor with an attached guest—"

"Then breaking up with Ashley turned out to be a gift?" She pressed on.

Brett uncrossed his legs. "You'll have to excuse my wife. She doesn't always respect personal boundaries."

Look who's talking.

"It's quite all right," Grant said, as the slideshow of the Tudor mansion played on the screen. "Yes, it was a gift. When I met Jason, I finally understood that my over-the-top reaction to the breakup was more about the lies I'd been telling myself than a true broken heart."

Rory sank back in her chair. "So you and Jason are happy?" she said weakly.

"Very happy." He beamed. "It turns out that Ashley had a good reason for breaking up with me, beyond the fact that the football player came along."

After that, Rory was forced to listen to a detailed description of a palatial mansion with a state-of-the-art chef's kitchen and Gaggenau appliances she'd never be able to afford.

"What time would be convenient for a showing?" Padderson said.

She blinked. "Sorry. I was distracted. I keep thinking about Ashley." She plunged in. "I just can't believe that football player killed her. He seems so nice. I wonder if she had any enemies. Did she ever say anything to you, Grant, that might be a clue?"

"No, she didn't." Grant's cold response told her she'd gone too far. "Are you from the press?"

"Absolutely not." Brett knew the game was over, and he rose. "DeeDee, you're obviously too upset about Ashley to talk about a new home now. Grant, I apologize for wasting your time. DeeDee is . . . delicate."

Grant showed them both out.

* _*

"Delicate"? They stood on the sidewalk bickering like the couple they weren't.

"What else was I supposed to say?" he countered.

"Nothing! You were supposed to say nothing! I was handling everything just fine before you and your gudzillion-dollar loafers barged in."

"Surely someone with a *Harvard* degree could have done better than ask questions that were about as subtle as a car crash."

"*Me?* I wasn't the one who wanted to start a Dumped by Ashley Hart Club."

"Okay, not my brightest moment."

She hated when he didn't fight back. His honesty made her like him even more.

"Padderson isn't a fool," he said. "I'll bet he's already Googling

DeeDee and Luther Meadows and coming up empty. We'll be lucky if he doesn't call the police."

She studied the toes of the sandals that didn't belong to her.

He studied the toggled toes of his designer loafers.

A UPS truck blew by.

He sighed. "Face it, Rory. We're lousy detectives."

"It looks a lot easier on TV," she said. "I still wish you hadn't gone to see Duncan Gilford after I told you he didn't know anything. And you had to have seen him. That's the only way you could have learned Padderson's name. It showed a lack of faith in me."

"What it showed is that the corner of your mouth tics when you lie. Did you really think I'd let you meet up with Padderson alone? He could have been a cold-blooded murderer."

"But he wasn't."

"Now we're fairly sure of that. Before today, we weren't."

She fumbled in her purse for her sunglasses. "How did you know when I'd be in his office?"

"I called the receptionist and told her I'd forgotten the time my *wife* scheduled the meeting. I guessed you'd use 'Meadows.' Fortunately, she didn't ask for your first name, or I'd have said Juliet."

"I had it under control. I didn't need your interference." She pushed on her sunglasses. "And now we can eliminate him as a suspect."

"Which puts us right back where we started."

"With Clint," she said glumly.

"I'm going to try to see him now." He glanced at his phone and then at her. "You said you need to get into my place. I should be home around seven. Why don't you meet me there, and I can show you around the kitchen. Give you a chance to try everything out."

Try *each other* out. That's what The River wanted, and they both knew it. "I'll think about it."

* *

Brett was pissed. Pissed at the universe for putting him in this situation. Pissed at Rory for being a splinter in his finger that wouldn't come out. Pissed at himself for letting his brain move into his pants and then blaming her for it.

He'd been so contemptuous of Nate Douglass for his stupid affair with Callie Capello, but this was worse. Callie lived for sex. She knew what she was doing. Rory, on the other hand, lived for laughter, chocolate, and feeding the homeless. Rory wasn't driven in the same way he was. She cared about making great chocolate, being a decent person, and driving him crazy.

He should never have told her he'd meet her at his condo tonight. He'd text her that something had come up, and he wouldn't be there. He'd say he needed to drive to Green Bay, and since he didn't like lying to her, he'd do it. He'd check in with a couple of his clients and spend the night in a suite at the Kohler resort reminding himself what was important in his life.

It was a good plan. All he had to do was follow through.

16

Rory left Brett's condo at six to make sure she was gone before he arrived. The wild mushroom lasagna rested in his now-sparkling refrigerator along with the cheeses, olives, and smoked salmon she'd bought at her favorite specialty shop. Wrapped packages of meat sat in neat stacks, and berries and figs waited for her on the counter. She'd double-checked with the rental company to make sure all the tables, linens, and dishes she'd reserved would arrive in time tomorrow. She'd even diagramed how she wanted the buffet arranged on Brett's one-of-a-kind glass and olive wood dining table that was as much sculpture as furniture. Of all the objects in his home, this was the only one she craved.

The table and the condo's owner.

Which made leaving before he appeared more necessary.

She parked the truck in the garage at her apartment and crossed the yard to the back door. If Claudia hadn't shown up last night, that tangled kiss would have reached its natural conclusion in the kind of ill-advised hookup that occurred when two people stopped thinking. Afterward, she could even have denied responsibility,

telling herself she hadn't made a real choice—it had simply occurred. But she couldn't use that excuse if she stayed at the condo
tonight because she knew exactly what would happen, and so did
Brett. This time she was doing the smart thing and letting her
brain rule. She couldn't build a future while she was getting naked
with a smooth-talking sports agent. Leaving was the right thing to
do, but that didn't mean she was happy about it.

She climbed the steps to her apartment, hitting each tread
harder than the last. She flung open the door.

Something was burning.

Spilled sugar crunched under her sneakers as she raced into the
kitchen. Kristin stood in front of the open window waving a dish
towel to dispel the smoke. Splattered mixing bowls littered the
flour-covered counter, and eggshells loitered in a brown puddle
of Rory's ninety-dollar bottle of vanilla extract. In the sink, her
eighteen-gauge commercial cookie sheet held the charred remains
of Kristin's cooking disaster.

Her stepmother looked as guilty as a family dog standing by a
shredded couch cushion. "I was going to surprise you with chocolate chip cookies."

Rory was furious at this desecration of her kitchen . . . and yet
touched. She stalked toward the mess in the sink, splashed water
over the cookie sheets, and threw a glare over her shoulder. "I
thought we talked about this. Unless Mommy's here, you're not
allowed to cook."

"I lost track of the baking time."

"Too busy mooning over your dreamy boyfriend?"

"Of course not." Kristin's snappish retort made her sound like
her old self. "And I've made chocolate chip cookies dozens of times
without this happening."

Sure she had. Kristin had made raw cookies, burned cookies, and cookies where she'd forgotten the sugar. People who didn't like sweets shouldn't try to make them.

And yet Kristin had done this to please her.

Her stepmother moved away from the window to dab at the counter mess. Rory nudged her out of the way. "Tell me about your breakfast date while I clean up."

"It wasn't a date."

"It was a date." Rory wrinkled her nose as she wiped up bargain chocolate chips that had no place in her kitchen.

"He's nice, but strange."

"How is he strange?"

"He's very literal. Everything is straightforward with him. It's . . . refreshing."

Rory regarded her curiously. "Unlike the way Dad was?"

"I didn't say that." Kristin brushed flour from the black top Rory had borrowed yesterday. Rory had returned all Kristin's clothes without her stepmother being any the wiser, although Rory had developed a fondness for the spatter-painted midi skirt. It would look great with a denim vest and moto boots. "Your father was a good man," Kristin continued. "He loved your mother very much."

Rory wasn't entirely surprised by the bitterness she heard behind Kristin's words, but only as Rory had grown older had she sensed the underlying tension in their marriage.

"I can see that you're in a mood," Kristin said. "I'll be across the hall at Toby's."

"Toby's? Since when are the two of you friends?"

"Since this afternoon. We met outside. He helped me unfreeze my phone, and I promised to proofread a document he's been working on. I probably won't understand a word, but I do know where to put a comma, and it's nice to be needed." With a pointed look, she flounced out.

Rory finished cleaning up the kitchen and set to work on the slow-cooked apple butter chicken she planned to turn into mini sliders tomorrow. She was a good cook, but not a trained chef, and for what Brett was paying her, this party had to be over-the-top special. The buffet menu she planned was creative without being pretentious, comfort food with a touch of luxe, things like lobster mac and cheese and skirt steak skewers with a balsamic reduction. For fun, she was serving hot dogs with melted Gruyère, caramelized onions, and a sprinkle of fresh thyme, all items she was fairly sure she could handle.

In addition to roping Toby in to tend the bar, Becky Evans, Jon's friend, would serve. Becky was meeting her at the condo early tomorrow afternoon to set up tables and prep the charcuterie tower, while Rory completed the main dishes and put the finishing touches on dessert. As the guests were enjoying the food, she'd stack the sample boxes with her precious chocolates on the table by the front door and say a little prayer.

She wondered how Brett had reacted when he came home to an empty condo. Maybe he, too, realized how insane it was for the two of them to be alone together.

* *

Instead of overnighting in Green Bay, Brett opened the door to his condo a little before seven o'clock, but no curly-haired chocolatier bopped out to greet him. She'd been here. Hell, yes, she'd been here. His refrigerator shelves were full of food, warming trays sat on his counters, and a paper towel held a single dark chocolate truffle along with a note that read: *Pairs with common sense.*

He wolfed it down in one bite, stormed into his bedroom, and grabbed his gym bag.

*

Rory had another fitful night's sleep on the couch, plagued by a nightmare in which she had to make dinner for the British royal family with only a banana and a can of Pringles, all while Brett and Callie were making out on a sandy beach in the next room. She awakened with a backache and a nervous stomach, but after she'd taken a shower and eaten a hard-boiled egg, she was ready to face the day. Until her phone pinged with an incoming text. And just like that, her day fell apart.

"What's wrong?" Kristin came out of the bedroom as Rory stared at her phone, her stomach twisting.

"I can't believe this . . . My server for tonight flaked out." Rory thought she'd planned for every contingency, but she hadn't planned for this.

"You look like someone died."

"Worse!" Rory shot up from the couch. "Becky was meeting me at the condo at noon to help with prep and to get ready to serve. Brett wants to sign Tyler Capello, so he's invited some of the city's top athletes to meet him. I can't cook and serve!" Rory hugged her stomach. If she still lived in Manhattan, she could find a friend to step in, but she had no one here.

"I'll help."

Rory spun to face her. "You?"

"If Toby can bartend, I'm sure I can serve."

"Toby bartended all the way through college."

Kristin pursed her lips. "You said this was a buffet. I'm sure I can manage setting out a few clean plates."

Kristin understood nothing about Rory's world. "It's more than setting out plates. A good server should be ready to describe what's in every dish. Food has to be replenished and refreshed. If someone drops a fork, they need a new one before they know it's gone."

"Hardly rocket science." Kristin sniffed.

"What if someone recognizes you? How am I supposed to explain Clint Garrett's mother on the catering staff?"

"People see what they expect to see. If anyone notices, they'll just think there's a resemblance."

Brett wouldn't think that. If he found his star client's mother mopping up spills, he'd freak. "Servers have to know when it's time to bus a dish. Nothing's worse than having your food whipped away before you can take your last bite. And I need help prepping this afternoon. Lots of help."

"Do you want me or not?" Kristin said belligerently.

Rory swallowed her misgivings. "You need to do exactly what I tell you. No ignoring me. No arguing."

Kristin gave her a smarmy smile. "As long as you don't make me eat liver, we'll do just fine." Her smile faded. "And I need something to keep me busy."

Rory understood, and she softened. "Thanks. I appreciate it."

★

Kristin was her normal disaster in the kitchen. She let the milk boil over for the lobster mac and cheese sauce, forcing Rory to start again. Pistachio shells ended up in the raw vegetable salad, and a carton of eggs met their fate on the kitchen floor. Rory didn't dare trust her with a knife, let alone a mandoline, to work on the charcuterie tower, but when the florist and rental company arrived, Kristin was in her element.

She quickly transformed Brett's stark black and gray interior into a warm party space, strategically positioning the tables in the living area, foyer, and on the patio balcony by the bar. She sweet-talked the men from the rental company into moving Brett's unwieldy concrete coffee table out of the way, something Rory hadn't thought of, and arranged the dining room chairs into casual seating groups with small tables nearby to hold glasses.

"Impressive." Rory eyed the flowers Kristin had rearranged by the painting of the rusty oilcan, making the artwork look chic instead of ridiculous. "If I were paying you, I'd give you a bonus."

"Go back to the kitchen where you belong."

"Yes, ma'am."

As Rory changed into black slacks, a white shirt, and the hunter-green chef's apron that complemented her Crayola-colored Vans high-tops, she listened for Brett's arrival. He'd be upset when he saw Kristin here. She wondered whether he'd also been upset about her ditching him last night. Refastening the bandana around her hair, she returned to the kitchen.

She'd just finished making the dressing for the raw vegetable salad when he appeared. Drawing his eyes away from her butt, he swiped some Marcona almonds from the counter. "How much is this costing me?"

"You didn't give me a budget." She tossed the strip steak in the marinade. "You also refused to look at the menu I emailed you. Something about how I shouldn't bother you with details because you're way too important to waste time listening to an insignificant person like myself who should already know how to throw an impressive party, even though she'd specifically told you she wasn't a caterer."

"I know I didn't say that."

"A loose interpretation. As for money, I'll send your assistant—who's a lot more informative than you are—an itemized bill." She flapped a hot pad at him before either of them could bring up last night. "Now please get out of my kitchen?"

"Technically my kitchen."

"Not tonight."

He smiled, grabbed a few more almonds, and disappeared . . . only to explode back in a few moments later. "What the hell is Kristin doing here?"

She stalled. "You'll have to ask her. I have no idea what goes through that woman's head."

"I'm asking you."

Her best strategy was to dodge and distract. She raked her eyes over him, letting her gaze travel from his slicked-back hair to his delectable chest, all the way down to his crotch. "You look so hot. And I mean that in a totally sexual way."

He narrowed his eyes at her. "You are nothing but talk, lady. And right now, the mother of my thirty-four-million-dollar quarterback is cleaning my guest bathroom."

"Don't worry. She'll do a good job."

The person who was her current employer emitted a sound resembling a growl. She scrambled for something to say that would derail this conversation. "We can't have an affair."

"We'll see about that. Right now, I want to know why Kristin's here."

She tried again. "It's not that I don't want to have an affair with you. Obviously, I do—you being you and all—but I'd only end up hating you."

"In what rusty corner of your brain did you draw that conclusion?"

"We clearly live in different universes, and you'd immediately dump me for a twenty-year-old beach volleyball player. Plus, childhood trauma. It's not good for me to have an affair with anyone who's part of my brother's world. As for Kristin, if you have issues, you'll have to talk to her. She and I barely speak."

He knew there was a flaw in her argument, but he couldn't quite find it. Muttering under his breath, he stalked off to find his quarterback's mother.

*
★

Kristin frowned at him. "Helping Rory tonight is exactly the distraction I need. I can hardly function from worrying about Clint."

"I understand." He called on all his diplomacy. "But Rory should never have let you—"

"She was shorthanded, and this was my decision."

He saw the same determination in her that he'd witnessed in her son and stepdaughter. These Garretts were going to ruin him.

She gestured toward her plain white blouse and black pants. "Don't worry. No one will recognize me. And if they do, I'll handle it. Now I need to finish setting up the buffet table before Rory sees me slacking. You know how unreasonable she is."

Did he ever. And she wasn't the only unreasonable one.

Giving up, he took a quick shower and changed into gray pants and a black sport shirt before he went out to survey what else had transpired since he'd left that morning.

The place had never looked more inviting: chairs rearranged into informal seating groups, navy linen tablecloths, flowers everywhere. The tantalizing smells coming from the kitchen reminded him that, with the exception of a couple of almonds, he hadn't eaten anything since a bowl of Cheerios that morning.

He went into the dining room, where Rory had constructed some kind of hors d'oeuvre tower as a centerpiece on his table. It was an impressive engineering feat, with assorted glass plates balancing different sizes of bowls. And the food . . . A mountain of fruits, cheeses, meats, olives, and nuts, along with crackers, flatbreads, and dips. Curls of smoked salmon, coins of chorizo, and bowls of shrimp flecked with lemon peel and onion. If tonight's party wasn't enough to impress Tyler, Callie, and the rest of his guests, he couldn't imagine what would be.

The balcony patio held a bar and potted trees that hadn't been there this morning. He was good with faces, and he recognized the bartender as the IT guy who lived across the hall from Rory. He opened the folding glass doors and stepped out. "Toby, right? I met you at Rory's place. Glad you could help her tonight."

"Happy to. What would you like?"

"Scotch on the rocks. Lots of rocks. It's going to be a long evening." As Toby made the drink, Brett decided to do some probing. "Rory's pretty upset about what happened to Ashley. Did you know her well?"

Toby didn't look at him. "I was crazy about her, but she only saw me as a friend."

Brett wondered if the police had investigated Toby's whereabouts that morning. As Toby handed over his drink, Brett heard Callie Capello's voice. His first guests had arrived. Taking a slug of his drink, he went to greet her.

Callie was decked out in a skintight white jumpsuit, long black hair extensions, and a palette of makeup. She dodged the hand he extended and kissed his cheek instead, landing too close to his mouth. He quickly drew back and looked over her shoulder for her son. "Where's Tyler?" Sensing she was getting ready to squeeze his ass, he took a quick step back.

"He's with some friends at Navy Pier. He'll show up soon."

Shit. The whole purpose of this party was to impress Tyler, and the kid wasn't here.

She slid her tongue along the seam of her lips. "You're looking as fine as ever, Brett Rivers."

"Let's get you a drink." And then, because he was the most reprehensible human being on earth . . . "You'll like the bartender. A nice young guy named Toby."

"Yum. But first . . . Where's your sexy assistant?"

He might be reprehensible, but he wasn't that reprehensible. "Hard at work." He caught her by the elbow and steered her toward the bar as Kristin emerged from the back hallway.

In the few minutes since he'd last seen her, she'd washed off her makeup and put on glasses. Her hair was parted severely down the middle and clipped behind her ears with barrettes. Those few changes had transformed her into one of those people no one tended to notice.

His doorbell rang. Lowering her chin like a servant in an English manor house, Kristin went to answer it.

*

By nine o'clock, the party was in full swing. Brett had mingled with every guest, and only a few of them had been thickheaded enough to mention Clint's arrest. Rory's demolished hors d'oeuvre tower had been replaced with a spectacular buffet offering something for everyone: meat lovers, vegetarians, big eaters, and dieters. The drinks were flowing, conversation was lively, and Rory had put together a great playlist. The party couldn't be going better except for one serious problem. Tyler Capello still hadn't shown up.

"You might want to rescue my husband." He gazed down at Annabelle Granger Champion, his boss's wife. "Mrs. Capello seems to have him cornered."

Like Rory, Annabelle had curly hair, but hers was auburn instead of honey blond, and she was a few inches shorter than Rory. "It would probably work better if you rescued him," Brett said. "But don't let her kiss you." And then, as an afterthought: "Unless you want her to."

She laughed. He'd been surprised when he'd first met Annabelle, having imagined Heath's wife as a turbocharged fashion model instead of this diminutive matchmaker to both the young and elderly.

"It's a great party, Brett."

That was true. More than the forty guests he'd invited had shown up: Chicago Stars and Bears players, a shortstop from the White Sox, a Cubs' starting pitcher, and one of the Blackhawks. Karloh Cousins had brought along a couple of his teammates. And still, Rory hadn't run out of food. He wished she were out here with him enjoying the party instead of doing all the work. As for Kristin . . . Each time he saw her carrying a dirty dish, he wanted to step in and do the job for her, but the one time he'd tried, she'd discreetly stepped on his foot. So far, not even Heath had recognized her. Her version of an invisibility cloak was working.

Heath had finally escaped Callie, and he sidled up next to his wife. "Where's Tyler, Brett?"

"Not here yet." It wasn't hard to pick up on Heath's displeasure. "How did you get along with Callie?"

"I still have my pants zipped, so I'm doing better than Nate. The question is, How are you getting along with her?"

"Still pure as the driven snow."

Annabelle frowned toward the woman who'd been hitting on her husband. "Signing Tyler Capello strikes me as more trouble than he's worth."

"You're wrong!"

"No way!" Brett and Heath exclaimed in unison.

Annabelle regarded Brett with disapproval. "You're still young, so I can understand your skewed view of life, but you . . ." She glared at her husband. "You should know better than to make your life harder."

Heath's expression softened in the way it did only when he was with his wife. "Not mine. Brett's."

Witnessing the intimacy between them made something ache inside Brett. He'd never know this kind of relationship.

The feeling passed as quickly as it had appeared. The kind of unspoken communication he had with Rory proved people didn't have to be married to have a close relationship. He and Rory could practically read each other's minds. People made life way too complicated.

Kristin emerged from the kitchen with a clean tray. Annabelle was staring at her, and he quickly tried to distract her. "What have your kids been up to?"

It was too late.

"Mrs. Garrett?"

Kristin turned at the sound of Annabelle's voice. They must have met at the annual bash the agency threw for its clients. Kristin nodded at her. Clearly confused, Annabelle took in her server's uniform. Not one for subtlety, she cut to the chase: "But why?"

Kristin moved closer, keeping her voice low. "I'm helping out my stepdaughter. She's catering the party."

Brett winced.

Heath moved to his wife's side, speaking as pleasantly as a Python could before it squeezed the life out of its victim. In this case, the victim being Brett. "Your stepdaughter is catering this party? Clint's sister?"

"Half sister," Kristin replied. "She's a wonderful cook, as you can see."

Annabelle nodded. "And you don't want anyone to recognize you."

Kristin gave her a wan smile. "How am I doing?"

"We won't tell a soul."

As Kristin returned to her duties, Heath caught Brett's shoulder in a viselike grip. "My office. First thing Monday morning."

*
*

Rory's feet hurt, her back ached, she'd cut her finger and burned her hand, but none of it mattered. The evening was going perfectly. The perishable leftovers were stacked in the refrigerator, the rest in containers on the counter. She'd run out of French onion hot dogs and been down to her last few lettuce wraps, but other than that, she'd made enough to feed everyone. The sample boxes of chocolates were stacked by the front door. She prayed her investment would pay off. Now, all she needed to do was pull off her showcase dessert.

"It smells like heaven in here." Callie Capello stood inside the doorway.

Callie wasn't the first guest who'd popped into the kitchen, but none had stayed long. Tyler's mother, however, looked as though she wanted to settle in for a chat. Rory gave her a brief nod. "Mrs. Capello."

"It's Callie, remember?" She gestured toward the dishes waiting for space in the dishwasher, which hummed quietly in the background. "The food was delicious. You're a talented woman."

"I hope you're having a good time." Rory bent down to check the last of her oversized chocolate lava cakes. Her bake timing had to be perfect. The cakes needed to be cooked all the way through without burning the edges or drying up the gooey centers.

"It's a great party," Callie said.

The dishwasher beeped, signaling the end of the last load. A cloud of steam escaped as Rory opened the door. She'd been using the machine's express function all evening, so she had to hand-dry the hot dishes, and she grabbed a towel. "Is Tyler enjoying himself?"

"He's not here."

Rory's hands stalled as she reached for a plate. "What do you mean? He's not at the party?"

"He met some friends at Navy Pier earlier." Callie adjusted the neckline on her clinging white jumpsuit, nudging it a bit lower on her cleavage instead of tugging it up. "He said he'd be here, but he must have gotten sidetracked."

In none of Kristin's trips to the kitchen had she mentioned that the guest of honor was missing, but they'd been too busy for anything more than a quick exchange of instructions. "I don't understand. Brett planned the party just for him."

Callie shrugged.

Rory grabbed a dry dish towel. "This is so not cool. Call him and tell him he needs to be here."

Callie lifted a perfectly arched dark eyebrow at her. "You're very bossy."

"What he's doing isn't right. Brett threw this party just for him."

"I suppose." As Rory removed another hot dinner plate with the dish towel, Callie pulled her phone from a small silver shoulder bag and made a call. "Tyler, get over here. Now."

Apparently, Tyler wasn't used to arguing with *madre*, because she hung up without waiting for a response. "He'll be here." She rested her hips against the counter, a position that thrust her impressive breasts forward, and purred at Rory. "So how have you been?"

Rory was tired, the dishes were hot, and she had to pee. "Honestly, I'm into guys, but you're an excellent kisser."

Callie laughed. "I've been around so many bullshitters lately. It's refreshing to be with someone who's upfront."

Rory added another clean plate to the plastic crate that held the growing pile of rented dishes. "This is a perfect opportunity for me to point out that Brett is the king of no-bullshitters. At least with his clients. I'm not so sure about his personal relationships. Not that I care."

Callie smiled. "You're adorable."

"Thanks." The oven timer pinged. "Excuse me. I need to take care of this."

"I'll leave you alone. Thanks for the memory."

Rory laughed.

★

Brett had given up on Tyler appearing when his guest of honor finally walked through the door. Unfortunately, he wasn't alone. Tommy Landom was attached to his side.

"Nice crib you got here, Rivers," Landom said, his speech slurred, gait unsteady.

Without apologizing for being late, Tyler broke away from Landom and made a beeline for the Cubs' pitcher. Heath, standing near the fireplace, spotted both Tyler and Landom. He shot Brett a fiery glare that made Brett feel as if the senior vice presidency was in danger of melting.

Brett moved toward Landom. He reeked of cologne and whiskey. "What are you doing here, Tommy?"

"Keeping an eye on my boy, that's all."

"Doesn't seem like he's your boy anymore."

"It ain't over till it's over."

Just as Brett prepared to forcibly walk Landom back out the door, Kristin appeared from the kitchen carrying an ornate serving tray displaying an array of dome-shaped chocolate cakes in various sizes. Rory came next. She'd straightened the curly ponytail under her bandana since he'd last checked up on her, and instead of the green apron she'd had on earlier, she wore a pristine white one. Whatever makeup she'd begun the evening with had worn off, but she still looked cute as hell.

She carried a bowl holding a wire sieve filled with what looked like powdered sugar to a table Kristin had cleared in the living area. Clearly something was up, and the guests gathered round to see, even Tyler.

Kristin set down the tray. Rory lifted the sugar-filled wire sieve from the bowl and positioned it over the cakes to dust them. From the pocket of her apron, she pulled a small butane kitchen torch. "Ready for dessert?"

The mood was upbeat, and someone in the crowd blew a whistle. Rory held the sieve in one hand, the torch in the other. With a quick press of her thumb, the torch flared, the sugar drifted down from the sieve, and a blazing orange fireball erupted over the cakes.

The onlookers gasped and erupted into applause as the fireball disappeared.

"Again!"

"How'd you do that?"

"Let's see it again."

His guests were clearly impressed.

She smiled, tapped the sugar over the cakes—simultaneously hitting the trigger on the torch—and produced another fireball. Damn, Rory was good at this. If only his boss didn't know he'd hired her as his caterer and Clint's mother weren't hauling dirty dishes, this would be a great party.

After a few more demonstrations, Kristin removed the bowl of sugar, and Rory cut into the first cake.

A river of chocolate gushed from the center.

As the guests lined up for their serving, she pointed out separate bowls of toasted nuts, coconut, raspberries, and whipped cream for anyone who wanted a topping. He intended to take his cake straight.

"Dude, this is a great party." Tyler Capello sidled up next to him. "I shoulda got here earlier."

You think? "Glad you could make it, Tyler. Have you met Akeem Deever yet? I'll introduce you to—"

The gauzy drapes by the patio doors burst into flames.

17

Someone screamed. Rory made a dash for the kitchen. Brett snatched up a pillow to smother the flames. Annabelle Champion stepped in to help, but Heath pushed her out of the way and grabbed another pillow. Callie dragged her baby boy to safety as acrid smoke began filling the room.

Out of the corner of his eye Brett saw Tommy Landom staring in drunken disbelief at the butane torch he was holding. That *asshole*! Landom dropped the torch and ran.

The draft from the open patio doors fed the flames as the guests fled the condo. Karloh Cousins helped up a woman who'd slipped on one of the many pieces of chocolate lava cake littering the floor. Toby shoved the portable bar to the end of the balcony, keeping the alcohol away from the fire. A tablecloth burst into flames, the overhead sprinklers came on, and the guests, with the exception of Heath and Annabelle Champion, ran for the door.

Rory raced from the kitchen with the fire extinguisher Brett had forgotten was there. "Stand back." She aimed the nozzle at the flames, pulled the pin, and squeezed the trigger, wielding the extinguisher as expertly as a Ghostbuster with a proton pack. The flames gradually died, but the sprinklers kept running.

Rory stood in the ruins of his party looking as miserable as a woman could look—clothes soaked, dripping bandana hanging from the end of her ponytail, fire extinguisher at her side.

By the time the building superintendent had the sprinklers turned off, only Brett, Rory, Kristin, Toby, and the Champions were left. "You sure know how to throw a party," Heath said through gritted teeth.

Brett dragged up his star quarterback's mother who was on her hands and knees, crawling through soggy paddies of lava cake to pick up broken plates. "I'll take it from here, Kristin."

Unlike her husband, Annabelle tended to look on the bright side. "The good news is, everyone will be talking about this party for years."

"That they will." Heath gave an ominous jerk of his head toward the untouched dining room. Brett followed, walking with the false confidence of a man whose career wasn't crashing around him.

The Python stopped by the table. "Let's do a roundup here. Your top client is charged with murder, his mother is crawling on the floor doing cleanup, his *sister* has been working her ass off in your kitchen when she should have been a guest, and topping it all off, Tyler Capello—a player you have *not* signed—shows up at your party with his slimy ex-agent who sets your place on fire. Is that about right?" He punched out the words. "Am I missing anything?"

The River was never at a loss for words. Until now.

"I've seen some fuckups over the years," Champion said, "but this just moved to the top of the list. What exactly is going on with you that I don't know about?"

So much. "A weird set of circumstances, that's all."

"This had better be the last weird circumstance." The Python wasn't done with him. "Do you know what I planned for tomorrow? I planned to be out on the lake with my family enjoying the sun in a sweet little thirty-two-foot sailboat. Instead, I'll be fielding phone calls, and that puts me at the top of my wife's shit list, which is not a place I want to be and where I wouldn't be if you weren't dropping the ball!" He coiled. "I never thought I'd have to say this to you, of all people, but I'm disappointed." He turned away and headed back to the living room, possibly taking Brett's future along with him.

The Champions left, and Kristin accepted Toby's offer to drive her back to the apartment. On her way out the door, she stopped and went over to Rory. "I'm sorry," she said. "You worked so hard."

Technically, he was the one who deserved condolences since this was his place and his career, but Rory was taking it hard. Her shoulders drooped, her arms hung listlessly at her sides—the feisty spirit so fundamental to her character kicked right out of her. A painful constriction gripped his chest. "Do you have dry clothes here?" He sounded both gruff and gentle, not sure how he felt.

She shook her head, turned her back on him, and retreated to the kitchen, her wet Crayola high-tops squeaking on the floor.

Only the sprinklers in the main living area and foyer had been activated, but the whole place reeked of smoke, his lungs burned, and they needed to get out of here. He headed to his bedroom and tossed a change of clothes into his weekender.

*
*

Rory stared at the crates the rental company provided for dishes and glassware, immobilized by the shock of what had happened. Brett came up behind her. Soot streaked his face and neck, his black shirt was ruined, and he had a hole in his pants.

"I'll take care of everything tomorrow," he said. "Let's go."

"I can't leave all this."

He reached around to the front of her waist and untied her wet apron. "There's nothing more we can do tonight."

Bewildered, she stared at him. "But I don't understand. I set the torch on the back of the table. It wasn't close to anything."

"Tommy Landom spotted it. He was drunk, and I'm guessing he wanted to attempt your sugar trick for himself."

She wrung her hands. "This is all my fault."

Brett regarded her with so much pity she wanted to choke him. "You didn't do anything wrong," he said. "It was a great party. Right up to the end." He slipped his arm around her and steered her from the kitchen.

She'd thought the worst was behind her, but she was wrong. As she reached the foyer, she saw all the sample boxes of her finest chocolates lying on the floor in a soggy pyramid.

*
*

Brett didn't trust Rory's broken-down truck, so he followed her home and walked her up to her apartment. It still held the lingering scents of the cooking she'd done for the party. This shabby place with its squeaky floors, saggy couch, and homey smells felt more welcoming than his condo ever had. Her face was pale, and he touched her cheek. "You're not going to start crying on me, are you?"

She blinked her eyes hard. "I'm a thug. Thugs don't cry."

She was breaking his heart. Or at least she would be breaking his heart if he had one. Her dirty white T-shirt had a trio of tiny burn marks near her breast, she'd lost her bandana, and she looked as dispirited as a field goal kicker who'd missed the uprights from the twenty-yard line.

"What are you going to do?" she said numbly.

"Check into a hotel for a couple of days. I'll deal with insurance tomorrow." An easy task compared with facing Heath again. Only a few weeks ago, Brett had been on top of the world, ready for the next upward swing in his star-kissed career, and now here he was.

"You can't check into a hotel looking like that," she said. "Use my shower."

"You go first. You need it worse."

Twenty minutes later, she came out of the bathroom wearing one of those white robes that looked like an old-fashioned bedspread, and she had a towel wrapped around her head. Since she hadn't taken any clean clothes into the bathroom, he guessed she was naked underneath, an erotic image that made him forget about his own damp clothes. He pulled himself together. "Feeling better?"

"The bathroom's yours."

She hadn't answered his question. He grabbed the suitcase he'd just brought up from his car. "There's a grilled cheese sandwich waiting for you in the kitchen. I'm betting you didn't have time to eat."

"You made me grilled cheese?"

"I have skills."

"Thanks." Her smile was so sad it barely registered.

*

The bread was perfectly toasted and the cheddar deliciously gooey. He'd even cut it into two triangles. Brett Rivers did everything well, but she could take only a few bites. The image of those small, waterlogged boxes of her sample chocolates was forever imprinted in her mind.

She abandoned the sandwich on her coffee table and slumped into the couch. So much for introducing her chocolates to Chicago's moneyed athletes. She'd used up her remaining supplies, failed miserably, and it was time to give up. Sell the Royal Palace of Sweets, pay off her debts, and support herself working catering jobs. Jobs that would take up all her time and suck her soul right out of her. Once again, she'd walk away. Once again, she'd prove that she wasn't tough enough to dig in.

But she still had the ability to work hard, didn't she? And she still knew how to make exceptional chocolate. What if she didn't quit? What if, despite this failure, she didn't walk away? What if, instead, she dug in deeper?

Brett emerged from the bathroom in the clothes she most loved seeing him wear: gym shorts and a T-shirt. She had nothing on under her robe, and she pulled it closed over her legs as she welcomed the distraction of those neat comb marks scoring his wet hair. "Your hair always puts me in a bad mood."

"Interesting. Your hair puts me in a good mood. Now why don't you say everything you need to say so you'll feel better?"

"I'm sorry." She met his gaze. "I wanted everything to be perfect."

"Everything you did *was* perfect," he said. "This is on me. I should have kicked Tommy's ass out the second he walked in."

"You're not the one who decided to light the dessert on fire." She dropped her head into her hands. "I was showing off, and now your home is ruined."

"The place is insured, and a restoration company will take care of the mess." He picked up the grilled cheese triangle she'd abandoned. "Sit up straight and stop feeling guilty." He set the sandwich back on the coffee table without taking a bite. "I'm more worried about my career than about my condo."

She'd never heard him express any vulnerability, and she studied him more closely. He looked away. "Forget about it. I'll be fine."

He regretted even this small display of insecurity, and she experienced a stirring of pity. Would anything ever be enough for him? She touched his bare thigh and said quietly, "Because you're The River."

He stared straight ahead. "Exactly."

She rested her head on his shoulder. "You don't have to be invincible, you know. Sometimes rivers dry up or maybe overflow their banks. Shit happens."

He wrapped his arm around her. "Not to this River."

The door swung open. Kristin froze as she saw them cuddled on the couch. "Oops."

Rory and Brett sprang apart.

An awkward silence fell.

Rory leaped up and tried to deflect. "Where have you been, young lady?"

"Toby and I were hungry. We went to Denny's. I'll be right back." She disappeared into the hallway.

Rory dropped back on the couch. "As if everything isn't already awful enough, now she's going to get all up in my face about what do I think I'm doing hooking up with a guy where there's no future?"

Brett had also come to his feet. "We aren't hooking up, and you're thirty-four years old. I seriously doubt she's going to get up in your face about anything." Still, he'd already put a good ten feet between them and looked as uncomfortable as she did. And the more uncomfortable he looked, the sadder she felt.

Theirs was the classic forbidden relationship. She posed a threat to his career, and he was a direct pathway to heartbreak. The only reason their relationship had lasted this long was because they were trying to help Clint. In an ideal world, maybe they'd be real friends. That was what she needed. A good friend. That was what they both needed. She'd left her friends behind when she'd moved, and Brett had clients instead of friends. And he had her. But the sexual heat that kept flaring between them was ruining everything.

Kristin popped back in from the hallway. "Toby's letting me move into his second bedroom."

"You don't have to go anywhere," Mr. Cool said from the kitchen doorway, as far as he could get from Rory. "I'm going to a hotel."

"I think it's better if I leave," Kristin said.

Rory pulled the sash of her robe tighter as she protested. "It's not like that. It's— We're friends. Brett believes his clients are his friends, but they're not because he always has to be on his guard when he's around them. But with me, he has nothing at stake."

Kristin held up her hand. "I see nothing. I know nothing. Let me get a few things, and then I'm out of here."

Rory gazed at Brett. Two sharp ridges had formed between his eyebrows. Kristin quickly reappeared with a toothbrush and a pair of pajamas draped over her arm. "Enjoy yourselves."

"We're not going to enjoy—"

She was already out the door.

Rory drew her hands into fists. "All I want is for us to be *friends*!"

"Not realistic," he said stonily.

"Of course it is!" She jumped up and stalked toward him. "We just have to set our minds to it."

He advanced on her. "And how am I supposed to do that when I'm around you? You with your—your gin-bottle eyes—"

"'*Gin* bottle'?!"

"—and ridiculous clothes that don't cover anything up!"

"My clothes cover *everything* up!"

He loomed over her. "And your sass and those legs—"

"Don't you dare criticize my legs! Just because my thighs rub doesn't mean—"

"And your hair!"

"My hair again! I can't help—"

"All those curls I want to sink my hands into." To her shock, he did just that. His fingers tugged, not hurting, the harsh angles of his face softening. "And that smart mouth of yours."

She gazed into his gray gangster's eyes. "What's wrong with my mouth?"

His voice dropped to a whisper. "Not a damn thing."

Their lips hovered. His thumbs cradled her jaw, brushed the corners of her mouth. The two of them alone in the world.

He tilted up her chin and kissed her, the sweetest kiss she'd ever received. Until the sweetness turned fierce.

She pressed against him. His hands slipped under her butt, drawing her off her feet. Her bathrobe gaped at the neck, pressing the inner curves of her breasts against the soft fabric of his T-shirt. She looped her arms around his neck.

He carried her to the bedroom, their kiss deepening, growing restless, all thrust and parry. She slid down his body. As her feet touched the floor, the robe slipped on her arms, catching on her elbows, freeing her breasts. He dropped his gaze. She hijacked their kiss. He tugged at the sash of her robe, and it slithered to the floor.

He took in her body as if he'd never seen a naked woman, and for the first time since they'd met, the smooth-talking River seemed to be at a loss for words. Until he wasn't. "God, you're beautiful."

She should have felt self-conscious, but she didn't. This was her body: trim waist, curvy thighs and hips, a little bow to her stomach. She'd had no reason to wax, and she needed to shave her legs. But her body was healthy, strong, and all hers. "I'm not beautiful," she said. "I'm just me."

"More than enough," he said hoarsely. His hands cupped the backs of her thighs, once again pulling her up. She wrapped her legs around his waist, opening herself to his agile, searching fingers.

It was crazy time. Wild, wild kisses. An awkward landing on the bed. She grabbed the waistband of his gym shorts. "Off."

He sat upright, but only removed his T-shirt. Eyes glazed, he kissed her again.

They tangled. Her hands slipped inside the elastic waistband of his shorts. It didn't take her long to find what she wanted.

He groaned as she explored. She didn't remember his body. It was as if she were seeing it all for the first time.

The gym shorts disappeared, and his hands were all over her, using his masterful mind-reading powers to discover what pleased her the most.

Legs splayed. Wet. Open. Fingers. Mouth.

An eternity passed in minutes, hours. She fell apart.

He barely gave her time to recover before he moved on top of her. His face was flushed, his eyes tarnished. "Beautiful," he whispered.

And then he was inside her, and it started all over again.

Rory awakened the next morning with Brett still asleep next to her. Instead of brooding over the challenges that lay before her, she let herself enjoy his scent—sex, spice, and the remnant of his aftershave. She propped herself on her elbow and gazed at his bare torso, glad that he didn't manscape. She wasn't used to seeing him at rest, and yet even in sleep, there were subtle movements. A twitch of his foot, the flutter of his eyelids. In some part of his brain, he was still alert. She wanted him all over again. God, she loved this man.

She bolted straight up. She most certainly did *not* love this man!

Except she did love him. Despite every lecture she'd given herself, she'd fallen in love. What was *wrong* with her? She grabbed her pillow and whacked him over the head. "Get out!"

He groaned and gradually peeled open one eye. "Very . . . grouchy."

His gravelly morning voice made him even more irresistible. She fought the urge to trace the contour of his cheekbones with her finger. He propped an arm behind his head and studied her through half-lidded eyes.

She jumped out of bed and snatched up her chenille robe from the floor. "You're trying to figure out how fast you can get out of here, right?"

"Wrong." He sat higher against the headboard, watching as she slipped her arms into the sleeves. "It's complicated, that's all." He ran his hand through his rumpled hair. "I didn't use a condom. I didn't even think of it."

She grabbed the pillow from the bed and whapped him again. "I'm on the pill! And we don't have any STDs. You know all that, so chill!"

He confiscated the pillow and dropped it over the far side of the bed out of her reach. "I always use a condom."

"I'll be sure to let you know if I'm pregnant." She jerked the sash closed on her robe. "You can raise it."

"Not funny."

More upset with herself than with him, she stepped over his gym shorts and Nikes on her way to the bedroom door. She stopped, determined to erect an unbreachable barrier between them. "I do not love you," she said. "Not even close. Get that idea right out of your egotistical head."

"It wasn't exactly in my head, but thanks for clarifying."

"I mean it. Your asshole personality is of no interest to me. Only your body."

The tightness around his mouth gave way to a lazy grin. He slid out of bed. "Speaking of bodies . . ." The man was sexual dynamite, all naked, hot, and hunky, with the devil in his eyes. "Let me see yours again." The bow she'd just tied in the sash of her robe came undone with a tug of his hand.

Just one more time. One more time and never again.

She didn't try to stop him as he took control, tossing her back in bed, moving her this way and that, dominating her in the most thrilling way.

But he wasn't the only one who knew how to take charge, and

after he'd given her his best, she set aside every one of her misgivings and took her turn. "On your back."

She was almost shocked when he complied, although he looked wary.

"Now," she said, in her newly discovered dominatrix voice, "you'll do exactly what I tell you." She splayed her fingers across his bare chest. "Or else . . ."

*
*

Rory showered, twisted her hair into a messy bun, and, not bothering with makeup, pulled on capris and a faded black tank top. She was worrying her bottom lip when Kristin came in without knocking, still in her pajamas. "I heard Brett leave."

"Nothing happened between us," Rory lied, as she padded on bare feet into the kitchen to make coffee. Brett hadn't given her a good-bye kiss when he'd left half an hour ago to get doughnuts, but they'd exchanged more than their share of kisses in the bedroom.

Kristin followed her to the kitchen, looking exactly as she'd looked when Rory had told her she'd been at the mall with Jenna Willis when she'd really been in Jenna's basement making out with Will Gibson. But this time, Kristin didn't feel like the enemy, and lying seemed another example of taking the easy way out. Rory carried the carafe to the sink. "Fine. *Everything* happened between us, and he went out for doughnuts, and I don't want to talk about it."

"Oh, Rory . . ." Kristin's sigh sounded more troubled than disapproving.

"You never like any of my boyfriends."

Rory's pathetic attempt at humor fell flat, and Kristin's look of concern only deepened. Rory abandoned the carafe in the sink. "I know, I know. Hooking up with him is stupid. He's Clint's agent, and all he cares about is his job and making money. Plus, he's him, and I'm me."

"There's nothing wrong with you," Kristin said sharply, "but there's a lot wrong with him."

Rory bristled, but before she could defend him, Kristin went on. "I like Brett Rivers. He's smart and ethical, he knows the business, and he takes excellent care of his clients. But as a romantic partner . . . ? The man does nothing but work." She leaned against the refrigerator, crossing her arms. "Rory, you deserve so much more."

"Who said anything about romance?" Rory could only be so forthcoming. "This is purely about sex," she muttered.

"He oozes testosterone. I get it. But women are extraneous to his life. If he does decide to let one in, she'll be a distant second to his career."

"I've always understood that."

Kristin nodded, and her hand came to rest gently on Rory's shoulder. Rory wanted to lean her cheek against it. Instead, she turned on the faucet and filled the coffee carafe.

Kristin stepped away. "I have to get dressed. I invited Daniel to a picnic in Millennium Park this afternoon, but first, I need to move my things into Toby's apartment."

Rory stared at her. "What are you talking about?"

"Toby's company is sending him to Washington for a week, and I'm staying at his place while he's gone."

"You don't have to do that."

"Somebody needs to take care of Luther, and it's time you got your bedroom back."

*

Brett returned not long after Kristin left. "I wasn't sure what you like, so I got one of everything." He set a big box of doughnuts on the coffee table. "Except chocolate. I didn't want to mess up your palate."

"Thoughtful. I'll get the coffee." She filled two mugs and returned to the living room. He was sitting on the couch, legs extended, staring at nothing. The easiness between them had disappeared. She handed over his mug and sat next to him without touching him. "This is the longest I've seen you off your phone, except in Michigan when you didn't have a choice."

"I sneaked in a few calls while I was on the doughnut run."

"Good to know you haven't lost your edge." As he lifted the lid on the box, she took in its contents. "Two dozen?"

"Options."

Like last night, she thought. So many options. She bypassed a vanilla frosted doughnut with sprinkles for a French cruller only to set it back down, acting as if she couldn't make up her mind when, in reality, the awkwardness between them had stifled her appetite.

His dark blue mug read, "Got Chocolate?" He took a sip. "I saw what happened to those little boxes of chocolates you made. You were going to give them to everyone when they left, weren't you?"

"Great idea I had." She forced herself not to sound bitter. "Strictly self-promotion for my business. I didn't charge you for them."

"For your business?"

"Despite what you might think, I haven't been drifting."

"I didn't say you were."

"But that's what you think." She gazed into her mug, her reflection distorted in the coffee's surface. "I have a plan. It's going to take a little longer to get it off the ground than I'd hoped, but I'm going to do it."

"Tell me about it."

She braced herself, praying he wouldn't laugh. "I'm going to refurbish the truck and sell my chocolates from it," she said in a rush.

He nodded. "Interesting."

She didn't want to hear him list all the obstacles, and she hurried on. "Starting Monday, I'm applying for jobs with as many catering companies as I can find to raise some cash. I'm also going to find a roommate. As soon as I pay off the fine, I'll start saving for truck repairs. By winter, I want to be back on the streets. Not the best time to launch a food truck, I know, but I'll add some really inventive hot chocolate to the menu, a few other things."

He wasn't frowning yet, so she told him about the website she'd build, the commercial kitchen space she intended to rent, the specialty ingredients she'd eventually be able to buy so she could make the kind of chocolates she dreamed of.

"You did a great job with the party," he said. "Why don't you start your own catering company?"

"I'm not a good enough chef to offer more complicated meals than what I served you. Catering takes capital, too, and there's a low profit margin. Also . . . I'd be miserable."

"I'm paying you for the chocolates you lost," he said firmly.

"Oh, no, you aren't. Chocolates weren't part of our contract."

He picked up his mug and studied her over the rim. "Look, Rory . . . if you need some cash . . ."

She jumped off the couch. "Not another word!" She forced herself to speak more calmly. "I appreciate the offer, but I've got this."

He nodded. "I'm sure you have."

But he wasn't sure, and neither was she.

*　*

As Brett watched her pretend to be a badass, he wondered what realm of his brain had decided it would be a great idea to offer her money only a few hours after they'd had sex.

Nothing last night had felt choreographed. She hadn't tried to make fake porn-star moves. He hadn't worried about whether his hands were always in the exact right places. Everything had felt . . . real.

She set her doughnut aside before taking a bite. "The rental company is coming to your place this afternoon to pick up everything. I need to go over there and explain why you'll be paying for one of their tables and a couple of tablecloths."

"I'll take care of it."

"It's my job. And don't worry. I won't jump you while I'm there."

He was more worried about jumping her.

She looked right through him in the way only she could. "You're regretting this. What happened between us."

"Not regretting . . ." He gave her the same practiced smile he gave his clients. "How could I regret something so enjoyable?"

"Because with you, business always comes first. Until last night."

He had a gift for soothing people, for finding the right words in any situation, but everything he'd been aiming toward seemed to be slipping away—two decades of hard work and grueling self-discipline. He rubbed the back of his neck. "What do you want me to say, Rory? If I say you're right, I'm a jerk. If I say we didn't cross all kinds of boundaries last night, I'm a liar. Boundaries that are important to both of us."

She was stone-faced. "Emotionally important to me. Practically important to you."

"Maybe I have an emotional stake in all this, too," he said hotly. "I'm not a robot, and you mean a lot to me."

"Of course I mean a lot! I'm your only real friend. And how pitiful is that?"

An unemployed, debt-ridden chocolate maker had just called him pitiful. It should have made him furious, but it hurt. As she'd so astutely observed, his friends were his clients. He didn't have the luxury of ever completely relaxing with them. Not the way he did with this quirky, curly-haired woman.

She must've gotten herself all worked up—or maybe he'd gotten her that way—because she was on her feet. "Put this in your bank account and smoke it. The sexual part of our relationship was great—more than great—but we've scratched that itch, and we're done."

He didn't want her to be right, but his options were clear. Either he could have his career or he could have sex with Rory Garrett, but he couldn't have both. The rules for successful agents were written in stone. No personal entanglements with a client's mother, aunt, cousin, or, especially, a client's sister—not as long as he wanted to stay employed by Champion Sports Management.

Her Cupid's bow lips formed a light oval. "If you're concerned about being alone with me at your condo, go to the gym or jump on your private jet and fly to Vegas with a couple of your clients."

She was hurting. He could see it. And he was responsible. "I don't have a private—"

She jabbed her finger at him. "Whatever you do, understand this. I won't be your dirty little career-ending secret."

It was a shot straight to his heart. "Rory, I never meant for things to go this far."

"You're not the one who made all the decisions, Rivers. Now get your things and clear out."

18

It hurt. It hurt so badly. Rory hugged her knees to her chest and tried not to cry, because giving in to the hot tears squeezing against the backs of her eyelids could only mean she had a broken heart. And she didn't want to admit that. Didn't want to acknowledge how deeply she'd fallen in love with that asshole Brett Rivers, who wasn't an asshole at all but a brilliant, kind, generous, maddening, and altogether decent human being. With warped values.

Her throat closed, and the tears spilled over. She'd understood him right from the beginning. Whip-smart and iron willed, the classic overachieving workaholic. Despite their differences, they had connected, and not just sexually. There had been something unfiltered about their relationship. Something raw and real. They'd seen the best and worst in each other and accepted both.

Through the open door, the rumpled sheets mocked her. She could have pretended she didn't notice his regret over last night— his regret over her. She could have let this affair go on longer in secrecy, let herself be with him for another few days, weeks, a month, but instead of holding on, she'd done the right thing, the hard thing. She'd kicked him out.

But the tears wouldn't stop. She'd stupidly, idiotically fallen in love with him, and her heart was broken into a thousand pieces. She couldn't even hide. She had to go to his place this morning and deal with the mess from last night, the rental company, the leftover food, her pans and utensils. She wasn't going to do any of it. She was locking her door, pulling the curtains shut, and letting herself mourn what she couldn't have.

She gave in to her ugly cry. When she was done, she washed her face and grabbed her keys.

She was a person who could do hard things, and she had a job to finish.

*

Kristin found a picnic spot for them on a bench nestled into the tall hedge that bordered Millennium Park's Lurie Garden. The twenty-five-acre park had once been a blighted railroad shipping yard, but now, with Chicago's magnificent skyline as a backdrop, it was one of the most beautiful public spaces in the country. Kristin offered Daniel the ham and Swiss sandwich she'd picked up at the deli, along with fresh corn salad, fruit compote, and toffee bars. A bottle of wine would have been nice, but the park police frowned on alcohol.

Daniel finished a neat bite of his sandwich. "Did you know we're sitting on top of one of the world's largest green roofs?"

"Yes, I do know that." She hadn't meant to be so abrupt, but she was nervous about what she needed to say today. She tried again. "Most tourists don't realize parking garages and rail lines are underneath them. Chicago is like a larger version of Minneapolis. It gets a lot of things wrong, but it gets a lot of things right, too."

Daniel made a small gesture toward her with his sandwich. "It was nice of you to do this."

"My pleasure." She sounded as if she were working for Chick-fil-A. "I'm glad it didn't rain, although I guess we could use some. My stepdaughter's landlord has been complaining to me about having to water his tomato plants every day."

"I don't want to talk about the weather."

Neither did she, but she also didn't want to talk about what she needed to talk about. "You look very nice." He was well coordinated in a white polo and olive shorts, both of which appeared to be new, as did his low-top Converse sneakers. "Your daughter picked your outfit, didn't she?"

He smiled. "She tried to talk me into not wearing socks, but I can only go so far."

"Understandable." She gazed at the garden's vast patchwork of ornamental grasses and flowers. Some she didn't recognize; others she did—fields of pink and purple coneflowers, salvia, Russian sage, all of them hearty Midwestern blooms.

Daniel braced his arms on his thighs. "Kristin, I need to know where we stand with our . . . relationship."

Direct as always. She pulled a piece of crust off her sandwich. "I like you very much, but you need to know that I have a lot going on in my life right now."

He sat straighter. "You're breaking up with me."

"No, I—"

"I understand. I don't like it, but I understand." He set his sandwich on the paper it had been wrapped in and stood. "I'll be going now."

"No! No, that's not what I—"

"I'd rather not talk anymore." He began to walk away, his spine straight, dignified.

She jumped up, spilling the container of corn salad and reaching for his arm. "Wait!"

He regarded her gravely, only his innate good manners keeping him from pulling away. "I'm too serious, and I have difficulty interpreting social cues. It's a lot for a woman to deal with."

"You're not too serious. You're genuine and honest. You're intense, but you're also the most open man I've ever known."

"But you don't want to see me anymore? Or am I reading things wrong again?"

His confusion tugged at her heart and made her say what she shouldn't say, not yet. "I'm crazy about you." A smile caught the corners of his mouth as he studied her, looking into her eyes. She gave him the time he needed to catch up with her before she went on. "I know it's too early to admit that. Counting today, we've had exactly three dates, and I guess I'll understand if I'm scaring you off."

"Why is that? Why are you crazy about me?"

"Because I don't have to be on guard with you. If I'm not sure how you feel about something or what you think, all I have to do is ask, and you'll tell me the truth." She released his arm. "With my husband, I was always guarded. I felt like I had to make it up to him because I wasn't his dead wife. His real wife. It was exhausting."

He nodded, processing. "That's very complicated. Then you're not breaking up with me?"

"I'm not. But there's something I have to tell you." Now she was the one who needed to give herself time. She began scooping up the corn salad from the walkway with the lid of the container. Daniel bent down to help, but she stopped him. "Let me. It's messy."

Messy, just like the other important relationships in her life.

He sat on the bench, taking her at her word. A couple pushing a stroller walked past along with chattering teenagers and women in bright summer dresses. A few kernels of corn had somehow ended up on the toe of his white sneaker. She picked them off, but they left an oil smear behind.

With the worst of the mess finally cleaned up, she sat on the bench next to him and reached for the sanitizer she kept in her purse. She took her time cleaning her hands because there was no need to rush her thoughts or her actions with a man like Daniel.

When she was done, she gazed out at the gardens. Monarch butterflies flitted through the milkweed and red-winged black-birds called out from the trees. "You asked me if I had children," she said. "I told you about Rory."

"She's an interesting young lady."

"Definitely interesting. But that's not what I wanted to tell you." She clasped her hands in her lap. "I also have a son."

Daniel regarded her quizzically. "Is there something wrong with him?"

"No. Not at all. He's wonderful. But I've learned to be cautious where he's concerned. Especially now."

"I don't understand."

"My last name . . . It's not Meadows, it's Garrett." She looked at him fully. "Daniel, my son is Clint Garrett."

Daniel blinked his eyes, his gaze focused, his internal wheels turning. "Clint Garrett?"

"The Chicago Stars quarterback."

"I know who Clint Garret is." He pondered. "That's amazing. But why would you not tell me?"

"Because too many people have tried to use me to get close to him. And with everything that's happening now . . ."

His eyebrows drew together. "That's what you thought I would do? Use you?"

"I didn't know. Not until I spent time with you and got to know you better."

He studied her long and hard, his thoughts impossible to read. Finally, he stood up. "Kristin, I have to go."

"But—"

"It's hard for me when people don't tell me the truth."

"I'm sure it is." She rose next to him. "But I have to take care of myself, and I won't apologize for that."

He gave her a slow nod and walked away.

When Gregg had walked away in the middle of an important discussion, she'd been devastated. She'd ended up crying silently in the bathroom, unwilling to let him see how he'd hurt her. But Daniel Hanbridge wasn't Gregg Garrett, and she finished her lunch. The food didn't go down easily, because she had to swallow around the lump in her throat. But it was a beautiful summer day, and she'd done what she needed to.

⋆⋆

Rory maneuvered the Royal Palace of Sweets into one of the guest parking slots. Her head still ached from her crying jag as she took the elevator to his condo, but God was merciful, and Brett wasn't there. She cleaned up the rest of the food mess in the kitchen, collected her serving dishes, and settled with the rental company. Driving back home with the truck streaming a sooty ribbon of exhaust, she wondered how she would get through the next few days.

She unloaded the truck and carried everything upstairs, past Toby's open door, and into her kitchen. On the way, she caught sight of herself in the mirror. She looked like hell, but at least her eyes were no longer puffy. She needed to check on Kristin.

Anyone going into Toby's apartment would know a single guy lived here by its decor: black leather couch, matching armchair, bare wood floor, no curtains, and industrial shelving crammed with cables and electronic equipment. Luther's litter box occupied a place of honor under a rectangular mirror decorated with *Tetris* stickers.

Kristin emerged from the small second bedroom where Toby stored his bike and where she'd presumably slept. It was both weird and not surprising to see her carrying a roll of paper towels and a bottle of Windex. Toby was about the same age as Clint, she'd bonded with him, and she liked to mother young men.

Kristin took in her appearance as Luther arched his back against her ankles. "What happened? You look awful."

"Not enough sleep." She gestured toward the paper towels. "Why are you cleaning Toby's apartment?"

"I need to keep busy," she said tightly. "I got dumped."

Rory finally had something to focus on other than her own problems. "Daniel dumped you? He adores you."

Kristin slammed the Windex bottle on Toby's black metal desk. "Clearly he doesn't adore me enough. It turns out that he has issues with women who aren't truthful."

It took Rory only a few seconds to understand. "You finally told him you're Clint's mother."

"And I wouldn't apologize for not telling him from the beginning."

"You did the right thing. He doesn't understand what it's like."

"He didn't see it that way. Everything with Daniel is either black or white. I'm used to shades of gray. A lot of gray."

Like Kristin's life with Rory's father?

"I can't believe how dusty this place is." Kristin attacked Toby's desk. "Anyway, it's over, and we only went on three dates, so it's not like it's the end of the world."

"But you're crazy about him."

"Maybe." Kristin wiped under the computer keyboard. "Look at us. Both falling for inaccessible men."

Rory considered denying it, but she was emptied out. "Brett and I are done, too. Not that we were ever together, but . . . Anyway, it's over."

Kristin set aside the spray bottle. "I need to put in my contacts, and then let's go to your place and talk." Luther followed her into the bathroom.

Rory gazed around Toby's apartment. He had a big vinyl collection and, as Kristin had mentioned, an aversion to dusting. She'd never been here when his bedroom was open, and now she peeked in. An unmade double bed rested on a plain metal frame. He had a dresser and a bedside table holding a lamp, an alarm clock, and a framed photo. In her experience, bedside photos held keepsake images: a beautiful landscape, friends having fun, a romantic shot with a lover, but even from the doorway, she could make out that this photo showed a woman and a corner of the garage behind their building.

She looked more closely. The woman was walking away from the camera to her car, her face and body turned at an awkward angle toward the photographer. The image was blurry. Why would Toby have such a mundane—

Rory shivered. The woman in the photo was Ashley.

* *

Rory told Kristin what she'd seen over frosted doughnuts and a bottle of zinfandel, a combination that didn't pair with anything except dejection. "People keep important photos next to their bed, not an out-of-focus shot of a neighbor."

Kristin crossed her legs beneath her on the couch. "What are you saying?"

Rory shook her head. "I don't know what I'm saying."

"Toby wouldn't hurt anyone."

"That's what they said about Ted Bundy. I mean, I don't actually know they said that about Ted Bundy, but they might have."

"Toby is no Ted Bundy."

"You have to admit that photo is creepy."

"They were friends. Maybe that's the only photo he has of her, and since she just died, he wants it nearby."

"Maybe."

Kristin exchanged her strawberry doughnut for a sip of zinfandel. Eventually she broke the silence that had fallen between them. "What happened with you and Brett?"

"Idiocy. That's what happened. You know I'm good at it."

"Stop putting yourself down, Rory. I don't like it."

Rory wiped her fingers on a napkin. "I'm too impulsive when it comes to relationships, something Clint and I seem to have in common. Although, unlike Ashley, Brett has a stellar character, except for the workaholic part."

"And you love him."

Rory made a business out of picking doughnut crumbs off her shorts only to stop what she was doing and look back up. "I never meant to. I always understood exactly what his priorities were, but you've been with him. Exactly how was I supposed to resist?"

"He's definitely an impressive man."

"If it hadn't been for Clint, we would never have spent so much time together, but neither of us trusts the police to look past their most obvious suspect, and we teamed up." She told Kristin more about the trip to Michigan, about talking to Ashley's boss, and about her meeting with Grant Padderson.

Kristin set down her wine goblet with a thud. "I had no idea all this was going on. You've been doing something tangible about Clint's arrest while I've been sitting around wringing my hands."

"You don't have a guilty conscience haunting you."

"What are you talking about?"

Rory had endured enough secrecy. She sat on the couch, wineglass and doughnuts abandoned, and told Kristin everything.

"Oh, Rory . . ." A tear slithered over Kristin's bottom eyelashes. "I would never have been able to think so fast."

"It was a terrible thing to do!"

"Terrible?" Kristin dashed away the tear trickling down her cheek. "He didn't listen to you when you tried to tell him the truth. How is what you did terrible?"

"Ashley's dead because of it!"

"You don't know that. Whoever killed her was looking for opportunity, and he—or maybe she, although I doubt it—found opportunity at Clint's house."

Kristin had no way of knowing that was true, but it still made Rory feel better. "You don't think I'm awful?"

"I think you're a good person and the best sister he could have had. And look how much you and Brett have done to try to clear his name."

"With no results."

"I wouldn't say that." She gave a wry smile. "You fell for each other."

"One of us fell harder than the other, and last night shouldn't have happened. Now can we talk about something else? You and Daniel."

"I don't want to talk about him. Tell me what happened with your business. First, you were selling candy from that truck, and then you weren't."

Since Rory's defenses had already broken down, she told her stepmother the whole story. Kristin was gratifyingly outraged. "What a horrible person that Jon is! You should sue him."

"I should sue myself for going into business with him in the first place."

"You're too hard on yourself."

"Am I? Do you know why I decided selling bubble gum was a viable path toward becoming a chocolatier? Because I didn't have the courage to go after what I really wanted."

"Stop it, Rory. You're doing your best." She brushed her hands together. "The best cure for heartbreak is to stay busy. Make new plans and move forward."

"I've already made plans," she said hesitantly. Sharing anything about her life with Kristin opened her to criticism, but since they were drinking wine with doughnuts, she took a chance. "I'm going to convert the Royal Palace of Sweets into a chocolate emporium on wheels."

"Another food truck?" Kristin abandoned her doughnut. "I'm surprised."

"Meaning you don't approve."

"You don't need my approval. Stop being so defensive."

"But I've had all these years of practice."

Kristin set her jaw. "Rory, I simply meant it's nothing I would have thought of, but I have no concept of what that involves or whether you can support yourself doing it."

"Forget I mentioned it."

Kristin sighed. "Can we start over? I'd like to hear more. Tell me how you envision your business?"

Rory weighed her reticence to open herself up to more of Kristin's judgment against her longing to talk about her idea. She took a deep breath. "Imagine coming out of work at the end of a long day. Or maybe you've just had a fight with your boyfriend, or you've been shopping and your feet hurt. You deserve a little luxury, and there I am—affordable luxury parked right in front of you. An array of beautiful, handmade chocolates on display in the front window. If you want to play it safe, you choose a buttercream or a sea salt caramel, but if you're more adventurous, you try something exotic: blackberry amaretto, maybe, or cinnamon chili—some combination that's full of flavor without being gimmicky. As soon as you taste it, you decide one truffle isn't enough, or maybe you think about how much your sister or your girlfriend loves chocolate, so you buy a few four-packs. Maybe you come back to buy a larger assortment as a hostess gift or Mother's Day present."

Warming to the topic, she described the business districts where she planned to park; her ideas for gourmet hot chocolate in the winter and, if she could figure out the refrigeration, chocolate-dipped ice-cream balls in the summer. "The business won't make me rich," she said as she finally wound down, "but I should be able to *support myself.* And maybe, eventually, make enough money to open my own shop."

Kristin ignored the barb. "When are you going to start?"

"First I have to save the money. The truck needs repairs and a new paint job. I have supplies to buy, packaging. I need to rent space in a commercial kitchen. I'll get there, but it's going to take a while."

"Complicated."

Rory could have taken offense, but Kristin seemed more thoughtful than critical, so she let it pass. They finished their doughnuts and wine, each occupied with her own thoughts.

*

Not long after Rory woke up the next morning, she received an email from the City of Chicago notifying her that her parking fine had been paid online. She hadn't mentioned the fine to Kristin, so only one person could have done this.

She grabbed her ball cap and set off for the cemetery. The homes she passed on her way had well-tended postage-stamp lawns and big front porches adorned with hanging baskets of Boston ferns, geraniums, and colorful impatiens. American flags flew from some porches, rainbow flags from others. She usually enjoyed walking along these streets, but today, her heart was as heavy as the humid air.

She entered the shady cemetery and strode along the paths, feeling the full weight of the power imbalance that had been part of her relationship with Brett from the time she'd awakened in that hotel room with five hundred dollars on the desk. Now, they'd broken up immediately after sex, and he felt guilty about it. He'd decided the best way to assuage the guilt he shouldn't be feeling was with his wallet.

She couldn't un-pay the fine, so she only had two options. She could either make a scene or keep her dignity by writing him a polite thank-you note and living for the moment she could repay her debt.

*
*

She'd written him a fucking *thank-you* note!

> Dear Brett,
> I received notice this morning from the city that the parking fine my former partner incurred has been paid. I will, of course, repay you as I'm able. Thank you for your unnecessary generosity.
> Sincerely,
> Rory Meadows Garrett

What the *hell*? "Rory Meadows Garrett," like he wouldn't know who the hell she was! The note didn't have a stamp, so she'd hand-delivered it to the reception desk. She wouldn't even talk to him face-to-face.

He crushed the note in his fist and tossed it in the trash.

Paying that fine hadn't made a dent in his bank account, but it would mean everything to her. The least she could do was to show up in person to acknowledge it. Not to thank him. God, no. The last thing he wanted was her thanks. He wanted—

He didn't know what he wanted other than to see her. But they were over. That monkey was off his back.

He'd never felt worse.

*

Rory returned to her apartment at one in the morning from her third job that day. She'd worked a corporate breakfast, prepped for an outdoor barbecue, and served at a charity dinner. She stumbled into her bedroom, kicked off her sneakers, and contemplated whether she had enough energy to brush her teeth, let alone scrape together the very last of her supplies to experiment with the tiramisu chocolate bar she'd been thinking about all day. Going to bed without brushing her teeth was the first step toward keeping all her belongings in a shopping cart. Just a few minutes' rest, and then she'd get up and . . .

*

"You didn't lock your door. Again."

Rory peeled open her eyes to dim morning sunlight and an indignant stepmother looming in her bedroom doorway. She grabbed her alarm clock. 7:15. Relieved, she sagged back into the pillows. She didn't have to be at work for an hour and a half.

"Rory, where is your common sense?" Kristin demanded. "Lock your door at night. And why do you still have your clothes on?"

Rory groaned and rolled over, her muscles screaming like a desperate politician. An hour and a half wasn't enough time to work on her chocolate bar. Holding up her hand to ward off the Step-mother from the Netherworld, she staggered to the bathroom for a quick shower.

Kristin was still there when Rory emerged wrapped in the che-nille robe she'd taken off for Brett only five days ago. Her chest ached at the memory. All she had to do now was keep putting one foot in front of the other and focus on her work.

Kristin extended a mug of coffee that, upon first taste, proved to be almost drinkable. "We need to talk."

"Oh, God." Rory headed for the couch. "You want to break up with me, too."

"If only I could."

Kristin looked so put-upon that Rory would have laughed if she had any laughter left. Kristin stalked toward her, waving a blue spiral notebook. "You left this on the coffee table."

"What are you doing with that?"

"Snooping. Like I did with your diary. Which is how I found out you were going way too far with Ryan Amos. And note that I never told your father about that."

"Noted and appreciated. Ryan was a douche. I should have aimed higher."

"Not the point." Kristin plunked down beside her, the open pages of the notebook showing Rory's rough financial calcula-tions. Kristin pointed at the figures. "This is what you need to get your food truck up and running. Am I right?"

Rory curled her fingers around the coffee mug. "A rough es-timate, which is why I'm currently working for Satan's catering company."

"You need investors."

"An astute observation, Veronica Mars. Unfortunately, I don't have the kind of track record that attracts investors."

"You should have asked me."

Rory reared back. "Asked you? Why?"

Kristin pursed her lips. "Because you should have."

"But why would you help me? You don't even like me."

"What's to like? You're irreverent, prickly, and generally difficult."

"And those are my good points."

But Kristin wouldn't be distracted by a wisecrack. "No matter what I say, you take offense."

Rory could have pointed out the same in reverse, but she didn't.

Kristin sucked in air. "Besides, you don't like me, either."

Rory thought about it. "That's not entirely true. We have sarcasm in common, and we've been getting on surprisingly well."

Kristin's brow furrowed. "You liked me for a while when you were little, but then—" She waved her hand in one of those *forget it* gestures, only to have her eyes fill with tears. "I gave up too soon. I'm sorry."

Rory wanted to annoy Kristin, not genuinely upset her. "Five nights ago, you were on your hands and knees picking up smashed lava cake. I'd hardly call that giving up too soon."

"I'm not talking about the cake." Kristin's voice caught. "I should have done better from the beginning. You were a child who'd lost her mother, and I was the strange woman who moved into your house much too soon. Of course, you needed someone to take out your anger on."

Rory saw Kristin crouched underneath the dining room table with a row of Barbies, Kristin pushing her in the playground swing. *Higher, Kissy! Higher!* Kristin comforting her when Rory got bullied and being calmly upfront about sex and birth control. "You did the best you could considering what a mouthy, disrespectful brat you had to deal with."

"My best wasn't good enough."

Rory didn't like Kristin's regret. "Stop it. You were only twenty-one when you married Dad. You took on a lot."

Kristin twisted her hands in her lap. "I was twenty-two, pregnant, and desperately in love with a man who was still in love with his dead wife." Her gaze drifted back to Rory. "Your mother was everything to him. She never got frustrated, never raised her voice, never demanded anything of him. She was perfect."

"Is that what you believe?"

"No," she said softly, "but it's what he believed."

Rory remembered how frequently her father had been condescending to Kristin, how often he'd dismissed her opinions. "Dad could be a jerk."

"He loved you very much."

"He sure didn't show it. It was always about Clint."

"You reminded him too much of your mother. That was a cross Clint never had to bear."

Rory remembered something she'd nearly forgotten. "Dad didn't talk about Mom, but you did. You used to tell me how much she loved me. You'd remind me of the cute nicknames she gave me, and how she planted a garden with me. You never met her. How did you know those things?"

"Her friends. They talked about her. Too much. I was younger than the other wives in the neighborhood, and they wanted to keep me in my place." Kristin smiled. "You resemble her more than physically. From everything I've heard, she was a unique personality—funny, bighearted, artistic."

It was odd viewing the past from Kristin's perspective. "You're prettier than she was, and you have a big heart, too. You're also kind of funny."

"Not as funny as you."

"Hardly anyone is."

Kristin laughed and tapped the last figure on Rory's notepad. "Is this enough to give you a good start?"

"Yes, but—"

"Then let's do it. I'll lend you the money."

It took Rory a few seconds to find her tongue. "You would seriously do that?"

"Yes, but . . ." Kristin held up her hand. "I have conditions."

"Like what?" Rory said warily.

"We'll be partners in the business. We'll work together."

"Why would you want to work on a food truck? It can be drudgery. We'd also argue all the time."

"We worked together at the party, didn't we? You did your thing and I did mine."

"You don't know anything about making chocolate."

"But I do know how to clean counters and serve customers."

"You live in Minneapolis."

"I'm moving here."

Rory gaped at her. "Since when?"

"Since— I don't know. Maybe the night of the party. I like being busy."

"You're busy at home. You have friends. A house."

"I can visit my friends whenever I want. As for the house . . . I'm selling it."

"You're selling our house?"

"Your house and Clint's house, Gregg and Debra's house, but

never mine. I've lived with a ghost long enough, and I'm sick of it. I'm also too young to wake up every morning trying to figure out how to fill my day."

"I don't know. I . . ."

"It's settled. I'll lend you the start-up money in exchange for a job and a percentage of your business until the loan's paid off."

"But that might never happen."

"Then I'll have to rethink my future investment strategy, won't I?"

She looked so smug, so pleased with herself, that Rory wanted to hug her. Not that she would. The two of them weren't huggers. They were business partners.

And kind of friends.

19

Brett was a mess sitting in a mess. The restoration company had cleared out the burned drapes, a rug, and an upholstered chair. They'd removed sections of water-damaged flooring and a few pieces of wallboard, but nothing had been replaced yet, and Brett didn't care if it ever was. He hated this place. He wanted to live somewhere with comfortable furniture, maybe a garden that somebody else took care of, but where he could sit outside and have a beer. He wanted a coffee table he didn't keep banging his shins on and art he enjoyed looking at, like maybe a floozy poster.

Definitely not a floozy poster. He needed to stop thinking about her.

His phone buzzed. It was Heath. He picked it up on the fourth ring.

His boss wasted no time. "Tyler Capello signed with CAA."

This was the biggest setback of Brett's career, and he should care. He did care. "The kid's a flake," he said.

"That's never stopped you before."

"His mother's a nightmare."

"Nothing you couldn't handle if you'd been on your game. He should have been ours, Rivers. And now he's not."

The line went dead.

*
*

Kristin didn't want to challenge the fragile peace she and Rory had established by moving back in with her stepdaughter when Toby returned from his trip, so she talked to Oscar Reynolds, Rory's landlord, and ended up renting Ashley Hart's apartment on a month-by-month basis until he found someone more permanent. She could have afforded a nicer apartment—and certainly one that didn't have such a ghoulish connection—but living downstairs from Rory made good business sense for now. Also, Rory needed Kristin in a way her son apparently didn't. And maybe Kristin needed Rory, too.

While the truck was being repaired, Kristin found a furniture rental company and began moving into the apartment. Rory, in the meantime, was finishing her commitment to the catering company, ordering supplies, and—in her occasional free hours—creating a website.

Kristin located a nearby bakery where they could rent the licensed kitchen space Rory needed for a quarter of the price of a commercial kitchen. The catch was that Rory had to use it in their off-hours—anytime from four in the afternoon until four the next morning. Kristin didn't like that, but Rory wouldn't consider renting a more convenient—and more expensive—kitchen. "I have better ways to use your money," she said.

Kristin heard nothing from Daniel, but Clint texted her nearly every day, reassuring her that he was fine and also making it clear that he wanted to be left alone. Giving him space was the hardest thing she'd ever done, and she wasn't certain she could have stayed away if she hadn't been so busy.

She researched food truck design and discovered the best and most economical way to make their truck stand out was to install a custom-designed vinyl wrap with eye-catching graphics over the original pink paint. Rory sent her, along with a box of freshly made chocolates, to Duncan Gilford, Ashley's old boss, and a day later, he'd produced a sophisticated cocoa-brown design both Kristin and Rory loved. They sent it off to a local production company that promised a quick turnaround and got a lift from Toby to Burr Ridge to pick up Kristin's Volvo.

✦

Toby dropped them off in front of Clint's house, vacated now of the news vans and reporters. Kristin went inside to pack the rest of her clothes, but Rory never wanted to go in that house again.

She spotted the same gardener she'd seen a couple of weeks ago at the side of the house. He was probably in his thirties, big, with sleeve tattoos. "The flowers are beautiful," she said, as she approached him. "Have you worked here for long?"

He didn't look up from the bushes he was pruning. "A couple of years."

"I'm a friend of Clint's."

He took her in with small, bloodshot eyes. "Tough what happened."

"Really tough." She'd forgotten her sunglasses, and she squinted against the glare. "Did you ever talk to her? Ashley?"

"Why would she talk to me?"

"I don't know. Did she?"

"There was a dead chipmunk in the pool once when she wanted to swim, and she asked me to get it out."

"Why didn't she ask Clint?"

"He wasn't here."

"So she came to the house when he wasn't home?"

"I don't know anything about that." He swiped the sweat from his forehead with the back of his arm and walked away.

* *

Kristin hated driving on the Chicago expressways, so Rory drove back and parked the Volvo in Ashley's old space. After Kristin had gone into her new apartment to unpack, Rory called Detective Strothers from the backyard. "Did you know Ashley used to go to Clint's house when he wasn't there?"

"Who told you that?"

"The gardener—the guy who takes care of the yard. I didn't get his name, but there's something suspicious about him. Secretive."

"I asked you to leave interrogation up to the police."

"I will. As soon as you drop the charges against my brother."

"Ms. Garrett—"

"Meadows. And the fact that Ashley was holding his ring when she died doesn't mean anything. I told you. He only had it on for the reunion. Otherwise, he hasn't worn it in years, and he would have taken it off as soon as he got home."

"You don't know that for a fact."

"I know my brother."

The brother who never wanted to see her again.

*
*

Kristin gazed around at the apartment with its white walls and nondescript beige rented furniture. All signs of Ashley Hart had disappeared. Everything about the apartment was completely impersonal. No photographs rested on the table by the couch, no paintings hung on the walls to reflect the owner's aesthetic. The apartment was a blank canvas that demanded nothing of her, unlike the big house in Minneapolis.

"The door's unlocked," she called out in response to a trio of knocks.

But the knocks hadn't come from Rory. Instead, Daniel stood framed in the open doorway, filling the space with his lanky body, hand-combed straight hair, and baggy tan pants his daughter hadn't picked out. Her heart gave a traitorous little skip.

"I went to your stepdaughter's apartment to see you. She wasn't friendly, but once she understood my intentions, she told me you'd rented here." He took a single step inside. "I've thought it over, and although I wish you'd confided in me from the beginning, I've concluded your hesitation is understandable."

His firm, decisive nod seemed to indicate he'd said everything he needed to, and the matter was taken care of. She crossed her arms over her chest. "Oh, you have, have you? It only took you nine days to *conclude* my hesitation was *understandable.*"

Her reaction wasn't what he'd hoped, and he hesitated. "I'm sure there've been many instances when people have tried to take advantage of you because you're the mother of a famous athlete."

"Yes, there have been."

"Once I processed that fact, I understood your logic."

"It's unfortunate you couldn't *process* that fact without walking away from me in Millennium Park and disappearing for a week and a half."

His Adam's apple bobbed nervously in his neck. "I didn't mean to be disrespectful. There was a lot to think about, and I think better when I'm alone. It's my habit."

"Well, it's *my* habit when someone walks away from me to kick them out of my life. So now we're clear, and you can leave."

It hadn't been her habit at all. How many times had Gregg walked away from her when he decided she was being overly emotional? But she'd lost patience with the woman she'd been.

She offered Daniel her iciest glare and all the time he needed to *process* the fact that he was being kicked out.

He caught on surprisingly quickly. "You're angry."

"I'm angry, but more than that, I'm disappointed. You disappointed me."

His shoulders hunched in distress. "I didn't mean to. I would never deliberately disappoint you."

"But you did. It shouldn't have taken you nine days to understand why I can't be forthcoming about my son when I meet new people, especially in light of what's happened. In case you don't read the papers, he's been falsely accused of murder."

"I understand that. Very wise of you to be cautious."

"Then *what*? Use your words, Daniel."

He approached her, his big hands dangling awkwardly at his sides. "Kristin, you mean everything to me. I'm not an impulsive man, but that day in the coffee shop, I was drawn to you in a way I can't explain. You lit up my life from your first smile, and from that smile, I—" His Adam's apple gave another bob as he swallowed hard. "I believe I fell in love with you." He took a deep breath. "I know it's difficult to understand how something so important could happen so quickly. It's difficult for me, too, which is why it's taken me so long to figure this out. Please understand that I don't expect you to feel the same way."

Daniel wouldn't say he loved her if he didn't believe it, but she needed more than that. Gregg used to say he loved her, but it had been more his love of the familiar than real passion for her.

Her lack of response didn't seem to deter him. "Assuming at some point you might still be interested in seeing me—and I'm assuming no such thing—the logistics are troubling. I have a business here that I can't abandon. You have a home in Minneapolis and a life there. Why would you consider leaving it behind? Of course, until today, I didn't know you'd rented this apartment, which gives me some hope, but I don't understand the ramifications."

"You've been dwelling on all this for nine days, and it didn't once occur to you that we should discuss it together?"

"It seemed presumptuous to unburden myself when I know your feelings don't run as deeply as mine."

"How would you know what my feelings are without asking me?"

"Logic. Look at you. You could have any man who interested you."

"The men who interest me are men who can communicate."

He gave a jerky nod. "If possible, I want to fix this."

"I'm not sure it is possible."

He set his jaw, refusing to give up. "I'm an engineer. It's my job to solve problems."

"This is a human problem, not an engineering one, and I can't be in a relationship with someone who walks away from me as you did instead of having an honest conversation. I had years of enduring the silent treatment from my husband, and I won't ever go through that again."

"I understand that now."

"Understanding isn't enough. I need to be in a relationship with someone who will discuss things as they happen instead of taking off on his own."

"A valid point." He gave a brusque nod. "I can do that."

"Can you? I'm not sure."

"I'm very sure," he said earnestly. "Because I'm doing it right now. Instead of leaving like I want to, I'll stay right here to discuss this if you'll reconsider kicking me out." When she hesitated, he closed the remaining distance between them and gazed down at her. "I can't change who I am, Kristin. I know I won't pick up on emotional nuances as quickly as you do, but now that you've told me what's important to you, I understand how I hurt you and why I need to communicate better. Can you be patient with me?"

He was so earnest, so dear, with all his feelings visible on his face, but she was still wary. "I don't know. I have to think about it."

"Let's think together, then." Instead of leaving, he gestured toward the couch. "I won't say anything, just hold your hand and give you all the time you need to consider the obstacles I've mentioned."

He'd somehow managed to turn the tables on her, and she didn't mind at all. "I suppose we could do that."

They moved to the couch and sat down.

"Your stepdaughter told me you have a gun. If that's true, which I doubt, I hope you have it locked up. Research shows that people with handguns in their house have twice the homicide rate of their neighbors without guns."

"I don't have a gun. My stepdaughter is a troublemaker."

"She cares about you."

"I guess she does."

"I like her. She reminds me of you."

"I thought we weren't going to talk."

"That's what I said, but I'm afraid if I give you too much time to think, you'll realize how much trouble I am."

"Oh, I realized that the day we met."

He picked up her hand and rubbed the palm. "I'll be quiet now."

"Good. There's nothing worse than kissing a man while he's talking." And there was nothing better than kissing an honest man willing to tell her exactly who he was.

Between kisses, he gazed into her eyes in a way that made her feel as if she were the most beautiful, sexiest woman he'd ever met. In so many ways, he was an old-school gentleman, and she was the one who led them to her bedroom. She was glad she didn't have time to worry about what happened next, or she'd have stressed over the loose skin around her thighs, the pale stretch marks on her belly, her slightly shopworn body. But as he undressed her, he regarded her only with admiration.

He turned out to be as deliberate with his lovemaking as he was about everything else. Attentive to every nuance of her body and meticulous when it came to detail. He was also slow. Maddeningly slow. She wanted to scream at him to hurry up, except she didn't really want him to hurry because she was going out of her mind in the most delicious way.

At the end, right before it was over, he told her he loved her, and she heard herself whisper the same words back to him.

*
*

Rory stood in a pool of light doing what she'd been born to do. Despite its generous size, the bakery kitchen was cozy in the deep night quiet. Harry Styles sang about lost love in the background while Rory added a fresh supply of chocolate callets to her new, larger tempering machine. Thanks to Kristin's partnership, she had what she needed to produce bigger batches.

Being in this kitchen in the dead of night with its gleaming stainless-steel counters, triple sinks, and industrial mixer was all she could have wished for. She wanted to tell Brett about it. She wanted to tell him which flavors she'd chosen to sell first, to describe the logo Duncan Gilford had come up with for their packaging, to share the name they'd decided on, and to let him know the refurbished former Royal Palace of Sweets would be ready to hit the streets in two days. He'd be genuinely interested. He'd ask good questions, point out something useful she'd overlooked, and be happy for her.

But she didn't need him to be happy for her. She was happy for herself. She was working harder than she'd ever worked—working with so much concentration, so much creativity, that she didn't think about him at all. Except when she did.

*
*

Brett felt like a stalker as he skulked in the alley behind Benik's Bakery at one in the morning when he should be in bed. Through the barred back window, he could see her working at the gleaming counter. A red bandana restrained her curls, and a tank top peeked from under the bib of denim overalls that looked as if they might have been worn by a sexy, 1950s dairy farmer. The tools of her trade lay around her on the counter: chocolate molds, squeeze bottles holding different colors of cocoa butter for decoration, an airbrush, some kind of cardboard booth she'd jury-rigged to protect the area around her when she was spraying decorations on her chocolates.

Earlier that evening, he'd met her neighbor Toby for a beer, ostensibly to tip him for bartending at the party—something Brett had understandably forgotten to do in the chaos of the evening—but really to make sure Rory wasn't living on the street because she couldn't make rent. The bakery was less than a mile from her apartment, but the thought of her walking home alone in the middle of the night scared the hell out of him. This was Chicago!

He rapped on the window harder than he intended. She reared up, her hand shooting to her chest, her expression turning murderous as she recognized him. She stormed toward the metal door. Seconds later, it swung open. "What do you *want*?" She didn't look even marginally glad to see him.

Sometimes the best defense was a strong offense. He charged inside, the door closing behind him. "I want to know what you're doing working by yourself in the dead of night where any thug off the street could barge in."

"Like you?" As she glowered at him, she pulled her bottom lip between her teeth, drawing his attention to a mouth he hadn't gotten to kiss nearly enough.

His life's path had been so much simpler before he'd entangled himself with Rory Garrett. Until he'd met her, there had been no potholes, side roads, or construction detours. Now, his straightforward life had hit a traffic snarl, which he needed to straighten out.

He bought time by looking around. Music played faintly in the background, and a larger version of the tempering machine she kept in her home kitchen hummed away. Three different kinds of molded chocolates sat in rows on the counter ready for packaging: one batch with white shells airbrushed in different shades of green, another with metallic purple domes speckled in black and white, and a third—hot pink bonbons piped with chocolate-brown squiggles.

"Go ahead," she said begrudgingly. "I know you want to."

The fact that she wasn't making him leave gave him hope that they could have a sensible conversation. Her all-or-nothing attitude toward their relationship was unnecessary. Nonsensical. That was why he was here. He needed to make her understand that they could continue to quietly see each other.

Although his appetite had deserted him these past few weeks, seeing what she'd created brought it back. Each piece was an exquisitely executed piece of art, and eating any of them felt like a desecration. Not that he'd let that stop him. He selected a white-coated bonbon and felt the distinctive snap of the glossy shell as he bit into it. A minty dark chocolate ganache bloomed in his mouth followed by the sharp tang of bourbon. It was incredible. "You've made a perfect mint julep."

She forgot to glower at him. "That's what I was going for. Adults only."

He temporarily set aside the uneaten half and picked up a glossy purple bonbon. This time, he experienced an explosion of blackberry and creamy vanilla that managed to be both simple and over-the-top luxurious. He'd never been a fanciful person, but everything she created seemed infused with a special kind of magic. "I can't ever eat cheap chocolate again."

Her gaze clung to his for only a moment before she looked away. "Thanks for the taste test. You can go now." She turned her attention to the large sheet of empty teddy bear molds on the table. Each one had a space for a stick to be inserted to make teddy bear lollipops. She'd already painted in the eyes, nose, and paws. Now she picked up a brush, dipped it in the bright blue cocoa butter sitting on some kind of mini warmer, and began painting the indentation that marked the bear's scarf.

Instead of leaving, he finished his two chocolates and observed the meticulous way she worked, a master of her craft, every movement purposeful. Finally, he broke the silence. "When is quitting time?"

"When I start making mistakes." Her hand wobbled. "Damn it! Will you get out so I can concentrate?"

Stalling for time, he reached for the bright pink bonbon with the brown squiggle. "I need to try this last one."

She stopped what she was doing and watched him. Something expectant in her expression should have warned him but didn't.

The roof of his mouth took the first hit, followed by his tongue, right up into his sinus cavities—an inferno that made sweat pop out on his brow. He wheezed. "This thing needs a warning sticker."

"It'll have one," she said smugly. "That's a specialty piece."

As he got his breath back, he detected a trace of espresso beneath the heat, a whisper of orange. This was the perfect tangle of sweet and spice, pain and pleasure, all in one fiery bite. He wanted to eat another. Eat her. The chocolates were an aphrodisiac. He yearned to lay her on the counter, smear chocolate all over her naked body, and lick it right off.

He quickly stepped back to hide his hard-on and knocked a spatula to the floor. He retrieved it and carried it to the sink where an array of dirty pots and bowls waited cleanup, and where he could give his body a chance to recover before she noticed, and where he could plot his next move. He had to make her understand how unnecessarily stubborn she was being.

He located the dish soap and began filling one of the three tubs with hot, soapy water.

"You don't have to do that," she said.

"I know." He glanced over his shoulder without turning. Her stiff posture had thawed. Her hands were still, her shoulders relaxed, her lips parted, and those gin bottle–blue eyes no longer icy.

When she realized he was watching, her armor went back on. "Suit yourself."

He bought more time by redirecting his attention to the dishes. He searched for something to talk about other than how much he missed her and how flat his world had become without her. "I met your friend Toby for a beer—I forgot to tip him the night of the party. He told me you and Kristin have gone into business together."

A glance behind him showed she was accenting the folds of the bears' cocoa butter scarves with purple. Apparently, plain blue scarves weren't special enough for a master chocolatier.

"You could have Venmoed Toby a tip," she said. "Why did you have to meet him?" The way she shoved aside the tray of bear molds told him she wasn't happy with her work.

"I wanted to make sure you were okay."

She carried the unfinished bear molds to the sink and dumped them in the soapy water. "Why wouldn't I be?"

He spotted a dab of blue cocoa butter on her cheek and yearned to kiss it off. "Because there's a murderer on the loose, and you've been asking questions."

She elbowed him out of the way at the sink and plunged her hands in the water. "Toby needs to mind his own business instead of gossiping about me. And I take Kristin's car at night, even though it's less than a mile. Not my choice. Kristin's prone to giving herself random job titles whenever she feels like it, and she declared herself our health and safety manager."

"I was surprised to hear the two of you have gone into business together considering your past history."

"Not as surprised as me."

"How's it going?"

"We haven't killed each other, if that's what you mean." She took a sponge to the bear mold. "In two days we're making our maiden voyage, which is why I need to get my work done tonight. I can't concentrate with you here."

He nodded. "This thing between us . . . I've been thinking a lot about it, and walking away doesn't make sense." He spoke more firmly, The River at the bargaining table. "We like being together. We have fun. We're sure as hell good in bed."

She grabbed a towel to dry her hands. "You've got a female sexual smorgasbord waiting for you all over the city. You don't need me."

"You know I'm not just talking about sex. We can be friends, if that's what you want. Good friends. We get each other." He was lying. He couldn't have only a friendship with her, and they both knew it. He never lied at the bargaining table, and he hated himself for it even as he reached out to touch her.

*
*

Rory's skin prickled as his hand brushed the nape of her neck. Water dripped from the faucet into the sink in a slow *tat . . . tat . . . tat.* The air-conditioning wheezed, and the spell between them wove itself again. Instead of pulling away, she rested her cheek against his wrist. But only for a moment before she drew away. "I can't be friends with you. And from the way you're looking at me, you can't be friends with me, either."

"How am I looking at you?"

Her voice grew hoarse. "Like I'm one more obstacle you need to conquer."

"That's not fair." His thumb found the seam of her lips. She closed her eyes. His hand smelled of dishwashing soap, chocolate, and ambition. It would be so easy to be swept up in his single-minded charge for the goal line—this man who had to win at everything.

She pulled away. "I can't. This isn't a game. You're hurting me."

She might as well have hit him. He flinched, and something that might have been shame made him drop his gaze. "You're right. I shouldn't have come here."

Within seconds, she was once again alone in the kitchen.

20

Kristin ran from room to room trying to find shoulder pads so she could race onto the football field and warn Rory that she hadn't fed her pet turtle. The sound of knocking gradually pulled her from the dream. Rory had never had a pet turtle. Something was wrong. The pressure of opening the food truck in the morning had gotten to her.

Shaking off the remnants of the dream, Kristin stumbled out of bed, and without bothering to grab a robe, opened the door. Her disheveled son stood on the other side.

"Clint . . ." *My son . . . My heart . . . My darling little boy . . .* Her hand flew to her cheek.

He loomed over her, more than a head taller, broad shouldered, with Gregg's blue eyes and cheekbones. He gave her a too-brief hug, his beard scruff brushing the top of her forehead. "Hey, Mom. Sorry to bother you so late." He stepped away from her too soon. "I can only go out at night these days. Like a vampire. Otherwise, the press follows me."

Her heart ached for him. "Of course. It's no bother. Come in."

He was her kid, but she was flustered. When children were young, parents were in control, but when they grew up, the kids called the shots, and if she hovered, said the wrong thing, he might distance her again.

She closed the door behind him and padded barefoot to turn on the lights. Rory said Clint had never visited Ashley here, so the apartment shouldn't hold any memories for him.

"I got your text," he said.

Which text? She'd sent so many. Too many. Maybe he meant yesterday's text when she'd told him she'd rented an apartment in Rory's building, although she hadn't told him which one.

"Sorry it's taken me so long to see you," he said. "I haven't exactly been in a good place."

"I understand." She didn't understand. She was his mother. He could talk to her about anything. "Let me get you something to eat. A sandwich. I have some leftover tuna salad." Rory thought Kristin smothered Clint, but was it smothering to want to feed your kid?

"I'm not hungry."

"I have beer." She hurried into the kitchen. She'd bought a six-pack of some kind of Guinness for Daniel. She'd seen him that evening, and she already missed him. She loved making love with him, but she also loved when they simply held each other. They talked for hours, sharing their stories, their secrets, their strengths and foibles.

"You don't drink beer," he said from behind her.

"I have a friend who does." She'd tell him about Daniel later, when she wasn't so nervous. She retrieved a bottle from the refrigerator and set it on the counter. She didn't have beer mugs—she barely had dishes—but she had a bottle opener somewhere. Where had she put it? She needed to find it.

"Mom, what's this about? This used to be Ashley's place. Why did you rent it?"

She'd been worried about this. "I hope it doesn't upset you. Nothing of hers is still here. It's only temporary until I find a permanent place."

He frowned. "What about the house? What are you really doing here?"

Being near you. Near Rory. With Daniel. "Someone's looking after the house."

She didn't miss the house at all. Despite a renovated kitchen and a new addition at the back, despite fresh paint, refurbished floors—despite Debra having lived there for only four years while Kristin had been there for twenty-eight—despite all that, the house wasn't hers.

She opened another drawer. Maybe she didn't have a beer opener. Maybe she'd only thought about getting one.

"Are you still here because of me? You don't have to stay."

"I know that."

"You texted me that you're selling chocolate with Rory? That's crazy."

She reached the last drawer and started her search all over again, her movements growing increasingly clumsy. He hadn't said he wanted a beer, but if she didn't give him one, he might not want to spend time with her. As she sorted through the drawers and cupboards, she gave him a jumbled account of what she and Rory were doing, repeating herself, getting events out of order, leaving cupboard doors and drawers open.

He regarded her uneasily. "Mom, are you okay?"

The concern on his face brought everything into focus. She saw herself as he saw her—hands trembling, chest heaving, searching for a bottle opener as if she were looking for the Holy Grail. Going into business with Rory wasn't crazy. This was crazy—believing her relationship with her son hinged on finding a bottle opener.

She pushed her hair away from her face. Rory was right. Kristin smothered Clint. Ever since he was born, her life's purpose had centered on being his mother. Now that she'd met Daniel, was she going to start living in his shadow, too?

Being with Rory, seeing her stepdaughter's passion for her work, had awakened something inside, and that image of herself no longer fit. She was a competent woman with energy and ambition, a woman who could match Rory snark for snark, who could throw herself over a wooden fence and stand up to the brilliant, eccentric man who'd won her heart. With a shock, she realized how much she loved this new version of herself.

She spotted the bottle opener, wedged between the toaster and coffee maker. She turned away from it toward her son. "Sorry. I can't find the opener."

He shrugged. "You and Rory have never gotten along. I don't understand why you've decided to operate a food truck with her. Do you need money? If you need money, I'll be glad to—"

"I don't need money. You know your father left me well provided for. And this is something I want to do. It's interesting. Challenging."

He set his jaw. "You have interesting things to do at home. You have friends there."

"I'm making friends here." Mr. Reynolds talked to her about his garden, Toby confided about his issues with his dad, but her best friend was now her stepdaughter. She met Clint's belligerent gaze. "Rory's your sister. I know you don't like what she did, but her heart was in the right place."

"And Ashley ended up dead!"

"Don't blame Ashley's death on Rory! You were ready to fly off to Las Vegas and elope with a woman who was clearly after your money. Rory cared enough to intercede."

Clint stuffed his hands in his pockets and left the kitchen. She went after him. "Do you have any idea how many times Rory has been on the phone arguing with the detective who's investigating your case?" The streetlight sent a trapezoidal pattern to the rug in front of the window where he stood. She advanced on him. "Rory tracked down one of Ashley's former boyfriends—did you know that? She talked to Ashley's boss, your housekeeper, even your gardener. She traveled to Michigan to find you!"

"She didn't have to do any of that," he mumbled.

"Look at me. Rory never once expressed any doubt about you. Never mentioned even the possibility that you might have been responsible for Ashley's death. And you've repaid her by cutting her out of your life."

"Ashley didn't deserve to die!" he exclaimed.

"Of course she didn't. And Rory doesn't deserve what you're dishing out. You're usually a good judge of character, but you misjudged Ashley and you're misjudging your sister."

He jerked his hands from his pockets. "I can't believe you're standing up for her."

Kristin finally understood what she'd missed, and her heart ached for him. "You're a natural leader. It's never been easy for you to admit when you're wrong. But you were wrong about Ashley, and instead of coming to terms with that, you've made Rory and Brett convenient scapegoats."

She'd never seen her son look at her like this—not so much with anger, but more as if she'd betrayed him. Her stomach sank, but as he stormed to the door, she didn't say a word. He was her son. She loved him beyond reason, but he would have to work this out for himself.

*
*

On their first day in the refurbished truck, Rory found a parking place near Union Station. Kristin, stylish in sunglasses, Lilly Pulitzer, and a straw boater, stood on the sidewalk looking as though she were on her way to a garden party in the Hamptons instead of trolling for customers. Rory watched from the truck window as the morning commuters leaving the train station passed her without a glance. It wasn't surprising no one recognized her as the mother of the city's most famous—now infamous—quarterback. Who would expect to see Clint Garrett's mother shilling chocolates in front of a food truck?

Rory had gotten up at six, after barely three hours of sleep, and found Kristin already awake and dressed. They'd driven to the bakery to pick up the chocolates stored there and headed for the Loop in the truck, Rory at the wheel.

"Excuse me, sir." Kristin politely addressed a man who had his suit coat draped over his arm. "Would you like to try our delicious handmade chocolates?"

The man moved on without looking at her.

"Pardon me, miss. We have handmade chocolates. Would you like to try our buttercreams?"

The woman didn't even glance in her direction.

Rory had known it was a waste of time to open the truck this early, but Kristin insisted, and Rory wanted to keep the peace between them.

"Enticing flavors," Kristin proclaimed to a Gen Z–er with ear-buds and a leopard tote.

"Handmade sea salt caramels." This to a millennial in khakis.

The longer Kristin kept at it, the more desperate she sounded, but Rory told herself it was too early to get depressed. She checked the videos she'd posted last night on her new TikTok and Insta-gram pages. With only a dozen followers, she was a long way from being an influencer, but she'd been DMing the ones who were and inviting them to visit the truck for free samples.

Even with the new brown-and-pink striped awning shading the window, it was already hot inside. Once the air-conditioning was repaired, she could begin making chocolates here during the day and use the bakery kitchen only at night when she needed to. But despite the lack of air-conditioning, she loved what they'd done with the truck. Not only was it running well, but Duncan Gil-ford's imaginative design for the vinyl wrap had transformed the tacky Royal Palace of Sweets into a chocolate emporium.

A cocoa-brown tree now enhanced the pink exterior, its branches curling to the roof and draping to frame the window. Instead of leaves, the tree sprouted colorful bonbons. And across the bottom of the truck in nut-brown script was the name they'd finally settled on:

SIMPLY THE BEST
Artisan Chocolates
Affordable Luxury

Kristin popped up at the window, whipping off her oversized sunglasses. "We need another location."

"The location's fine, and we're not moving until our four hours are up."

"But no one is stopping!"

"It's eight o'clock. People are still drinking their first cup of coffee. I told you so. Tomorrow we'll open at ten."

Kristin looked so defeated that Rory wished she'd held her tongue, and she softened her tone. "Things will pick up midmorning. You'll see." She prayed that was true.

A mulish expression settled over Kristin's face. "Not good enough." She strode away from the window and began shouting like a Sag Harbor carnival barker. "Kick-start your morning! Drop chocolate truffles in your coffee! Coffee and truffles! It's a new day!"

Rory's truffles were designed to be savored, not drowned in an ordinary cup of coffee, but she wouldn't let herself be a snob about it.

One of the busy commuters looked Kristin's way, and she marched right over to him. "You, sir! Truffles in your coffee or are you just glad to see me?"

Rory laughed, her first since Brett had walked out of the bakery kitchen.

The commuter Kristin had accosted scurried away, but she wasn't discouraged. "Madam! Chocolate in your coffee guarantees a productive day! It was Warren Buffett's secret to success!"

The first Rory had heard about it.

The commuter rushed past her. Kristin whipped off her boater and brandished it like a flag. "Best chocolate in the city! Truffles in your morning cup will make your day! Two for the price of one!"

They really needed to discuss these unilateral decisions Kristin was making.

A woman wearing a backpack slowed. With her Starbucks cup in hand, she hesitantly approached the window. "I'll try it."

As she set her cup on the sill and pulled off the lid, Rory selected two truffles for her and handed them over on a doily with a smile. "Stop by tomorrow and let me know how you like them."

The woman nodded, dropped the truffles in her coffee, and paid—half of what she should have, but they'd made a sale.

An older man with a beard appeared next, and Rory got in the spirit. "That's a big cup. You might need three."

Kristin heard that. "The more truffles you buy, the bigger the yummy!"

Rory stuck her head out the window. "The *'yummy'*?"

"Mind your own business."

Kristin's enthusiasm was contagious, and an older, executive-type woman appeared next who blessedly wanted to eat the truffles, not drown them in her coffee. By the time their four hours were up, all the cocoa truffles were gone, along with eighteen individual pieces and two sample packs. It was a start, and it was also time to move.

*
*

Brett had no trouble finding Rory's truck with its new color scheme and eye-catching design. She'd wisely listed her business on the city's most popular food truck location app, and her parking spot in the Loop near Clark Street and Lake Street was taking advantage of the business lunch crowd.

For a good ten minutes, he'd been ignoring the pinging of his phone as he watched from the window of the 7-Eleven across the street. At first, Kristin stood on the sidewalk luring customers, but then she and Rory switched places.

Rory's familiar yellow shorts showed off her sturdy, supple legs, and her red-and-white-checked sleeveless blouse was the one she'd been wearing the day they'd met at Clint's house. Her curly hair made a shiny cloud around her head as she called out to passersby, and although he couldn't hear what she was saying, either she or her legs were doing a great job, because people were approaching the window.

A weight settled deeper onto his shoulders. He'd grown used to thinking of Rory as a quirky, sexy, intriguing woman who could never quite get her act together. But now, as his phone pinged and he saw her in her element, brimming with energy, doing what she'd been born to do, he was the one who felt like the loser.

These days his head was fuzzy, and he was in a perpetual bad mood. Clients whose demands had never bothered him had begun to set his teeth on edge. Playing the game just to win the game felt meaningless as he compared himself to Rory, who didn't even know there was a game. She didn't care about owning the biggest condo, driving the fastest car, or showing up on ESPN with a hot new client. She only wanted to make great chocolate.

Yesterday, he'd been late for a meeting because his mind kept drifting to her—something she'd said that made him laugh, how she pushed a wayward curl off her cheek, the feel of her skin, the sounds she'd made when he was inside her.

He'd been happy before they met. Or maybe not happy, but he'd been content. Or maybe not exactly content, since he didn't entirely understand what that word meant. He was always on the move, going after the next big thing—the biggest client, the fattest deal. No grass would grow under his Gucci loafers. But what was he running toward or running from?

During a lull between customers, Rory approached a tamale truck parked next to her and handed them something. Later, she

did the same with a truck selling lobster rolls. He didn't understand what she was doing until he saw a man who'd bought a lobster roll approach Rory's truck and hand over that paper. She was
passing out coupons to the neighboring trucks—a brilliant move.
Suddenly he wanted to be selling chocolates with her. He wanted
to be the huckster on the sidewalk convincing the lunch crowd to
trade their money for the city's best chocolate.

But his phone kept pinging, and he had his own job to do. Playing the game. Being the best.

*
*

Exhausted and elated from the success of their first few days, Rory
and Kristin devoured the steamed dumplings they'd bartered for
from an Asian fusion truck. Kristin dabbed the last of the soy
sauce from her fingers and gazed across the kitchen at Rory standing at the sink. "You're not going back to the kitchen tonight."

"I have to. We're out of cocoa truffles."

"Thanks to my continued marketing brilliance," Kristin said
smugly.

"Thanks to you." Rory smiled, despite being tired all the way to
her bones, even though it was barely seven thirty. She rinsed the
dumpling container at her sink and tossed it in her recycling bin.
"I don't need to make a lot, so it won't take long. I'll be home by
midnight. We have enough of everything else for a couple more
days."

Kristin's expression sobered. "Rory, this isn't sustainable for
you."

"It's only until the air-conditioning is fixed. Then I'll be able to
work more in the truck."

"Which could take another few weeks. You can't work all night and be on the street at eight the next morning. You were right. We need to make a later start."

"We can't appear and then disappear. That's not the way food trucks work. Those early-morning customers are coming back. They're buying more, and not just to drown them in coffee." She took Kristin's unopened chopsticks from the table and stuck them in her junk drawer. "If the morning thing keeps working, we should think about adding a premium coffee and more truffle flavors." She smothered a yawn. "Maple, amaretto. Maybe something off-the-wall like cardamom."

"*Bleck.*" Kristin made a face.

"I'll take cardamom as a no." Rory moved into the living room, trying to remember where she'd dropped her bag.

Kristin followed her. "You make my head spin."

It was hard to connect this new version of Kristin with the reserved, anxious woman Rory had grown up with. "You've loved every second." *And I love you.* The knowledge was new, unexpected, and felt so right.

"I have loved it, but you can't have slept more than four hours a night all week."

Rory yawned. "I can handle it."

Kristin's chin set. "I'm taking the truck out tomorrow morning while you sleep in. You can get on the L and meet me later."

"You can't do that. You won't even drive your car in the city, let alone drive the truck."

"I'm tired of letting fear get in my way."

Rory gazed at Kristin and something tightened in her throat. "When I grow up, I want to be just like you." Kristin cocked her head, waiting for Rory to follow up the compliment with a jab, but Rory gave her a long hug instead. "We'll take driving the truck step-by-step. No need to rush. I'll help you get used to it."

"I already have help. Daniel's driven lots of trucks. He's going with me tomorrow morning."

"Daniel? You've already talked to him about this? Doesn't he have a business to run?"

"He's rearranging his schedule." Kristin's mouth curled in a dopey smile. "It's only for one morning."

Rory understood so much more now. "Dad would never have done something like that."

"He didn't like to be inconvenienced. And Daniel isn't like your father."

Rory smiled. "No, he's not."

*
*

As Imagine Dragons played in the background, Rory piped an extra-creamy ganache in generous, even domes on the parchment sheets laid out on the bakery counter. She relished having an abundance of ingredients to work with again. Once the ganache domes had set, she'd hand-dip them in tempered chocolate and finish them with a dusting of her fine French cocoa powder.

It was only ten o'clock. She was beyond tired, but she decided to make a separate amaretto-flavored ganache and take Kristin up on her offer. Even staying in bed until eight o'clock would feel decadent. She went into the bakery's storage room and grabbed a fresh bag of callets. One day they'd be able to afford a commercial roaster and roast their own beans.

As she emerged from the storage room, someone knocked on

the back door. The pain hit all over again. How was she going to stop thinking about Brett if he kept showing up?

But as she crossed the kitchen, the face that looked back at her through the barred window didn't belong to Brett. It belonged to Clint, the brother who'd said he never wanted to see her again.

She cautiously opened the door. He offered a small, polite nod. "Can I come in?"

She shrugged and stepped aside.

"It smells good in here."

Imagine Dragons had switched to "Demons." She set the bag of callets on the prep table and picked up her phone to turn off the music. He took in the counters and ovens. "How old were you when you tried to sell me to that lady in the park?"

She concentrated on her phone instead of looking at him. "Six and a half. Old enough to know better."

He stuffed his hands in the pockets of his shorts. "My favorite story. That took guts."

"It took stupidity." She set aside her phone, wondering why he'd come here. "A six-year-old carrying an infant along a cement sidewalk. I could have dropped you."

"You didn't."

She pretended to inspect the truffle centers on the counter. "Kristin wouldn't leave you alone with me for years afterward."

"She never should have left you alone with me. You were a shitty babysitter." He leaned his hips against the six-burner range.

"The shittiest." She opened the bag of callets, wishing he'd go away.

"When a tornado siren went off, you told me it meant there was a zombie invasion. You said zombies hated jalapeños, and the only way I could keep them from sucking out my brain was to eat one raw."

She finally looked at him. "It would have worked, too, if you hadn't rubbed your eyes and started screaming. I got in big trouble for that."

"You deserved it." He crossed the kitchen and poked his head into the storage room. "Christmas Eve when I was five, you told me Santa had accidentally crashed into the Hubble telescope and died."

"I know I've been an awful sister, and I understand why you're done with me. There's nothing you can say that'll make me feel worse. I'm sorry. Now, do you mind leaving?"

He approached the domes of sticky ganache. "Can I eat one of these?"

"They're not done but go ahead."

He picked up a truffle center, popped the whole thing in his mouth, and spoke around it. "The best was the time you taped me up in bubble wrap and rolled me down that big hill behind the Slaters' house." He ate another, not savoring the flavors the way Brett did, just enjoying it. "You wouldn't cut me out until right before you knew Mom and Dad were coming home."

She remembered too well. "I never understood why you didn't tell on me."

"It was fun, and I liked getting your attention. Mom and Dad I was sure about, but not you."

She finally looked at him. "You must have been a masochist."

"Maybe." His voice grew softer. "Do you remember when Frankie died?"

Rory would never forget. Frankie Spravic had been Clint's best friend in third grade. He'd died in a freak house fire, and the whole community had gone into mourning. "It was awful."

"You slept with me every night for at least two weeks. I told you I was afraid I'd die in my sleep, and you promised you'd stay awake all night and wake me up if I stopped breathing."

"I'm sure I was asleep as soon as you were."

"But I didn't know that." He wandered over to the sink to rinse off his sticky fingers. "I was always jealous of you."

She stared at him. "Of me? How could you have been jealous of me?"

"You were allowed to screw up. I never was."

"But they doted on you. Idolized you. You could do no wrong."

"And I felt like I had to live up to all of their expectations—especially Dad's. I had to be good at everything. I wasn't allowed to screw up. But you didn't have that pressure. You could flunk a test, and all he'd do was ground you for a couple of days. But if I goofed off at anything—classwork, sports, chores—I'd get these long lectures from Dad about responsibility, achievement, living up to my potential. He'd reminded me of all the advantages I had, the talent I was born with. Disappointing him was a hell of a lot worse than being grounded. And once you left for college, with only me to focus on, it got worse."

She understood intellectually what he was saying, but not what it meant emotionally. "You were jealous of me?"

"Hell, yes. I guess I still am."

She felt as if the floor were tilting under her feet.

He leaned his hips against the big commercial refrigerator. "You don't always have to perform at the top of your ability. You don't get trolled on social or have sportswriters make up shit about you. You can go anywhere you want without people asking for selfies." He shoved his hands through his hair. "Poor me, right? Millions of people want what I have, and here I am whining about it. What an entitled jerk."

She considered the constant pressure he lived under. The never-ending public scrutiny. And now, he'd been charged with a murder he didn't commit. "I guess being the Golden Boy isn't all it's cracked up to be."

"No pity needed. I love playing football."

"I know you do. But you don't love everything connected with it."

"Like I said. A million people would like to have my problems."

"Charged with a murder they didn't commit? Hardly."

"I was an idiot about Ashley. You tried to warn me. So did Brett. But I don't like being wrong, and I didn't want to hear it."

She wondered what had finally made him see the truth.

He stared at nothing then turned his attention back to her. "Lying about her wasn't the only time you lied to protect me."

"What do you mean?"

"I was maybe eight, and Dad kept warning me my bike was going to get stolen if I didn't lock it up in the garage at night."

"Sounds like him."

"It happened just the way he said. I forgot to put it away, woke up the next morning, and it was gone. When he found out, he lit into me. How ashamed he was of me, how he expected better, how could he be proud of me when I did stupid things? I started to cry. You sauntered downstairs, saw what was going on, and told Dad it was your fault. You said you'd taken my bike from the garage and left it out in the yard when you were done with it."

"I guess I vaguely remember."

"You must have been around fourteen. Apparently Dad never wondered why you'd want to ride a kid's bike because all I can remember is him telling Mom something like she should handle you because he gave up."

"Sounds familiar."

"I knew that was wrong even then, but I didn't say a word. I let you take the blame."

She smiled. "Your lack of character is music to my ears."

He smiled back at her. "Remember how I'd follow you around, stay right on your heels so you couldn't get away, and repeat everything you said? Man, that was fun. You'd get so pissed. The best was hiding under your bed and jumping out at you. You'd chase me through the whole house yelling."

"I could never catch you."

"Good practice for my future career. When you complained to Mom, she'd tell you that I was just a little kid, and you needed to be grown-up about it."

"That still makes me mad."

"Definitely unfair." He grinned.

She smiled even as she felt the sting of tears. "I forgot what a little shit you were. Why have I let myself feel guilty for so many years?"

"Beats me." He sobered. "I didn't kill Ashley."

She snatched a tissue from her bag, suddenly angry. "Why are you telling me that? I know you didn't kill her!"

"How do you know? I don't have an alibi, and I sure as hell had motive."

She threw up her hands. "God, Clint, anyone who knows you realizes you aren't capable of killing someone. That's why this is so horrible."

He rubbed his hand through his beard scruff. "Mom reamed my ass for giving you shit about what you told Ashley."

"She did?"

"She said you've been doing detective work."

"And I've come up with absolutely nothing. All the police do is patronize me."

He ducked his head, lifted it, gazed at her. "I'm sorry for what I said the other day. I was wrong. You were looking out for me like you always did."

This new vision of the past took her aback. She'd forgotten how much pressure her dad had put on Clint and how Kristin had tried to make up for it by doting on him. But Rory had doted on Clint, too, in her own way. He was her baby brother, and despite her childish mischief, she hadn't been quite the horrible sister she'd believed herself to be. She loved her brother—had always loved him. It was herself she hadn't been able to accept. "We both wanted what the other had," she said.

"But we never talked about it."

"Now we have. You're a good man, Clint Garrett." The last thing he needed was another female doting on him. "Even though you acted like an asshole when I came to see you."

"Guilty." He cocked his head. "I want things to be different between us."

"I do, too." She paused. "As long as you don't start following me around and repeating everything I say."

He deliberately bumped her with his arm. "As long as you don't start following me around and repeating everything I say."

"I'm going to kill you!"

"I'm going to kill you!"

She jabbed him in the chest. "I'm buying jalapeños."

He laughed and pulled her into a hug.

She hugged him right back.

21

Rory was still smiling as she packed up the fresh truffles for tomorrow in the food keepers she used for transport. What a distorted lens she'd been using to view her childhood. Clint had given her a gift tonight, and she hoped she'd given him one, too. Even though her life felt precarious now, at least her relationship with her brother had a future.

Unless he ended up in prison for murder.

She pushed away the thought, snapped the lids on the containers, and turned off the kitchen lights. Carefully balancing her night's work in her arms, she let herself out into the alley.

A dark figure appeared from nowhere.

She gasped, and the container on top—the one holding four dozen freshly made truffles—began to slip from her grasp.

The figure made a diving catch . . .

"Got it!" Brett rolled to his back, somehow holding up the truffles. "No damage done."

She stared down at him. He didn't look like himself, and not just because he was lying flat on the crumbling concrete with a plastic container of truffles balanced in his hands. The flood-lights mounted on each side of the back door showed a man who hadn't shaved and whose slicked-back hair was only a memory. Now, it fell over his forehead and stuck up in the back. His awkward sprawl had bunched his T-shirt, and he had one missing shoe. No one could confuse this rumpled deadbeat with the cocky titan of the sports industry she'd first met on that hotel balcony a month ago.

She snatched the food keeper from him. "What are you doing sneaking up on me like that?"

Still on the ground, he began brushing loose gravel from his bare legs. "Didn't mean to surprise you."

Her heartbeat slowly returned to normal. "Then what did you mean to do?"

A few dots of blood appeared in his leg hair, but he ignored them as he came to his feet. He bent over and picked off more gravel—maybe because he needed to, maybe because he didn't want to look at her. "I couldn't sleep," he muttered.

"So you decided to hang out in the alley with the rats?"

"I wanted to see you." He looked around for the shoe he'd lost during his rescue mission.

"We're done, Brett. There's nothing left to say."

"That's not true." He glanced at the scrape on the inside of his arm, seeming to forget about the shoe.

She finally noticed his car parked across the alley. "Brett, are you drunk?"

She'd never seen him like this—clumsy, uncertain—and despite every internal resolution to keep her distance, she set the truffles on the hood of Kristin's Volvo and moved to him. "What's wrong?"

"Pretty much everything." He finally put his shoe on only to take it back off, shake out the gravel, and try again.

"Your leg is bleeding."

"I don't care. I made a decision."

"What kind of decision?"

"I'm going to tell Heath everything."

"You're what?" She regarded him with growing alarm. "No you aren't."

He swiped his palm over his face. "You said I made you feel like a dirty little secret. I hate that."

"Let it go. Let everything go." She had to put a stop to this. "I can't have a relationship with you. You, more than anyone, should understand that. My work is everything to me right now. I can't get distracted by all kinds of messy feelings that won't take me anywhere but down."

"You think I don't have messy feelings?"

"Not as messy as mine." She could either hold on to her pride, or she could strip herself bare and finally put an end to this. She made herself meet his gaze. "The only future we have is heartbreak. Despite what I said, I fell in love with you, Brett."

He didn't move. Didn't blink.

"I knew what a mistake it was, but it still happened." She took a long breath. "Everything's a competition to you. It's in your DNA. But I'm not like that. And be honest with yourself. If you had me locked in, you know you'd get bored. The fun for you is the blitz, the scramble, the trick play. That's what your life is about. What your relationships are about."

"You're not a competition!" he exclaimed.

"Then what am I?"

He opened his mouth to respond. Closed it. She drilled in. "Do I mean enough to be the most important thing in your life? Before your career? Your ambition? Look me in the eye and tell me you're in love with me." Her voice trembled. She waited. "Go ahead," she whispered. "Do it."

A deafening silence stretched between them, and something broke inside her. "I thought so." She grabbed the truffles, climbed into Kristin's car, and left him behind.

⁎

Brett stared at the taillights of her car disappearing down the alley. His legs felt as if they'd been set in concrete. He'd always had fast reflexes, but the way she'd blurted it out like that—the way she'd challenged him . . . He'd clutched. If she'd given him a few minutes, he'd have—

"You fucker."

Clint shot around from the side of the Dumpster and grabbed him by the front of his T-shirt. "You've been playing her!" Clint shoved him hard against the brick wall of the bakery. "My sister!" He released Brett just enough so he could once again press him against the bricks. "You son of a bitch!" Another shove. "You're a snake! Even she should have been able to figure that out."

It was the word "even" that got him. As if Rory had something missing, as if she weren't the smartest woman he knew. He broke free, jammed Clint in the chest, and sacked him.

They wrestled in the gravel. Rats scurried in the Dumpster, and an ambulance siren screamed in the distance. They scrambled to their feet. Garrett got him in the shoulder, in the jaw. Brett hit him anyplace he could reach. Fueled by misery, he had the target he needed for everything he'd screwed up.

Garrett was seven years younger, a trained athlete, and had him by fifty pounds, but the fight still lasted longer than it should have. Eventually, though, with Brett's back once again pinioned to the wall and Clint's arm strapped across his chest, the fight was over.

"You're fired, you son of a bitch! And don't you ever go near her again!"

* *

Clint sped from the alley, adrenaline surging, barely resisting the urge to ram his car into Rivers's Benz. Defending his sister's honor might be old-fashioned, but it felt good, a little payback for acting like a jerk. Thank God, he'd come back. He'd driven around when he'd left Rory. Feeling almost good. He wanted to do something big for her. She'd always refused to take his money, but she was starting a business. Maybe he could convince her to let him invest.

He couldn't visit her in the daytime, and he didn't want to wait until tomorrow night to talk to her, so he'd headed back to the bakery, hoping she'd still be there. But as he'd pulled into the alley, he'd spotted Rivers's red Benz parked at the end. Something hadn't felt right. He'd killed the engine and walked the rest of the way up the alley until he heard Rory. A broken heart was something he knew too much about, and it took only seconds for him to hear the pain in her voice and understand what had been going on behind his back. Understand how Rivers had played her.

His leg cramped. Rivers had put up more fight than a pansy-assed sports agent should have, and that pissed him off even more.

By the time he pulled into the Owens-Shore garage, his cramp was gone, but not his anger. He grabbed his phone. He didn't care that it was the middle of the night. He wanted Heath Champion to know exactly why the company had lost a client.

* *

Brett got quietly drunk at an all-night dive bar with missing floor tiles and a Cash Only sign hanging between a set of deer antlers and a photo of the Pope. The varnish had worn off the sticky bar a good two decades earlier, and duct tape held the seats of the stools together. The blood had congealed on his leg, his jaw was swollen, and his dirty T-shirt had a rip at the shoulder. Nobody knew him here, and nobody wanted to know him.

At four in the morning, he finally settled his tab and staggered out. He forgot where he'd left his car, and he was too drunk to drive anyway, so he Ubered home. Filthy and unwashed, he collapsed on the couch of the place he hated.

He awoke around noon with a throbbing head and aching jaw. The smell of fresh paint and day-old sweat made his already-precarious stomach roil. Nobody fired The River, and yet that's what Clint Garrett had done.

Brett had to fix this. That's what he did. He cut problems off at the knees before they became bigger problems. Now he had to save his career. He rolled off the couch and staggered into the shower. He was still The River. He could do this.

Three cups of coffee later, he was on his way to break the unbreakable rule for every employee at Champion Sports Management: disturbing the boss on weekends when he was with his family. But Brett couldn't let this fester until Monday. He had to intervene now. Convince Heath that this had only happened because of the stress Clint was under.

No time to find his car now. He Ubered to the Champions' house in Lincoln Park. Annabelle answered the door, took one look at him, and grimaced. "Uh-oh."

She wore a turquoise bathing suit cover-up printed with dancing monkeys, possibly a reference to her children, the youngest of whom stood behind her in the hallway, one finger up his nose, the other hand hugging a deflated beach ball.

Brett caught a glimpse of himself in the hallway mirror behind her. Bruised and unshaven jaw with a black eye and bruised chin, he'd forgotten to comb his hair, and something wasn't right with his shirt. He glanced down and saw he'd buttoned it wrong.

Annabelle hurried out onto the porch with him, closing the front door firmly behind her. "Talking to him now isn't a good idea."

"I have to."

Light glinted off the sunglasses resting on top of her auburn hair. "Clint called him in the middle of the night."

Another gut punch. He'd hoped Clint would wait until Monday. Now, instead of getting to Heath first to do damage control, Brett had to play a dangerous game of catch-up. "That's all the more reason I need to see him now."

"I strongly suggest you give him the weekend to cool off."

"With all due respect, that's not going to work."

She shrugged. "Your funeral."

As she led him down the long hallway to the kitchen, he clumsily rebuttoned his dress shirt and dragged his hand through his hair.

Heath, wearing swim trunks and a T-shirt, stood at the counter stuffing trail mix into individual plastic snack bags. He saw Brett, and his eyes grew as cold as Chicago in January. With a worried glance between the two men, Annabelle moved to her husband's side. "I'll take over."

Heath jerked his head toward a side hallway. Brett followed him, bypassing a pair of kids' rain boots and a chair piled with beach towels on the way to Heath's home office, a sunny room with framed children's drawings on its light gray walls.

Heath stood between the windows and didn't invite him to sit. "Garrett called me at two in the morning."

Brett had to keep his cool. "He's under a lot of pressure. He had to take out his frustration on someone, and I was convenient. That's all this is."

Heath moved to his desk, leaving Brett standing like a kid in the principal's office. "You were supposed to be my senior VP. The one I could trust to take over. Next in line. The guy who could handle any situation. You were the man who was supposed to help me lead Champion Sports Management into the future."

"I'm still that man," Brett said, not as firmly as he wanted. "This is a speed bump, that's all. Look, Heath, I'll recover. I always do."

Heath shot up from his desk. "You don't have a clue how to recover from this. And do you know why?" He jabbed a hard finger in the general direction of Brett's head. "Because you don't have any fucking *practice*! You've never screwed up—not until last month. But, man, once you got the hang of it, you aced it! First Garrett gets accused of murder, and you can't find him. Then you decide to throw a party for Tyler Capello, who doesn't show up until the bitter end and then signs with CAA. And that party—it wasn't just any party, was it? In a staggering lack of judgment, you sign up Clint's sister and mother to be your hired help and top it off by trying to burn to death half the jocks in this town!"

"That's not quite fair. It was—"

"Shut up!" He came around the side of the desk. "You should have been able to sign Tyler without breaking a sweat. And now Garrett—one of the best players in the world—has fired you!"

"He's having a tough—"

"You know what's even worse? Now I—not you—*I* have to get down on my fucking knees to convince Garrett to stay with us. And the only way I can do that is by promising to personally represent him. Promise he'll never have to see your face again and hope that's enough to keep him!"

"Heath—"

"I don't want to represent Garrett!" he exclaimed. "I want to make my job easier, not harder, but here I am, at the beck and call of another demanding jock. *If* I'm lucky enough to convince him to stay."

"Garrett isn't a demanding—"

"Don't!" This time his finger connected directly with Brett's chest, landing close enough to a bruised rib to make Brett wince. "Here's exactly how we're moving forward. Instead of firing you— and believe me, I'm tempted—I'm transferring you to the West Coast office. From now on, you work for Portia Powers and Brodie Gray out of LA. You don't show your face in Chicago—you don't show your face in the entire state of Illinois unless I personally sign off on it."

Brett didn't want to go to LA. Chicago was his town. His people. His ugly condo was here. Rory was here.

"You had the world in the palm of your hand, but you blew it. And over what? Over a *woman*!"

The contemptuous way he sneered that word—as if Rory were garbage—made fire run through Brett's veins. He clenched his fists at his sides. "Watch it."

"You're telling me to watch it? You—the asshole who decided to fuck Garrett's sister? Yeah, I know all about that! You're telling me—"

Brett grabbed Heath by his shirt and slammed him against his office wall exactly as Clint had done to him. "Rory Garrett is not just *any woman*!" Lost in a white-hot rage, Brett thrust his face in Heath's. "You go to hell! You and your job and this whole fucked-up business can all go to hell because I quit!"

He stormed from the room, past Annabelle and two wide-eyed children—out the front door with all the fires of hell burning at his heels.

The front door slammed shut. Annabelle raised her eyebrows and slowly crossed the office carpet to her husband. She straightened his T-shirt, patted his chest, and brushed her lips over his. "Now *that* was interesting."

*
*

Rory gazed into the dark backyard from her kitchen window. It was one thirty Sunday morning, and she needed to sleep. Instead, she was wide-awake, standing in her dark kitchen, thinking about Brett.

The friendship he craved was something she couldn't give him. She ran her finger over the chipped paint on the window frame. Brett would never love her back, not more than he loved his job. He'd also never tell Heath about their relationship. The rules of his profession were written in stone and being intimate with a

member of a client's family was beyond forbidden. Look at what
had happened with Tyler. Brett had nothing to gain by being upfront with Heath and everything to lose.

She needed to get some sleep, but as she began to turn away
from the window, something moved in the backyard. She looked
more closely and saw a dark figure entering Mr. Reynolds's garden
shed. A light flickered inside and, a few seconds later, went off
again. The door opened. A man emerged and headed back toward
the house. As he stepped into the faint yellow glow from the porch
light, she saw it was Toby.

Goose bumps prickled her arms. Why would he be sneaking
into Mr. Reynolds's shed at one in the morning unless he was
hiding something there? She dug her fingernails into her palms.
She'd talked to Clint's housekeeper and gardener. She'd followed
through with Duncan Gilford and Grant Padderson. But because
she liked Toby, she'd ignored her uneasiness about him, the uneasiness that hadn't gone away since she'd seen that fuzzy photo next
to his bed. She couldn't ignore it any longer.

She listened for his footsteps coming up the stairs. Finally, she
heard his door opening and closing behind him. She retrieved a
flashlight from the kitchen and let herself out, muffling the sound
of the door closing behind her.

She made her way soundlessly down the stairs and along the
hallway to the back door. She hesitated, assessing the risk of what
she was doing, but Toby's apartment faced the street instead of
the alley. Even if he decided to look out his window, he wouldn't
see her. Padding quietly across the wooden porch, she retrieved
the key to the shed from underneath the ugly pottery frog at the
bottom of the steps. She obviously hadn't been the only one to see
Mr. Reynolds hide the key here.

Accompanied by the shrill cry of cicadas, she crossed the yard and opened the shed's padlock. Instead of pulling the cord on the single overhead bulb as Toby had done, she used her flashlight to search the interior.

The shed smelled of dirt, fertilizer, and gasoline from the red plastic container next to the lawn mower. A small workbench took up one wall; an array of tools hung on another. Shelves held hose nozzles, clippers, and enough bug-killing chemicals to destroy the ecology of a small country. Clay pots and bags of potting soil sat in a row on the concrete floor, and a tower of tomato cages filled one corner.

Toby hadn't seemed to be carrying anything out of the shed. Had he left something here? Hidden it? But why wouldn't he keep whatever it was in his apartment?

Rory remembered Kristin and her Windex bottle, the way she'd moved Toby's things around to clean under them. Maybe he'd been afraid she'd find something she wasn't supposed to see and brought whatever it was out here to keep that from happening.

The inside of the shed still held the day's heat, and sweat beaded on her skin as she began a more systematic search, looking into pots and watering cans, behind bags of fertilizer. She sorted through a collection of sprinkler parts and a cardboard box of hardware, upended a stack of plastic buckets. Just as she was about to give up, she spotted a small metal toolbox poking out from the darkest corner under the workbench.

She knelt on the dirty floor to retrieve it and set it on the workbench. Holding the flashlight in one hand, she unfastened the latch and flipped the lid open.

The beam bounced off a piece of silky, dark fabric. She touched it. Her stomach churned as she realized it was a lacy black demi-bra. Neatly folded beneath the bra were two pairs of string thong panties. Her stomach pitched in revulsion. There was an ivory camisole, a makeup brush, and a hair tie still holding a few long strands of auburn hair. At the very bottom of the toolbox lay an iPhone in a white leather Prada case. Ashley's missing phone.

Again her stomach heaved. All these objects had touched her body. This was the grotesque trophy collection of the man who'd murdered her.

Everything clicked into place. Toby hadn't just had a crush on Ashley. He'd been obsessed with her. Rory imagined Ashley racing to her car, hurrying to get to Clint's house so she could make everything right again. But her car wouldn't start. She'd asked Toby to drive her, just as Rory had asked him to take her and Kristin to Clint's house. That was why the police couldn't find a record of a taxi or lift service taking her there. Because Toby had brought her.

She imagined Ashley sitting in the car next to him, swishing her hair, telling Toby that she and Clint hadn't really broken up. They'd only been going through a temporary separation. She envisioned Toby growing increasingly agitated but unable to say anything. She could see him creeping into the house after Ashley had let herself in with the key she'd held on to. Maybe she hadn't closed the front door all the way, or maybe Toby had made an excuse to follow her inside—to get a drink of water or something. But instead of leaving afterward, he'd hidden somewhere and eventually followed her upstairs. If he couldn't have Ashley, Clint wasn't going to get her, either.

It all fit.

The door hinges squealed. She spun around and went weak with relief as she saw it was only Mr. Reynolds.

"What are you doing in here?"

She steadied herself. "I have to call the police."

"You shouldn't be here."

"I'll explain later. For now—"

Mr. Reynolds's arm shot up. He had something in his hand. Something he shouldn't have been—

He caught her on the side of the head and everything went dark.

22

It was two o'clock on Sunday morning and Brett couldn't get back to sleep. He should have been depressed. He had no job and an uncertain future, but instead of falling off the rails, his life was finally on track, and he felt good. He felt great!

Yesterday afternoon, when he'd shoved Heath against that office wall, every preconceived notion he'd carried about himself had vanished. Heath was a decent guy, a great boss, and an upright man who took care of his employees. One day Brett would apologize. It wasn't Heath's fault that Brett had been a clueless blockhead who didn't know his own mind.

After he'd left Heath's house, he'd retrieved his car, driven home, and gone for a long run to shake out the cobwebs. When he'd cleaned up, he'd visited three jewelry stores until he found what he was looking for, a one-and-a-half-karat cushion-cut sapphire ring the color of Rory's eyes. He wanted to buy something a lot bigger, but he knew Rory too well.

Before he'd gone to bed, he'd eaten his first decent meal in days and planned his strategy. By morning, Rory should have had time to cool off. He'd show up at the food truck, tell her how much he loved her, kiss the hell out of her, and shove that ring on her finger before she could argue with him. She was everything to him. He'd started falling in love with her in Michigan, but it was such an unfamiliar emotion that it had taken him this long to recognize it. She was more important than his career, his money, more important than the hectic, adrenaline-fueled life he'd created for himself. Now he understood what Rory had seen so clearly, that Brett had been playing at the game of life instead of living it.

His phone was ringing. He was used to middle-of-the-night phone calls, but he was no longer at the beck and call of every drunken client who wanted to cry on his shoulder because his wife had busted him with another woman or, even worse, who was demanding a clean urine sample that Brett wouldn't give him.

He couldn't sleep anyway, so instead of ignoring it, he leaned over and glanced at the screen. It was Kristin.

"What's wrong?"

"Is Rory with you?"

She sounded out of breath, frantic, and he shot to his feet. "No. Why? Where is she?"

"Not in her apartment or at the bakery. That's where I am. The truck is missing, and I thought she might have driven here to do some extra work, even though she normally would take my car. But she's not here. I don't know how long she's been gone or where she is." Kristin's voice trembled. "I had this awful dream about her, and I couldn't go back to sleep, so I went into her apartment to make sure she was all right. It seemed silly at the time, but— Maybe she's driving around. But it's two in the morning, and we have to work in a few hours."

Panic hit him like a fist as he remembered how dogged she'd been in her search for Ashley's murderer. Rory was too smart to have deliberately put herself in danger, but he had an ugly premonition that was exactly what had happened.

The city was huge. She could be anywhere. And he had no idea how to find her.

*
*

Rory's head throbbed, and the smell of gasoline pricked her nostrils. She squeezed open her eyes. She was curled on the floor of the food truck, city streetlights flashing through the windows, her ankles and wrists bound with black electrical tape. Icy dread shot through her veins. The shed . . . The toolbox with Ashley's lingerie and cell phone . . . Mr. Reynolds standing in the doorway with something in his hand. Lifting it—

The truck hit a pothole, and her shoulder banged against the floorboards. She gasped and craned her neck to see him at the wheel, his hands encased in gardening gloves. Toby wasn't the one who'd gathered that ghoulish collection of Ashley's belongings. It was Mr. Reynolds. He was Ashley's murderer.

Terror paralyzed her. She'd seen his obscene collection, and now he had to get rid of her. That gasoline can could only mean he intended to set the truck on fire with her inside.

She pulled her knees tighter to her chest, as if the smaller she made herself, the safer she'd be. But there was no safety. No one was coming to rescue her, and cowering in terror wouldn't save her life.

Her brain settled on the inconsequential. He'd used his landlord's key to get the truck's ignition key from her apartment while she lay unconscious. It was the same way he'd sneaked into Ashley's apartment to steal her things. She remembered Ashley's sister, Stacy, saying that Ashley intended to move because something was bothering her. Rory had assumed she was worrying about Grant Padderson, but she'd wanted to get away from Reynolds.

The smell of gasoline made her stomach roil. She whimpered, a pitiful, helpless sound audible only to herself. She wasn't ready to die, not now. Not when she was making beautiful chocolate and had a new relationship with her brother and stepmother. Not when she'd be leaving Brett behind. She'd never regret loving him, her boardroom warrior in Gucci loafers who believed every barrier could be smashed through with hard work and willpower. If she didn't go down fighting, he'd never forgive her.

She drew up her knees far enough to reach her ankles and fumbled for the edge of the electrical tape. The truck lurched around a corner, slamming her against the bottom cupboards. She lost the edge and found it again. Bit by bit, she began peeling it back. It stuck awkwardly to her fingers, but as the truck jostled along the road and streetlights flashed haphazardly through the windshield, she kept at it, a quarter inch by a quarter inch until her ankles were finally free.

She kept her legs pressed together in case Mr. Reynolds looked back. If she could free her wrists, she could reach the hammer in the bottom cupboard, the one she used to tap the stubborn hinges on the canopy over the serving window. She strained her neck, looking frantically around for something to cut through the tape, but there was nothing, no handy kitchen knife, no sharp-edged metal corner.

With a sob of despair, she curled tighter.

Mr. Reynolds glanced over his shoulder and spoke for the first time. "It would have gone easier for you if you'd stayed asleep."

She lay still, not saying anything.

"It's your own fault, poking around like that in my shed." He sounded his normal grouchy self, the same way he sounded when he complained about trash bags being left overnight in the hallway.

She had to know, and she pushed out the words: "You were in love with Ashley." *Not love. Obsession.*

"Swishing her ass around every man she saw, actin' like every one of them was special. Hangin' on to me. Tellin' me how much she loved older men when all she wanted was to cut a deal on her rent. And like a fool, I did it. Those other men she was screwin', they didn't mean anything to her. She told me that. But then she met that football player and went all moon-eyed and wouldn't even talk to me."

Rory twisted her hands, searching for an edge she could loosen. "That must have been hard."

"When they broke up, she came cryin' to me, and I paid off her car to cheer her up, and she was all 'Thank you, Oscar. You're the best man in the world.' But it turned out the football player was the one she loved all along."

The street had grown bumpier, the lights less frequent. Rory's little finger touched the edge of the tape.

"'Oscar, my car won't start.' That's what she said to me that morning—all ready to call one of those car companies to drive her to Garrett's house so she could make up with him. Made me see red the way she'd been leading me on after I paid off her car." Reynolds was no longer talking to her, only to himself. "I told her I'd take her. I could see she was nervous about it, but all she cared about was getting to him, and the whole way there, she kept talking about how much she loved him, making sure I knew I was nobody to her, so when we got there, I told her I had to use the john. She didn't care. She was callin' out his name, going up the stairs, not even remembering I was still around. I knew she was planning to move out, but I couldn't let her do that. I had it planned—the way she was going to trip on the basement stairs at home. But this was a better way."

Rory's head pounded and pain shot into her shoulders. He'd been planning to kill Ashley all along. She twisted her wrists, working at the tape.

"I followed her upstairs, and there she was poking around in his bedroom, losing her dignity, ready to crawl back to him. When she opened those doors to look out that balcony, I almost laughed because now she wouldn't have to die in my house."

He slowed, and the blue glare of a floodlight shone through the window. Rory glimpsed the side of a brick building—some kind of warehouse or industrial building, someplace that would be deserted this time of night. She tasted blood as she bit into her bottom lip. This was it. He'd run out of words, and she'd run out of time. The tape around her wrists wouldn't come loose. Her head was throbbing. She had no weapon. But a cold clarity cut through her panic, and she suddenly knew exactly what she had to do. Something grotesque. Repulsive. But not as repulsive as being burned to death.

She inched forward toward the front of the truck. As he concentrated on driving between the dark buildings, she reached the driver's seat. The truck slowed even more, seconds away from stopping. She scrambled to her feet and did the unthinkable. With a lunge, she looped her bound wrists over his head and jerked on his neck as hard as she could.

He clawed at her arms. The truck careened, throwing her off-balance, but she couldn't fall, not with her arms locked around his neck. Using her wrists as a garrote, she jerked harder, beginning to cry, nose running, bile rising in her throat. His head fell back, and his nails tore at her skin. He made a ghastly, gargling sound, the whites of his eyes rolling. She sobbed. Yanked harder. Harder still. Finally he went limp.

She still didn't let go. His foot flopped onto the gas pedal. The truck spun and screeched into the building.

*
*

Brett saw the side of the truck hit the corner of the warehouse. He slammed on his brakes, jumped out of his car, and ran as fast as he'd ever run. Through the window in the door, he glimpsed Rory's landlord slumped sideways in the driver's seat and saw Rory lift her arms from around his neck.

He grabbed the handle and yanked open the door as she slumped to the floor, curling into a ball. Her wrists were taped together, and she was making animal sounds he'd hear in his nightmares for the rest of his life.

He knelt beside her, cradled her in his arms. "It's okay. It's all right. You're safe. I'm here." As if his being here made any difference now. He should have been with her. He should never have left her alone.

She gasped for air, her cheeks wet with tears. "I— I think I killed him."

"Good." Whatever that bastard had done to her, he deserved to die.

"You're here," she whispered hoarsely, and he'd never felt lower in his life, because she'd had to save herself. All he'd done was use the food truck location app she'd signed up for. But even though he'd broken every speed limit tracking the truck—even though he'd ordered Kristin to call the police with the information—he hadn't gotten to Rory soon enough to stop this horror.

Sirens sounded in the distance. "I love you," he said. "I love you so much."

She squeezed her eyes shut. "That's nice."

He touched her bound wrists. Real men carried pocketknives, but he'd lost every one he owned to the TSA, and he had no way to free her. "I don't deserve you."

"I know," she murmured, as the sirens grew louder. "My head hurts."

An ugly welt had formed under the curls at the side of her forehead. If Reynolds wasn't already dead, he'd kill him himself. He couldn't leave her here a second longer. Swooping her up in his arms, he carried her from the truck.

*
*

While the paramedics tended to Rory, the police pulled Reynolds from the truck. As they strapped him to a gurney, Brett could see he was still alive. He pushed forward. "Don't you dare put that bastard in the same ambulance as her!"

"We won't," the paramedic told him. "Step back and give us room."

When they loaded her in the second ambulance, they wouldn't let him go with her.

★
★

The CAT scan showed no skull fracture, no brain bleed. Rory had a concussion, but she didn't have blurred vision, ringing ears, or memory loss. The only nausea she experienced was when she remembered what had happened.

Detective Strothers was waiting for her when they wheeled her back into her curtained cubicle in the emergency room. She wasn't in the mood for forgiveness. "I told you Clint didn't kill Ashley!"

"It turns out you were right," he said evenly.

"What about—" She couldn't say his name. "Did I kill him?"

"He's alive and raving. Why don't you start at the beginning?"

He took notes as she recounted it all. She swallowed as she got to the end. "I think he was going to set the truck on fire. And me."

Strothers nodded. "That seemed to be what he intended. Afterward, he planned to hike to the Irving Park CTA station and catch the Blue Line to get home."

The Blue Line ran twenty-four hours, something Mr. Reynolds would have known.

Strothers closed his notebook. "That's enough for now," he said gently. "I appreciate how forthcoming you've been." He rose from his chair and hesitated. "You seem to feel some responsibility for your friend's murder, but from what Reynolds has already told us, we have reason to believe he had prior victims. You may have stopped a serial killer." As she tried to take that in, a cart clattered on the other side of the curtain. He patted her foot through the blanket. "If you ever decide you want to join the force, let me know, and I'll be happy to write you a recommendation."

*
*

Brett paced the perimeter of the hospital waiting room. Even though a nurse told him Rory was doing well, he needed to see that for himself. But the police wouldn't let him in until they'd finished questioning her.

Kristin and Clint burst into the waiting room. Kristin reached Brett first. "How is she?"

Clint bristled with hostility. "What the hell are you doing here?"

Ignoring him, Brett rested his hand on Kristin's shoulder. "A mild concussion, but she's okay. The police are with her now."

Some of the other occupants of the waiting room were beginning to recognize Clint. Brett focused only on Kristin. "They want to monitor her for a few hours, but she seems to be doing as well as can be for someone who's been through what she has."

"We'll take it from here," Clint said flatly.

Brett finally acknowledged his former client. "I'm not going anywhere."

"You have no right to be here!"

"I guess Rory can decide that," Brett said.

Kristin grabbed Brett's arm. "Tell us exactly what happened."

Brett steered them into the quietest corner of the room and, ignoring the stares of the other occupants, quietly recounted everything he knew.

"Oscar Reynolds." Kristin pressed her fingers to her lips. "I can't believe it. I used to talk to him about his garden. I wish she'd killed him!"

"The feeling's mutual, but it's probably better that she didn't. She has an overdeveloped conscience."

Clint clenched his jaw. "And you, dude, have none."

Brett rounded on him. "Get used to me, Garrett, because I'm not going anywhere."

Belligerence narrowed Clint's eyes.

Brett stared back, not blinking, thinking how Rory had filled the empty hole inside him that he'd been trying to satisfy in all the wrong ways. Rory was his happiness. Now all he had to do was convince her she needed him in the same way.

The detective emerging through the automatic doors ended their staring contest. Strothers. He'd gotten a statement from Brett while Rory was being treated. "You should be able to see her now," the detective said.

Brett blocked Clint as the three of them made a dash for the doors. "You wait out here."

Clint looked mulish and Kristin intervened. "Let's give Brett a few minutes."

"Not a chance," Clint said. "Somebody has to watch out for her."

"I know this is going to shock you," Brett retorted, "but Rory is perfectly capable of watching out for herself, even with a concussion. I'm the one you should be worried about." He pushed past him through the doors.

Rory had fallen asleep. He pulled the room's single chair next to the bed and took her hand. Sitting quietly, the machines beeping softly in the background, he watched her sleep, and his heart filled with gratitude for each breath she took.

Kristin and Clint came in, and Rory's eyes gradually opened.

*
 *

Her headache had become a dull throb. Brett was sitting in the chair next to the bed and holding her hand. Kristin stood on the other side with Clint hovering at the foot. "The gang's all here," she murmured, only to come wide-awake. "The truck!"

"Don't worry about the truck," Kristin said. "You're the only thing that's important."

Brett understood Rory's priorities better than Kristin. "The truck has a few dents and scratches. Nothing that can't be fixed."

She gazed at him and remembered it all. Brett kneeling next to her, holding her in his arms, saying he loved her.

"I love you." He said those words again, but this time in front of God and everybody, and the intensity in his gaze told her he wasn't talking about friendship love.

She locked her eyes with his. "Say it again."

"I'll happily say it for the rest of my life. I love you, Rory Garrett, and you'd better have meant it when you said you loved me, too."

She had a headache, her truck was wrecked, she'd almost killed a man, and she wasn't in the best of moods. "If I have to almost die for you to decide you love me, forget I said anything."

He kissed her fingers. "I understand."

No way was she letting him weasel out of this. "I mean it."

"Of course you do."

Off to the side, Clint snorted in disgust.

Without releasing Rory's hand, Brett turned to face him. "Whether you like it or not—and you obviously don't—I love your sister, and, despite all the crap I've dished out, she loves me. Or at least she did a couple of days ago. I'm sorry if that upsets you, Garrett, but I don't work for you or for Champion any longer, and you don't get a vote."

"You what?" Rory sat straight up in bed, which made her head reel. She gripped the bed rails to steady herself. "What do you mean you don't work for Champion any longer?"

Brett nudged her back down. "I quit."

"You can't do that!" she exclaimed.

"It's all about priorities, sweetheart. And you're mine." He hadn't planned on doing it like this, but since he couldn't get her alone . . . "Will you marry me?"

She pushed the curls away from her face. "Seriously? You want to get married?"

"I do." He gave her hand a gentle squeeze.

"Not in a million years." She snatched away her hand and glared at Clint. "Please escort him out." She hesitated. "But don't hurt him."

Clint scratched his chin. "Under normal circumstances, I'd be happy to oblige, but he's guaranteed to put up a fight, and I can't afford to get in any more trouble right now."

Rory gazed at Kristin, who shrugged. "He's bigger than I am."

Brett had bargained with the most powerful operators in the NFL. He knew when to dig in and when to back off. "Don't stress, sweetheart. You need some rest. I'll go."

Was he really going to give up so easily?

"We'll talk later," he said.

"Don't count on it!" she exclaimed.

He kissed her on the good side of her forehead and left.

*★

The police held a press conference that afternoon exonerating Clint. Kristin refused to leave Rory alone in her apartment after the hospital released her and slept next to her in bed that night.

"You snore," Rory said, when she finally got up late the next morning. She still had a headache, but it was beginning to ease.

"That's what Daniel says."

Rory smiled and gave her another of the quick hugs that had become their habit. She sat at the kitchen table to eat the Mickey Mouse pancakes Kristin had made her. She'd burned the edges of the mouse ears, just as she'd done when Rory was a kid, but Rory ate them anyway.

Kristin, however, only poked at her pancakes. "I'm worried about what happens when you try to get back in the truck. About re-traumatizing you. We need to rethink everything."

Rory waved off her concern. "That's our truck, and there's a big difference between walking in voluntarily and being dragged in unconscious. I'm not letting that deviant ruin this."

Not long after, they saw the police digging up Mr. Reynolds's vegetable garden from the kitchen window. "That can't be good," Kristin said. "We definitely have to find a new place to live."

"As soon as we get the truck back on the street."

Kristin poured herself a fresh cup of Rory's coffee. "I've been reading some fascinating books about marketing, and I have a few ideas I'd like us to talk about. Opening an Etsy shop maybe. Approaching luxury buyers. We need to set up an ad budget. So much to talk about when you feel better."

After everything she'd been through, Rory's emotions sat close to the surface, and she swallowed a lump in her throat. "You're loving this, aren't you?" *Loving me.*

"I'm having the time of my life." Kristin got all dreamy-eyed. "I'm meeting Daniel's daughter today, but I already know I'm going to like her." She gently touched Rory's cheek. "Brett's pretty wonderful, too. If you'd seen how upset he was in that hospital waiting room, you'd know you have nothing to worry about."

"I'm not exactly worried," Rory replied. "More cautious."

⋆

By the next day, Rory's energy had returned and her headache had disappeared. She couldn't postpone this awkward conversation any longer, and she crossed the hallway to knock on Toby's door.

"I loved Ashley!" Toby exclaimed, after she'd told him everything. "I'd never have hurt her. How could you think something like that about me?"

"In my defense, you did have motive, and sneaking into the tool shed in the middle of the night was definitely suspicious."

Toby sulked. "You know I'm a night owl. Reynolds never let me borrow his tools, and I needed his wire strippers. I'm running new speaker wires."

"I'm sorry, Toby. I really am."

He tugged at his T-shirt. "I guess after everything you've been through, I can't be too pissed."

"Thanks." She supplemented her apology with a dozen mint creams and returned to her apartment to see that Brett had finally texted her.

B: How are you feeling?

R: Fine. Where's my truck?

B: Being repaired.

R: $$$?

B: Insurance covering most of cost.

R: Who's doing repairs?

B: Guy I know. Owes me a favor. BTW, you're getting new driver's seat. Old one accidentally ripped.

R: How did that happen?

B: Life is strange.

And he was gone.

She knew exactly why he hadn't yet come to see her. He understood how much she hated being pushed around, and he was giving her all the space she needed. But exactly how much was that?

*
*

The man who loved her didn't come to see her, didn't call. He was crafty that way. But the next morning, he texted again.

> B: Air-conditioning fixed. Truck ready on Friday.
>
> R: With A/C? How did you make everything happen so quickly?
>
> B: I'm damned good. You should marry me.

She smiled and tucked her phone away, only to have it ping again.

> B: I love you
>
> R: Since when?

It seemed important to know.

> B: Since Michigan. Not sure exact moment. You?

A long time before she admitted it to herself.

> R: Don't remember. What are you doing tonight?
>
> B: Getting drunk and entertaining hookers. Life sucks without you.

She laughed.

> R: Tell them hi from me.

*
  *

A letter arrived by FedEx that afternoon informing her that Simply the Best was now the official chocolatier of the Chicago Stars. She immediately called Clint. "You shouldn't have done that."

"Why not? You make the best damned chocolates in the country."

"I want to do this on my own, Clint."

"Then you should have been an orphan." He hung up on her.

Kristin came back all aglow from meeting Daniel's daughter. "She's wonderful. Smart and kind. Great sense of humor. We had so much to talk about."

Rory pursed her lips. "She sounds awful."

Kristin laughed and hugged her. "No need to be jealous. You'll always be my first girl."

"Don't you forget it."

*
  *

    B: New driver's seat brown with pink trim. Picked out colors
       myself.
    R: Sounds cheery.
    B: Gotta go. Closing deal on my condo.
    R: You sold your condo?
    B: Need place where you'll be happy. Also, don't like it.

She was glad he wasn't around to see the way her eyes misted up. She set her phone aside only to have it ping again.

    B: You want kids after we're married?
    R: I don't want to get married!!!
    B: Very immature attitude

R: We barely know each other!

B: You're funny.

* *

Clint came over for dinner. Instead of the haggard look he'd been carrying around, there was a new maturity about him. "I talked to Heath. Your boyfriend isn't answering his phone for either one of us."

"He's having a midlife crisis."

"He's not even forty, and he's having a Rory crisis. Put him out of his misery so he can get back to work."

"You're the one who fired him."

"Yeah, well, I'm having second thoughts about that. Brett understands me."

Rory threw up her hands.

Clint dug in. "You need to go see him and tell him you love him so he'll talk to Heath and me and life can get back to normal."

She pursed her lips. "Maybe."

"You're stupid. And I say that with love. The man has given up everything for you."

He was right. She loved Brett for quitting his job and, at the same time, hated that he'd done it. He needed to get back to work.

She knew what she had to do. Brett Rivers was the cagiest man in the world, but he loved her, and she loved him, and enough was enough.

R: I'm coming over to your place right now to talk.

B: Bad idea.

R: Why?

B: Because you're sex crazy, and I don't believe in sex outside a committed relationship.

R: Since when?

B: Since now.

R: Define "committed"

B: An engagement. True love kind, not open-ended. Six months and then we get married.

R: Two years and then we discuss it.

B: One year.

R: Deal. But only to discuss.

B: Coming over so we can shake on it.

★
★

He did come over, but instead of shaking hands, he was so hungry for the sight of her that she was in his arms before either of them could say a word. They kissed—him being oh-so-careful not to hurt her and her not being careful at all. He had no job, no home, no plan, but she loved him, and he'd never been happier.

"You're everything to me." He buried his face in curls that smelled of strawberry and chocolate.

She drew back, a world of feeling in her blue eyes. "That's nice to hear, but you have to get your job back."

He kissed her again. "Is work all you think about?"

She tugged gently on his bottom lip with her teeth. "I'm not supporting a deadbeat boyfriend."

Boyfriend. He inwardly scoffed. She'd forgotten who she was dealing with. He nibbled her earlobe. "You're my life."

She kissed the corner of his mouth. "Too much responsibility."

He laughed and thanked the universe for bringing him this woman.

They kissed some more, but as he slipped his hands under her top, she cradled his face in her strong, capable hands. "I'm experimenting with a new product, and I'd like your opinion."

"Now?" As much as he loved helping, he had something better in mind than product testing.

"Now." She twitched her fingers toward the bedroom and disappeared into the kitchen. "You might want to take off your clothes," she called out.

He raced to the bedroom. "Only if you do." He banged his elbow on the door as he ripped off his shirt.

She appeared a few minutes later, holding a very ordinary round container and naked except for a pair of exceptionally sexy purple lace granny underpants. He wanted to rip them off and forget everything else.

She came closer, taking in his aroused, very naked body with appreciative eyes that made every miserable second he spent in the gym worthwhile.

"I'll obviously need better packaging," she said, "but for now . . ." Tucking the container behind her back, she moved to the bed. "Lie down."

He didn't know exactly what was happening, but he intended to enjoy every second of it.

She knelt on the bed next to him. "Close your eyes."

He did as she asked and soon felt a warm, wet finger slide down the center of his chest. He smelled chocolate and opened his eyes.

She held up the container. "Artisanal chocolate body paint." Locking eyes with him, she extracted a fresh, gooey scoop with her finger and continued her downward journey. Dipping. Stroking. Dipping again. "I added a touch of cayenne pepper for extra heat," she said huskily.

He groaned as her chocolate-drenched finger meandered here and there. She finally found her target, and he nearly lost his mind.

She drew a series of intoxicating loops that made him dig his fingers into the mattress. Sweat broke out on his brow. She leaned closer. "Lots of body paint is on the market, but nothing of this quality."

And nothing like the woman applying it.

With a wicked look, she licked. "Maybe it needs a little whiskey." Her breath teased his skin. "Not too much. Only a dash."

She licked again and again. Circling. Stroking. He clenched his jaw. The room started to spin, and he grabbed her shoulders before it was too late.

Within seconds, he had those purple lace granny pants on the floor and her on her back. He grabbed the container, dipped in two fingers, and began painting her naked body just as he'd once imagined.

He circled her breasts, found their centers, closed his lips over them and tasted the best chocolate anyone had ever made. Now she was the one writhing on the bed. He drew ovals on her stomach. Tasted. Drew arrows on the insides of her thighs. Tasted. And then the very heart of her, until it was all too much for both of them.

He moved on top of her, smearing chocolate everywhere. She raised her hips to take him in, and they found the ancient rhythm of thrust and arch. Whispering love words. Promises. Pleas. She wrapped her legs around his hips. Dug her fingernails into his back. Cried out. With a groan, he followed her into the mystery.

Seconds later, a muffled scream assaulted his eardrums. "Cayenne!" she yelped. "Big mistake!"

He'd come back to himself enough to realize what had gone

wrong. He swooped her up and raced to the shower, his own body feeling the effects of that ill-conceived additive. She laughed and moaned as he washed them both and kissed her and loved her all over again.

Life would always be an adventure with Rory Garrett.

It took them forever to clean up the mess. Sheets, bedspread, pillowcases. Chocolate smeared the rug, the wood floor, the edge of the tub. When she finally put her product on the market, she'd better include a plastic sheet.

Halfway through their cleanup, he got distracted by her kiss-bruised mouth, and they made slower love on the floor underneath the floozy poster. She was a better person than he was. Kinder. Smarter. Braver. And God knew she had a superior sense of values. She was the love of his life, and he'd make certain he never disappointed her.

As he came up the steps from putting the bedspread in the basement washer, he pondered the fact that Rory wouldn't be able to live here much longer. He wondered how long it would take him to convince her they should find a place together. Not long, he suspected. She might be the best chocolatier in the country, but he was always and forever The River. Laser-focused. Decisive. And very much in love.

One way or another, he'd make the deal of a lifetime.

EPILOGUE

Sunlight splashed the Wedgwood-blue walls; glass-fronted, painted cabinets; and big, round, marble-top table with its chintz-covered chairs. But instead of the chocolate shop of her dreams, this was her home kitchen. Rory loved the old-fashioned design—the cozy window seat, generous work space, and quality appliances. Best of all was the view of their sweeping backyard, a grassy expanse that stretched from their gazebo to a winding creek with fern-covered banks and a wooden footbridge.

A woman was never too old to learn new things about herself, and she'd finally realized owning her own shop was only appealing in fantasy. In reality, managing a store and waiting on customers would take her away from what she really wanted to do: make impeccable chocolate.

Heath Champion sat at her marble-top table with a cup of her best coffee and the crumbs from one of the biscotti she'd made this morning. Now that she had her own roaster for cocoa beans, she was obsessed with experimentation. She'd made the biscotti with an organic cocoa powder she'd created from the earthy notes of fair-trade Ecuadorian beans and the fruitier beans of Peru's eastern Andes. When she had the proportions exactly right, she'd talk to Kristin about adding the cocoa mix to their growing line of products.

Since Heath was Brett's boss, the close friendship that had developed between the couples should have been awkward, but it wasn't. She and Brett even babysat the Champion children when their parents needed a weekend away. Brett said it was preparation for having their own kids.

Rory sipped her coffee. She and Brett had a shockingly easy marriage. They laughed far more than they argued, loved instead of sparred, and were always there for each other. On the first anniversary of the day they'd met, Brett had given her the best gift she could ever have imagined—her mother's red evening bag beautifully restored. But lately, he'd been carrying more than his fair share of the load, something she needed to fix.

A blade of afternoon sunlight struck her sapphire wedding ring as she moved an earthenware pitcher of garden flowers out of the way so she and Heath could meet eye to eye. It was time for the serious conversation that had been brewing between them for months. She met Heath's steely gaze with her own steelier one. "I need him."

The Python curled his lip. "I need him."

She curled her lip back. "What you need is to let him go. His loyalty to you is holding him back from doing what he really wants to do."

"Says you."

His childish retort told her she had an edge. "This is the next logical step for him."

"The next logical step is for him to take over as CEO of Champion Sports Management when I retire."

"No, it's for him to take over as CEO of Simply the Best so I can stop doing what I hate and get back to doing what I love."

He kicked back in his chair. "You don't need him. You're doing a great job running the company."

"I'm barely hanging on and only because Brett spends all his free time coaching me. I hate every minute of being an executive. I want to make chocolate and invent new products, not run a company. I'm holding us back."

Their battle continued for the heart and soul of Brett Rivers, although technically Rory already had his heart and soul. It was his brains and talent they were bargaining for.

Heath tried another angle. "He loves the sports world too much to leave it."

"Not as much as he used to. He got more excited helping me negotiate a deal with my last supplier than he did working on Clint's new contract."

The Python's eyes strayed to the serving plate.

"Go ahead," she said. "You know you want to."

He chose an almond-chocolate biscotti and pointed it at her. "What I want is for you to leave my senior vice president alone."

"Brett's ready for a fresh challenge, and all that's holding him back is his loyalty to you." She drilled in. "You have at least three other agents ready to move up the ladder at Champion—thanks to Brett's excellent mentoring. Unlike you, *he's* never been forced to *rehire* anyone he's fired."

"Low blow." He took a moment to savor the biscotti.

She leaned on the table. "Follow your conscience, Heath. You've had Brett's best work for years. Now it's my turn. We're creating a family business here."

"A family empire is more like it," he grumbled. "In two and a half years, you and Kristin went from operating a food truck to running a company with eighteen employees, and a new building."

"A modest, well-worn building," she said.

"Eight offices, an attached warehouse, and a big test kitchen is hardly modest. At the rate you're going, you'll need a larger space soon."

Rory crossed her arms over her chest. "It's Kristin's fault. Who knew she'd turn into such a marketing whiz?"

"All the marketing skill in the world means nothing if you don't have a great product." He pointed the uneaten half of his biscotti at her. "Which you do."

It had happened so quickly. Clint had given them their first big push by ordering over a hundred gift boxes for his teammates and the coaching staff. Many of the recipients had appreciated the quality of the products enough to place their own large orders. Rory and Kristin quickly had to accept the fact that they'd grown out of their food truck.

They sold it to a pastry chef, took on two assistant chocolatiers, and hired Daniel's brainy daughter, Chloe, to run their online business. Kristin relentlessly courted the buyers at high-end retailers whose orders kept growing as they began carrying more products: bars, truffles, colorful bonbon assortments, and Simply the Best Gourmet Chocolate Body Paint. One of the elegant, cupcake-sized porcelain jars ended up in the hands of a famous actress who'd featured it on her social media platforms, and business had exploded after that.

But rapid growth meant less time in the kitchen, until Rory was hardly there. If this kept up, the products would eventually begin to suffer. They also couldn't continue to expand without a more professional financial plan, something she didn't have the experience or desire to take on.

They didn't call Heath "The Python" for nothing, and he sank his fangs into the weakest part of her plan. "Your business is growing, but Brett would still have to take a pay cut to leave me."

"All the more motivation for him to work hard." She took a sip of her now-cold coffee. "We're discussing setting up kiosks in major airports, but I'm a chocolatier, not a captain of industry, and I can't take that on without him."

Heath cut to the chase. "I need him."

She leaned forward. "You *want* him, but you can do fine without him. I can't." She played her trump card. "I'm pregnant."

He came out of his chair, sprinkling crumbs on her kitchen floor. "That is the sneakiest, most unethical, unprofessional, manipulative . . . ! How am I supposed to compete with that?"

"Easy." She rose, too. "All you need to do is remind him how much you've done for him, and he'll stay. You know the value he places on loyalty." She cocked her head. "But even you aren't heartless enough to do that, now are you?"

When he emitted a long-suffering sigh, she knew she'd won. "I'll talk to him this afternoon."

It wasn't nice to gloat, and they weren't done. "What's a good time frame for letting him go?"

"How soon do you need him?"

"Yesterday. But I'm nothing if not fair. Two weeks."

"One month."

Even better than she could have hoped for. "Deal."

They shook hands just as Brett and Annabelle returned from an ice-cream run with the Champion kids, who immediately headed to the backyard teepee.

Brett lifted an eyebrow at Rory.

She gave him a faint nod along with a smile.

He smiled back.

Heath sneered at them both. "This was a setup. You sent your wife to do your dirty work."

Brett put his arm around her. "She's more ruthless than I am. Even I'm scared of her."

Totally untrue, but she did like the vision of herself as a mercenary. "I learned from the best."

Heath shook his head. "You've got your hands full with that one."

"And don't I know it." Brett kissed the tip of her nose.

They drank more coffee, ate the rest of her biscotti, and played with the kids while she contemplated a new product—the Empire Builder—dark chocolate covered in twenty-four-karat gold leaf enrobing a luxuriously creamy vanilla-and-cognac filling. She envisioned selling it for an outrageous price in a custom-designed box that would hold only two bonbons, each one nestled in a marbled chocolate cup resting on a bed of glistening sugar pearls.

She waited until bedtime to discuss the idea with her new CEO. When she was done, he curled his hand over her belly and kissed her curls. "Convince me," he whispered.

She stroked his chest. "I'll do my best."

He smiled into her eyes. "I couldn't ask for more."

Early the next morning, sated from what had happened the night before, she slipped quietly out of bed. She had a baby to grow, a husband to love, and chocolates to make. It was going to be a busy day.

ACKNOWLEDGMENTS

I t is common, during a writer's career, to have many editors, but I have been blessed for the last thirty years with only one, editor extraordinaire Carrie Feron. As happens in a long relationship between two women with so many common interests (besides me ☺), we have formed a deep friendship. We have been through births and deaths together, laughter and tears. We've watched our families grow and our chicks leave the nest.

Carrie is now moving on from her distinguished career at HarperCollins/Avon Books, taking a piece of history with her. Carrie's vision, innovation, and insights have all left an indelible mark on the publishing industry.

Simply the Best is both the last of my books she will edit and the beginning of another chapter in our long personal relationship. I like to think we've made each other better people. I know she has made me not only a better writer, but also a more perceptive human being.

Thank you and I love you, my dear friend and editor.

Susan Elizabeth Phillips
Naperville, Illinois
susanelizabethphillips.com

ABOUT THE AUTHOR

SUSAN ELIZABETH PHILLIPS is a multi-award-winning best-selling author whose books have been published in over thirty languages. Guided by the motto "Life is better with happily-ever-afters," she loves writing about love in all its forms. Among her accomplishments, Susan created the sports romance genre with her novel *Fancy Pants*.